YASUNARI NAGATOSHI

This is me, asleep in my chair
in the middle of writer's block.

I'm sorry, dear Editor.
Tomorrow—I promise...!!

ZOMBiE BOY'S METAMORPHOSiS COLLECTiON

MUSCLE ZOMBIE BOY

BiCEP

He's just a muscle, so he's super-athletic and loves sports! He's especially good at running, so he's always jogging around town. Muscle Zombie Boy doesn't get along with Fat Zombie Boy, and forces him to do push-ups or crunches whenever they see each other. His dream is to be champion at a bodybuilding competition.

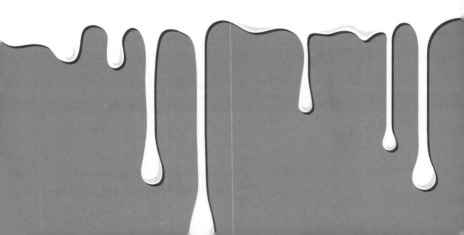

ZO ZO ZOMBIE

VOL. 8

RAINY SEASON

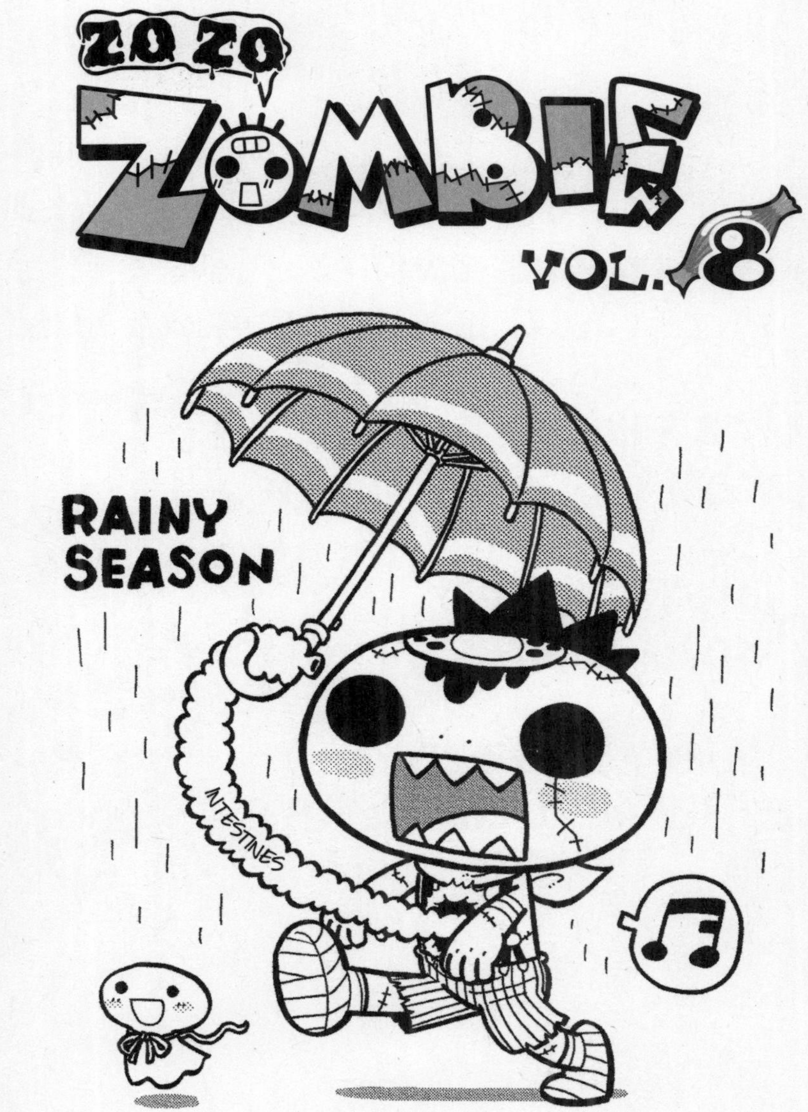
INTESTINES

YASUNARI NAGATOSHI

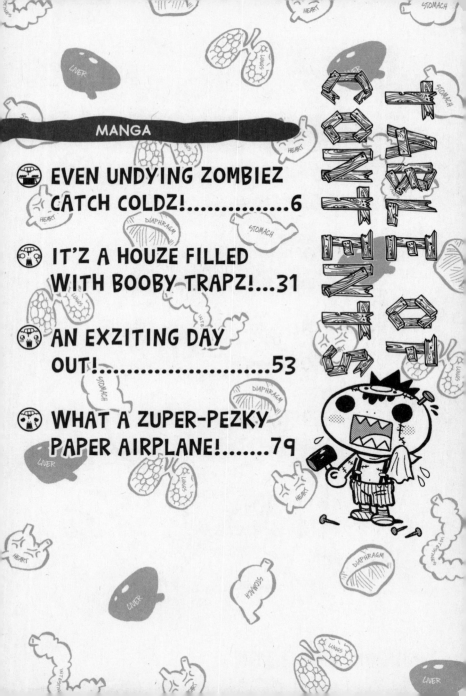

TABLE OF CONTENTS

MANGA

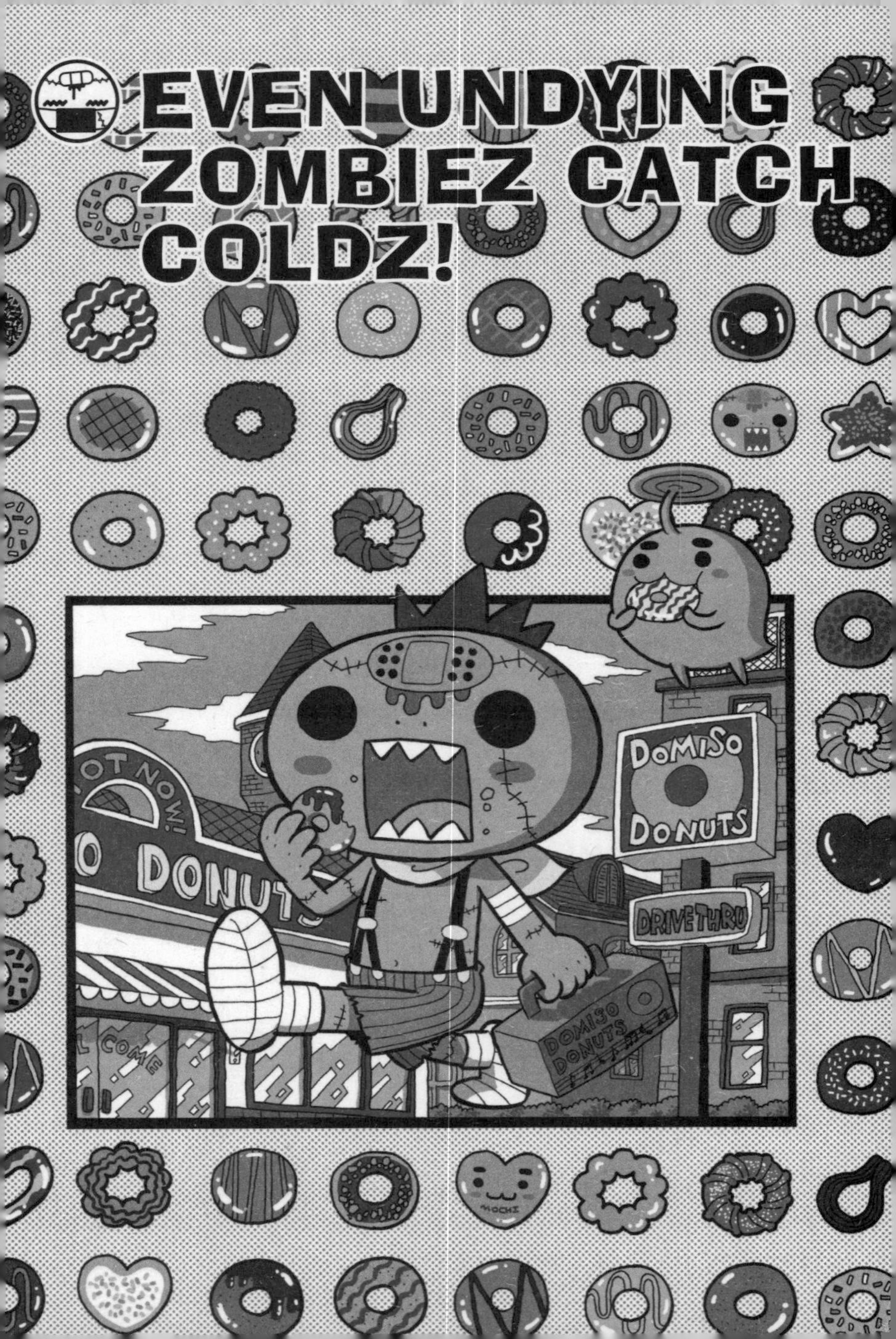
EVEN UNDYING ZOMBIEZ CATCH COLDZ!
DOMISO DONUTS
DRIVE THRU
DOMISO DONUTS
MOCHI

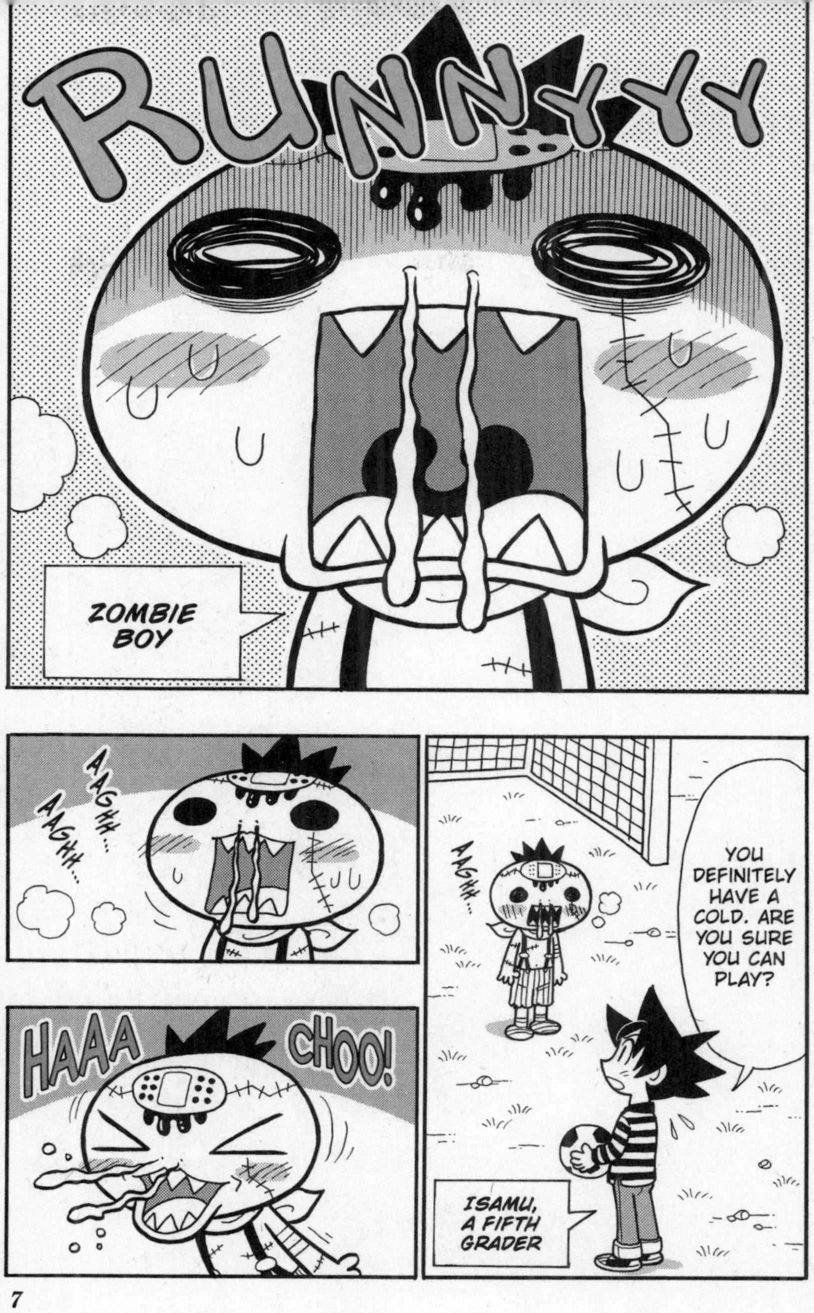
RUNNYYY
ZOMBIE BOY
YOU DEFINITELY HAVE A COLD. ARE YOU SURE YOU CAN PLAY?
AAGHH...
ISAMU, A FIFTH GRADER
AAGHH... AAGHH...
HAAA CHOO!

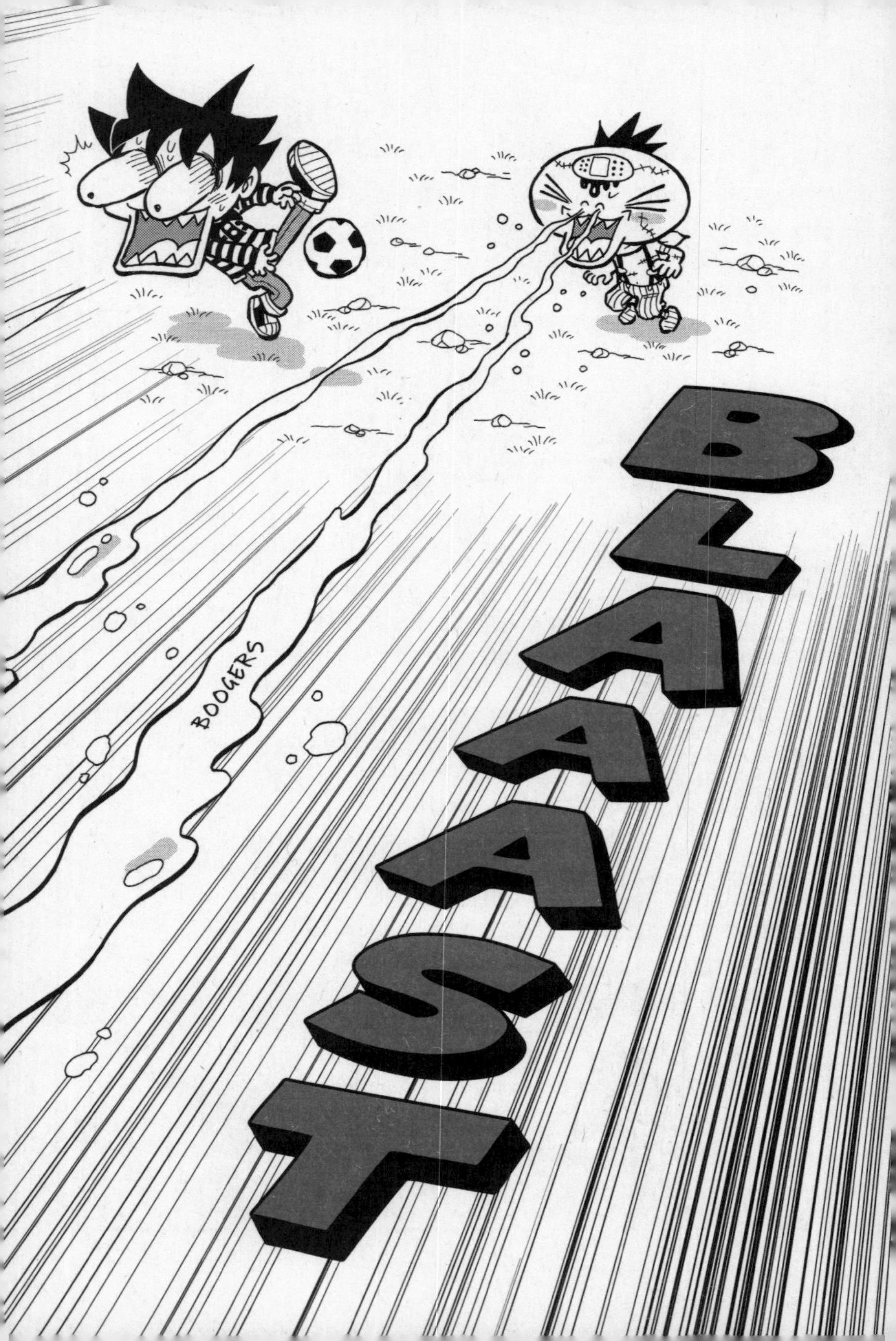
BLAAAST
BOOGERS

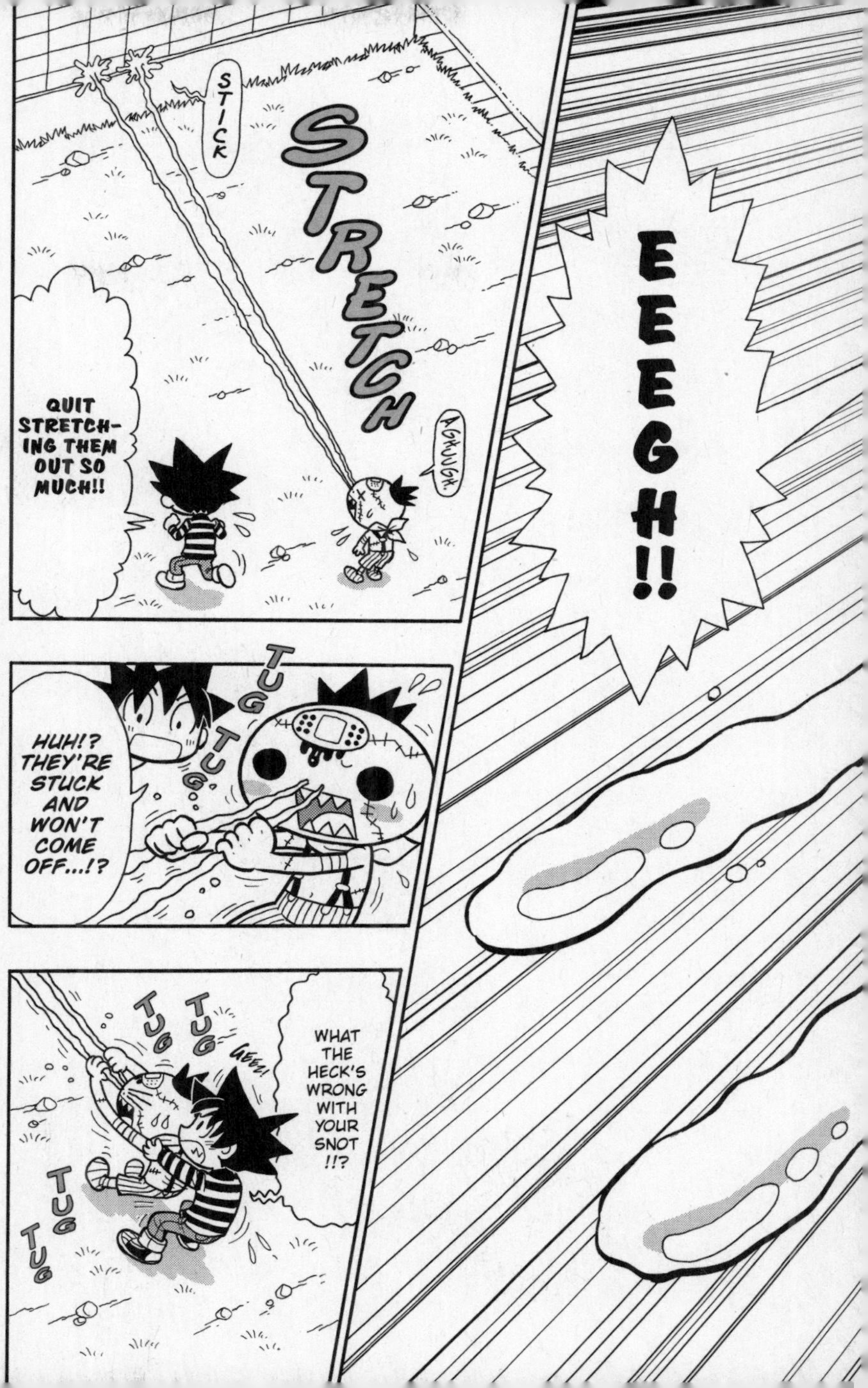
EEEEGH!!
STICK
STRETCH
AGKUUGK.
QUIT STRETCHING THEM OUT SO MUCH!!
TUG TUG TUG
HUH!? THEY'RE STUCK AND WON'T COME OFF...!?
TUG TUG
GEEZ!
WHAT THE HECK'S WRONG WITH YOUR SNOT !!?
TUG TUG

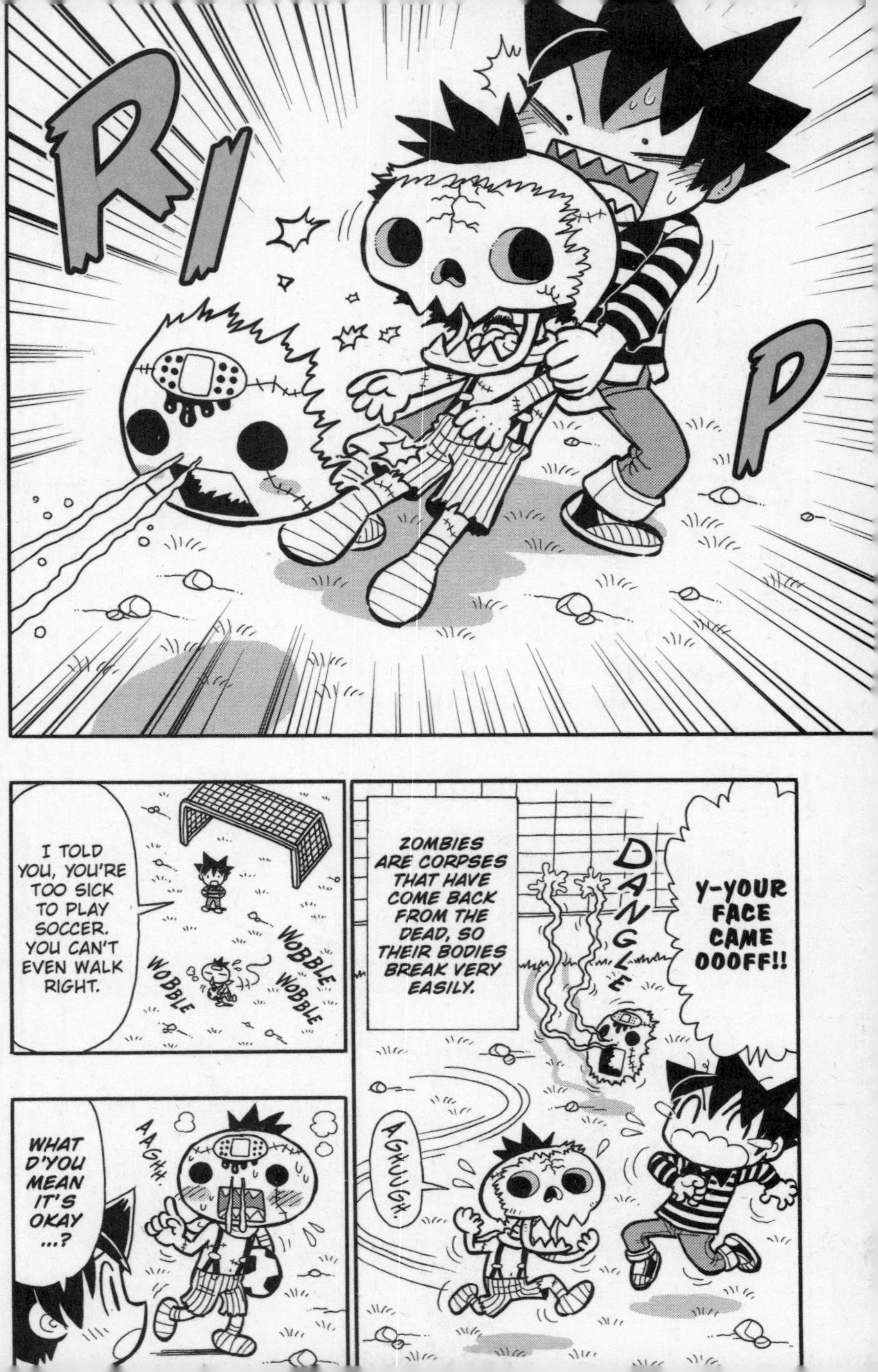
RIP
Y-YOUR FACE CAME OOOFF!!
DANGLE
ZOMBIES ARE CORPSES THAT HAVE COME BACK FROM THE DEAD, SO THEIR BODIES BREAK VERY EASILY.
AGHUGH..
I TOLD YOU, YOU'RE TOO SICK TO PLAY SOCCER. YOU CAN'T EVEN WALK RIGHT.
WOBBLE WOBBLE
WOBBLE
AAGHH.
WHAT D'YOU MEAN IT'S OKAY ...?

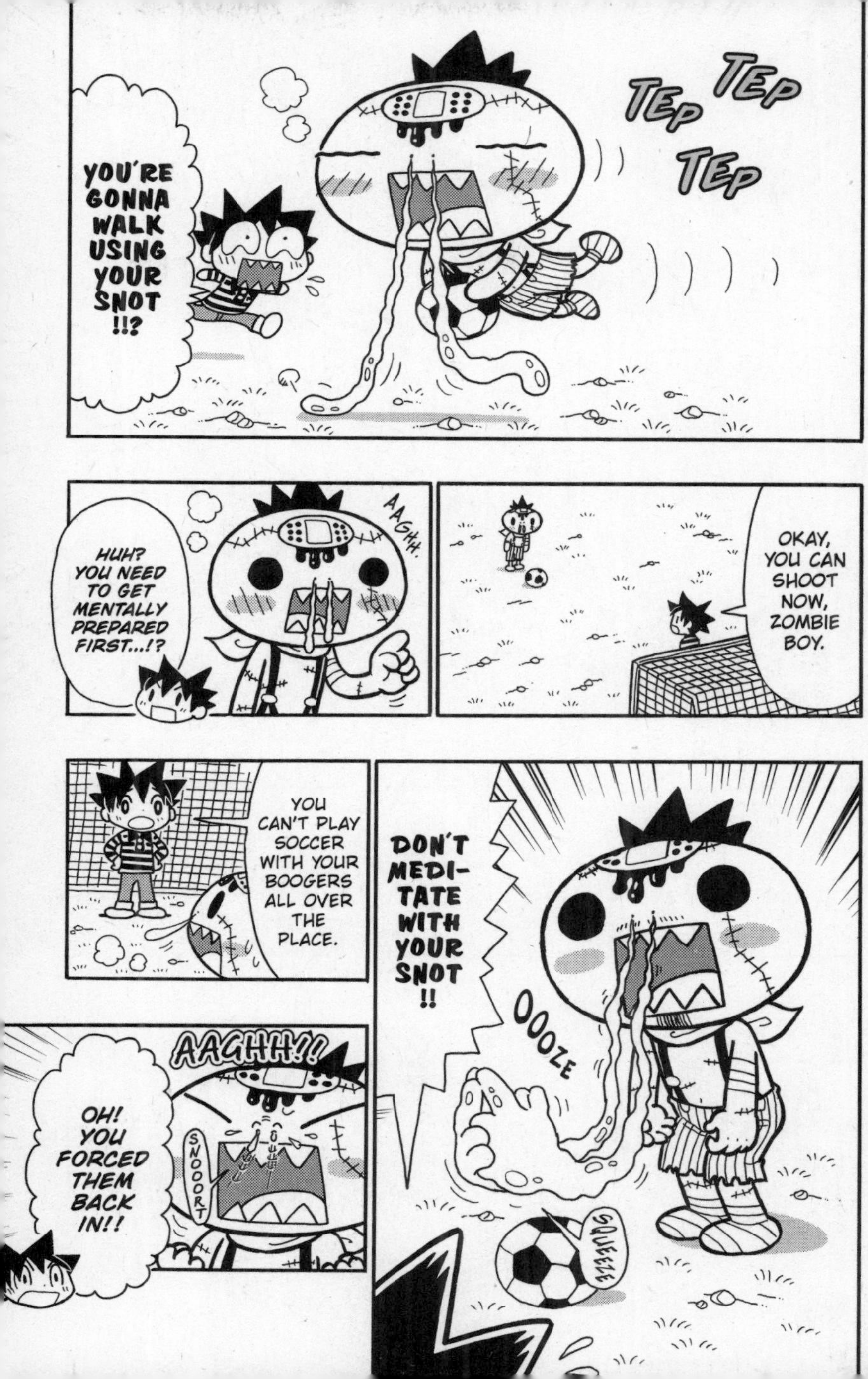
TEP
TEP
TEP
YOU'RE GONNA WALK USING YOUR SNOT !!?
OKAY, YOU CAN SHOOT NOW, ZOMBIE BOY.
AAGHH.
HUH? YOU NEED TO GET MENTALLY PREPARED FIRST...!?
DON'T MEDI-TATE WITH YOUR SNOT !!
OOOZE
SQUEEZE
YOU CAN'T PLAY SOCCER WITH YOUR BOOGERS ALL OVER THE PLACE.
AAGHH!!
SNOOORT
OH! YOU FORCED THEM BACK IN!!

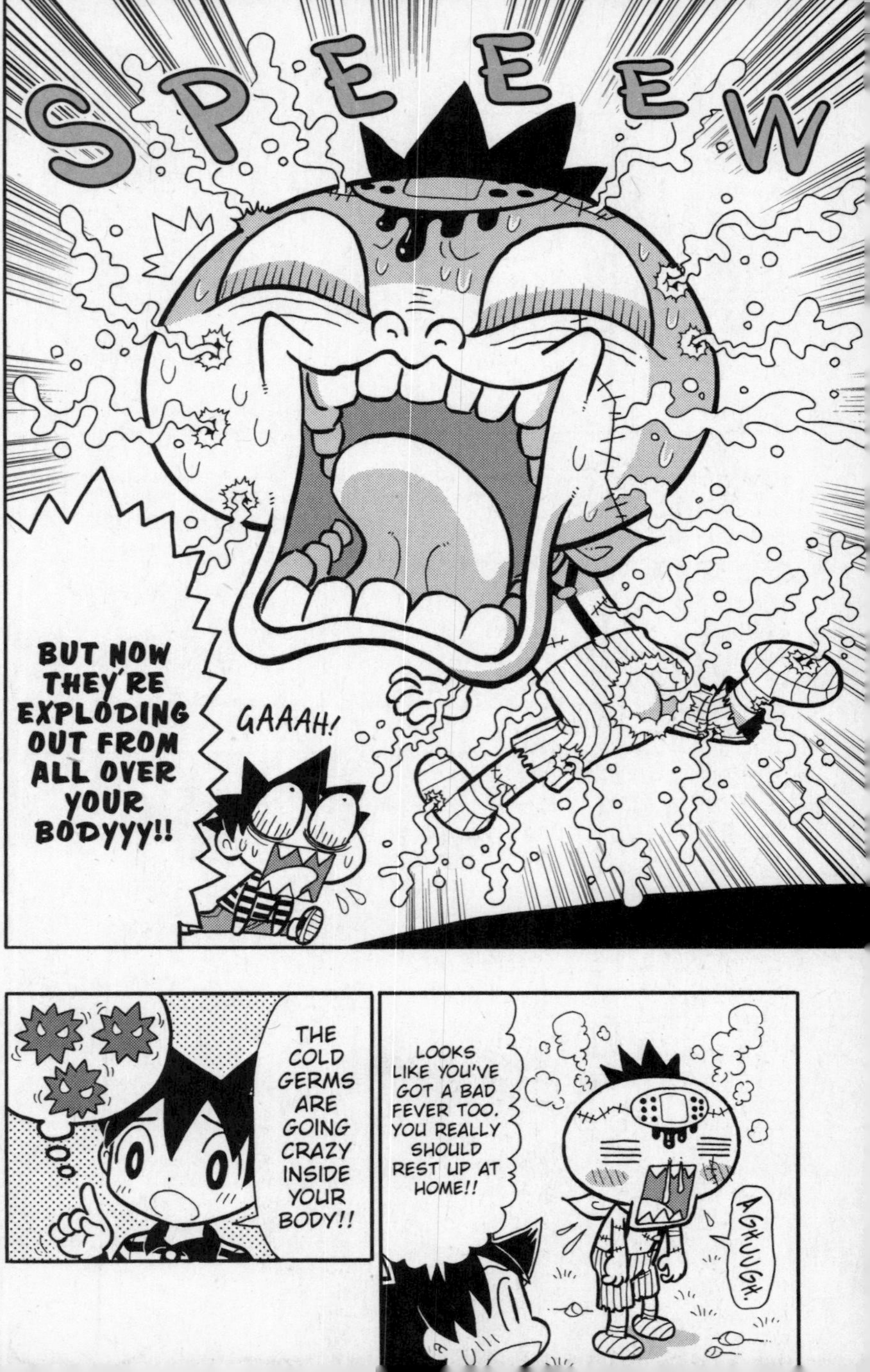
SPEEEW
BUT NOW THEY'RE EXPLODING OUT FROM ALL OVER YOUR BODYYY!!
GAAAH!
LOOKS LIKE YOU'VE GOT A BAD FEVER TOO. YOU REALLY SHOULD REST UP AT HOME!!
AGHUUGH.
THE COLD GERMS ARE GOING CRAZY INSIDE YOUR BODY!!

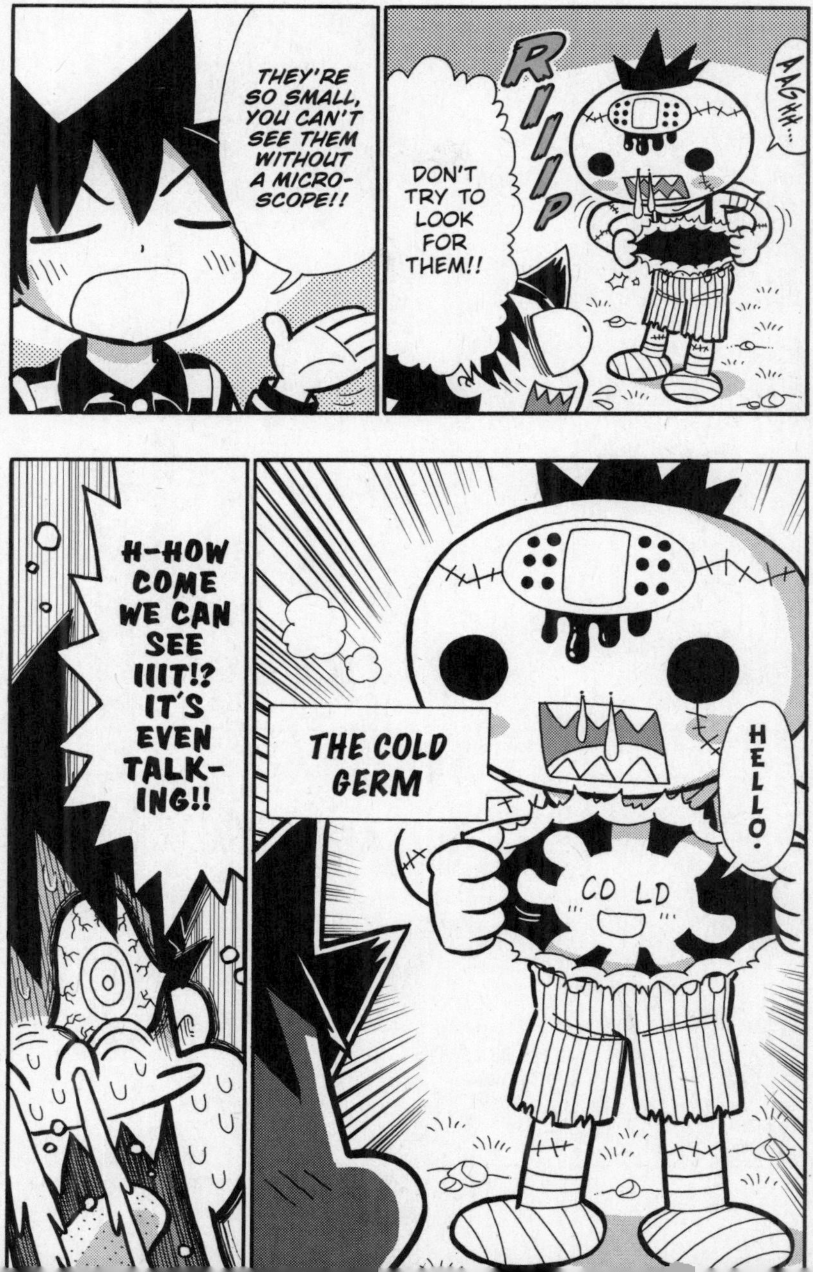

AAGHH...
RIIIP
DON'T TRY TO LOOK FOR THEM!!
THEY'RE SO SMALL, YOU CAN'T SEE THEM WITHOUT A MICRO-SCOPE!!
HELLO.
THE COLD GERM
CO LD
H-HOW COME WE CAN SEE IIIT!? IT'S EVEN TALK-ING!!

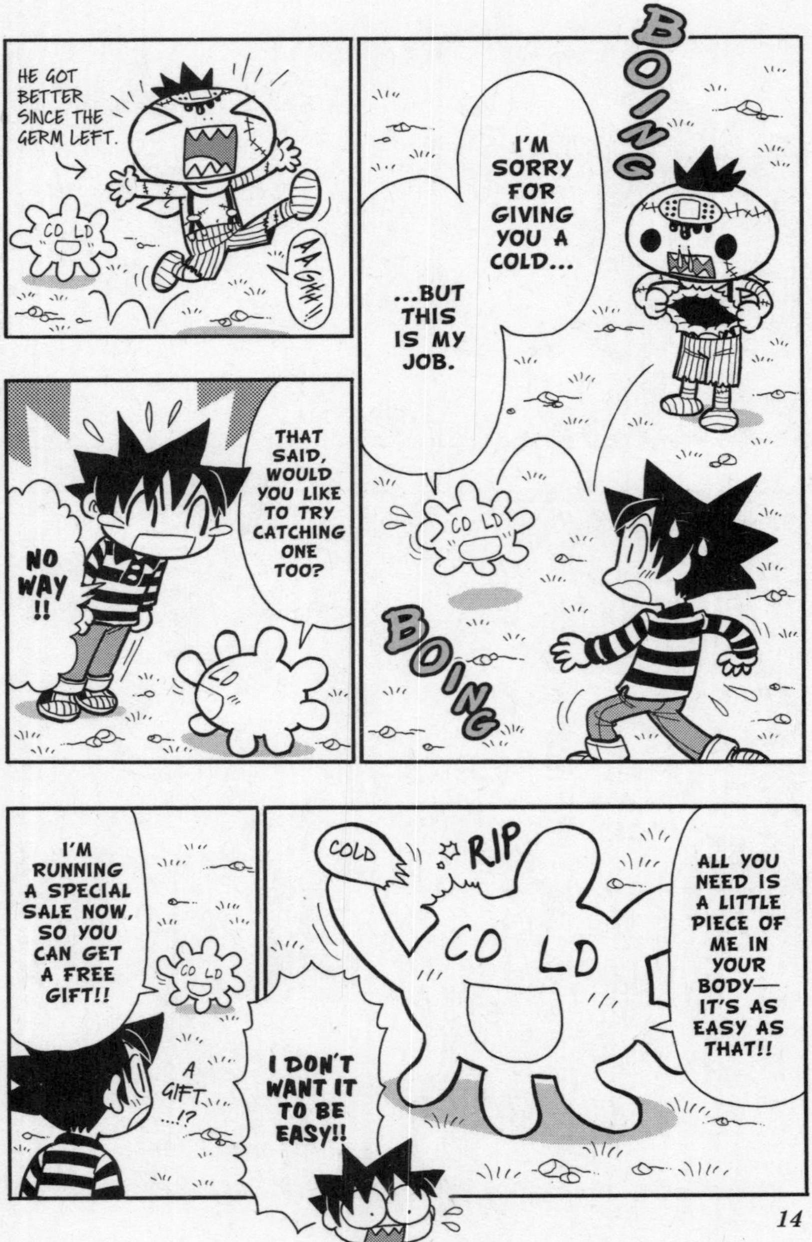
BOING
I'M SORRY FOR GIVING YOU A COLD...
...BUT THIS IS MY JOB.
CO LD
BOING
HE GOT BETTER SINCE THE GERM LEFT.
CO LD
AAGHH!!
THAT SAID, WOULD YOU LIKE TO TRY CATCHING ONE TOO?
NO WAY!!
LD
ALL YOU NEED IS A LITTLE PIECE OF ME IN YOUR BODY— IT'S AS EASY AS THAT!!
RIP
COLD
CO LD
I'M RUNNING A SPECIAL SALE NOW, SO YOU CAN GET A FREE GIFT!!
CO LD
A GIFT ...!?
I DON'T WANT IT TO BE EASY!!

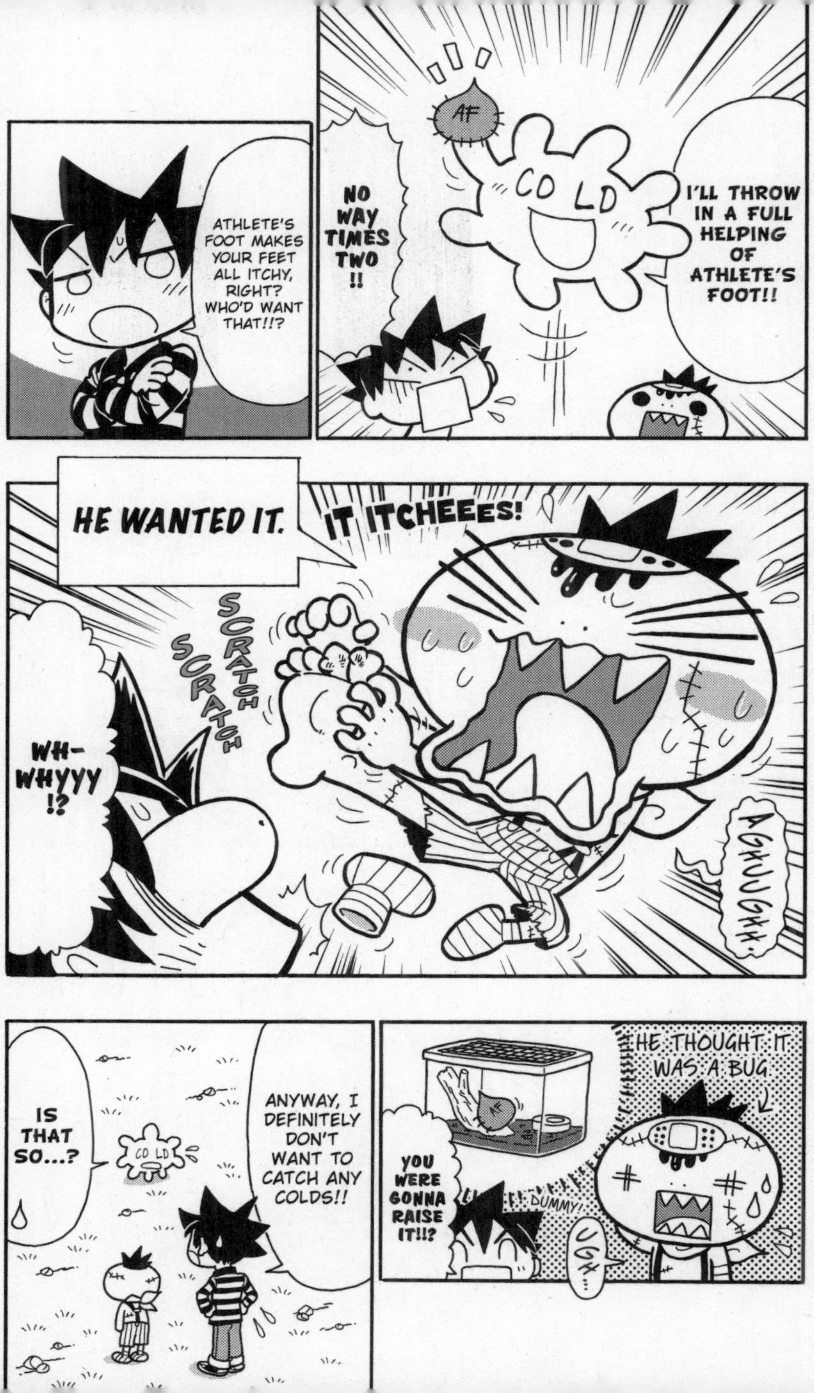
AF
I'LL THROW IN A FULL HELPING OF ATHLETE'S FOOT!!
CO LD
NO WAY TIMES TWO!!
ATHLETE'S FOOT MAKES YOUR FEET ALL ITCHY, RIGHT? WHO'D WANT THAT!!?
IT ITCHEEES!
HE WANTED IT.
AGHUUGHH.
SCRATCH SCRATCH
WH-WHYYY!?
HE THOUGHT IT WAS A BUG
YOU WERE GONNA RAISE IT!!?
DUMMY!
UGH...
ANYWAY, I DEFINITELY DON'T WANT TO CATCH ANY COLDS!!
CO LD
IS THAT SO...?

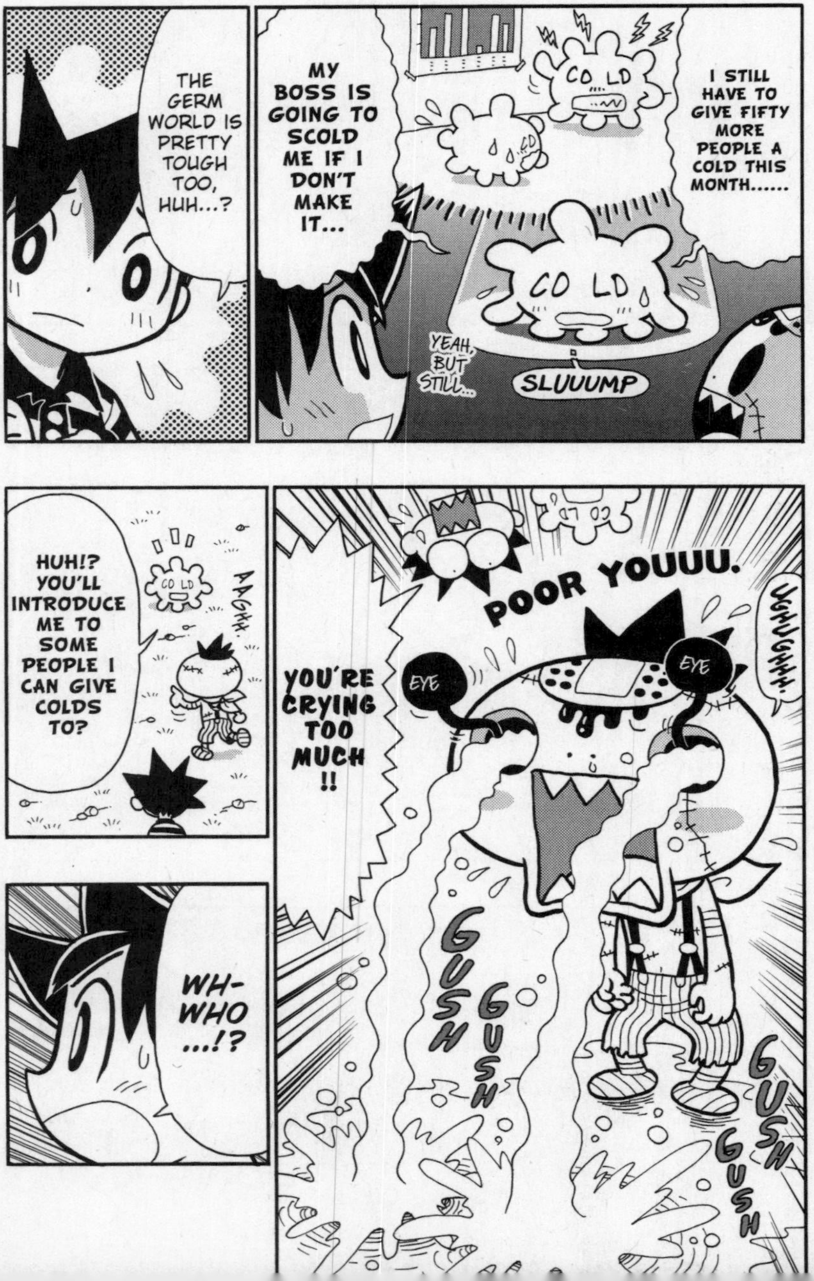
I STILL HAVE TO GIVE FIFTY MORE PEOPLE A COLD THIS MONTH......
CO LD
MY BOSS IS GOING TO SCOLD ME IF I DON'T MAKE IT...
CO LD
YEAH, BUT STILL...
SLUUUMP
THE GERM WORLD IS PRETTY TOUGH TOO, HUH...?
UGHUGHHH.
POOR YOUUU.
EYE
EYE
YOU'RE CRYING TOO MUCH!!
GUSH
GUSH
GUSH
GUSH
HUH!? YOU'LL INTRODUCE ME TO SOME PEOPLE I CAN GIVE COLDS TO?
AAGHH.
CO LD
WH-WHO...!?

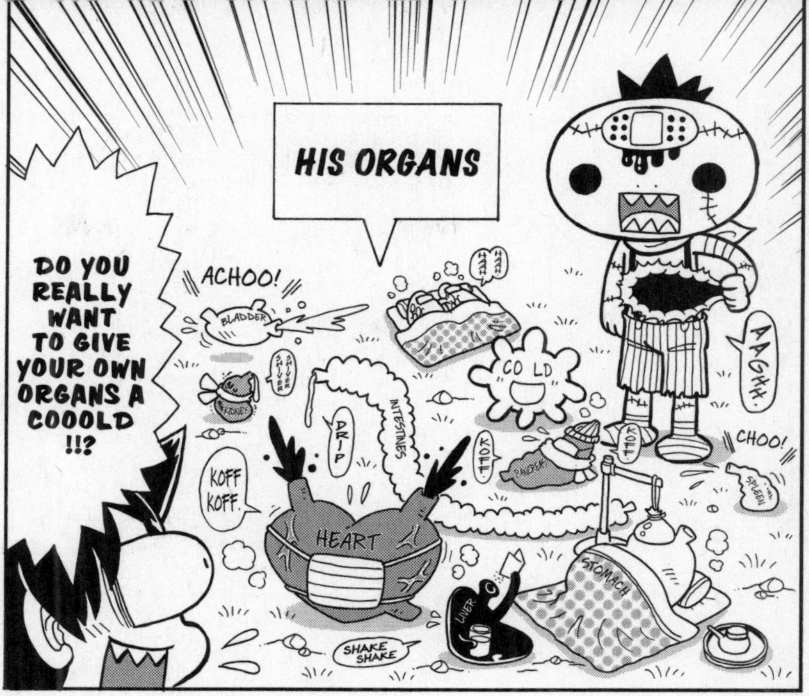
HIS ORGANS
AAGHX.
HAAH HAAH
CHOO!
SPLEEN
KOFF
KOFF.
PANCREAS
CO LD
STOMACH
LIVER
SHAKE SHAKE
HEART
INTESTINES
DRIP
KOFF KOFF.
SHIVER SHIVER
KIDNEY
BLADDER
ACHOO!
DO YOU REALLY WANT TO GIVE YOUR OWN ORGANS A COOOLD !!?

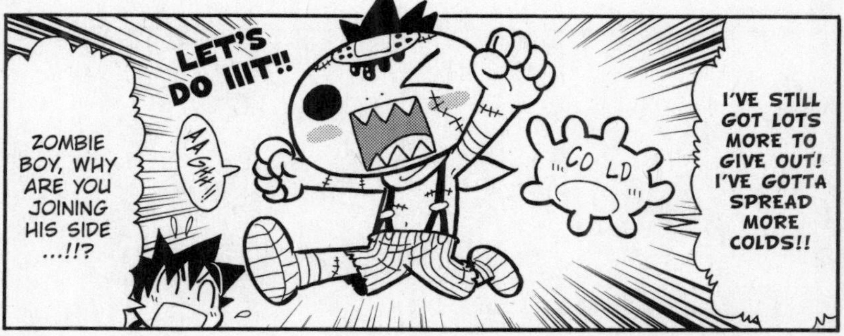
I'VE STILL GOT LOTS MORE TO GIVE OUT! I'VE GOTTA SPREAD MORE COLDS!!
CO LD
LET'S DO IIIT!!
AAGHX!!
ZOMBIE BOY, WHY ARE YOU JOINING HIS SIDE ...!!?

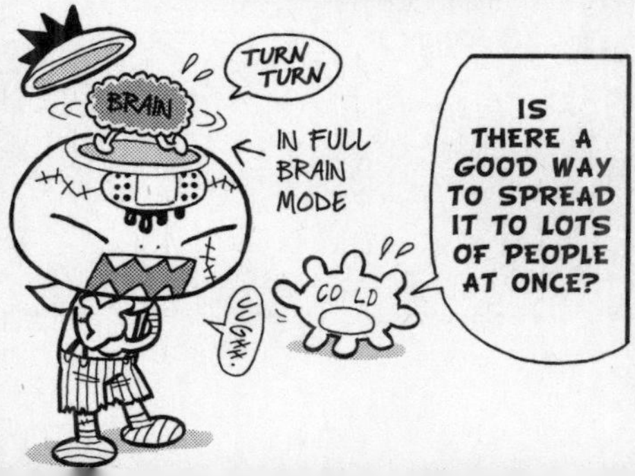
IS THERE A GOOD WAY TO SPREAD IT TO LOTS OF PEOPLE AT ONCE?
TURN TURN
BRAIN
IN FULL BRAIN MODE
CO LD
UGHX.

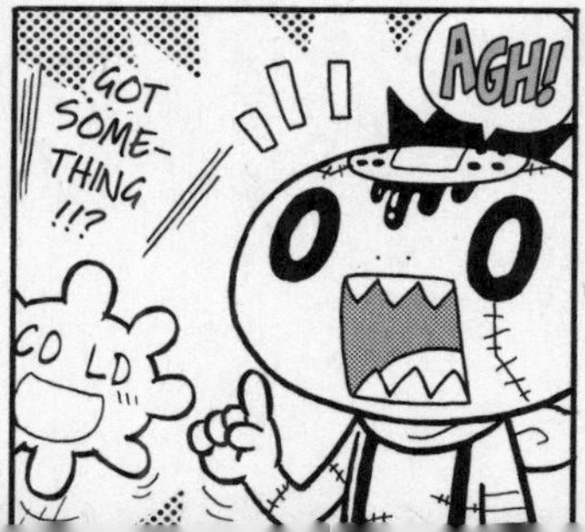
AGH!
GOT SOME-THING !!?
CO LD

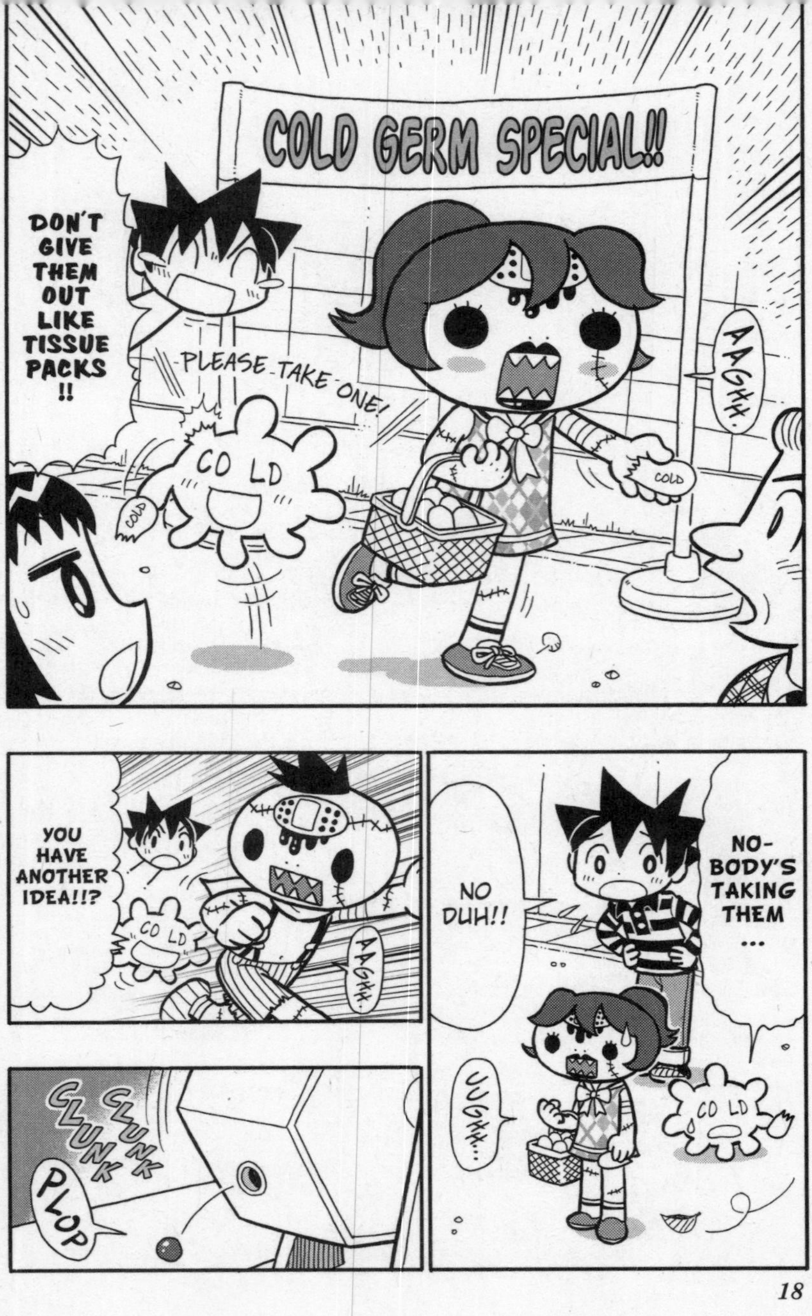
COLD GERM SPECIAL!!
AAGHX.
PLEASE TAKE ONE!
DON'T GIVE THEM OUT LIKE TISSUE PACKS!!
CO LD
COLD
COLD
NO-BODY'S TAKING THEM...
NO DUH!!
UGHX...
CO LD
AAGHX.
YOU HAVE ANOTHER IDEA!!?
CO LD
CLUNK CLUNK
PLOP

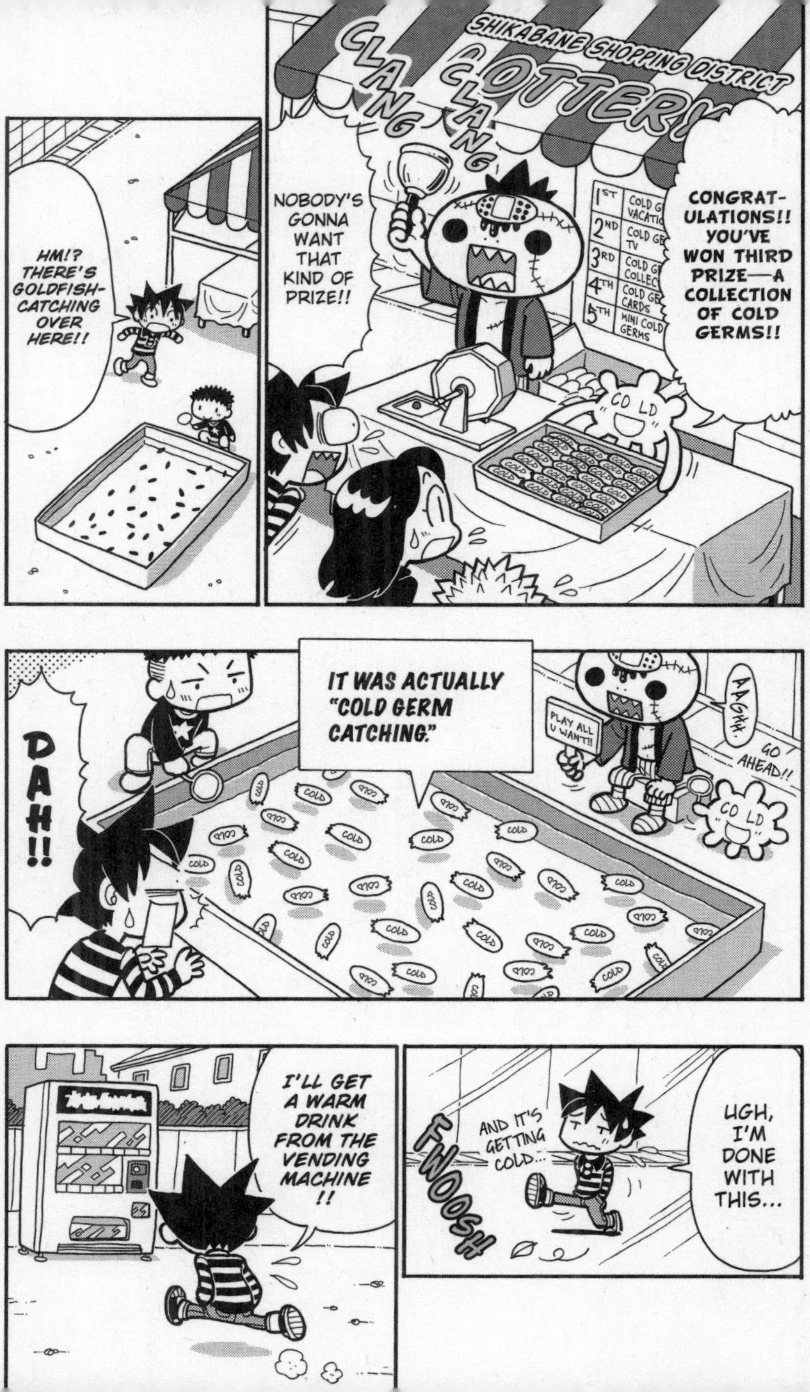
SHIKABANE SHOPPING DISTRICT
LOTTERY
CLANG
CLANG
CONGRATULATIONS!! YOU'VE WON THIRD PRIZE—A COLLECTION OF COLD GERMS!!
NOBODY'S GONNA WANT THAT KIND OF PRIZE!!
HM!? THERE'S GOLDFISH-CATCHING OVER HERE!!
AAGHH.
GO AHEAD!!
PLAY ALL U WANT!!
IT WAS ACTUALLY "COLD GERM CATCHING."
DAH!!
UGH, I'M DONE WITH THIS...
AND IT'S GETTING COLD...
FWOOSH
I'LL GET A WARM DRINK FROM THE VENDING MACHINE!!

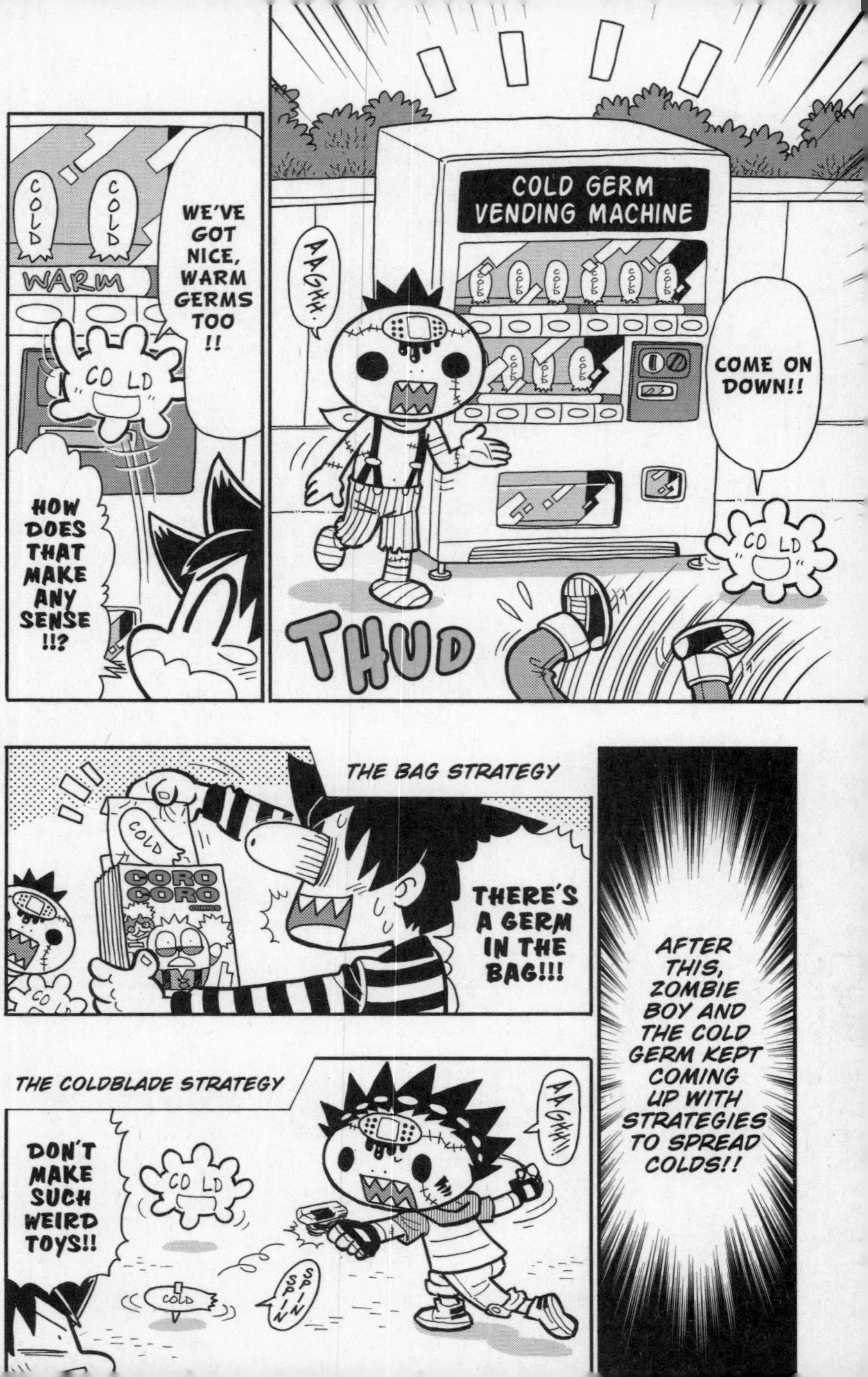
COLD GERM VENDING MACHINE
COLD
AAGHH.
COME ON DOWN!!
COLD
THUD
COLD
WARM
WE'VE GOT NICE, WARM GERMS TOO!!
COLD
HOW DOES THAT MAKE ANY SENSE!!?
AFTER THIS, ZOMBIE BOY AND THE COLD GERM KEPT COMING UP WITH STRATEGIES TO SPREAD COLDS!!
THE BAG STRATEGY
COLD
CORO CORO COMICS
THERE'S A GERM IN THE BAG!!!
COLD
THE COLDBLADE STRATEGY
AAGHH!!
COLD
DON'T MAKE SUCH WEIRD TOYS!!
SPIN SPIN
COLD

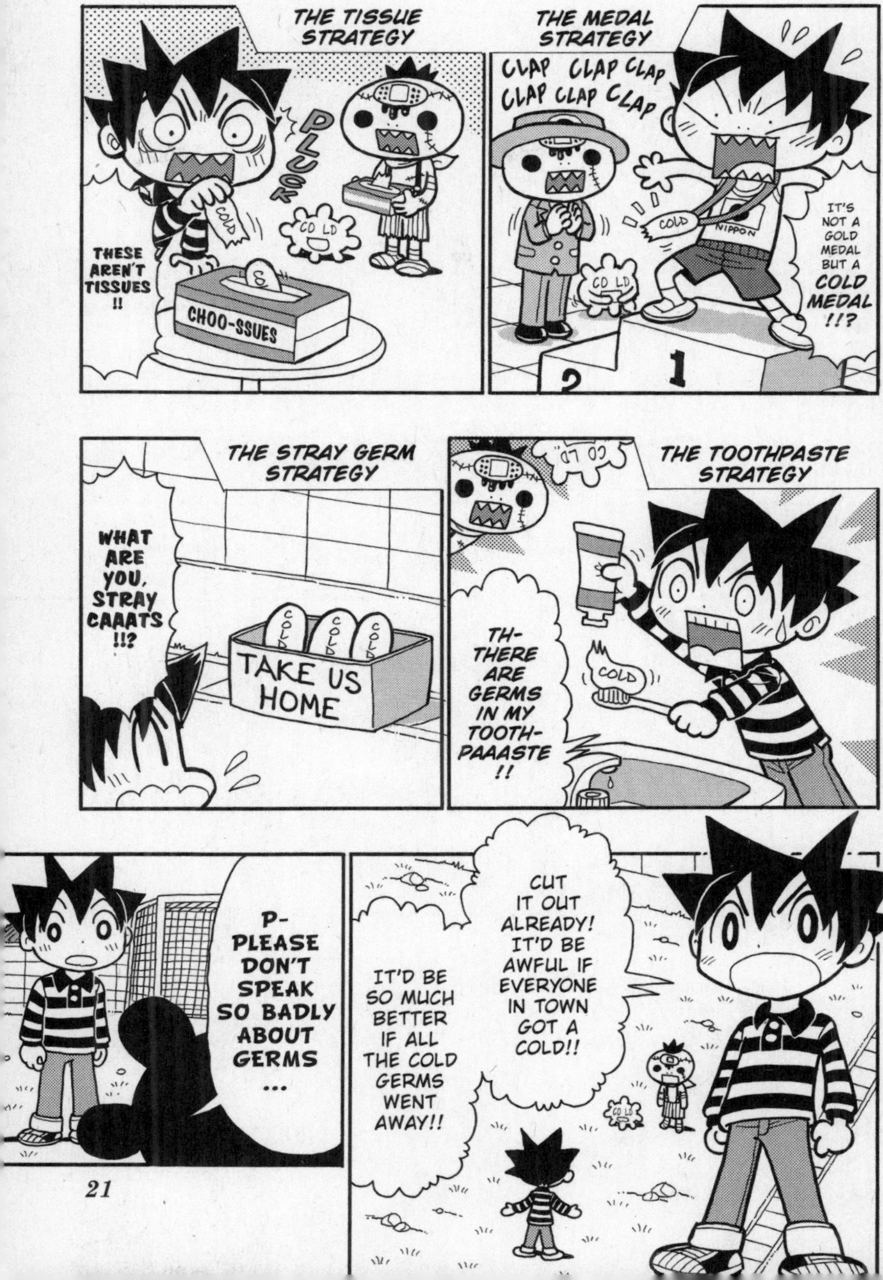
THE MEDAL STRATEGY
CLAP CLAP CLAP
CLAP CLAP CLAP
COLD
NIPPON
CO LD
IT'S NOT A GOLD MEDAL BUT A COLD MEDAL!!?
1
2
THE TISSUE STRATEGY
PLUCK
COLD
CO LD
THESE AREN'T TISSUES!!
CHOO-SSUES
CO LD
THE TOOTHPASTE STRATEGY
COLD
TH-THERE ARE GERMS IN MY TOOTH-PAAASTE!!
THE STRAY GERM STRATEGY
WHAT ARE YOU, STRAY CAAATS!!?
COLD
COLD
COLD
TAKE US HOME
CUT IT OUT ALREADY! IT'D BE AWFUL IF EVERYONE IN TOWN GOT A COLD!!
IT'D BE SO MUCH BETTER IF ALL THE COLD GERMS WENT AWAY!!
CO LD
P-PLEASE DON'T SPEAK SO BADLY ABOUT GERMS...

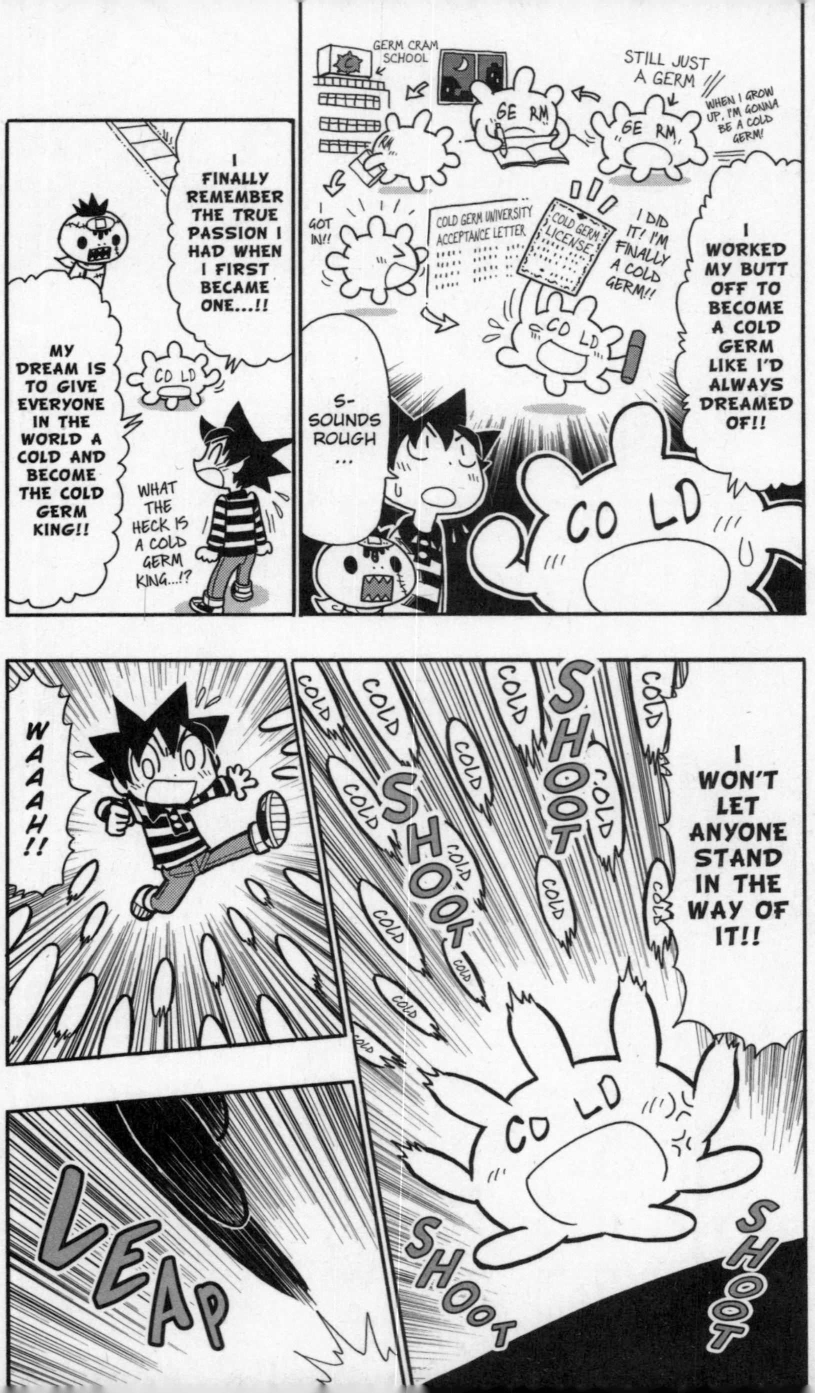
STILL JUST A GERM
WHEN I GROW UP, I'M GONNA BE A COLD GERM!
GE RM
GE RM
GERM CRAM SCHOOL
I WORKED MY BUTT OFF TO BECOME A COLD GERM LIKE I'D ALWAYS DREAMED OF!!
I DID IT! I'M FINALLY A COLD GERM!!
COLD GERM LICENSE
CO LD
COLD GERM UNIVERSITY ACCEPTANCE LETTER
I GOT IN!!
S-SOUNDS ROUGH...
CO LD
I FINALLY REMEMBER THE TRUE PASSION I HAD WHEN I FIRST BECAME ONE...!!
MY DREAM IS TO GIVE EVERYONE IN THE WORLD A COLD AND BECOME THE COLD GERM KING!!
CO LD
WHAT THE HECK IS A COLD GERM KING...!?
I WON'T LET ANYONE STAND IN THE WAY OF IT!!
SHOOT
SHOOT
SHOOT
SHOOT
COLD
CO LD
WAAAAH!!
LEAP

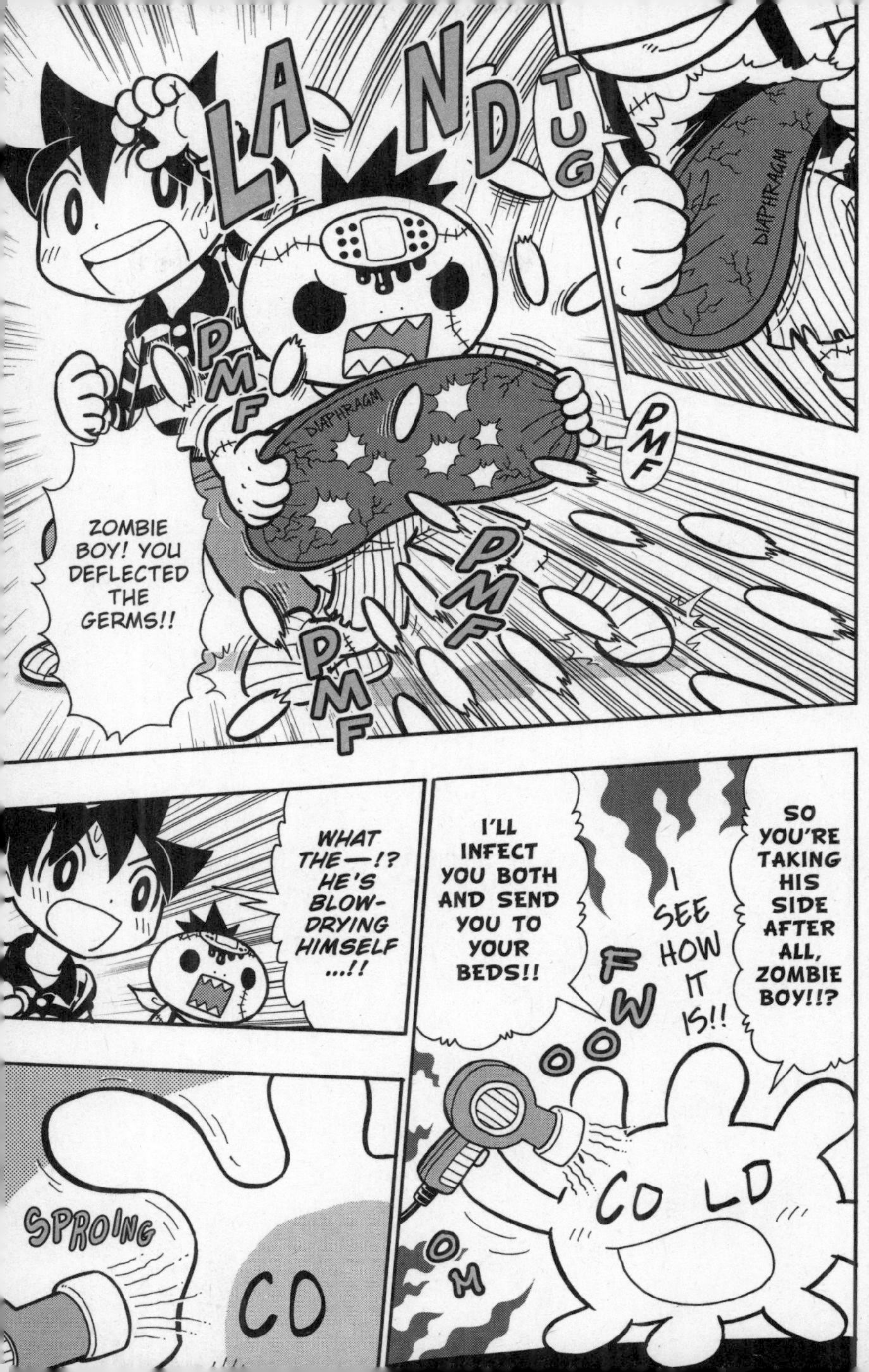
TUG
DIAPHRAGM
LAND
DIAPHRAGM
PMF
PMF
PMF
PMF
ZOMBIE BOY! YOU DEFLECTED THE GERMS!!
SO YOU'RE TAKING HIS SIDE AFTER ALL, ZOMBIE BOY!!?
I SEE HOW IT IS!!
I'LL INFECT YOU BOTH AND SEND YOU TO YOUR BEDS!!
FWOOO
WHAT THE—!? HE'S BLOW-DRYING HIMSELF...!!
COLD
OM
SPROING
CO

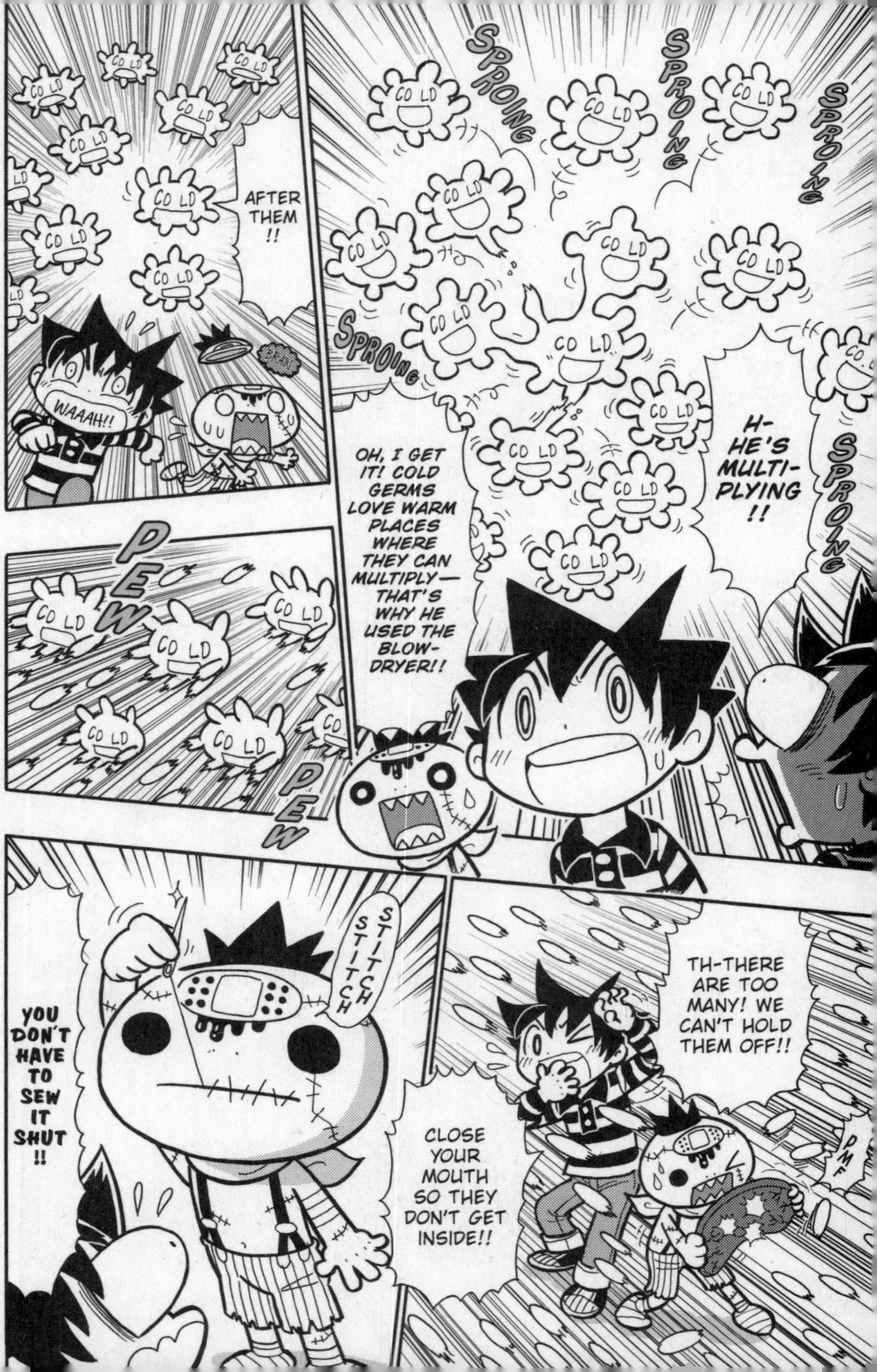
SPROING
SPROING
SPROING
CO LD
H-HE'S MULTI-PLYING!!
OH, I GET IT! COLD GERMS LOVE WARM PLACES WHERE THEY CAN MULTIPLY—THAT'S WHY HE USED THE BLOW-DRYER!!
SPROING
SPROING
AFTER THEM!!
WAAAH!!
PEW
PEW
TH-THERE ARE TOO MANY! WE CAN'T HOLD THEM OFF!!
DMF
CLOSE YOUR MOUTH SO THEY DON'T GET INSIDE!!
STITCH STITCH
YOU DON'T HAVE TO SEW IT SHUT!!

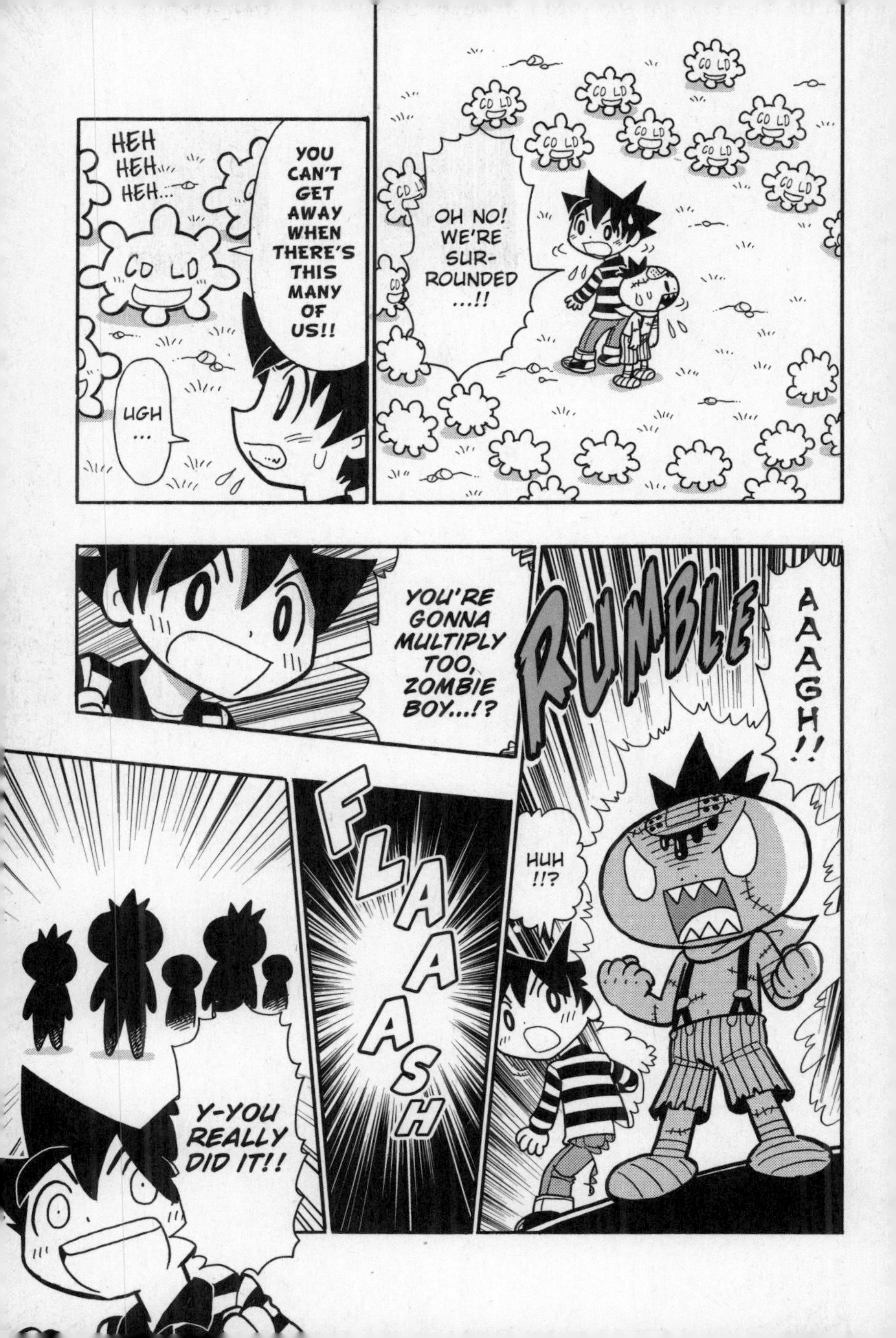
CO LD
OH NO! WE'RE SUR-ROUNDED...!!
HEH HEH HEH...
YOU CAN'T GET AWAY WHEN THERE'S THIS MANY OF US!!
UGH...
RUMBLE
AAAGH!!
HUH!!?
YOU'RE GONNA MULTIPLY TOO, ZOMBIE BOY...!?
FLAAASH
Y-YOU REALLY DID IT!!

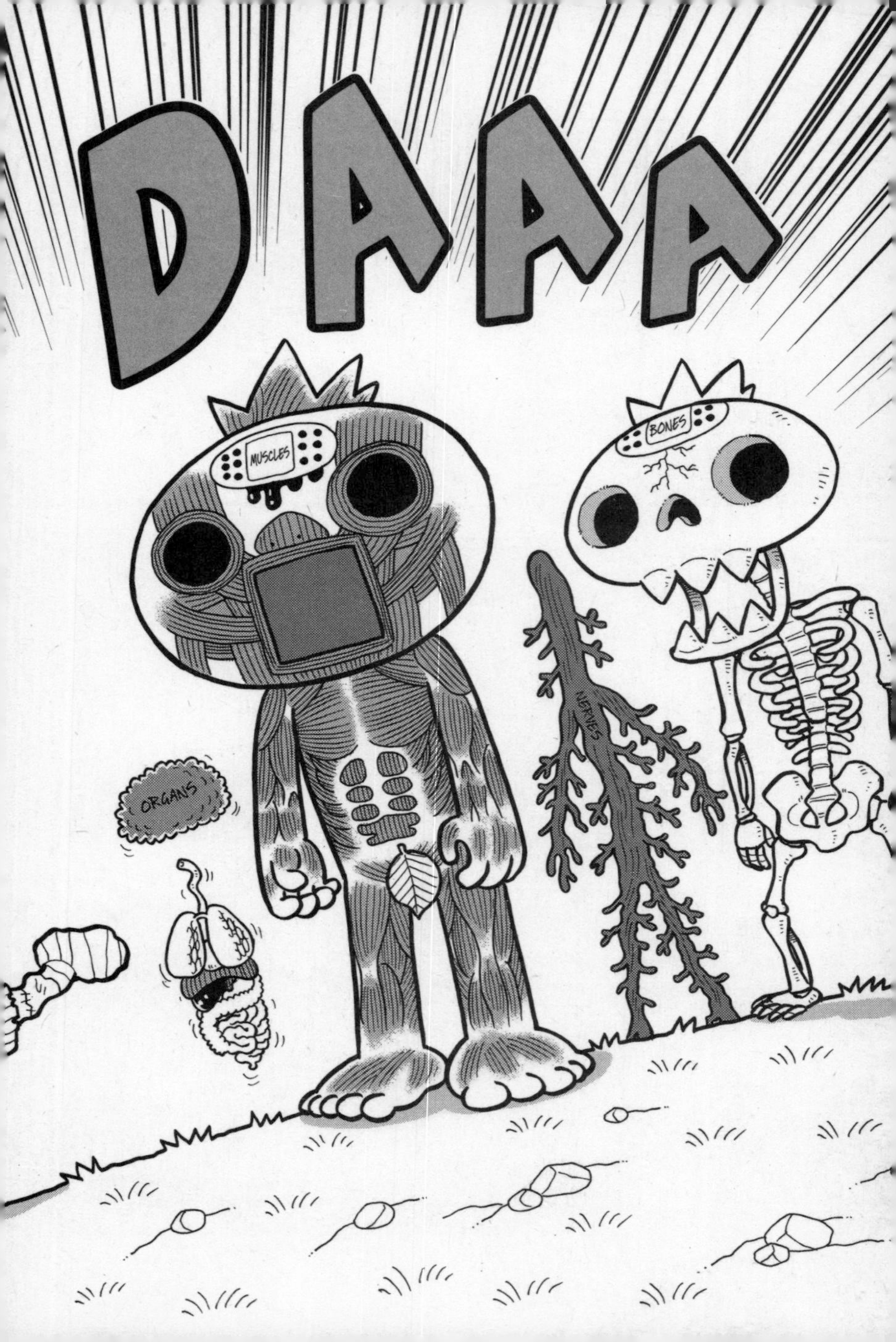
DAAA
MUSCLES
BONES
NERVES
ORGANS

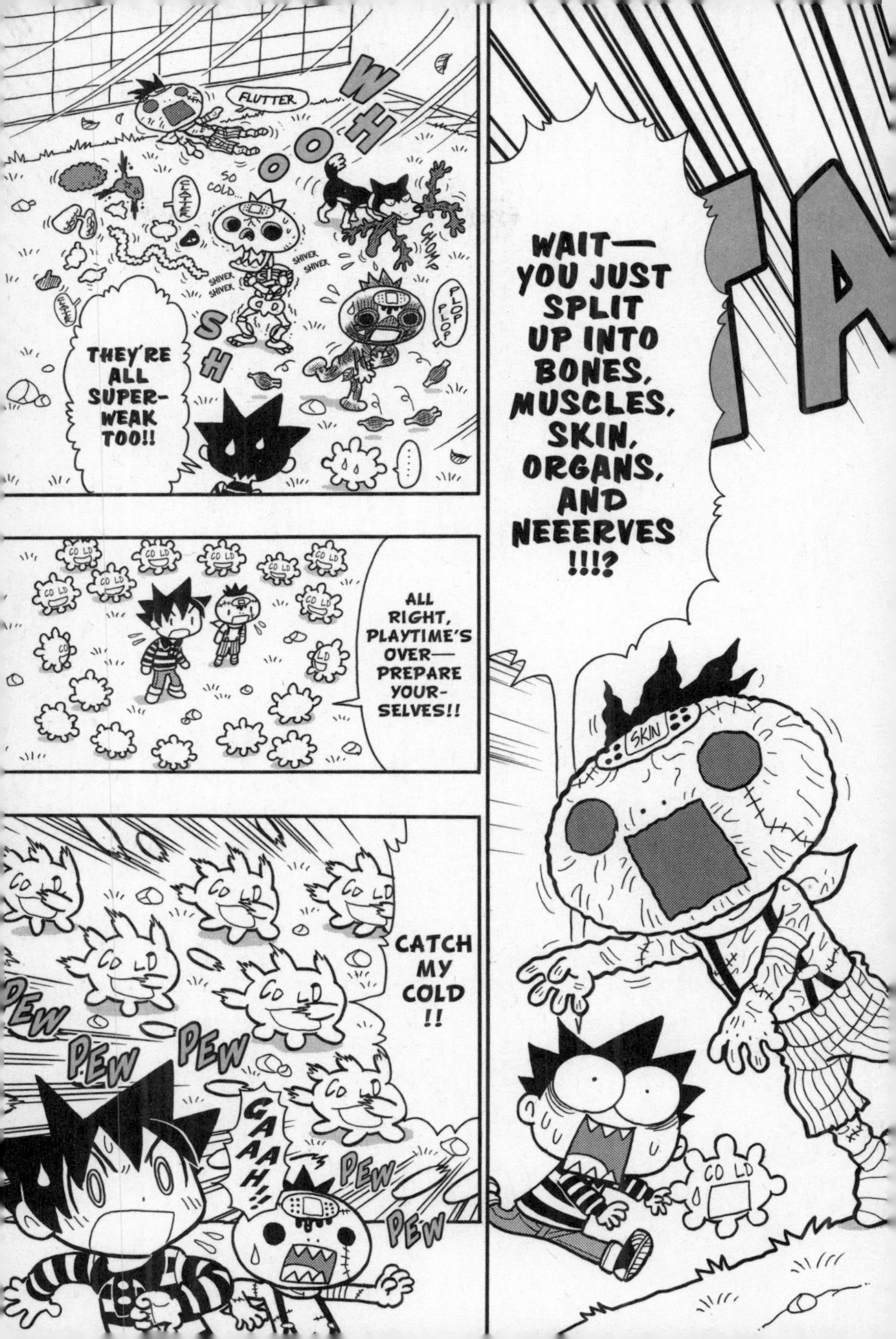
WAIT— YOU JUST SPLIT UP INTO BONES, MUSCLES, SKIN, ORGANS, AND NEEERVES !!!?
SKIN
CO LD
FLUTTER
WHOOOSH
SO COLD...
CLATTER
CHOMP
SHIVER SHIVER
SHIVER SHIVER
PLOP PLOP
THEY'RE ALL SUPER-WEAK TOO!!
...
ALL RIGHT, PLAYTIME'S OVER—PREPARE YOURSELVES!!
CATCH MY COLD!!
PEW
PEW
PEW
GAAAH!!
PEW
PEW

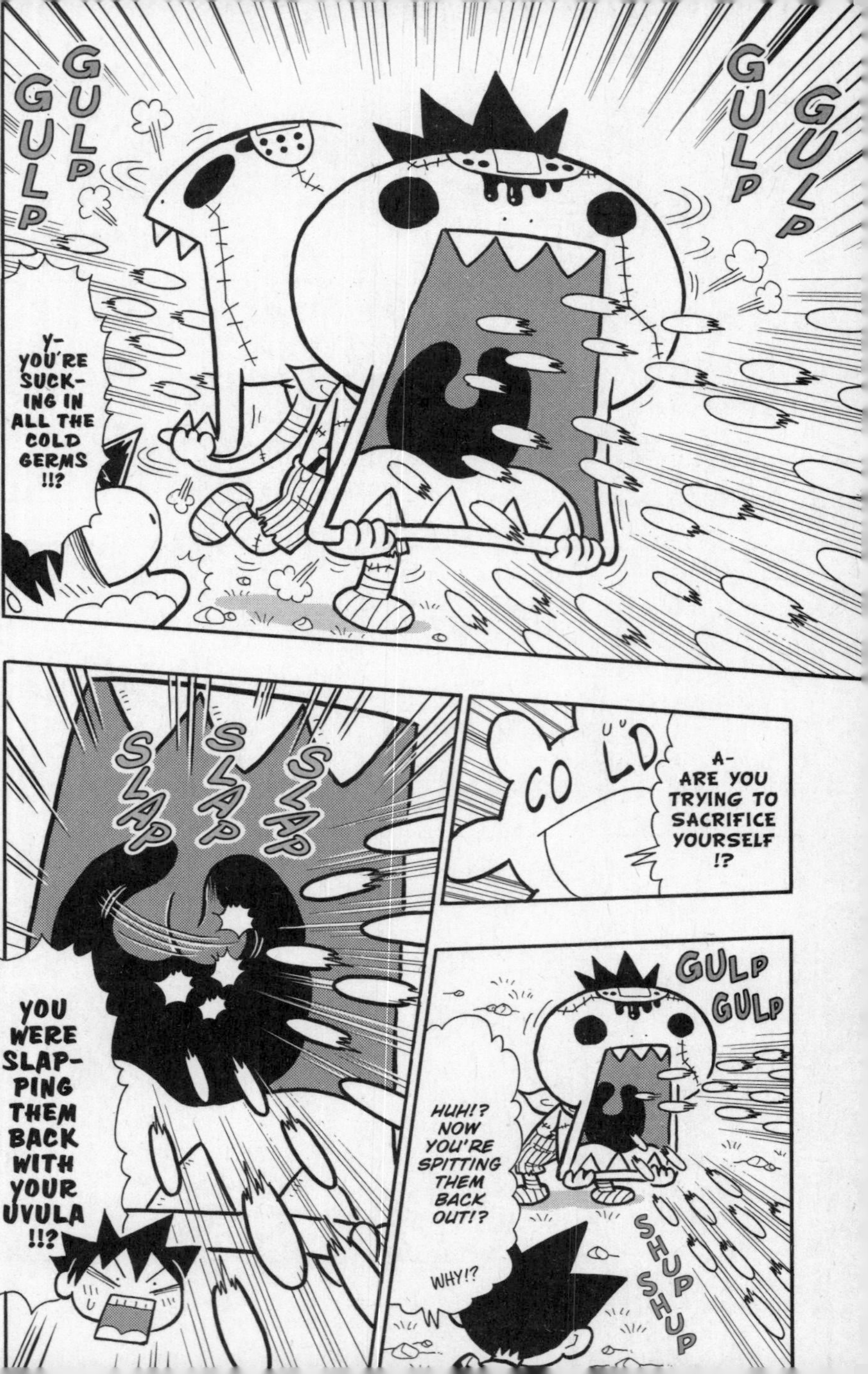
GULP GULP
GULP GULP
Y-YOU'RE SUCKING IN ALL THE COLD GERMS!!?
COLD
A-ARE YOU TRYING TO SACRIFICE YOURSELF!?
GULP GULP
HUH!? NOW YOU'RE SPITTING THEM BACK OUT!?
SHUP SHUP
WHY!?
SLAP SLAP SLAP
YOU WERE SLAPPING THEM BACK WITH YOUR UVULA!!?

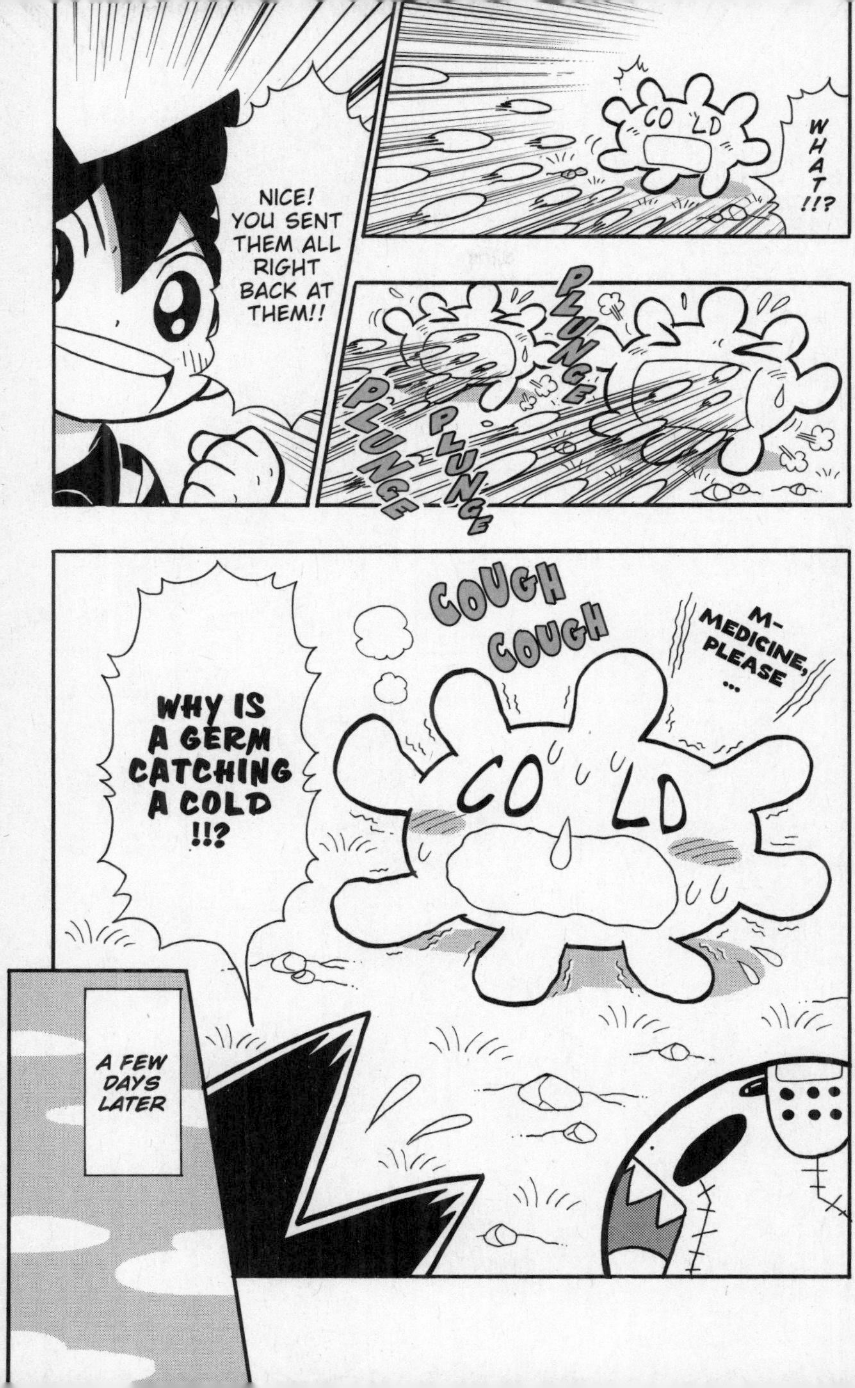
CO LD
WHAT!!?
PLUNGE
PLUNGE
PLUNGE
NICE! YOU SENT THEM ALL RIGHT BACK AT THEM!!
COUGH
COUGH
M-MEDICINE, PLEASE...
CO LD
WHY IS A GERM CATCHING A COLD!!?
A FEW DAYS LATER

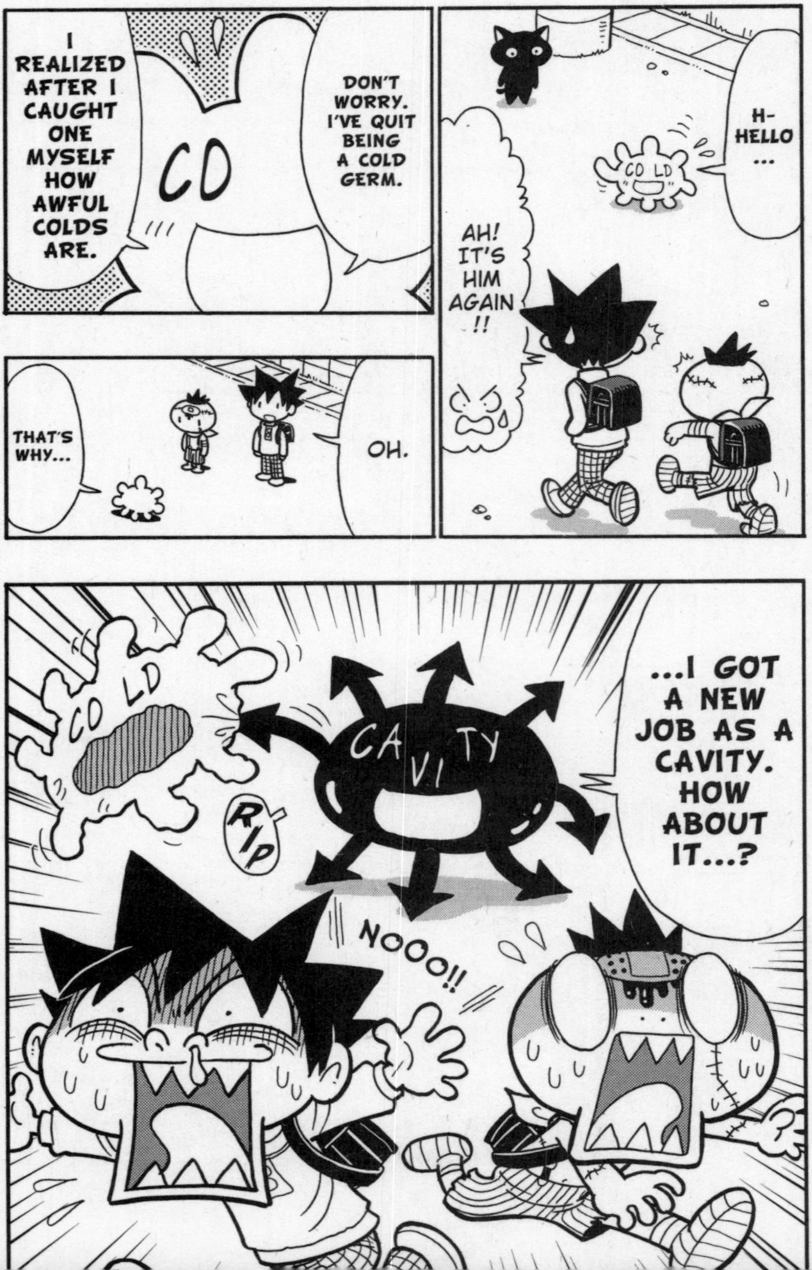
H-HELLO...
CO LD
AH! IT'S HIM AGAIN!!
DON'T WORRY. I'VE QUIT BEING A COLD GERM.
CD
I REALIZED AFTER I CAUGHT ONE MYSELF HOW AWFUL COLDS ARE.
OH.
THAT'S WHY...
...I GOT A NEW JOB AS A CAVITY. HOW ABOUT IT...?
CAVITY
CO LD
RIP
NOOO!!

IT'Z A HOUZE FILLED WITH BOOBY TRAPZ!

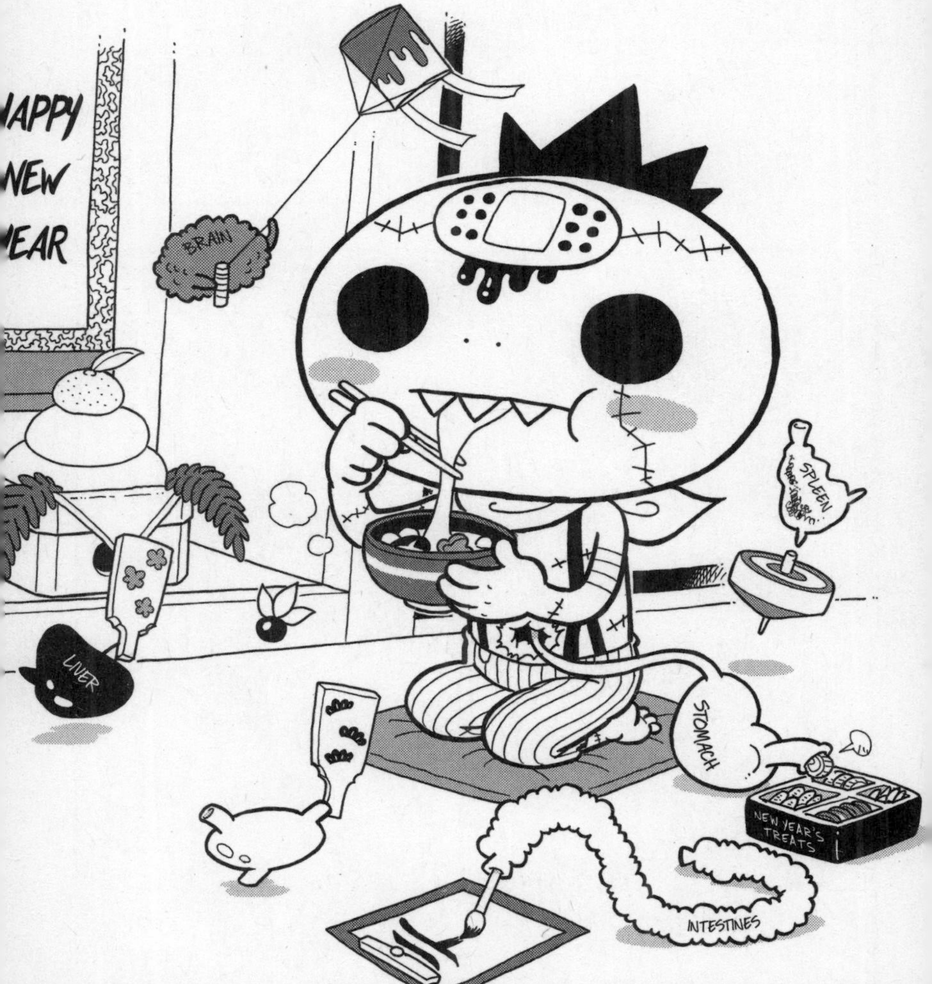

HAPPY NEW YEAR
BRAIN
SPLEEN
LIVER
STOMACH
NEW YEAR'S TREATS
INTESTINES

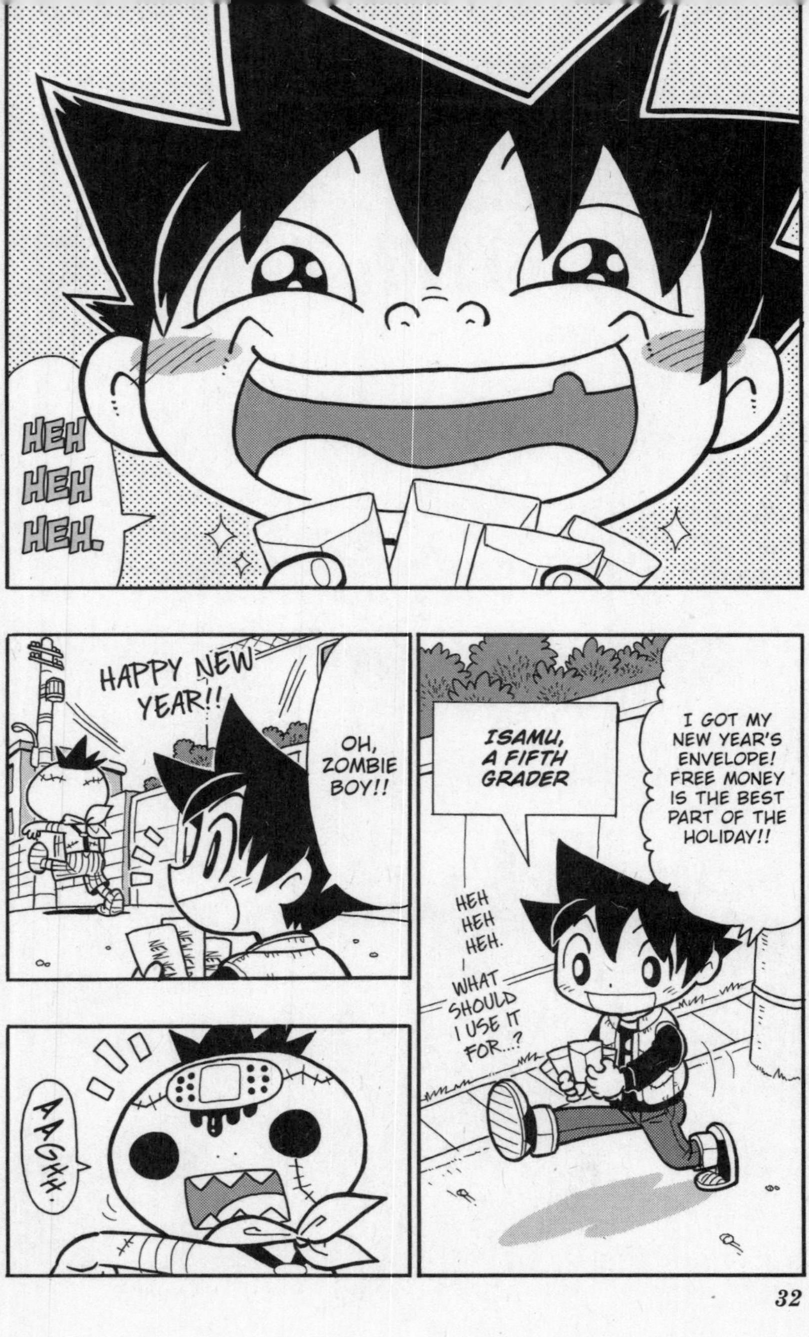
HEH HEH HEH.
I GOT MY NEW YEAR'S ENVELOPE! FREE MONEY IS THE BEST PART OF THE HOLIDAY!!
ISAMU, A FIFTH GRADER
HEH HEH HEH.
WHAT SHOULD I USE IT FOR...?
OH, ZOMBIE BOY!!
HAPPY NEW YEAR!!
AAGHH.

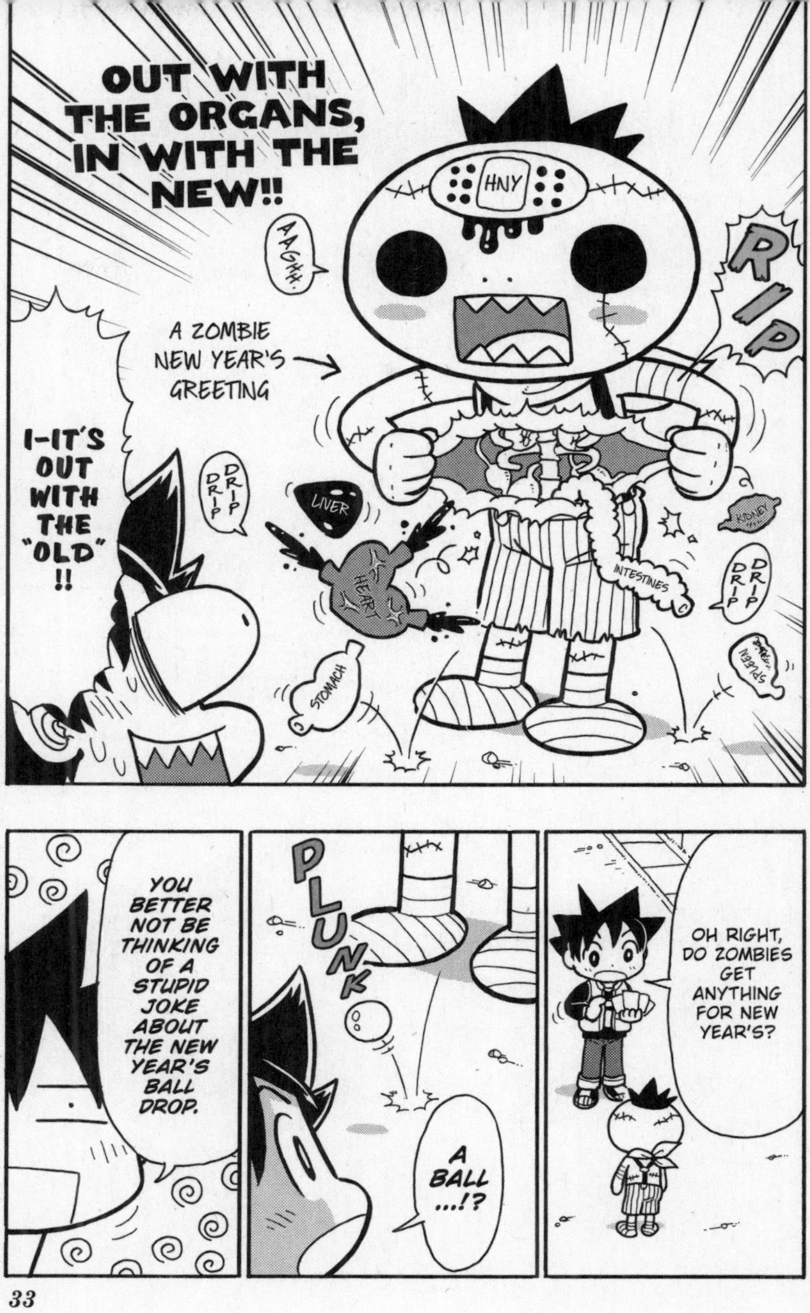
RIP
OUT WITH THE ORGANS, IN WITH THE NEW!!
HNY
AAGHX.
A ZOMBIE NEW YEAR'S GREETING
KIDNEY
DRIP DRIP
INTESTINES
LIVER
DRIP DRIP
HEART
SPLEEN
STOMACH
I-IT'S OUT WITH THE "OLD"!!
OH RIGHT, DO ZOMBIES GET ANYTHING FOR NEW YEAR'S?
PLUNK
A BALL ...!?
YOU BETTER NOT BE THINKING OF A STUPID JOKE ABOUT THE NEW YEAR'S BALL DROP.

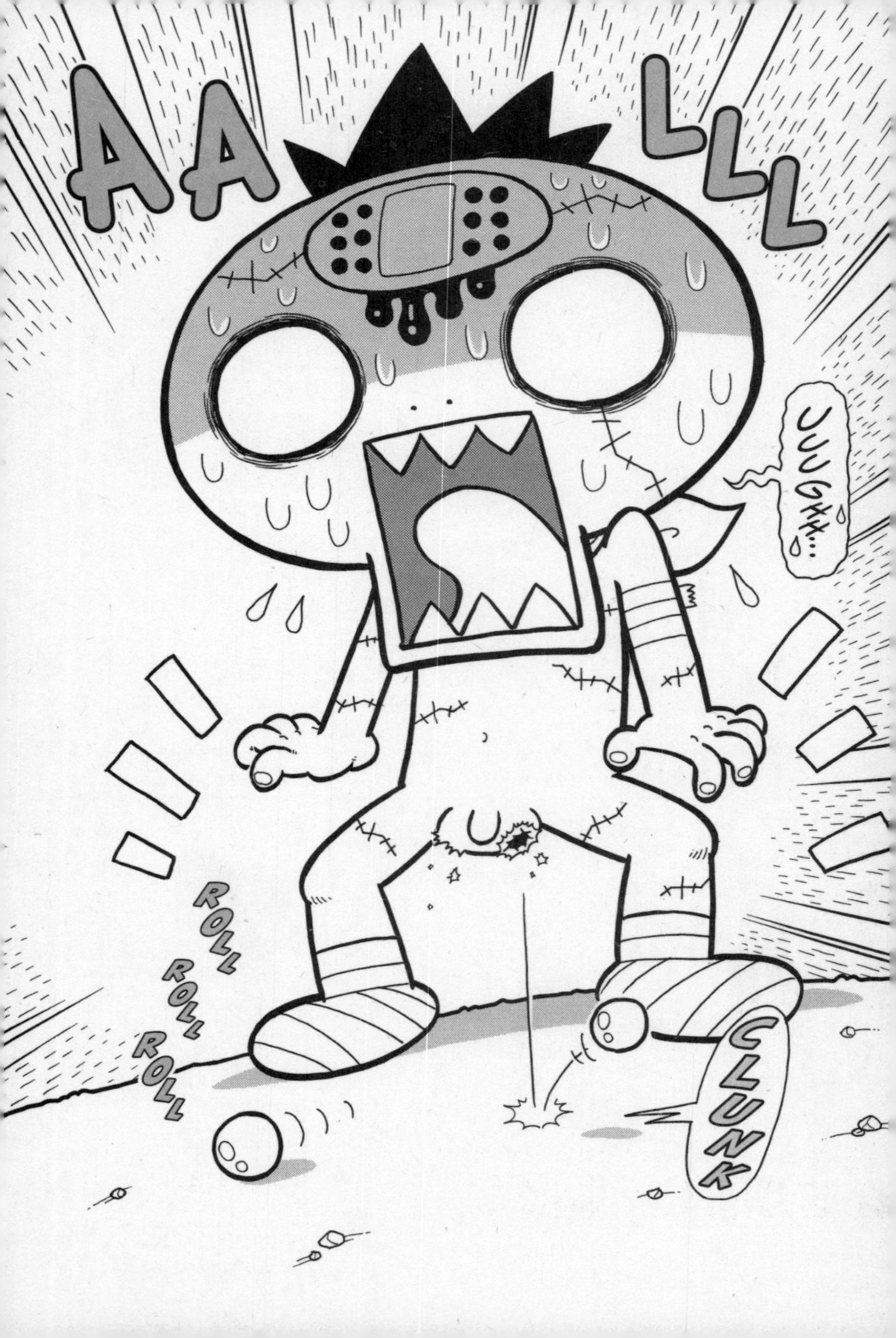
AAAALLLL
UUUGHH...
ROLL ROLL ROLL
CLUNK

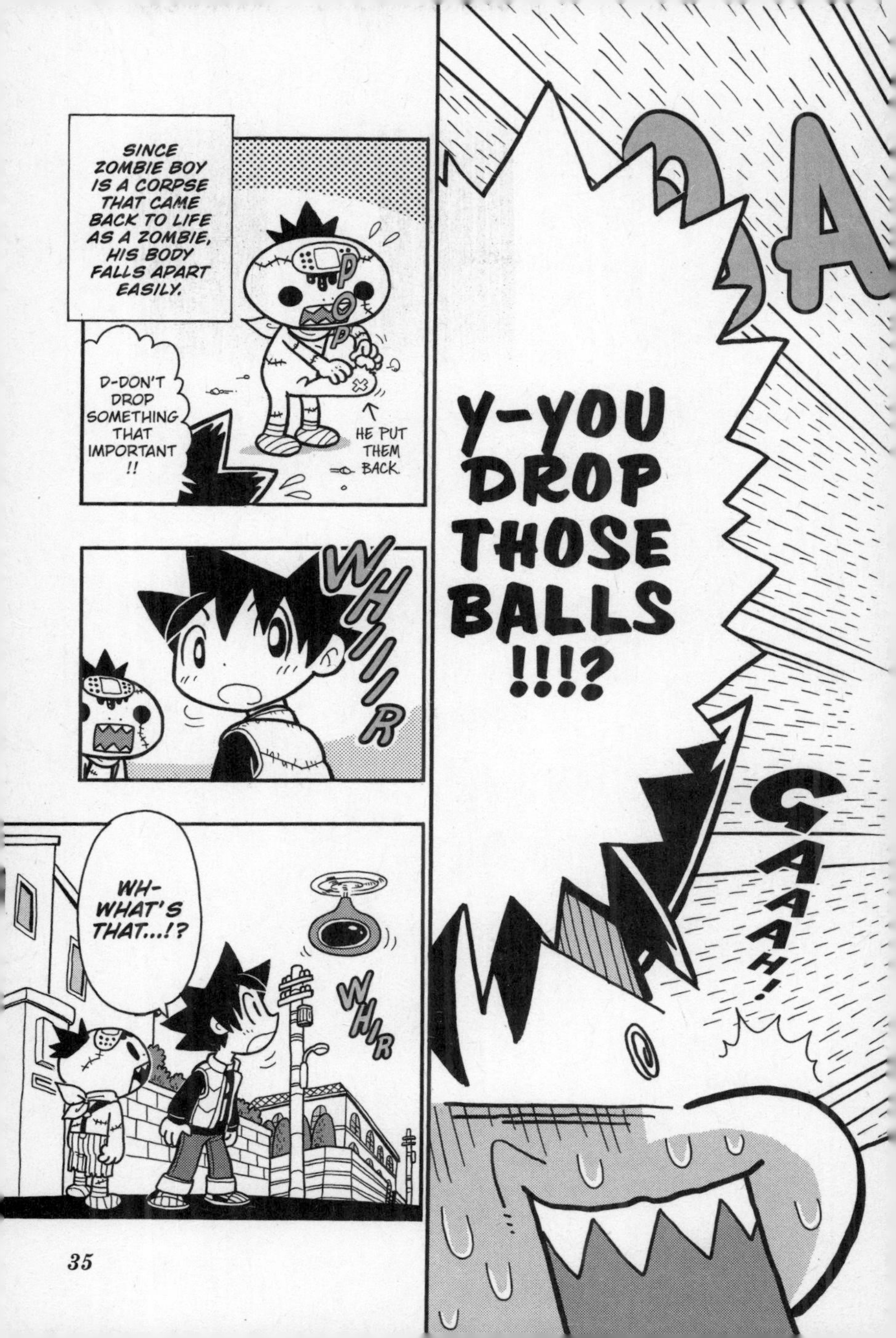

DA
Y-YOU DROP THOSE BALLS !!!?
GAAAAH!
SINCE ZOMBIE BOY IS A CORPSE THAT CAME BACK TO LIFE AS A ZOMBIE, HIS BODY FALLS APART EASILY.
POP POP
D-DON'T DROP SOMETHING THAT IMPORTANT !!
HE PUT THEM BACK.
WHIIIR
WH- WHAT'S THAT...!?
WHIR

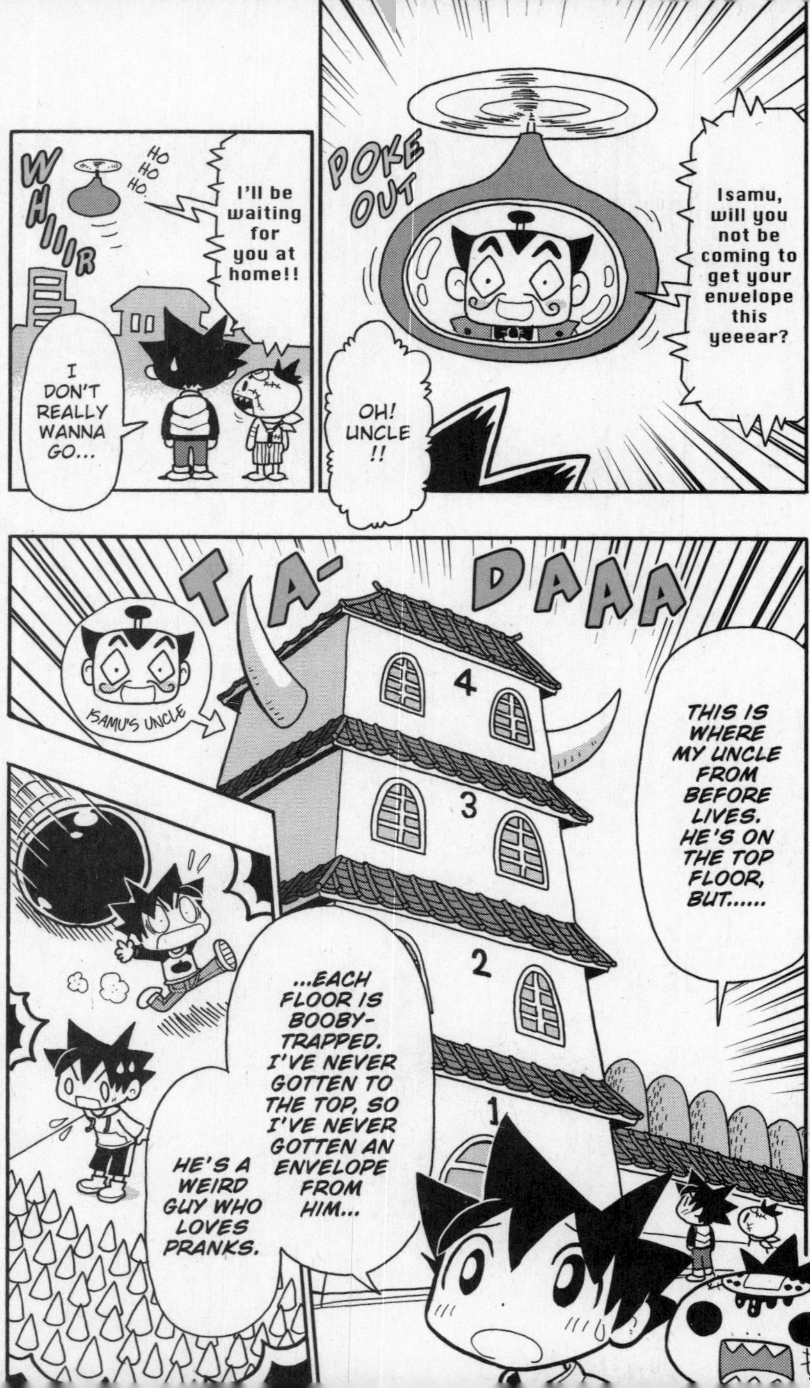
POKE OUT
Isamu, will you not be coming to get your envelope this yeeear?
OH! UNCLE!!
WHIIIR
HO HO HO.
I'll be waiting for you at home!!
I DON'T REALLY WANNA GO...
TA-DAAA
ISAMU'S UNCLE
4
3
2
1
THIS IS WHERE MY UNCLE FROM BEFORE LIVES. HE'S ON THE TOP FLOOR, BUT......
...EACH FLOOR IS BOOBY-TRAPPED. I'VE NEVER GOTTEN TO THE TOP, SO I'VE NEVER GOTTEN AN ENVELOPE FROM HIM...
HE'S A WEIRD GUY WHO LOVES PRANKS.

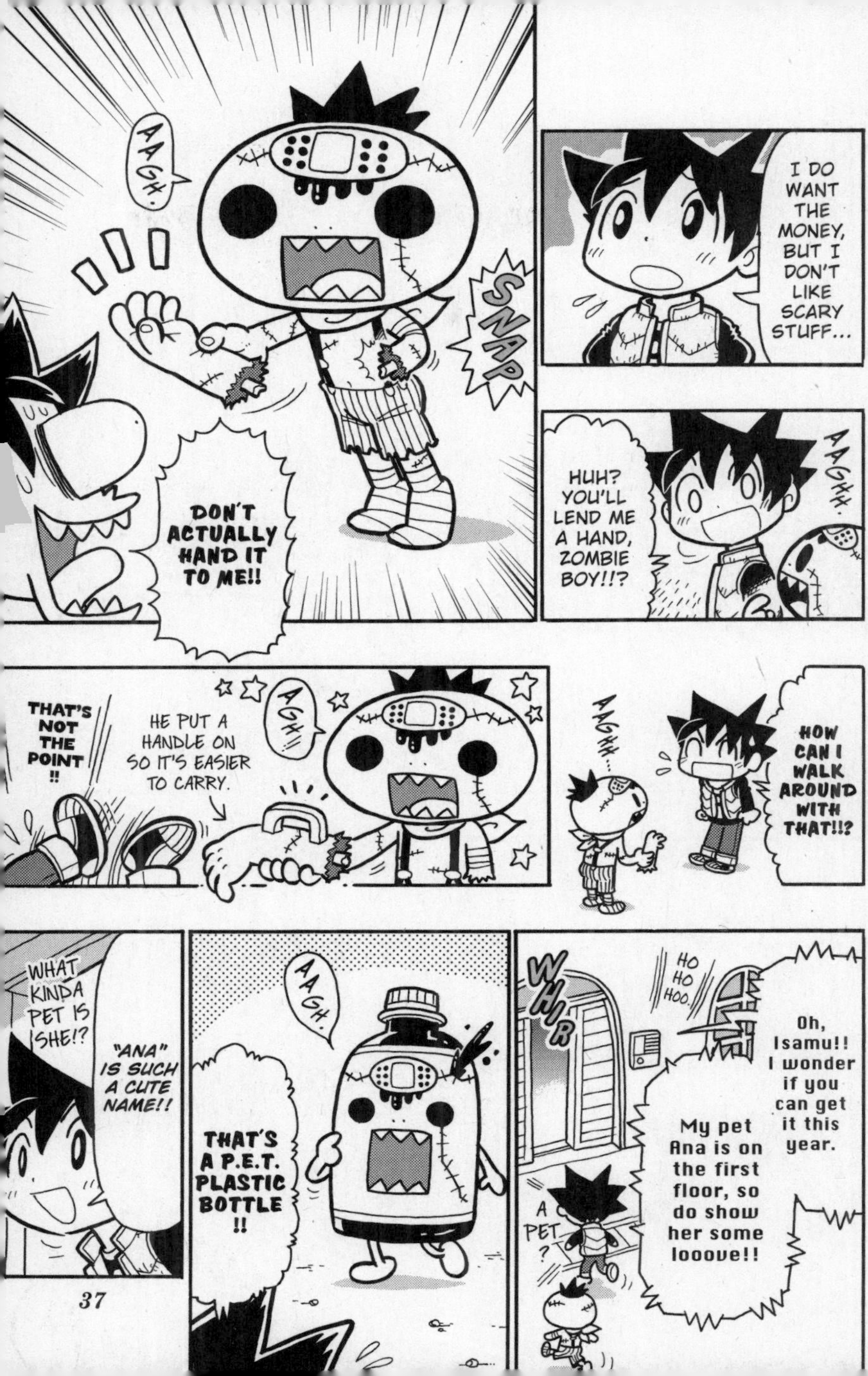
I DO WANT THE MONEY, BUT I DON'T LIKE SCARY STUFF...
AAGHH.
HUH? YOU'LL LEND ME A HAND, ZOMBIE BOY!!?
AAGH.
SNAP
DON'T ACTUALLY HAND IT TO ME!!
AAGHH...
HOW CAN I WALK AROUND WITH THAT!!?
AGH.
HE PUT A HANDLE ON SO IT'S EASIER TO CARRY.
THAT'S NOT THE POINT !!
Oh, Isamu!! I wonder if you can get it this year.
HO HO HOO.
WHIR
My pet Ana is on the first floor, so do show her some looove!!
A PET?
AAGH.
THAT'S A P.E.T. PLASTIC BOTTLE !!
WHAT KINDA PET IS SHE!?
"ANA" IS SUCH A CUTE NAME!!

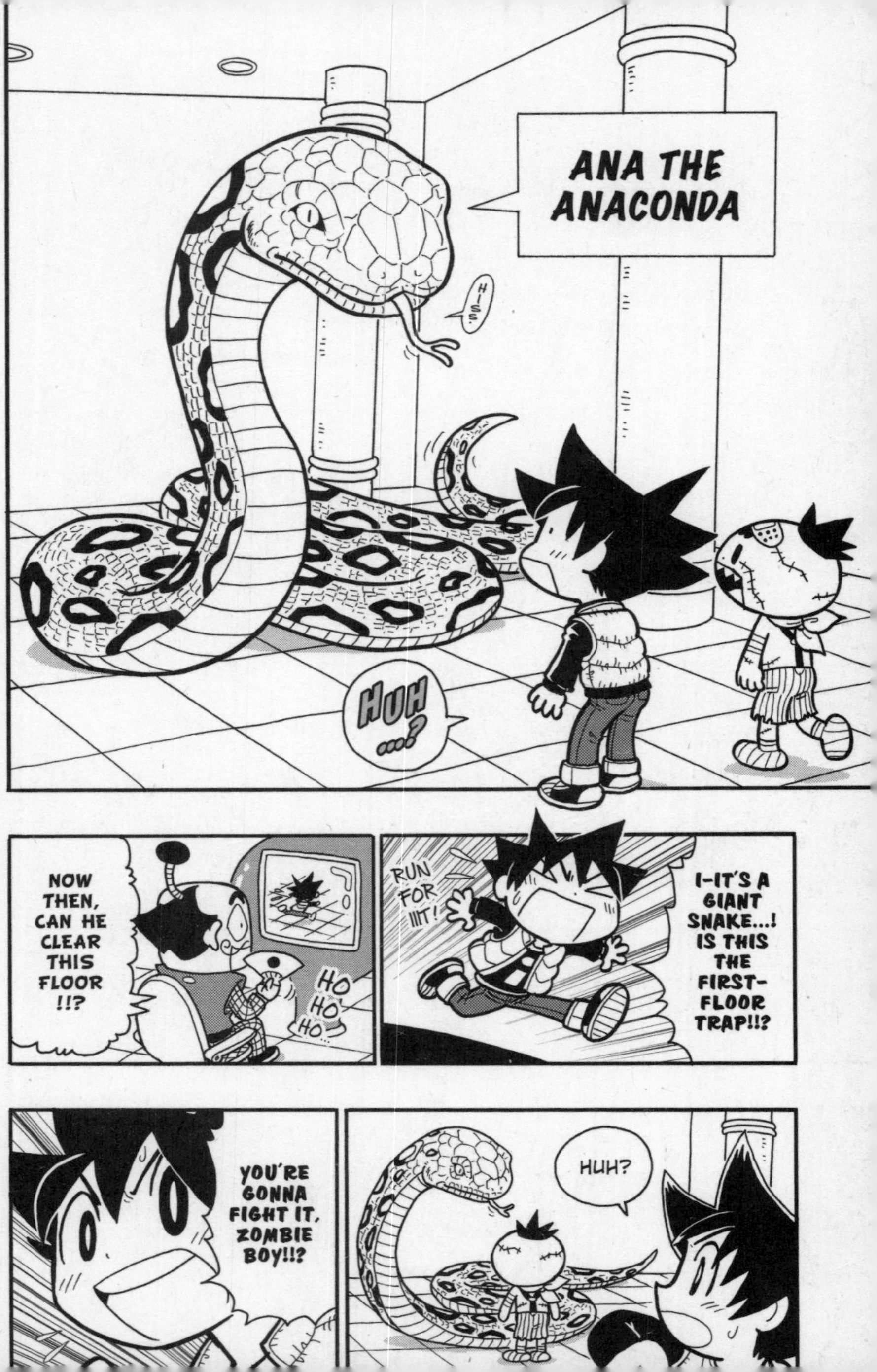
ANA THE ANACONDA
HISS.
HUH...?
I-IT'S A GIANT SNAKE...! IS THIS THE FIRST-FLOOR TRAP!!?
RUN FOR IIIT!
NOW THEN, CAN HE CLEAR THIS FLOOR!!?
HO HO HO...
HUH?
YOU'RE GONNA FIGHT IT, ZOMBIE BOY!!?

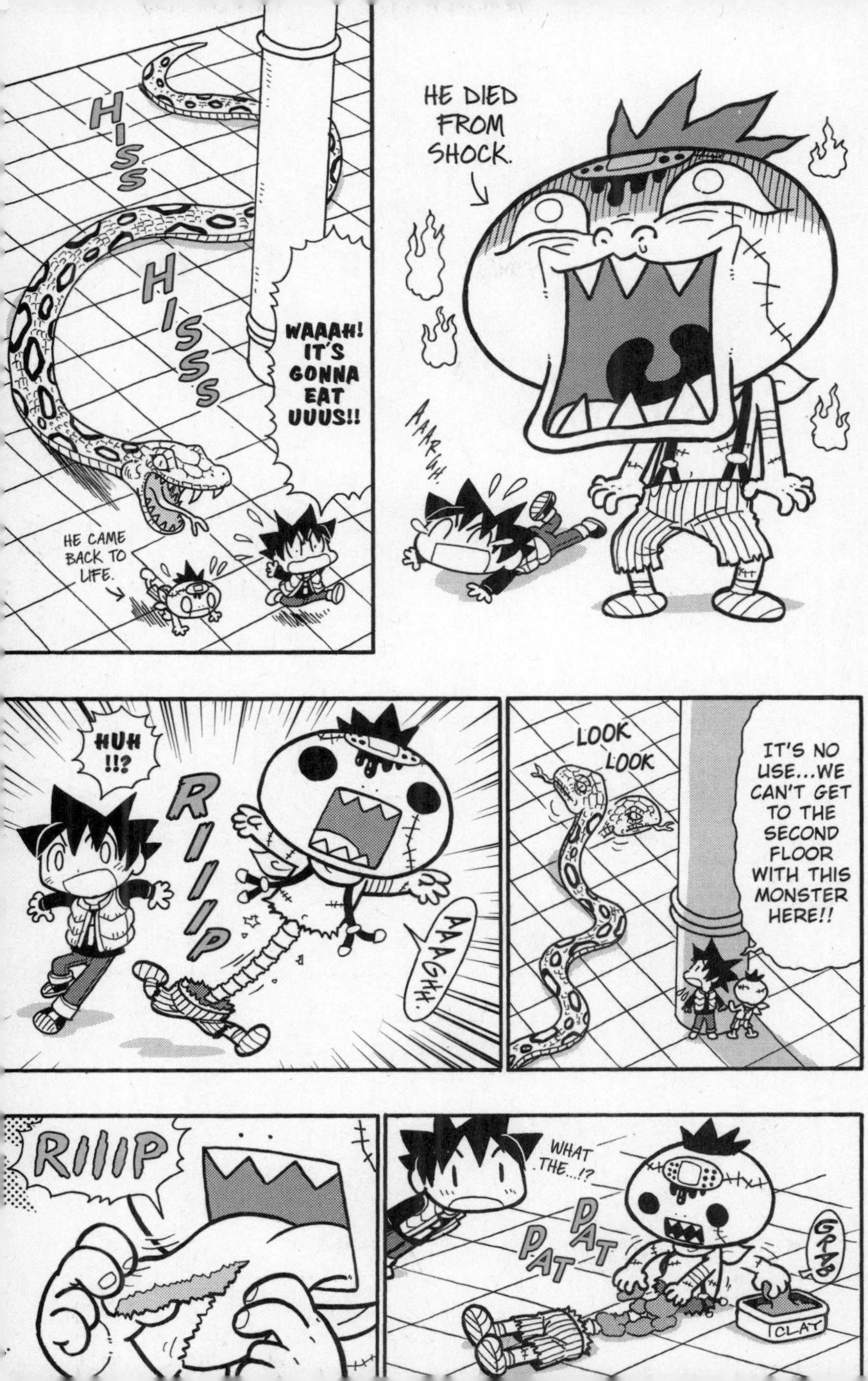
HE DIED FROM SHOCK.
AAARUH.
HISS
HISS
WAAAH! IT'S GONNA EAT UUUS!!
HE CAME BACK TO LIFE.
LOOK
LOOK
IT'S NO USE...WE CAN'T GET TO THE SECOND FLOOR WITH THIS MONSTER HERE!!
HUH!!?
RIIIP
AAAGHH.
WHAT THE...!?
PAT
PAT
GRAB
CLAY
RIIIP

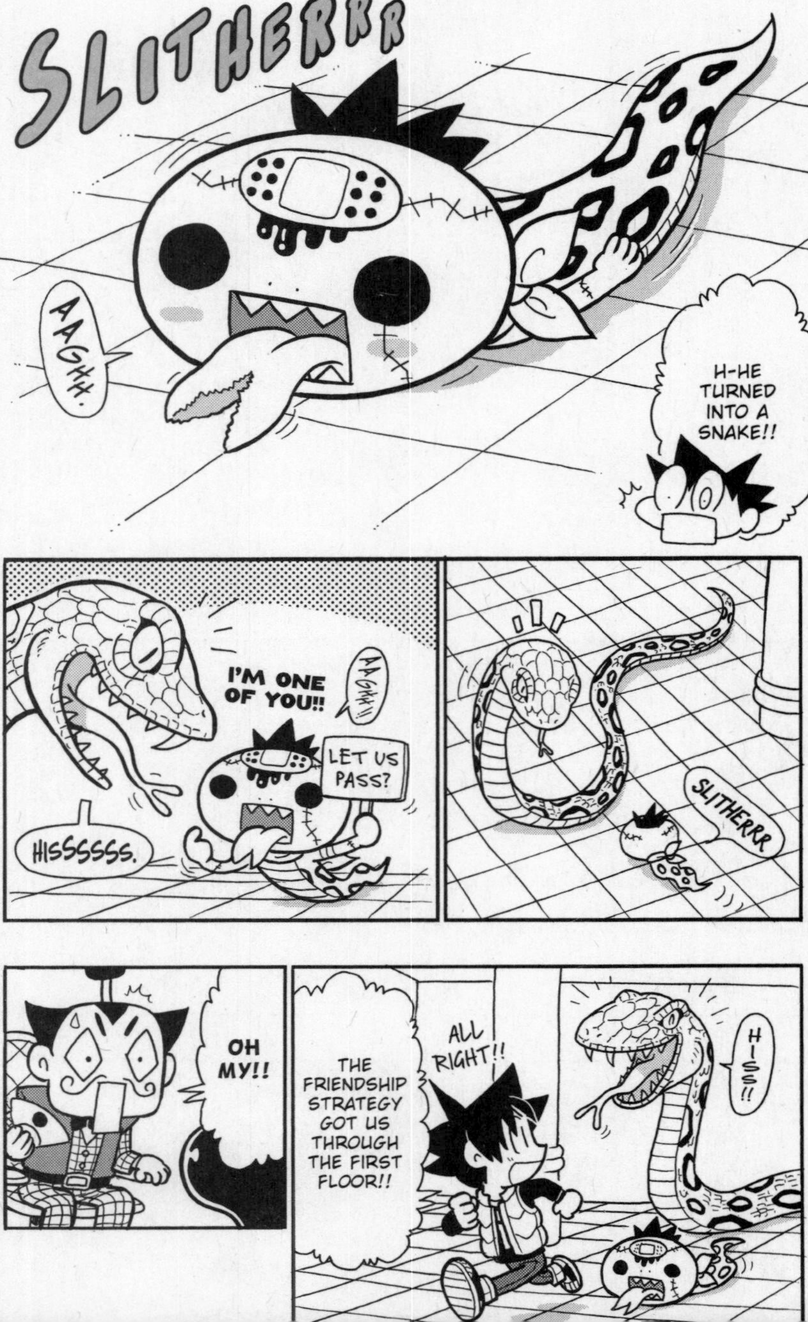
SLITHERRR
H-HE TURNED INTO A SNAKE!!
AAGHX.
SLITHERRR
AAGHX!!
I'M ONE OF YOU!!
LET US PASS?
HISSSSSS.
HISS!!
ALL RIGHT!!
THE FRIENDSHIP STRATEGY GOT US THROUGH THE FIRST FLOOR!!
OH MY!!

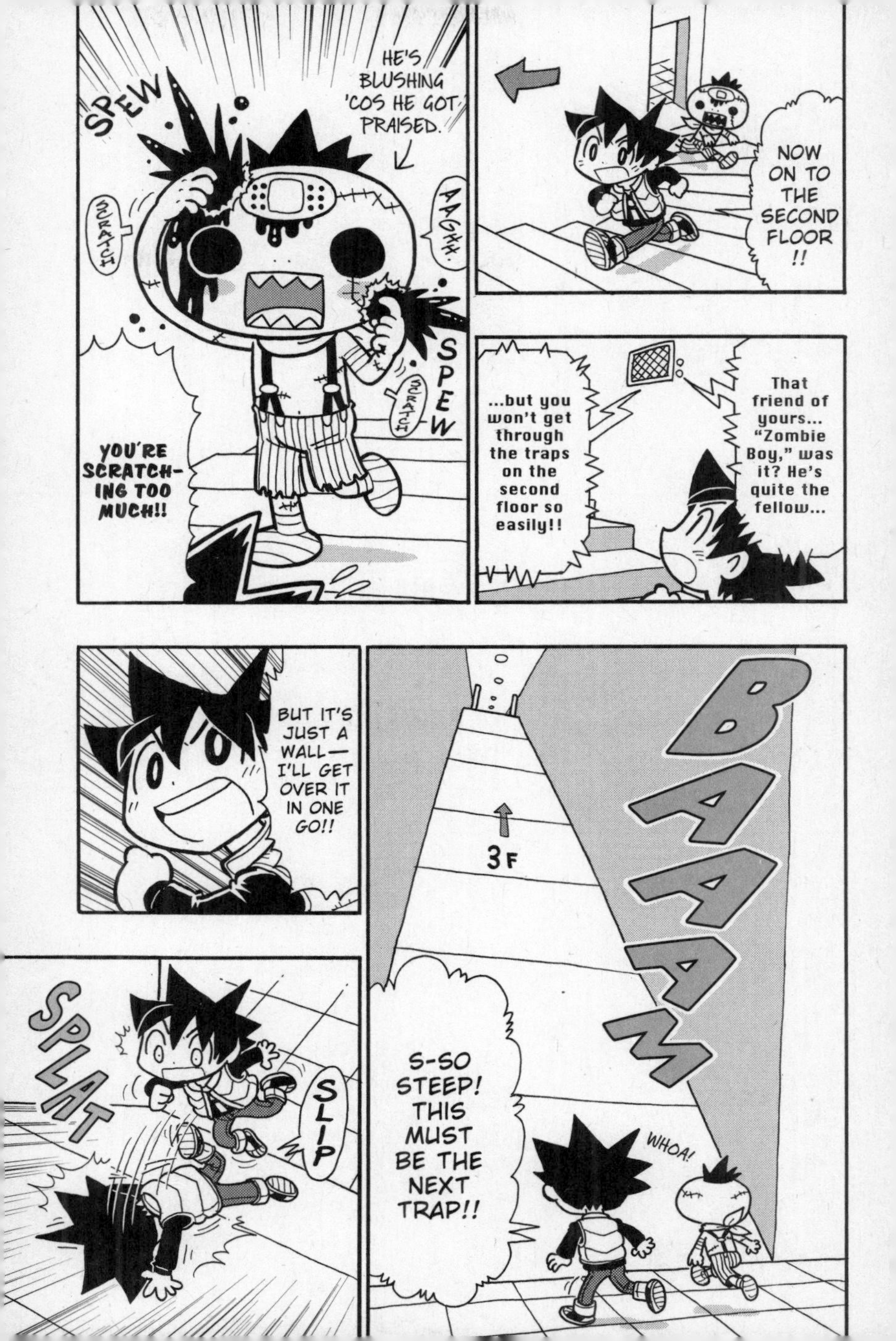
NOW ON TO THE SECOND FLOOR!!
That friend of yours... "Zombie Boy," was it? He's quite the fellow...
...but you won't get through the traps on the second floor so easily!!
HE'S BLUSHING 'COS HE GOT PRAISED.
SPEW
AAGHX.
SCRATCH
SPEW
SCRATCH
YOU'RE SCRATCHING TOO MUCH!!
BAAAAM
3F
S-SO STEEP! THIS MUST BE THE NEXT TRAP!!
WHOA!
BUT IT'S JUST A WALL—I'LL GET OVER IT IN ONE GO!!
SLIP
SPLAT

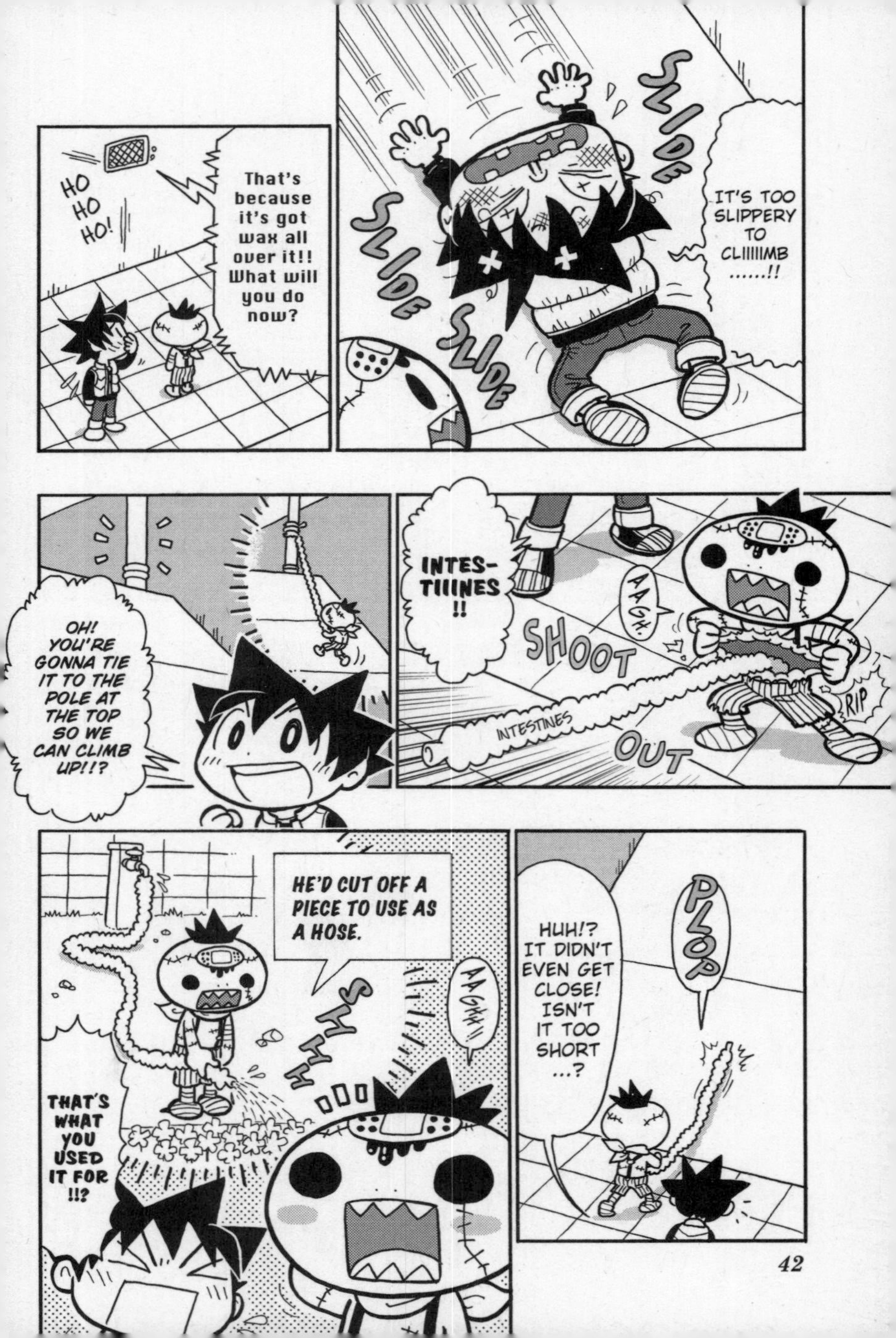
SLIDE
SLIDE
SLIDE
IT'S TOO SLIPPERY TO CLIIIIIMB ......!!
HO HO HO!
That's because it's got wax all over it!! What will you do now?
INTES-TIIIINES !!
AAGH.
SHOOT OUT
INTESTINES
RIP
OH! YOU'RE GONNA TIE IT TO THE POLE AT THE TOP SO WE CAN CLIMB UP!!?
HUH!? IT DIDN'T EVEN GET CLOSE! ISN'T IT TOO SHORT ...?
PLOP
HE'D CUT OFF A PIECE TO USE AS A HOSE.
AAGHH!!
SHHH
THAT'S WHAT YOU USED IT FOR !!?

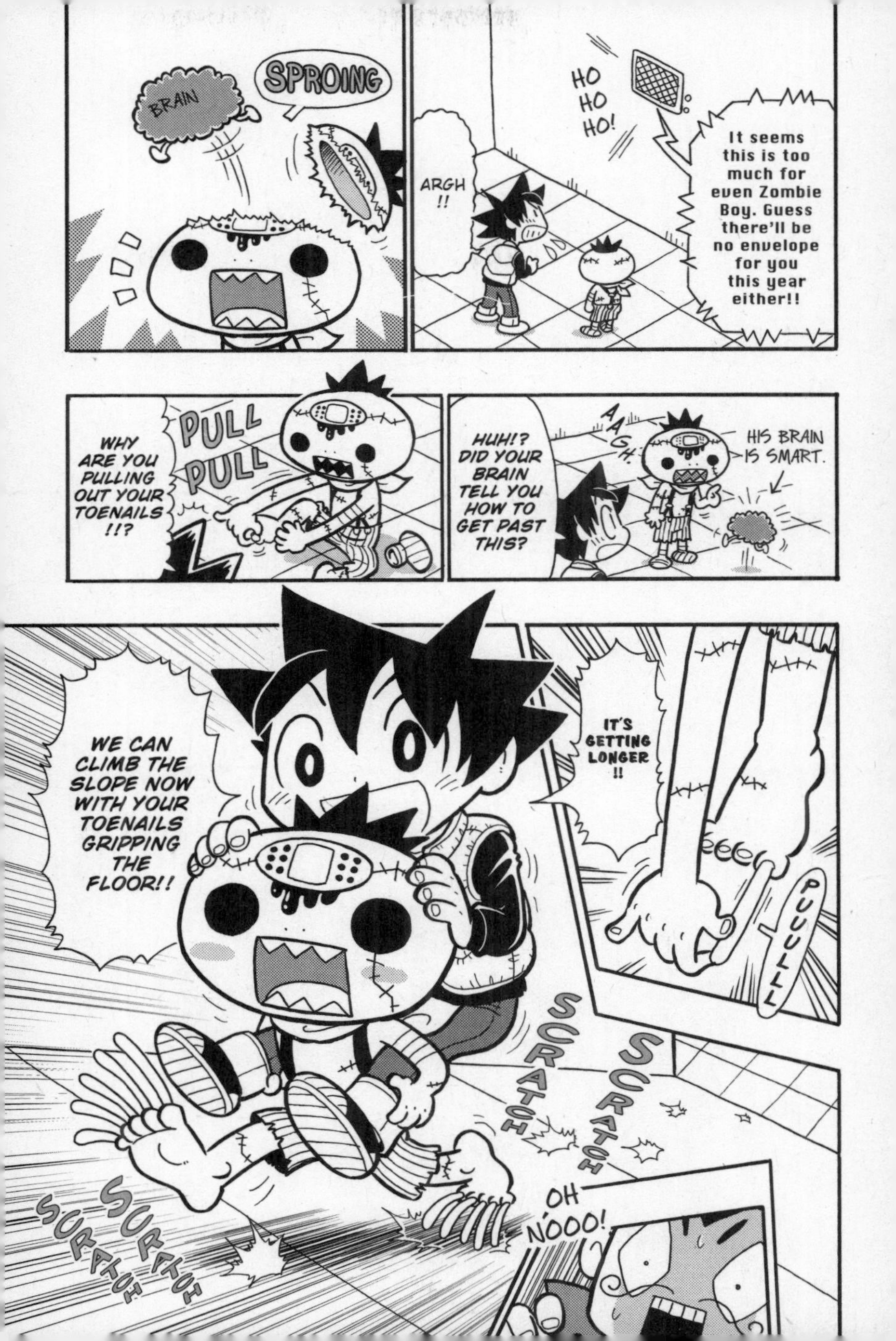
HO HO HO!
It seems this is too much for even Zombie Boy. Guess there'll be no envelope for you this year either!!
ARGH !!
SPROING
BRAIN
AAGH.
HIS BRAIN IS SMART.
HUH!? DID YOUR BRAIN TELL YOU HOW TO GET PAST THIS?
PULL PULL
WHY ARE YOU PULLING OUT YOUR TOENAILS !!?
IT'S GETTING LONGER !!
PUUULLL
WE CAN CLIMB THE SLOPE NOW WITH YOUR TOENAILS GRIPPING THE FLOOR!!
SCRATCH SCRATCH
SCRATCH SCRATCH
OH NOOO!

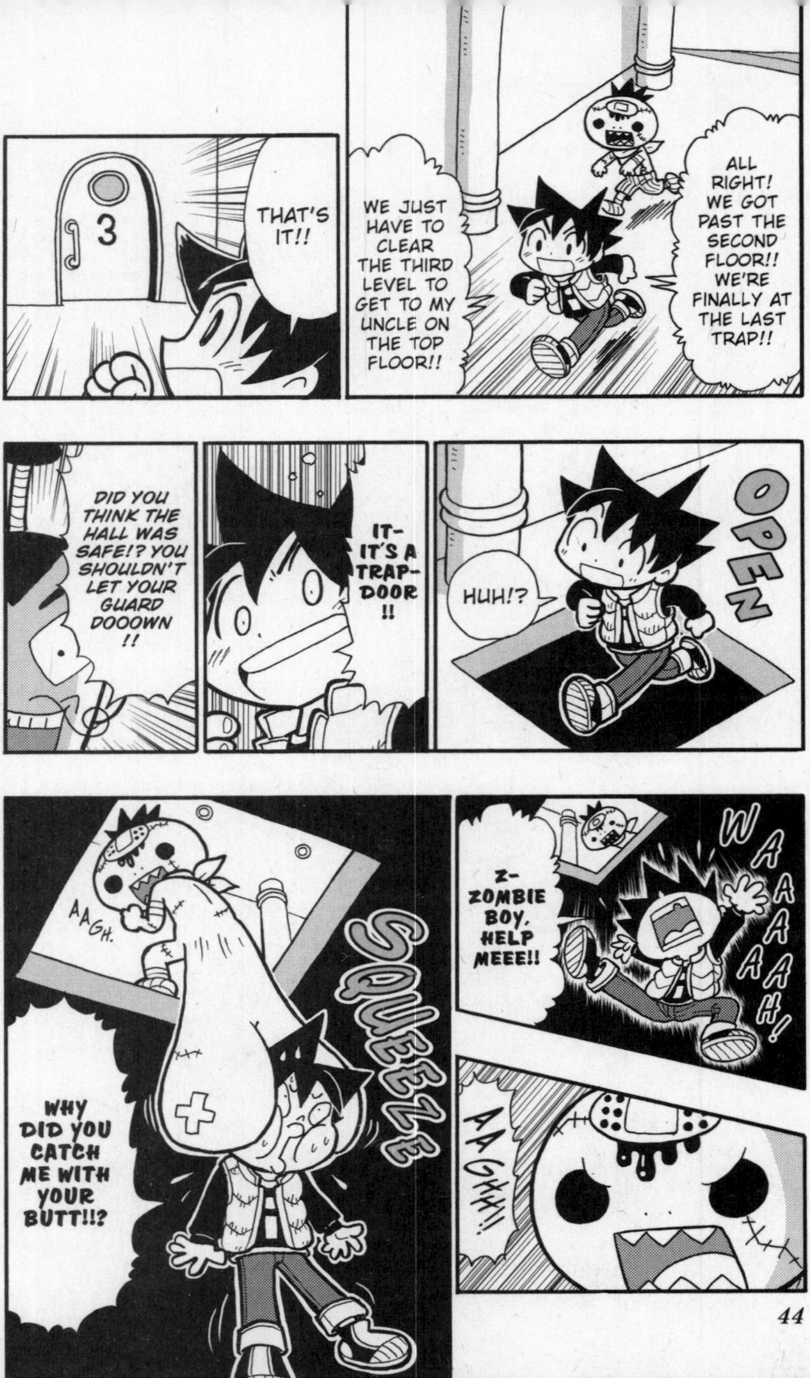
ALL RIGHT! WE GOT PAST THE SECOND FLOOR!! WE'RE FINALLY AT THE LAST TRAP!!
WE JUST HAVE TO CLEAR THE THIRD LEVEL TO GET TO MY UNCLE ON THE TOP FLOOR!!
3
THAT'S IT!!
OPEN
HUH!?
IT- IT'S A TRAP-DOOR!!
DID YOU THINK THE HALL WAS SAFE!? YOU SHOULDN'T LET YOUR GUARD DOOOWN!!
WAAAAAAAH!
Z-ZOMBIE BOY, HELP MEEE!!
AAGHH!!
AAGH.
SQUEEZE
WHY DID YOU CATCH ME WITH YOUR BUTT!!?

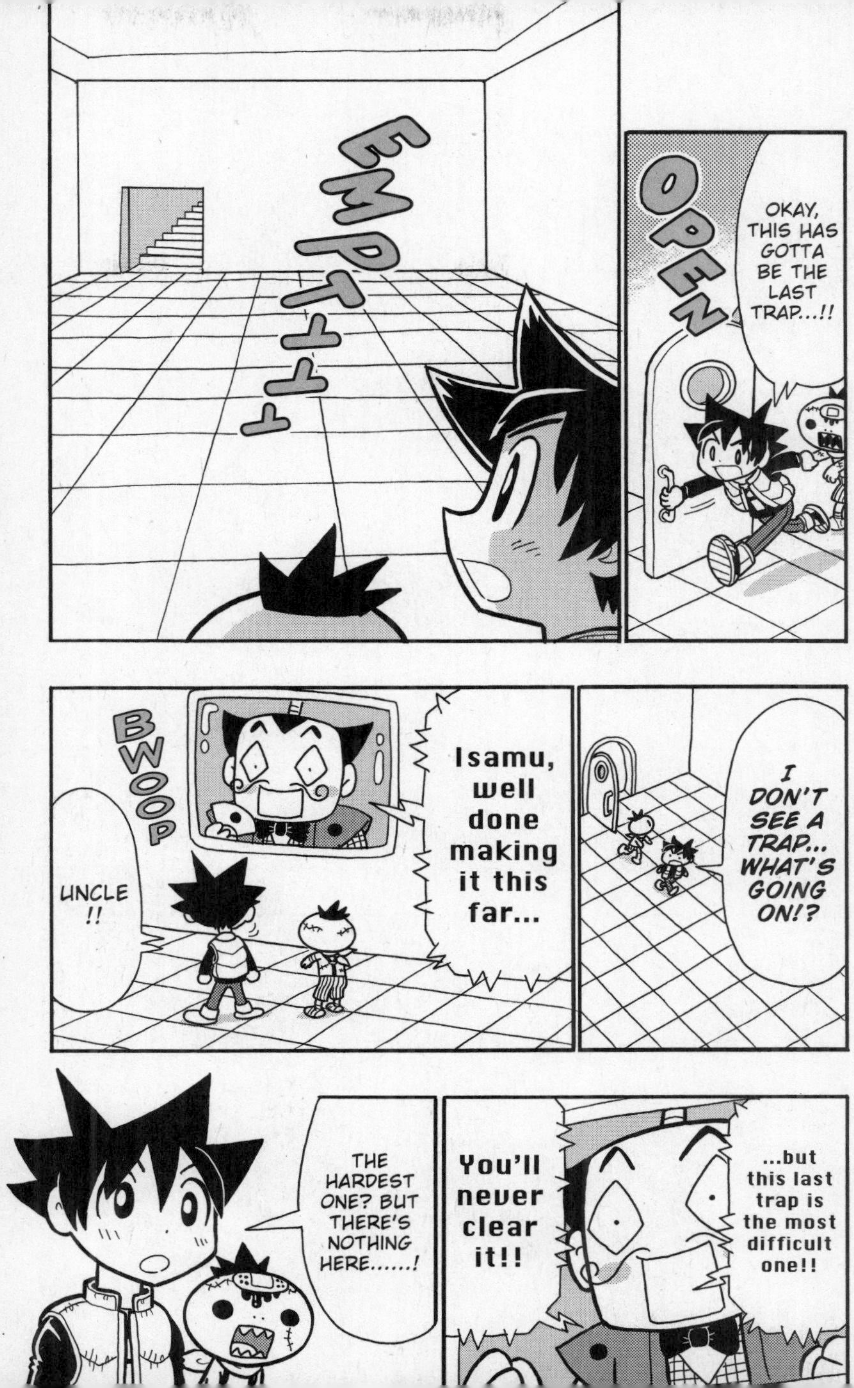
OPEN
OKAY, THIS HAS GOTTA BE THE LAST TRAP...!!
EMPTYYY
I DON'T SEE A TRAP... WHAT'S GOING ON!?
Isamu, well done making it this far...
BWOOP
UNCLE !!
...but this last trap is the most difficult one!!
You'll never clear it!!
THE HARDEST ONE? BUT THERE'S NOTHING HERE......!

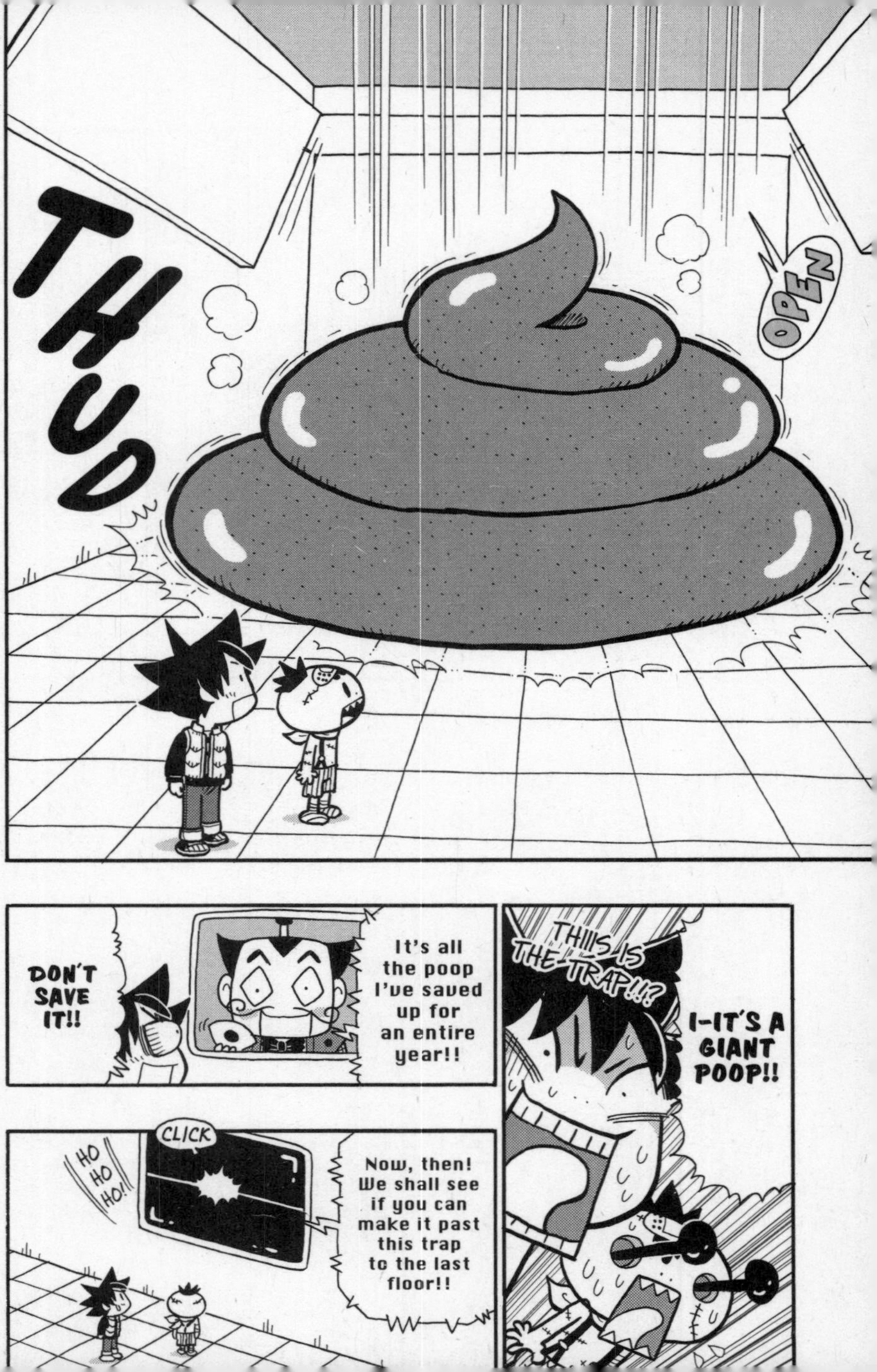
OPEN
THUD
THIIIS IS THE TRAP!!?
I-IT'S A GIANT POOP!!
It's all the poop I've saved up for an entire year!!
DON'T SAVE IT!!
CLICK
Now, then! We shall see if you can make it past this trap to the last floor!!
HO HO HO!

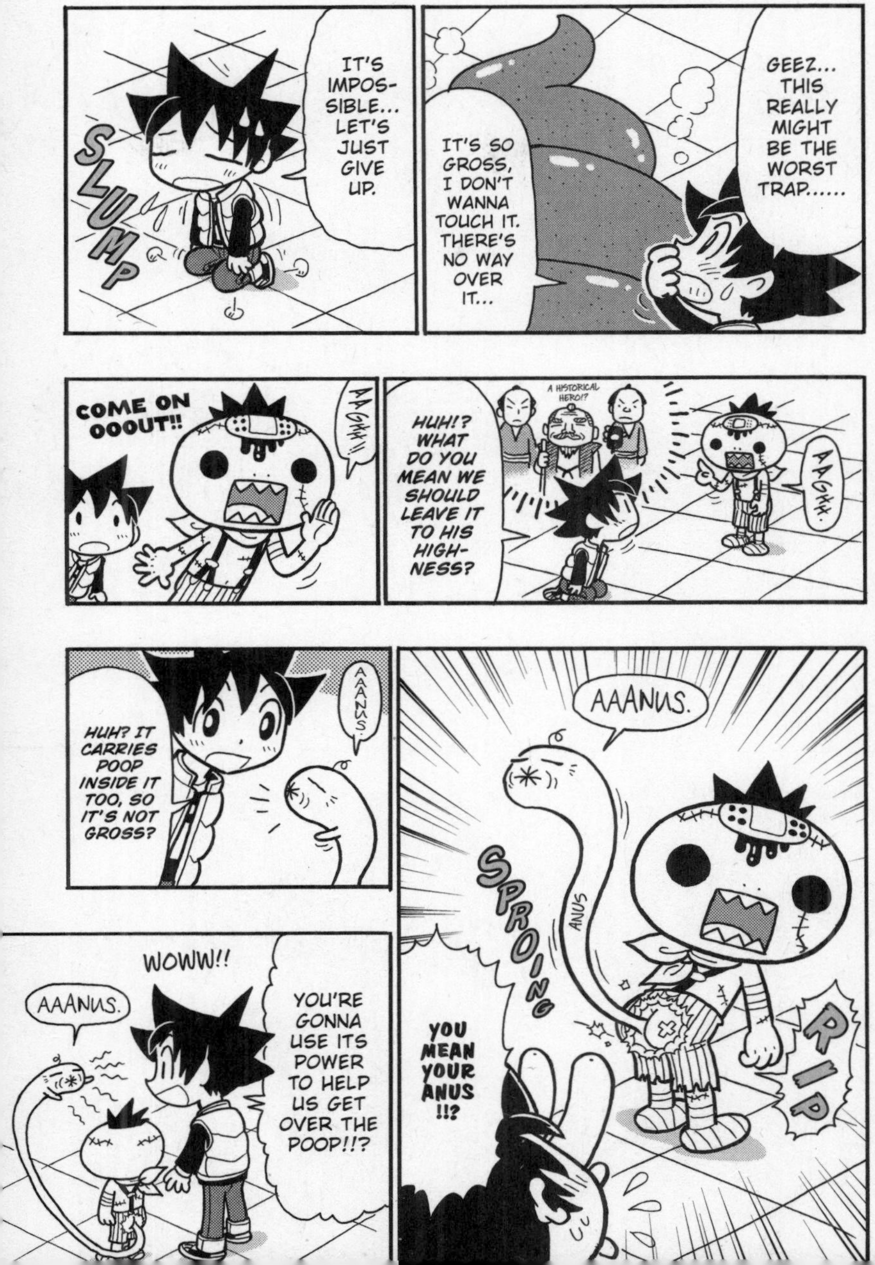
GEEZ... THIS REALLY MIGHT BE THE WORST TRAP......
IT'S SO GROSS, I DON'T WANNA TOUCH IT. THERE'S NO WAY OVER IT...
IT'S IMPOSSIBLE... LET'S JUST GIVE UP.
SLUMP
AAGHH.
HUH!? WHAT DO YOU MEAN WE SHOULD LEAVE IT TO HIS HIGHNESS?
A HISTORICAL HERO!?
AAGHH!!
COME ON OOOUT!!
AAANUS.
SPROING
ANUS
RIP
YOU MEAN YOUR ANUS!!?
AAANUS.
HUH? IT CARRIES POOP INSIDE IT TOO, SO IT'S NOT GROSS?
YOU'RE GONNA USE ITS POWER TO HELP US GET OVER THE POOP!!?
WOWW!!
AAANUS.

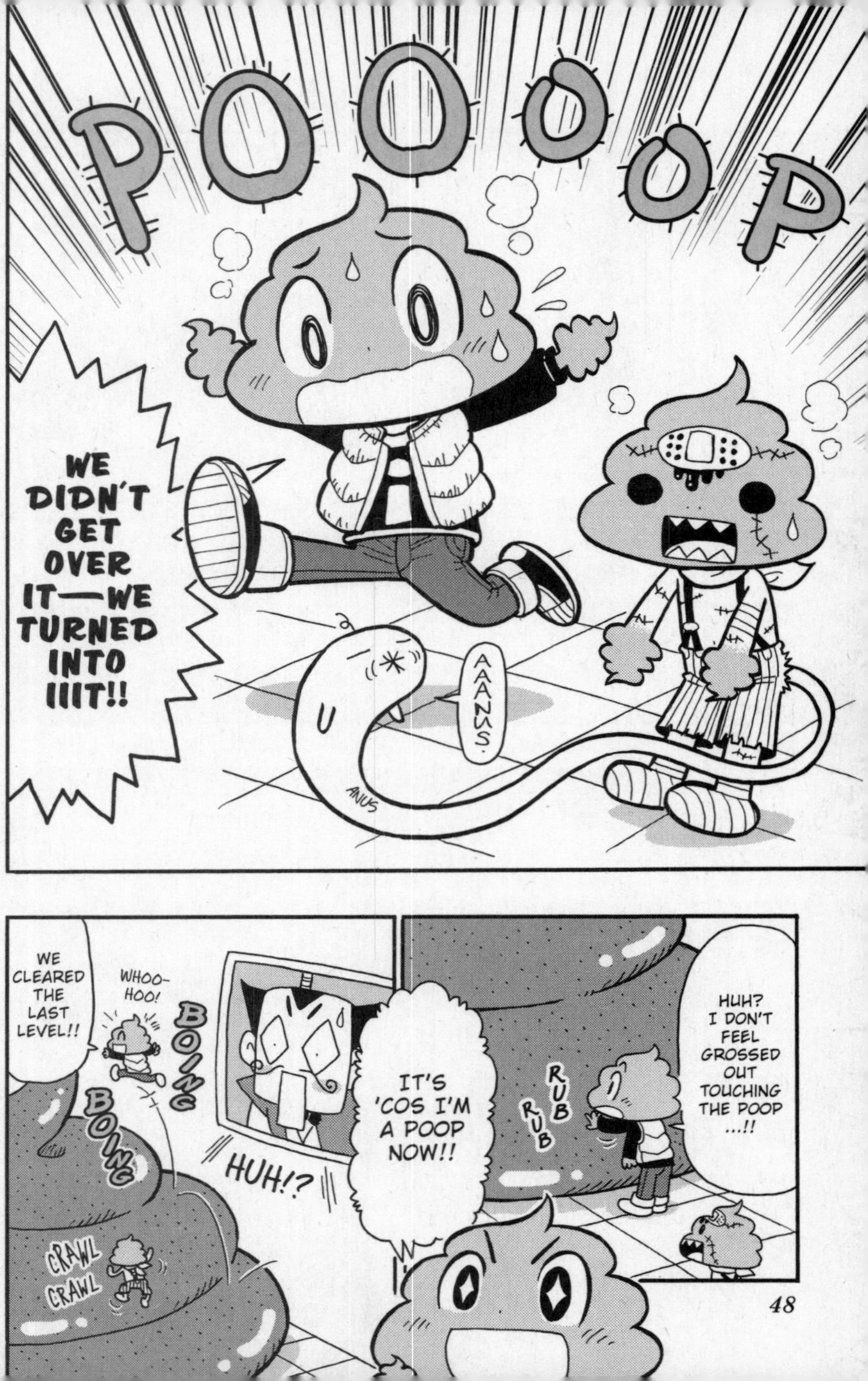
POOOOOP
WE DIDN'T GET OVER IT—WE TURNED INTO IIIT!!
AAANUS.
U
ANUS
HUH? I DON'T FEEL GROSSED OUT TOUCHING THE POOP ...!!
RUB RUB
IT'S 'COS I'M A POOP NOW!!
HUH!?
WHOO-HOO!
WE CLEARED THE LAST LEVEL!!
BOING BOING BOING
CRAWL CRAWL

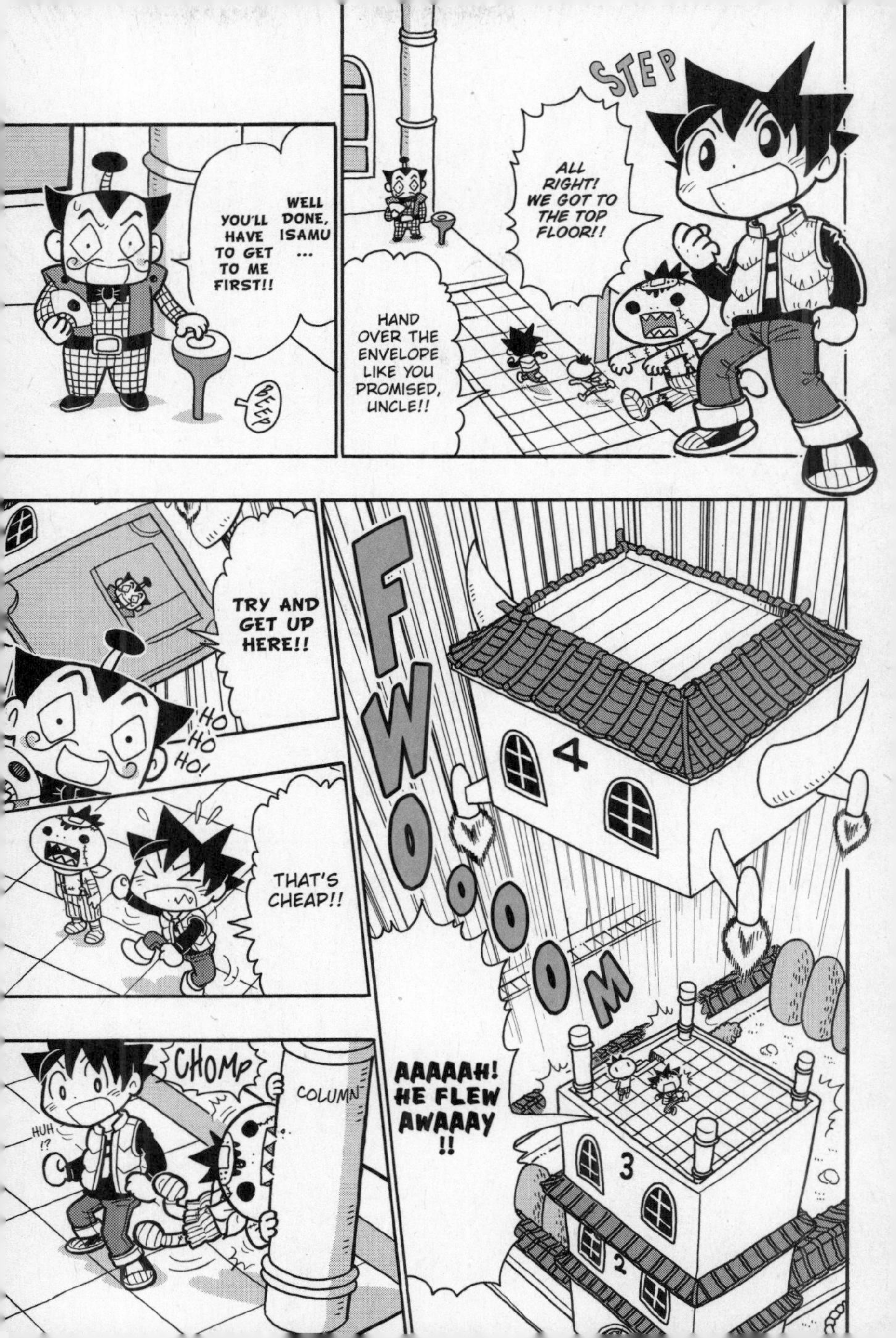
STEP
ALL RIGHT! WE GOT TO THE TOP FLOOR!!
HAND OVER THE ENVELOPE LIKE YOU PROMISED, UNCLE!!
WELL DONE, ISAMU ...
YOU'LL HAVE TO GET TO ME FIRST!!
BEEP
FWOOOOOM
4
3
2
AAAAAH! HE FLEW AWAAAY!!
TRY AND GET UP HERE!!
HO HO HO!
THAT'S CHEAP!!
CHOMP
COLUMN
HUH!?

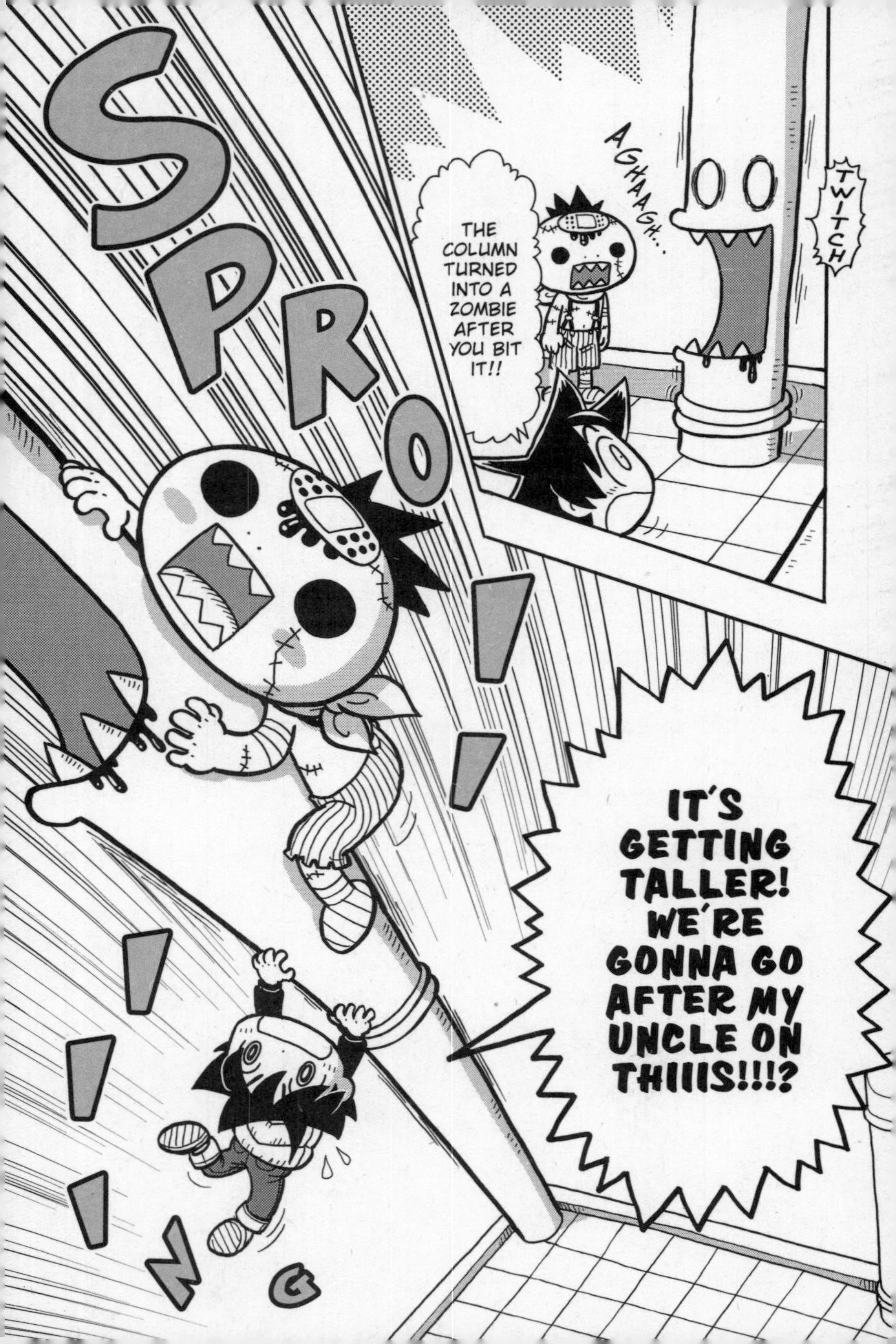
TWITCH
AGHAAAGH...
THE COLUMN TURNED INTO A ZOMBIE AFTER YOU BIT IT!!
SPRO!!!!!NG
IT'S GETTING TALLER! WE'RE GONNA GO AFTER MY UNCLE ON THIIIS!!!?

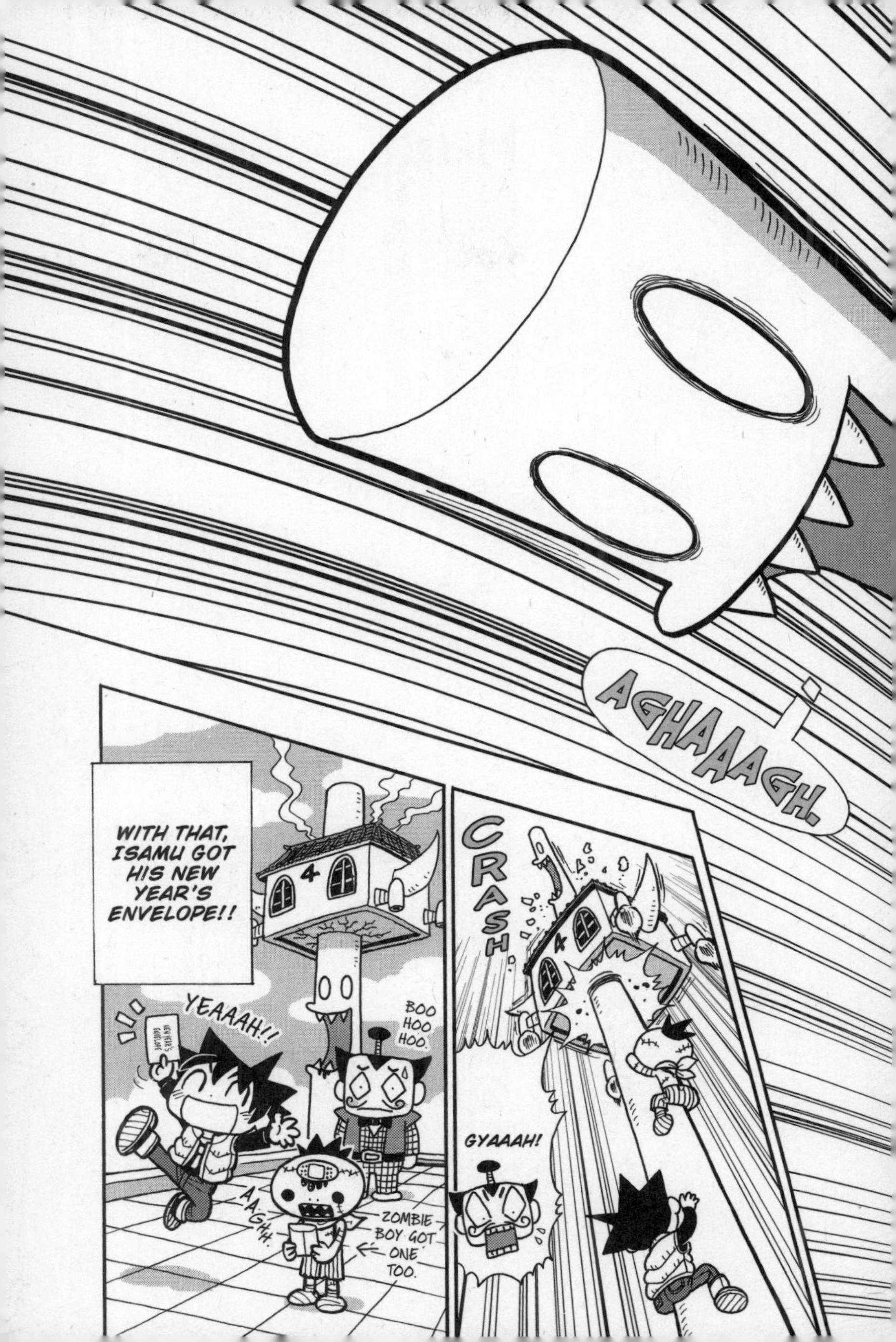
AGHAAAGH.
CRASH
GYAAAH!
WITH THAT, ISAMU GOT HIS NEW YEAR'S ENVELOPE!!
YEAAAH!!
NEW YEAR'S ENVELOPE
BOO HOO HOO.
AAGHH.
ZOMBIE BOY GOT ONE TOO.

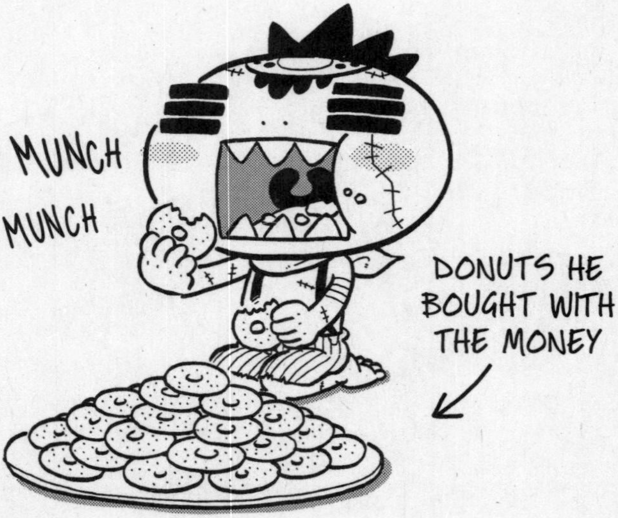
MUNCH
MUNCH
DONUTS HE BOUGHT WITH THE MONEY

AN EXZITING DAY OUT!

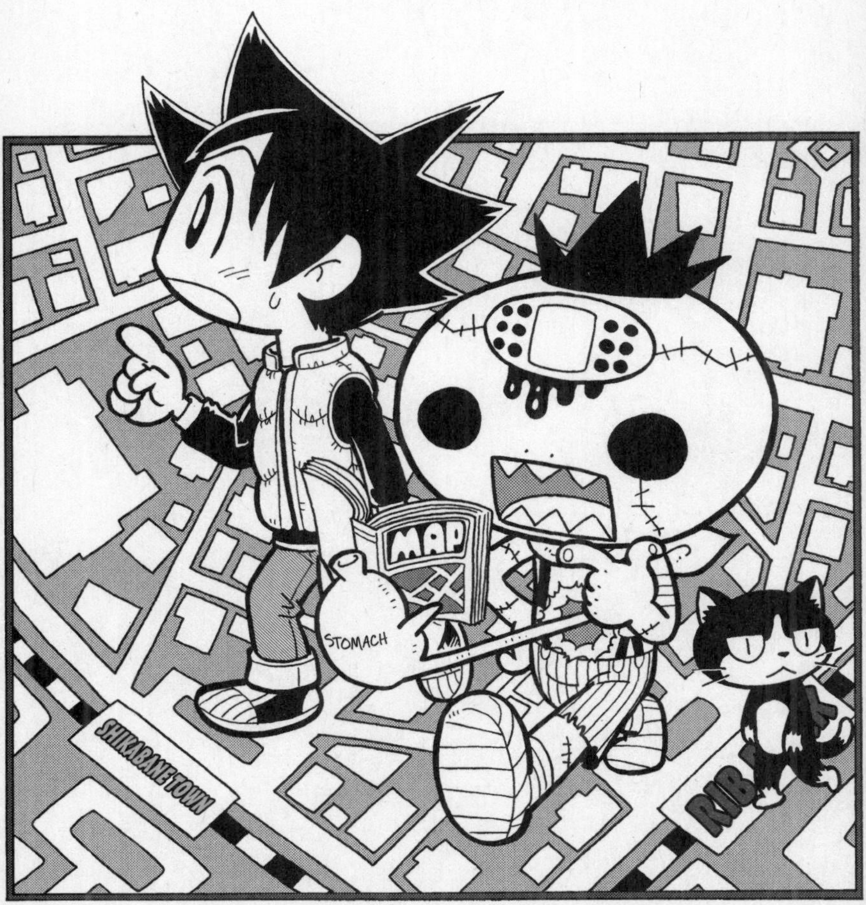
MAP
STOMACH
SHIKABANE TOWN

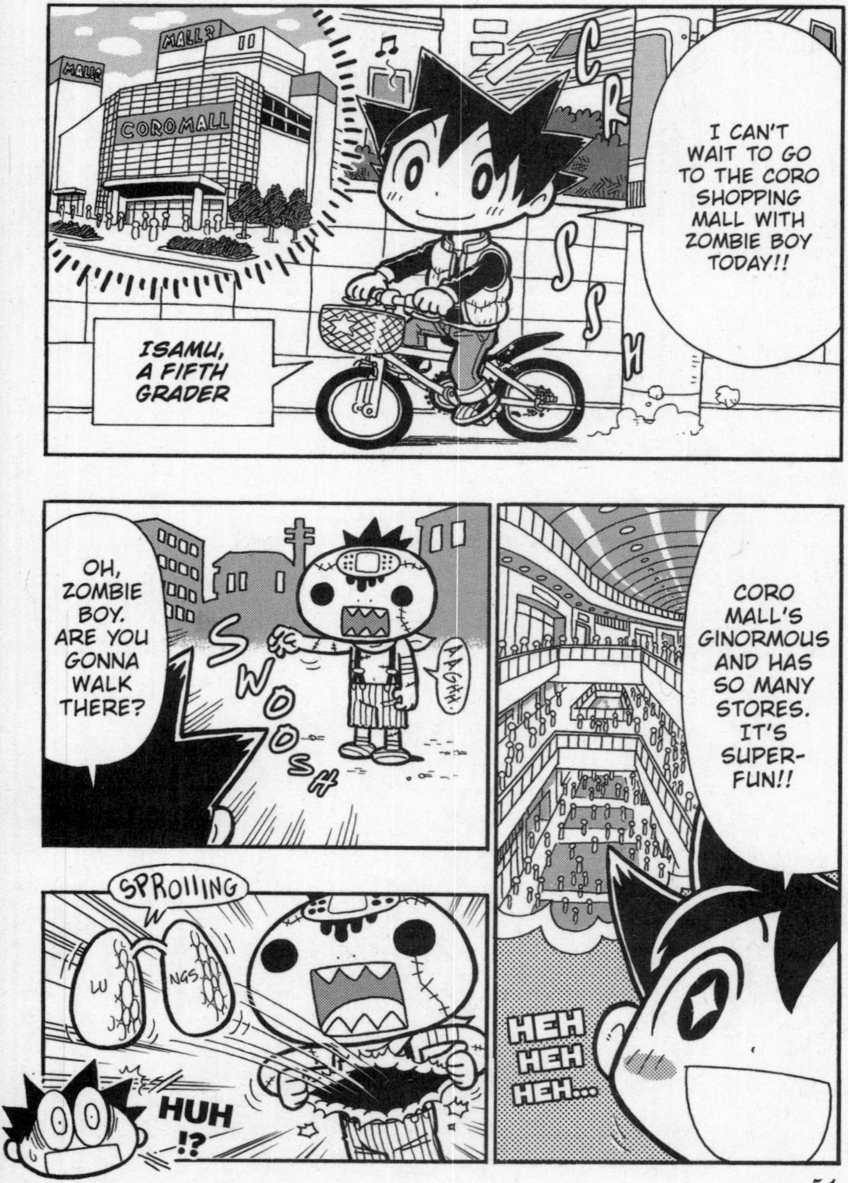
MALL3
MALL2
COROMALL
I CAN'T WAIT TO GO TO THE CORO SHOPPING MALL WITH ZOMBIE BOY TODAY!!
CRSSSH
ISAMU, A FIFTH GRADER
CORO MALL'S GINORMOUS AND HAS SO MANY STORES. IT'S SUPER-FUN!!
HEH HEH HEH...
OH, ZOMBIE BOY. ARE YOU GONNA WALK THERE?
AAGHH
SWOOSH
SPROIIING
HUH!?

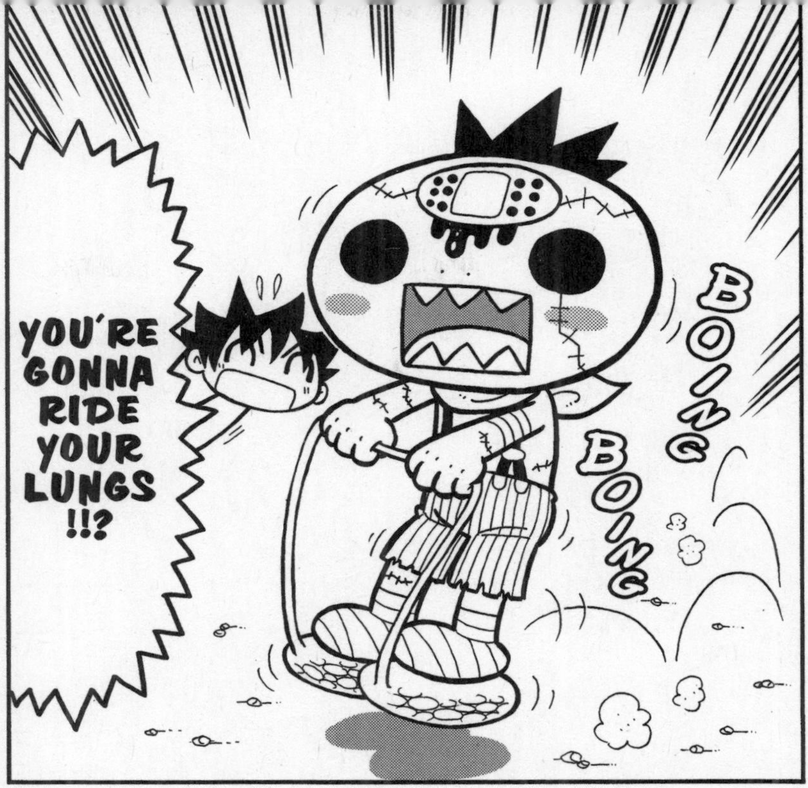
YOU'RE GONNA RIDE YOUR LUNGS!!?
BOING
BOING
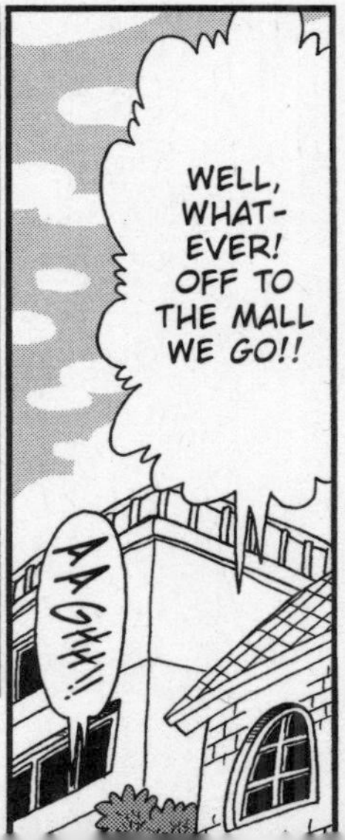
WELL, WHAT-EVER! OFF TO THE MALL WE GO!!
AAGH!!
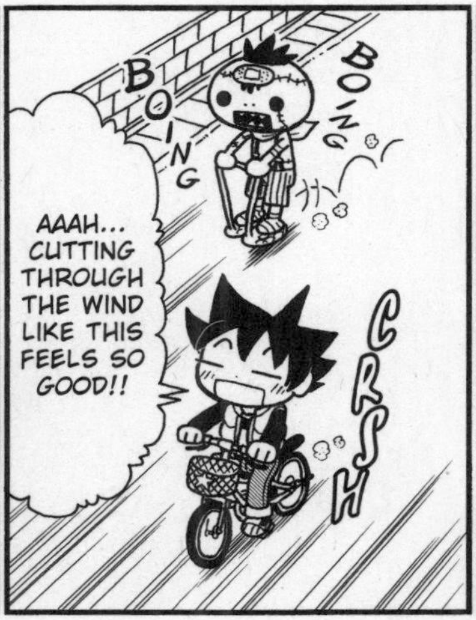
BOING
BOING
AAAH... CUTTING THROUGH THE WIND LIKE THIS FEELS SO GOOD!!
CRSH
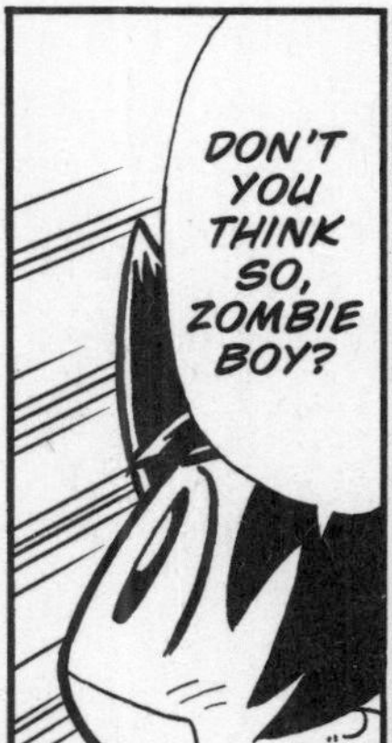
DON'T YOU THINK SO, ZOMBIE BOY?

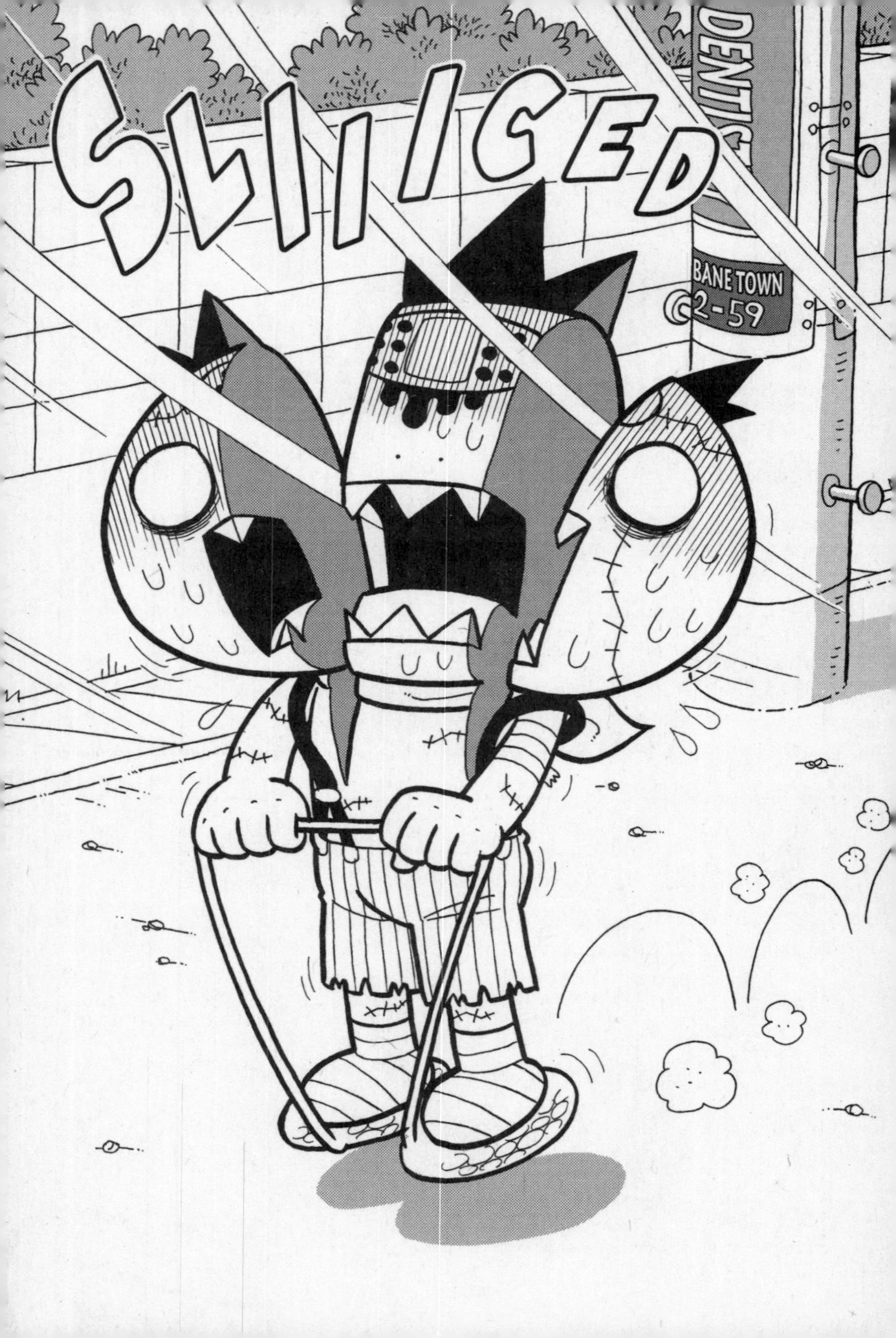
SLIIICED
BANE TOWN
2-59

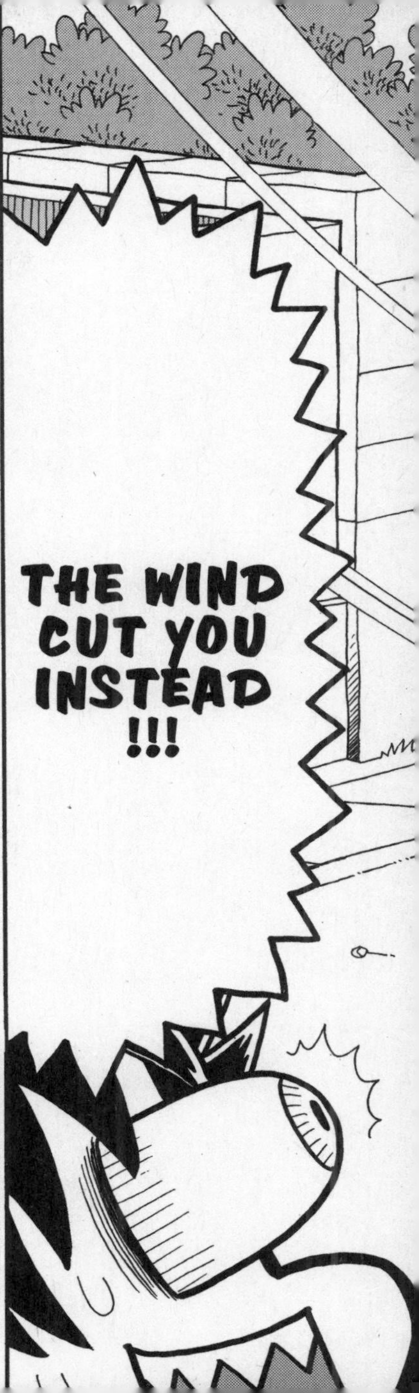
THE WIND CUT YOU INSTEAD !!!

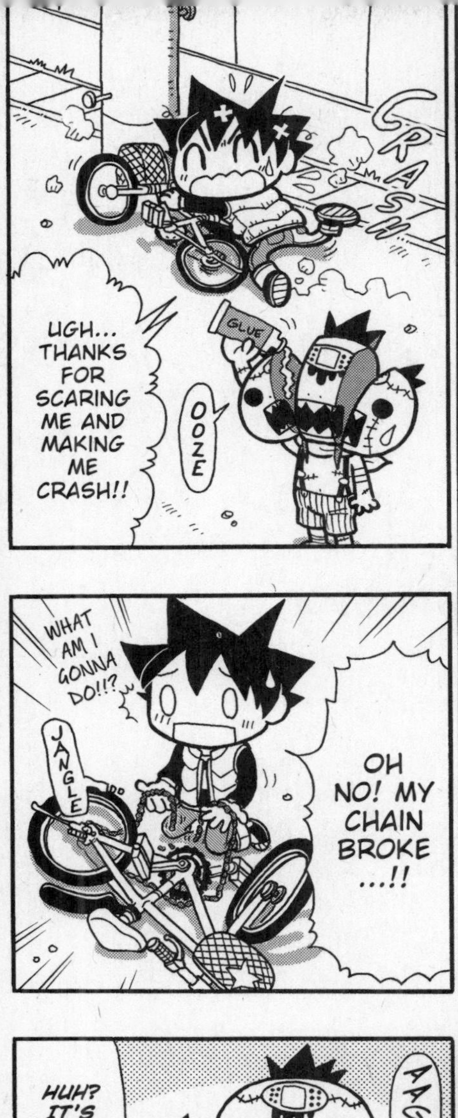
CRASH
GLUE
OOZE
UGH... THANKS FOR SCARING ME AND MAKING ME CRASH!!
OH NO! MY CHAIN BROKE ...!!
WHAT AM I GONNA DO!!?
JANGLE
AAGHH.
HUH? IT'S GONNA BE OKAY ...!?

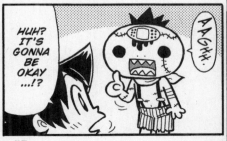

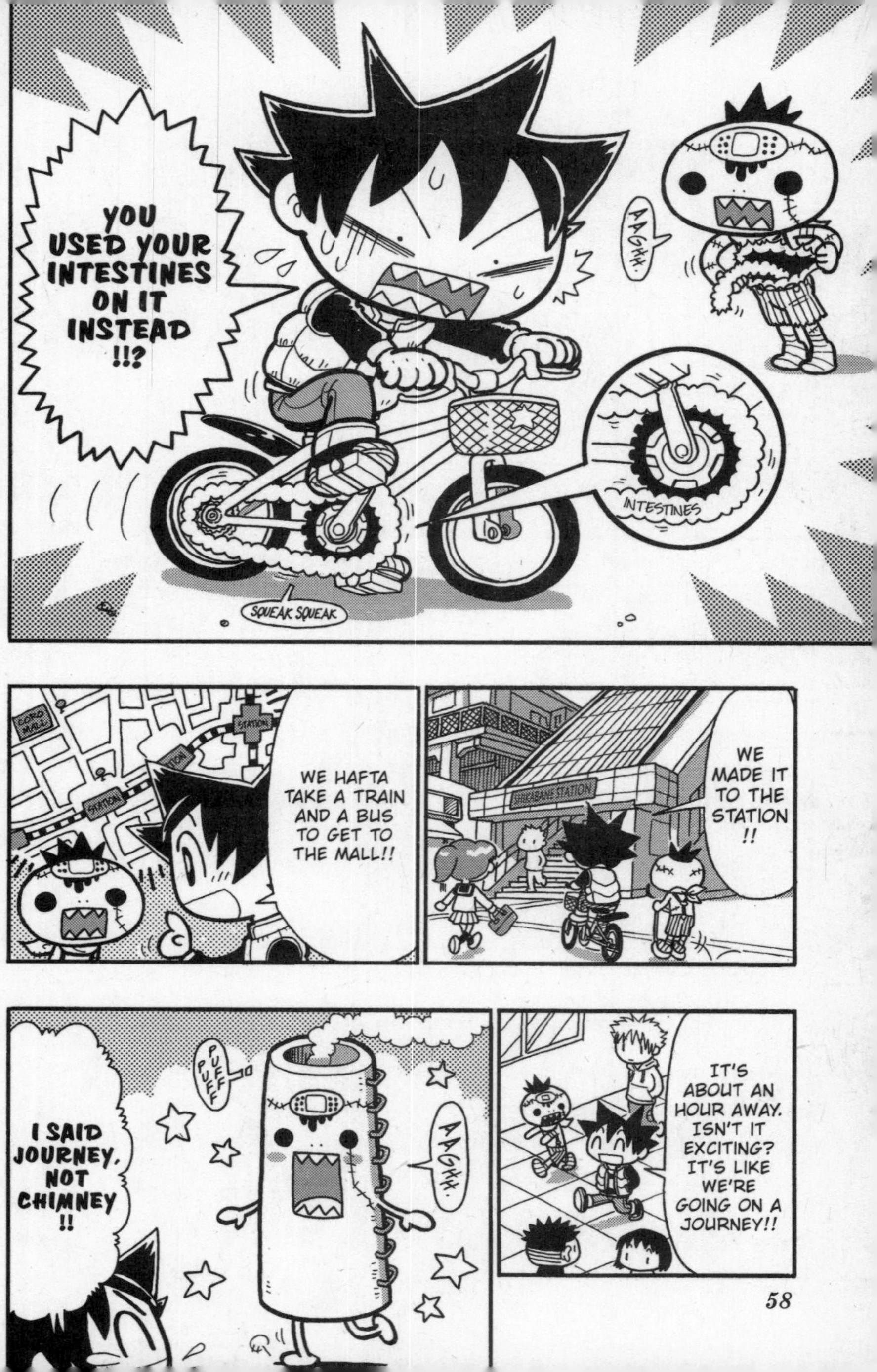

AAGHX.
YOU USED YOUR INTESTINES ON IT INSTEAD !!?
INTESTINES
SQUEAK SQUEAK
WE MADE IT TO THE STATION !!
WE HAFTA TAKE A TRAIN AND A BUS TO GET TO THE MALL!!
IT'S ABOUT AN HOUR AWAY. ISN'T IT EXCITING? IT'S LIKE WE'RE GOING ON A JOURNEY!!
PUFF PUFF
AAGHX.
I SAID JOURNEY, NOT CHIMNEY !!

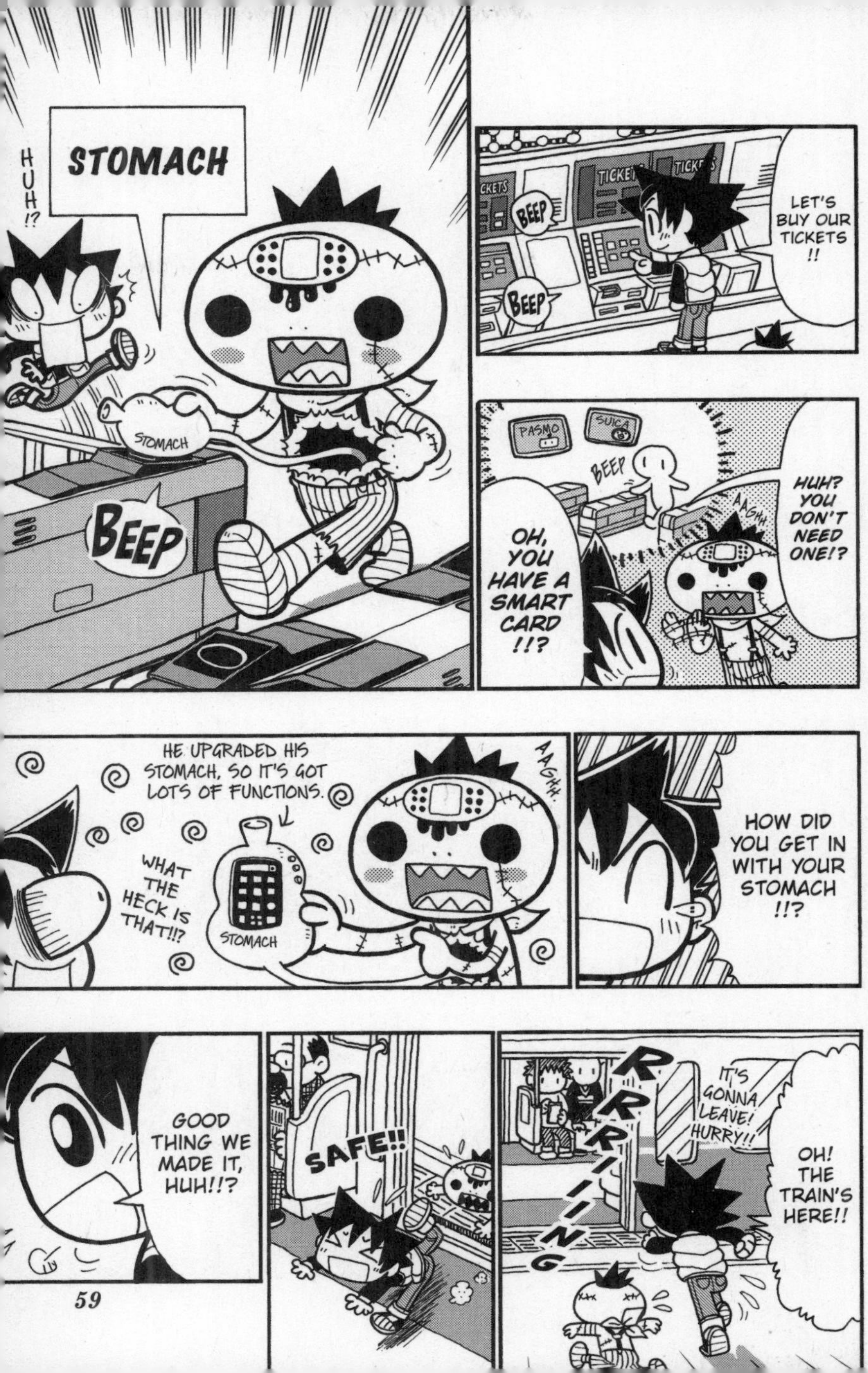
LET'S BUY OUR TICKETS!!
TICKETS
TICKETS
TICKETS
BEEP
BEEP
HUH? YOU DON'T NEED ONE!?
OH, YOU HAVE A SMART CARD!!?
PASMO
SUICA
BEEP
AAGHH
STOMACH
HUH!?
STOMACH
BEEP
HOW DID YOU GET IN WITH YOUR STOMACH!!?
AAGHH
HE UPGRADED HIS STOMACH, SO IT'S GOT LOTS OF FUNCTIONS.
WHAT THE HECK IS THAT!!?
STOMACH
OH! THE TRAIN'S HERE!!
IT'S GONNA LEAVE! HURRY!!
RRRIIIING
SAFE!!
GOOD THING WE MADE IT, HUH!!?

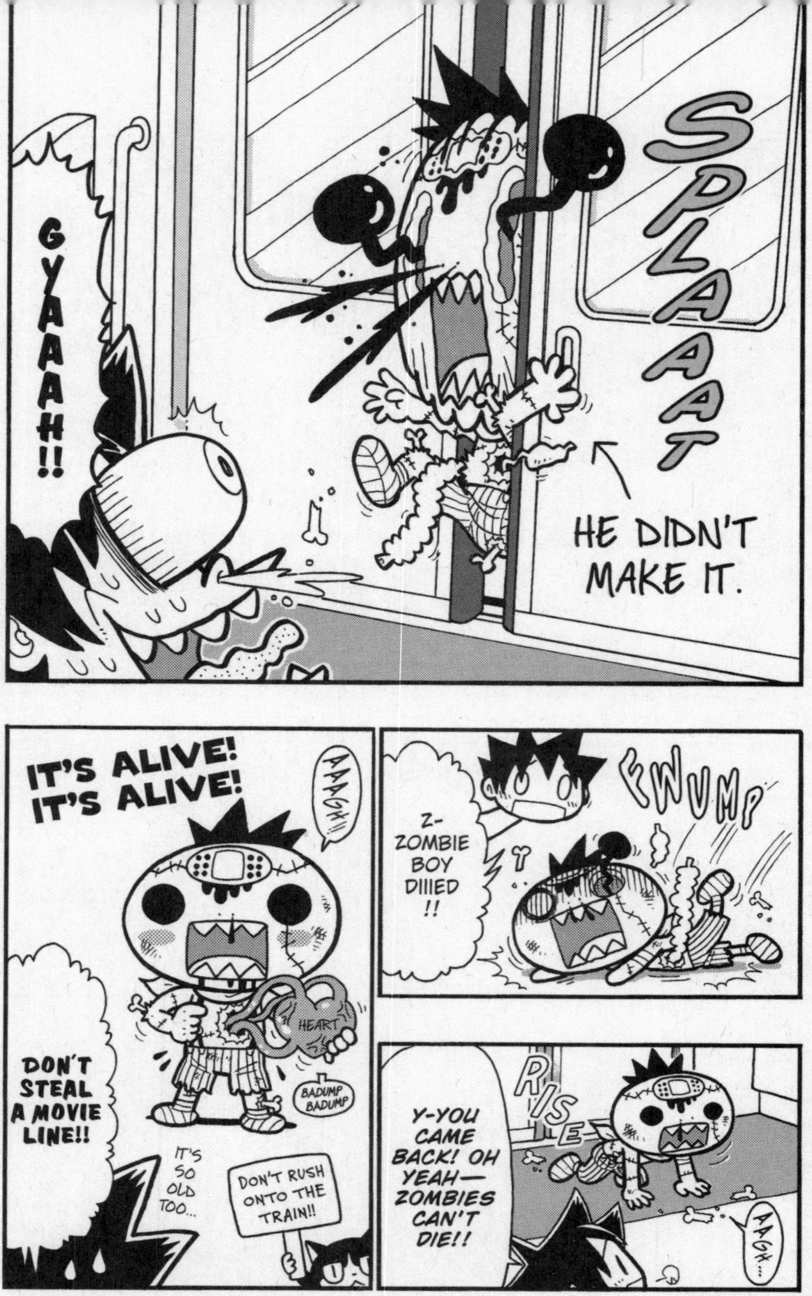
SPLAAAT
HE DIDN'T MAKE IT.
GYAAAAH!!
FWUMP
Z-ZOMBIE BOY DIIIED!!
RISE
Y-YOU CAME BACK! OH YEAH—ZOMBIES CAN'T DIE!!
AAGH...
AAAGH
IT'S ALIVE! IT'S ALIVE!
HEART
BADUMP BADUMP
DON'T STEAL A MOVIE LINE!!
IT'S SO OLD TOO...
DON'T RUSH ONTO THE TRAIN!!

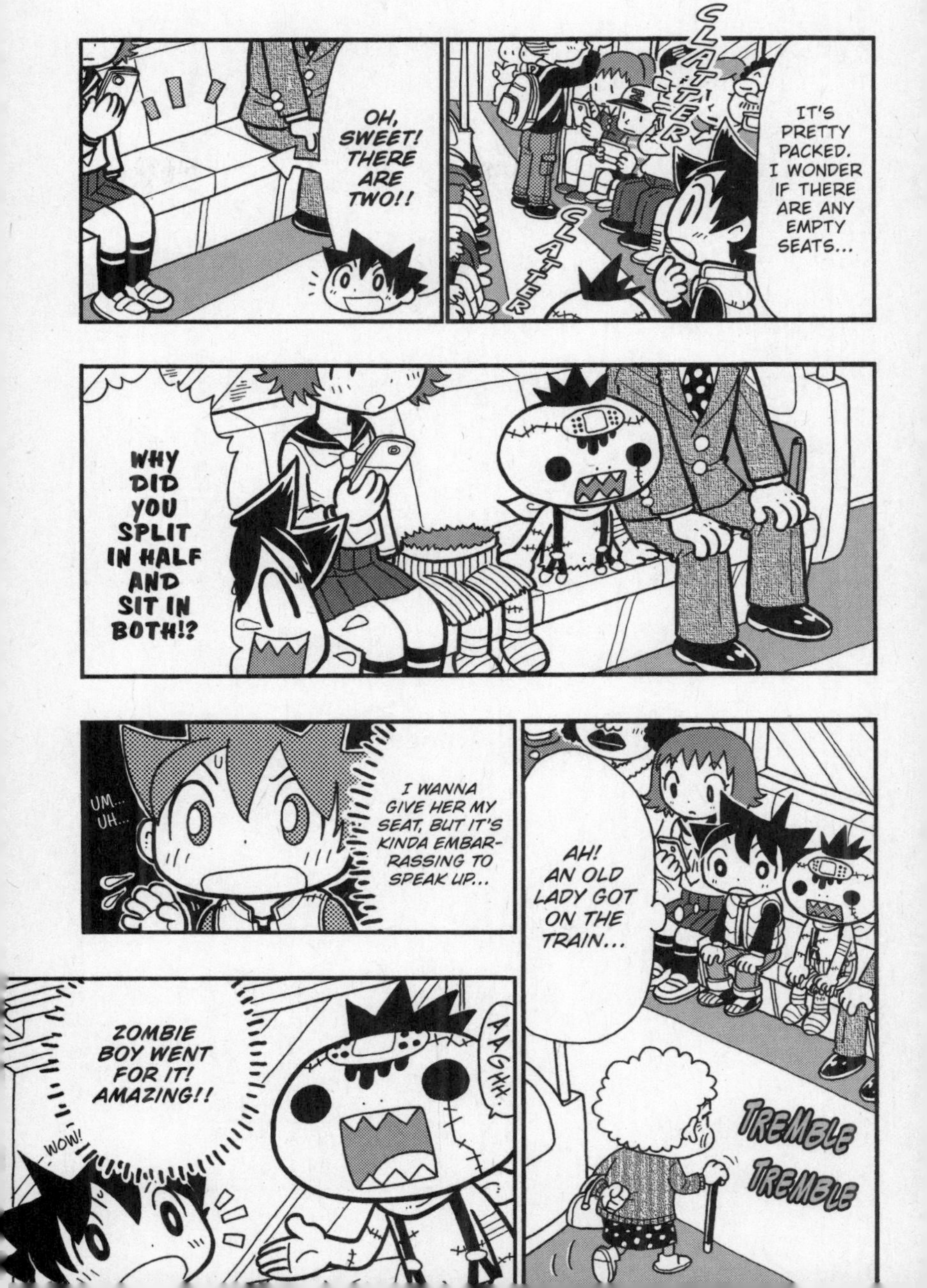
IT'S PRETTY PACKED. I WONDER IF THERE ARE ANY EMPTY SEATS...
CLATTER
CLATTER
CLATTER
OH, SWEET! THERE ARE TWO!!
WHY DID YOU SPLIT IN HALF AND SIT IN BOTH!?
AH! AN OLD LADY GOT ON THE TRAIN...
TREMBLE
TREMBLE
I WANNA GIVE HER MY SEAT, BUT IT'S KINDA EMBARRASSING TO SPEAK UP...
UM... UH...
AAGHH.
ZOMBIE BOY WENT FOR IT! AMAZING!!
WOW!

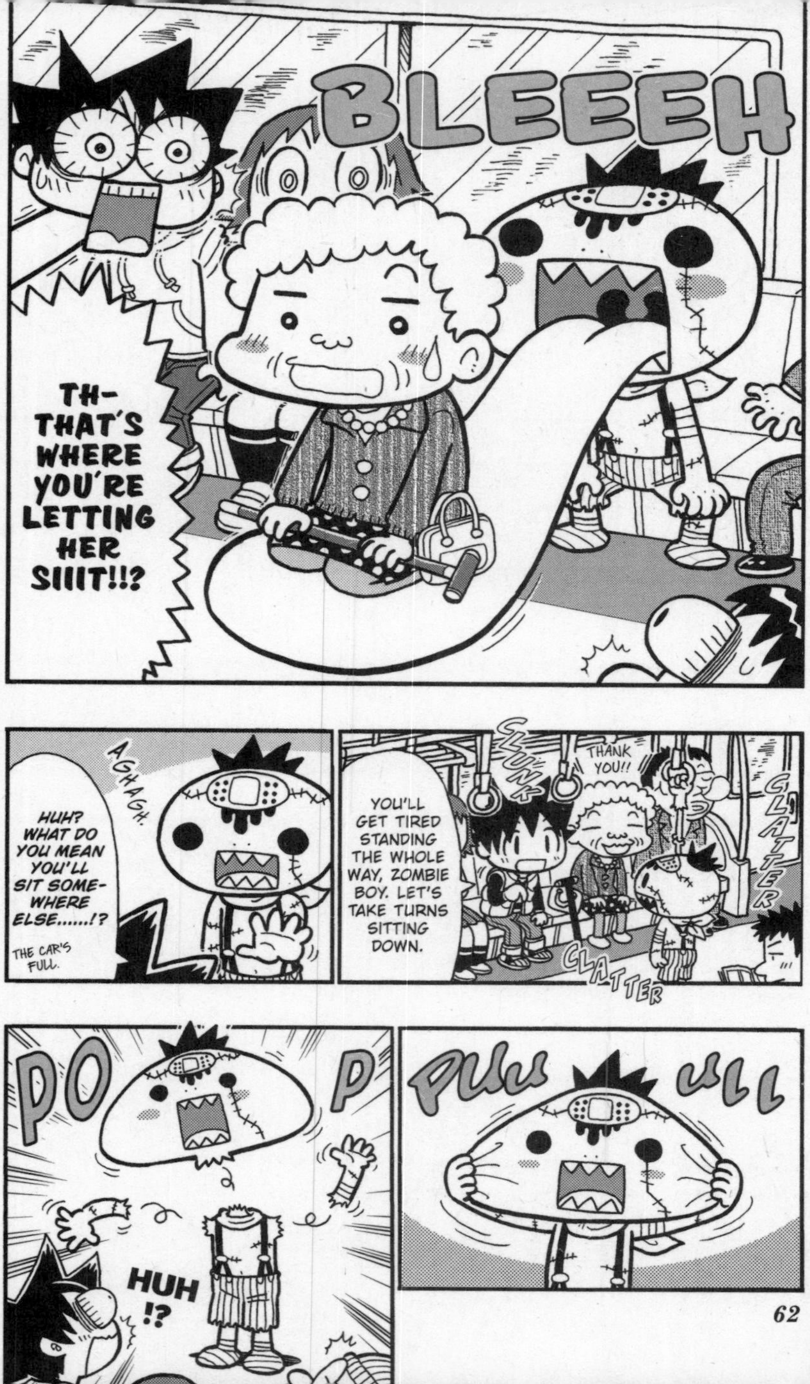
BLEEEH
TH-THAT'S WHERE YOU'RE LETTING HER SIIIT!!?
CLUNK
THANK YOU!!
YOU'LL GET TIRED STANDING THE WHOLE WAY, ZOMBIE BOY. LET'S TAKE TURNS SITTING DOWN.
CLATTER
CLATTER
AGHAGH
HUH? WHAT DO YOU MEAN YOU'LL SIT SOME-WHERE ELSE......!?
THE CAR'S FULL.
PUUUULL
POP
HUH !?

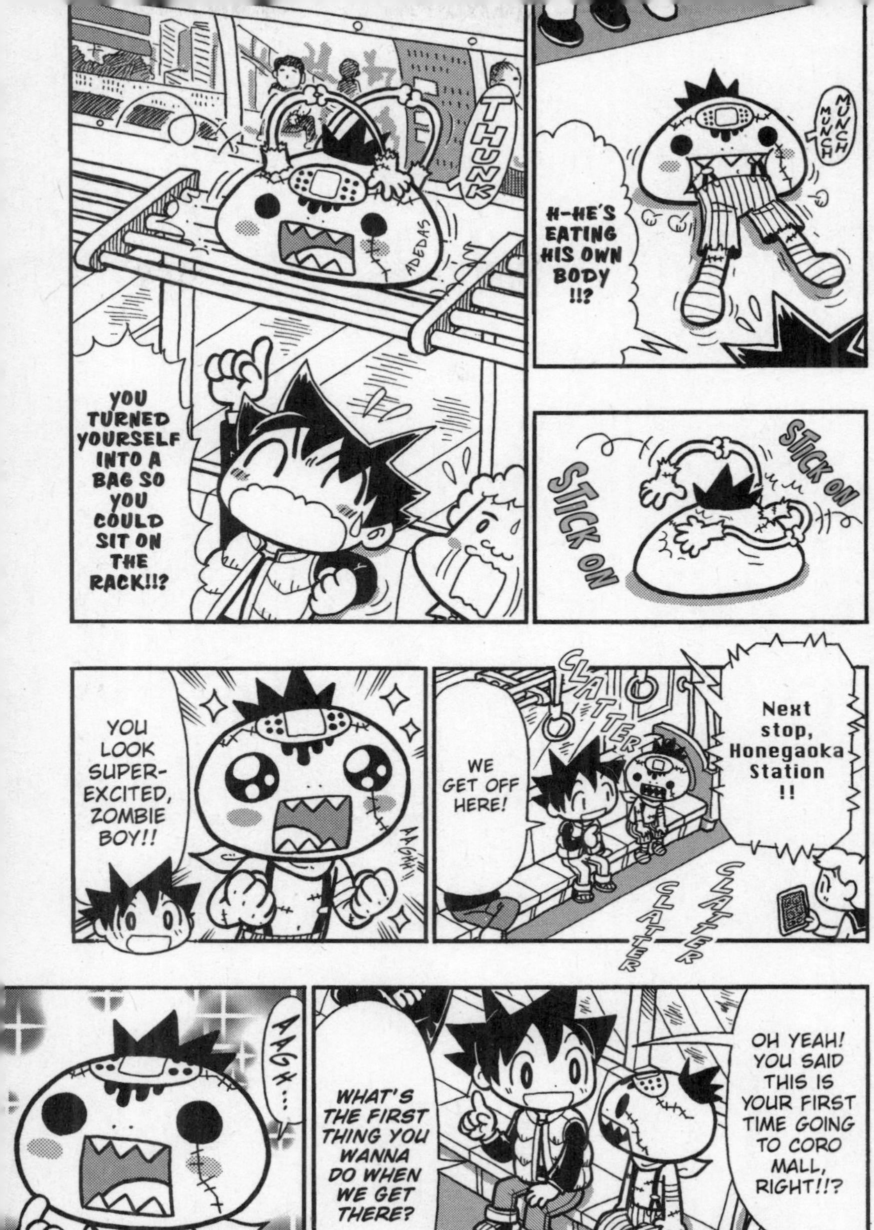
MUNCH MUNCH
H-HE'S EATING HIS OWN BODY!!?
STICK ON
STICK ON
THUNK
ADEDAS
YOU TURNED YOURSELF INTO A BAG SO YOU COULD SIT ON THE RACK!!?
Next stop, Honegaoka Station!!
CLATTER
WE GET OFF HERE!
CLATTER
CLATTER
YOU LOOK SUPER-EXCITED, ZOMBIE BOY!!
AAGH!!
OH YEAH! YOU SAID THIS IS YOUR FIRST TIME GOING TO CORO MALL, RIGHT!!?
WHAT'S THE FIRST THING YOU WANNA DO WHEN WE GET THERE?
AAGH...

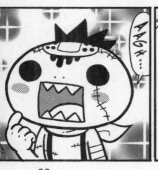

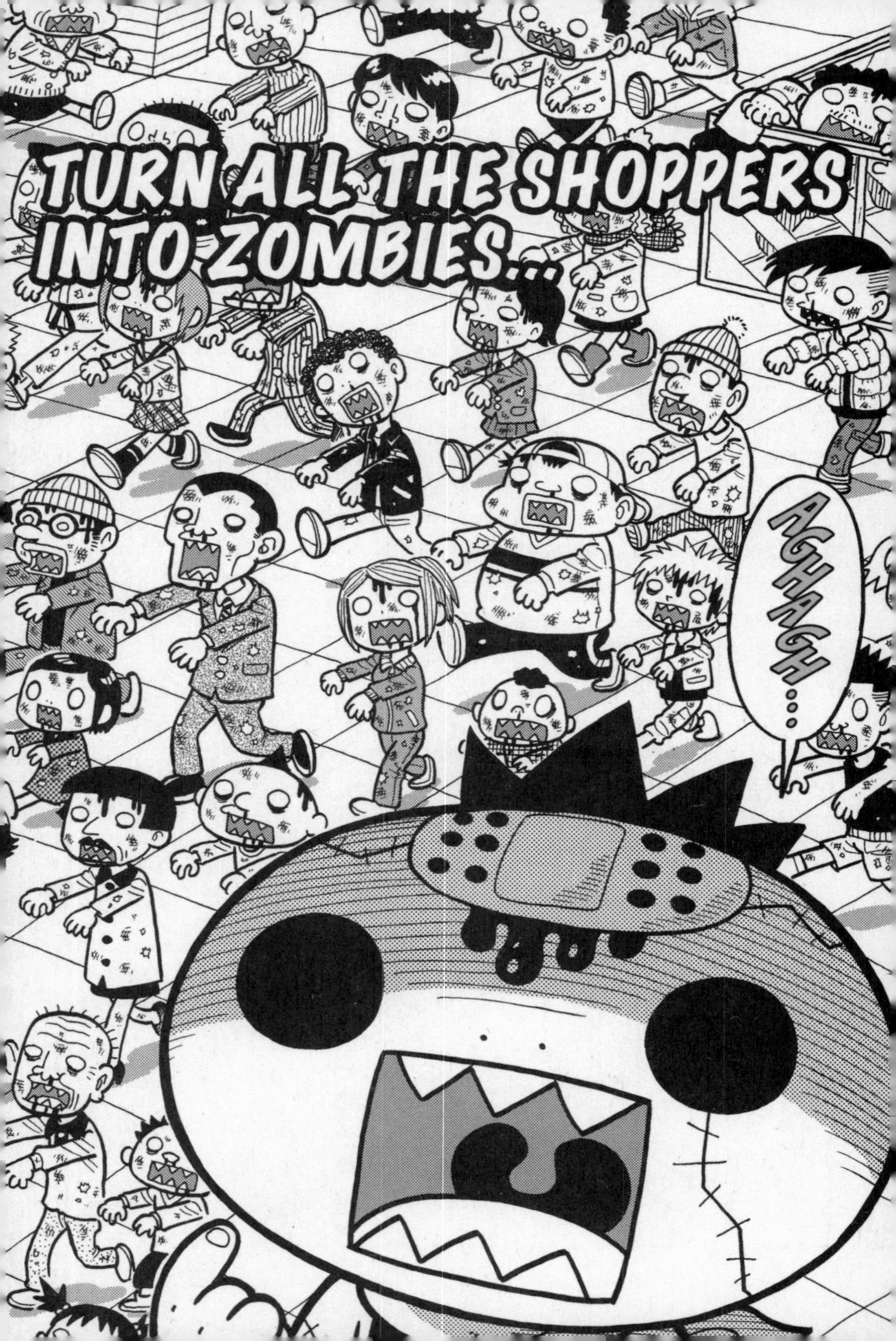
TURN ALL THE SHOPPERS INTO ZOMBIES...
AGHAGH...

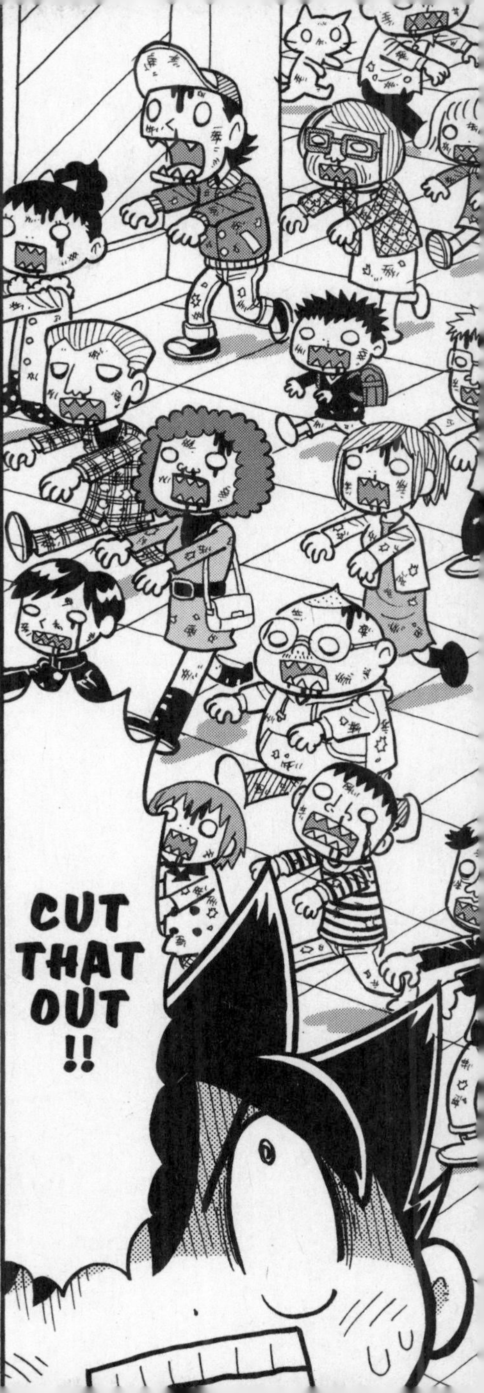
CUT THAT OUT!!

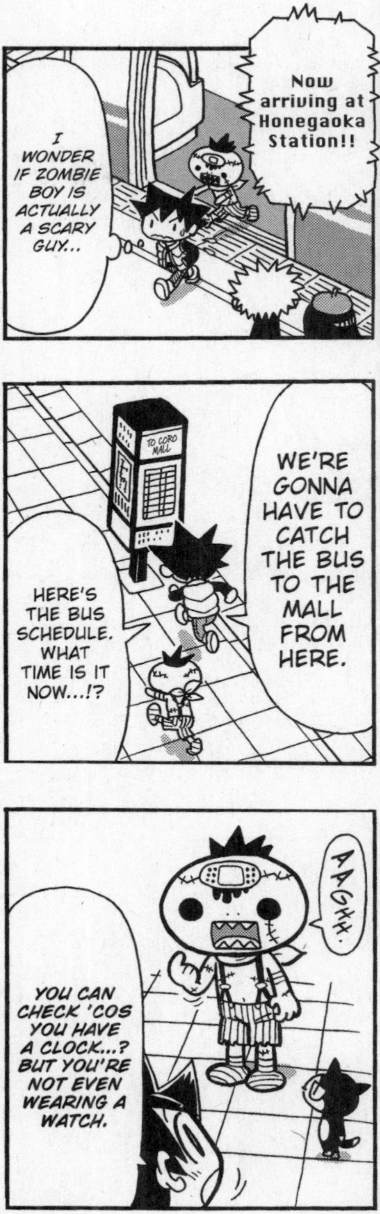
Now arriving at Honegaoka Station!!
I WONDER IF ZOMBIE BOY IS ACTUALLY A SCARY GUY...
TO CORO MALL
WE'RE GONNA HAVE TO CATCH THE BUS TO THE MALL FROM HERE.
HERE'S THE BUS SCHEDULE. WHAT TIME IS IT NOW...!?
AAGHH.
YOU CAN CHECK 'COS YOU HAVE A CLOCK...? BUT YOU'RE NOT EVEN WEARING A WATCH.

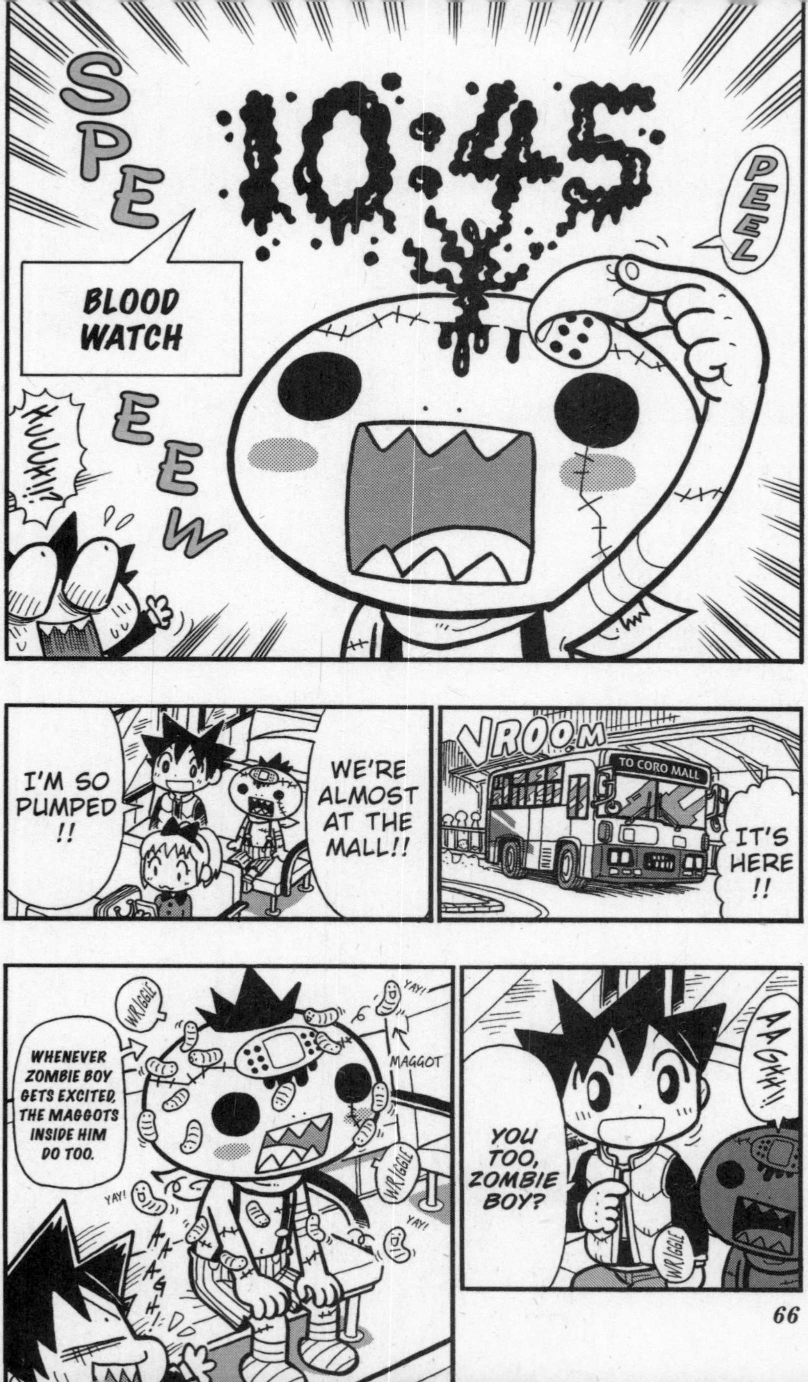
PEEL
10:45
SPEEEW
BLOOD WATCH
KUUUX!!?
WE'RE ALMOST AT THE MALL!!
VROOM
TO CORO MALL
IT'S HERE!!
I'M SO PUMPED!!
AAGHXX!!
YOU TOO, ZOMBIE BOY?
WRIGGLE
YAY!
MAGGOT
WRIGGLE
WHENEVER ZOMBIE BOY GETS EXCITED, THE MAGGOTS INSIDE HIM DO TOO.
YAY!
WRIGGLE
YAY!
AAAGH!

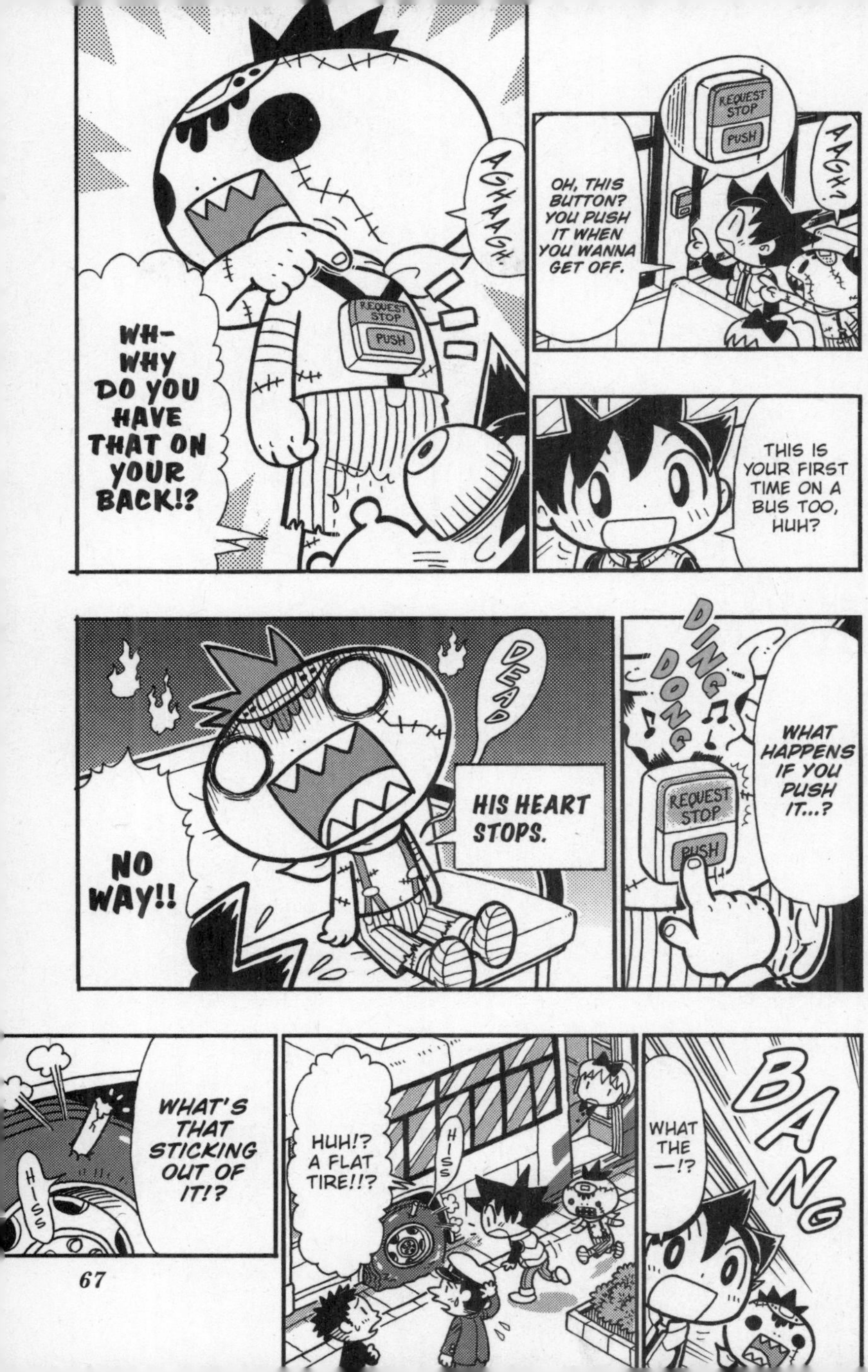
REQUEST STOP
PUSH
AAGH!?
OH, THIS BUTTON? YOU PUSH IT WHEN YOU WANNA GET OFF.
THIS IS YOUR FIRST TIME ON A BUS TOO, HUH?
AGHAAAGH.
REQUEST STOP
PUSH
WH-WHY DO YOU HAVE THAT ON YOUR BACK!?
DING
DONG
WHAT HAPPENS IF YOU PUSH IT...?
REQUEST STOP
PUSH
DEAD
HIS HEART STOPS.
NO WAY!!
BANG
WHAT THE—!?
HISS
HUH!? A FLAT TIRE!!?
WHAT'S THAT STICKING OUT OF IT!?
HISS

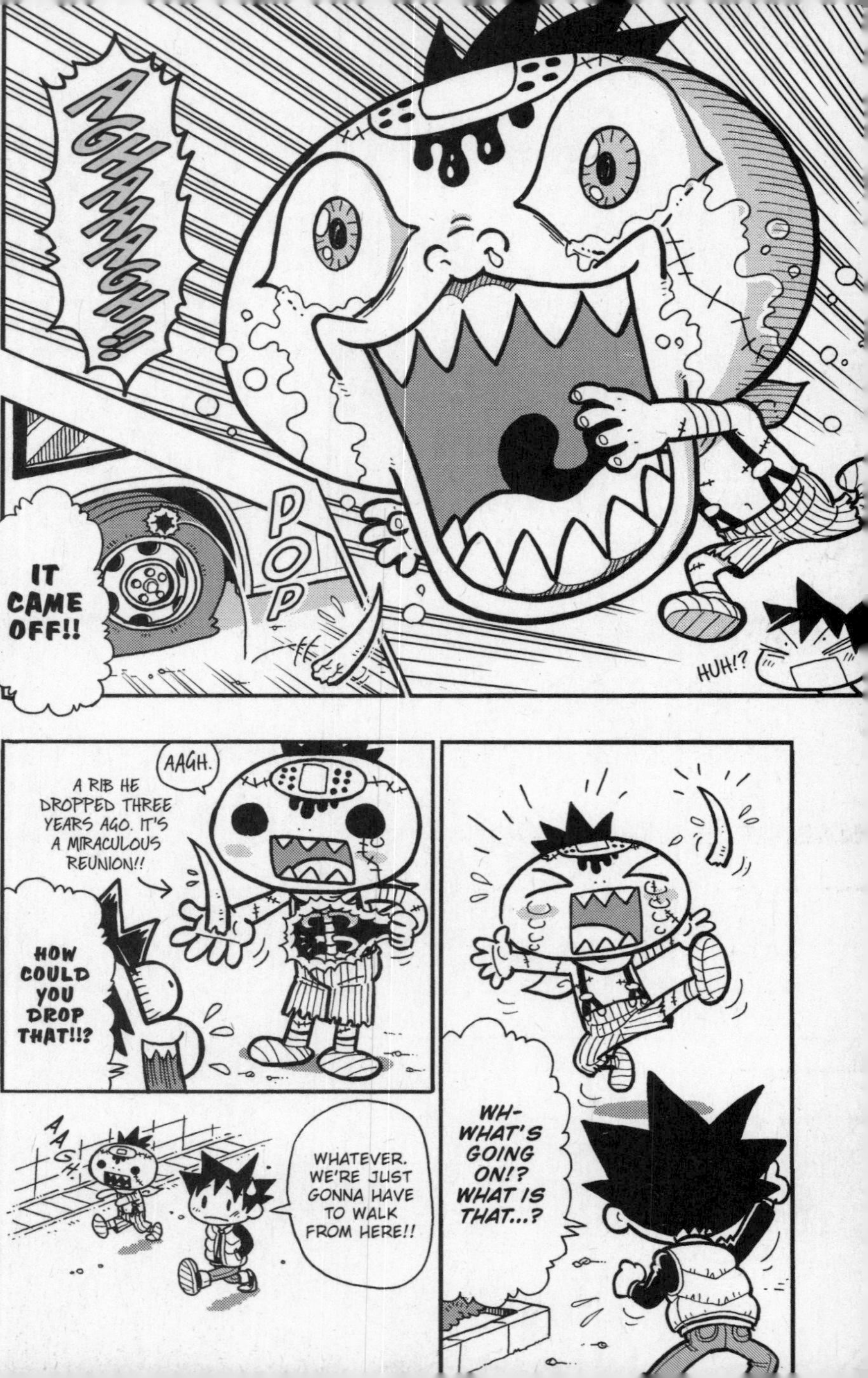
AGHAAAAGH!!!
HUH!?
POP
IT CAME OFF!!
WH- WHAT'S GOING ON!? WHAT IS THAT...?
AAGH.
A RIB HE DROPPED THREE YEARS AGO. IT'S A MIRACULOUS REUNION!!
HOW COULD YOU DROP THAT!!?
AAGH.
WHATEVER. WE'RE JUST GONNA HAVE TO WALK FROM HERE!!

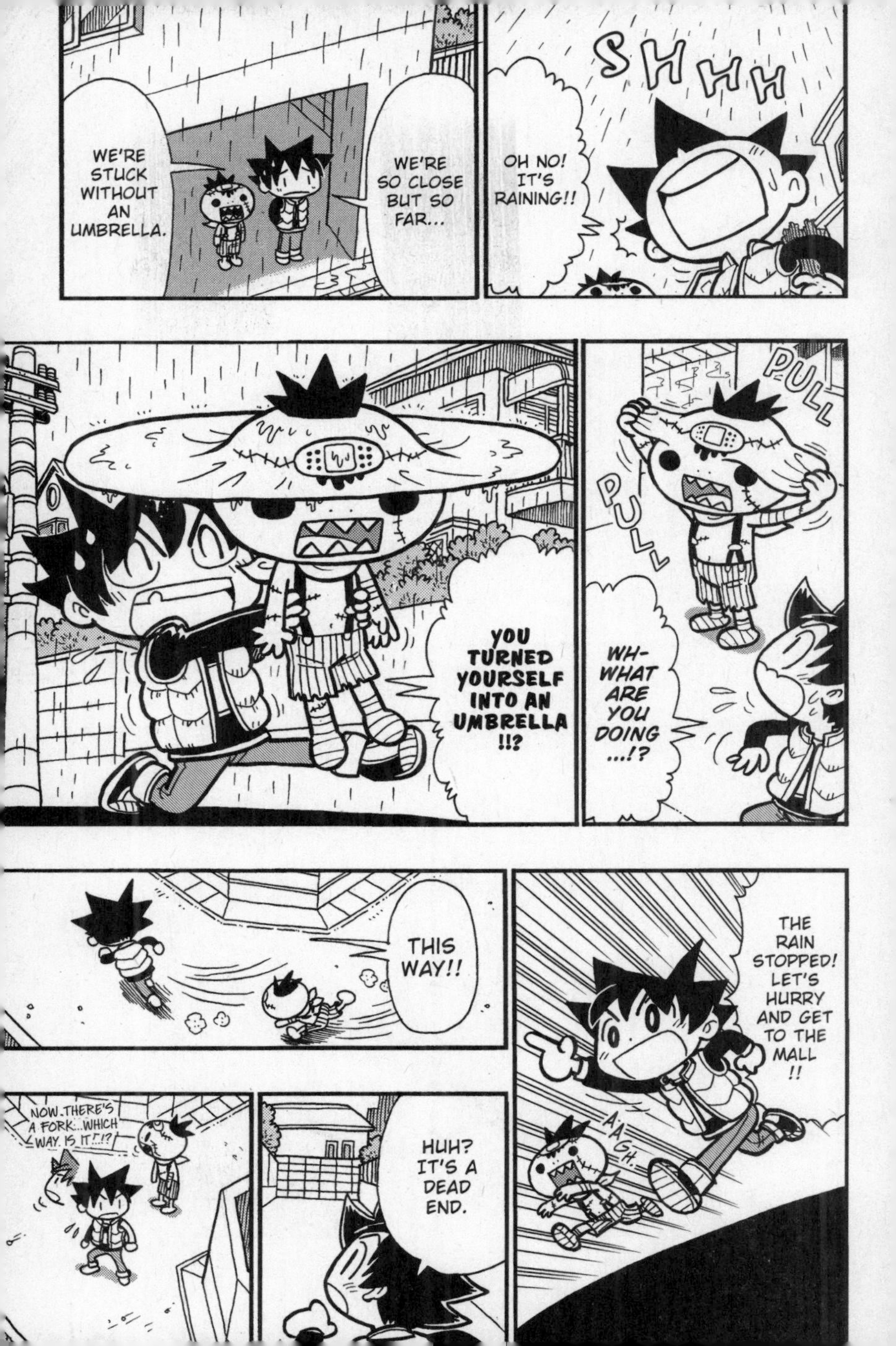
SHHH
OH NO! IT'S RAINING!!
WE'RE SO CLOSE BUT SO FAR...
WE'RE STUCK WITHOUT AN UMBRELLA.
PULL
PULL
WH-WHAT ARE YOU DOING ...!?
YOU TURNED YOURSELF INTO AN UMBRELLA !!?
THE RAIN STOPPED! LET'S HURRY AND GET TO THE MALL !!
AAGH.
THIS WAY!!
HUH? IT'S A DEAD END.
NOW THERE'S A FORK...WHICH WAY IS IT!?

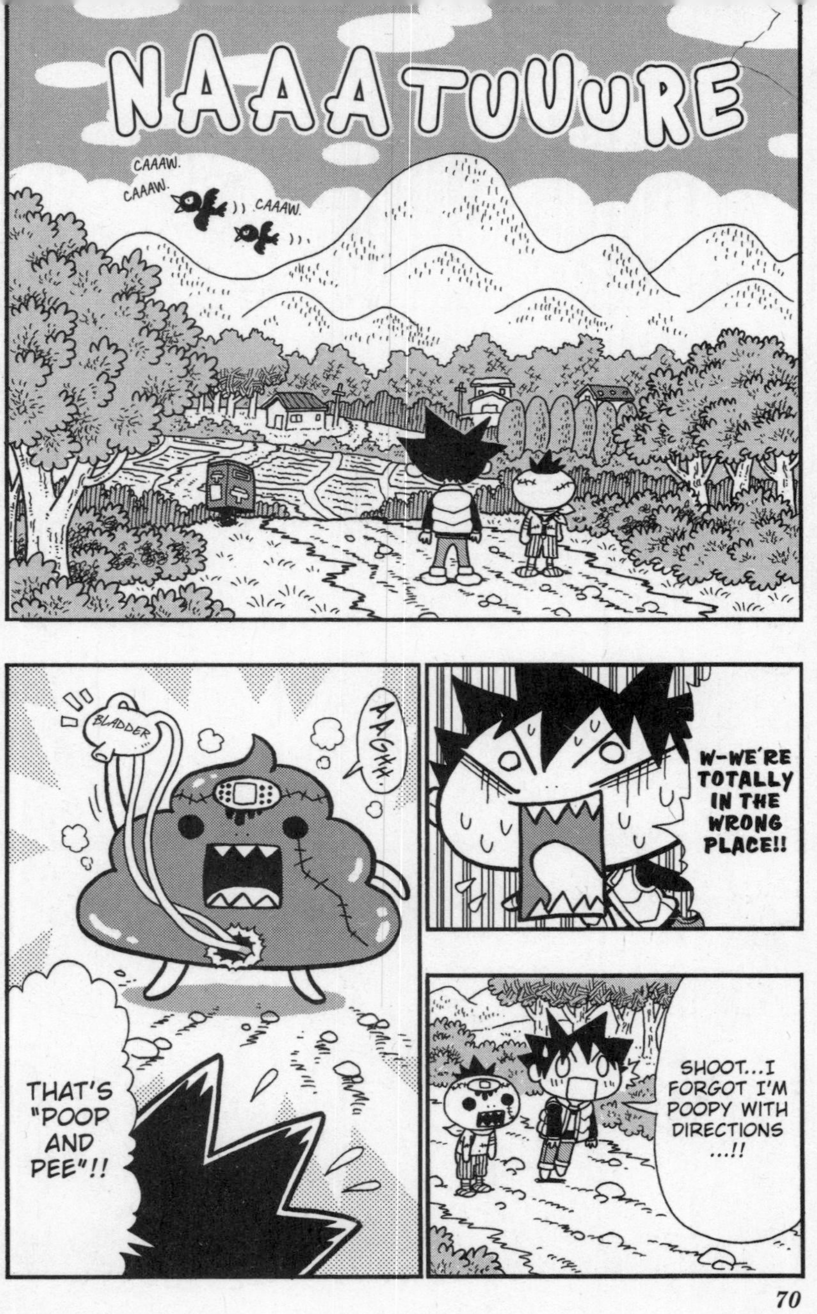
NAAATUUURE
CAAAW.
CAAAW.
CAAAW.
W-WE'RE TOTALLY IN THE WRONG PLACE!!
SHOOT...I FORGOT I'M POOPY WITH DIRECTIONS ...!!
AAGHX.
BLADDER
THAT'S "POOP AND PEE"!!

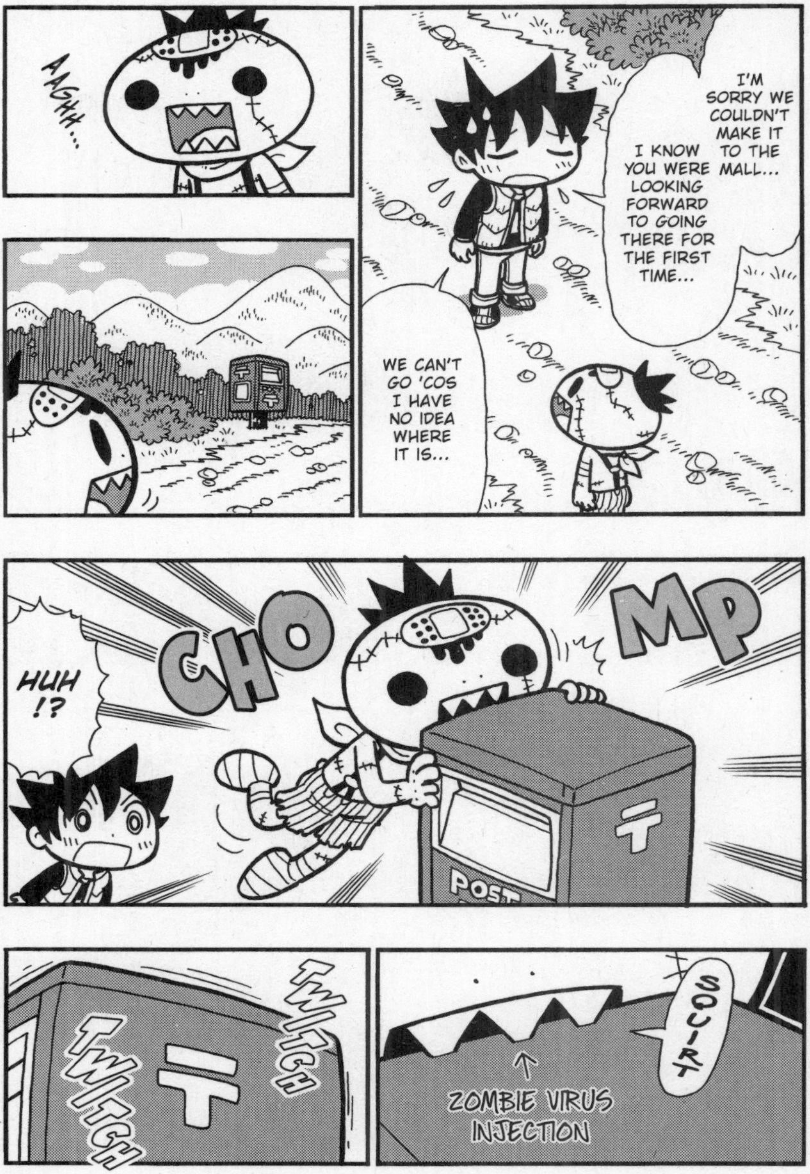
I'M SORRY WE COULDN'T MAKE IT TO THE MALL...
I KNOW YOU WERE LOOKING FORWARD TO GOING THERE FOR THE FIRST TIME...
WE CAN'T GO 'COS I HAVE NO IDEA WHERE IT IS...
AAGHH...
CHOMP
HUH!?
SQUIRT
ZOMBIE VIRUS INJECTION
TWITCH
TWITCH

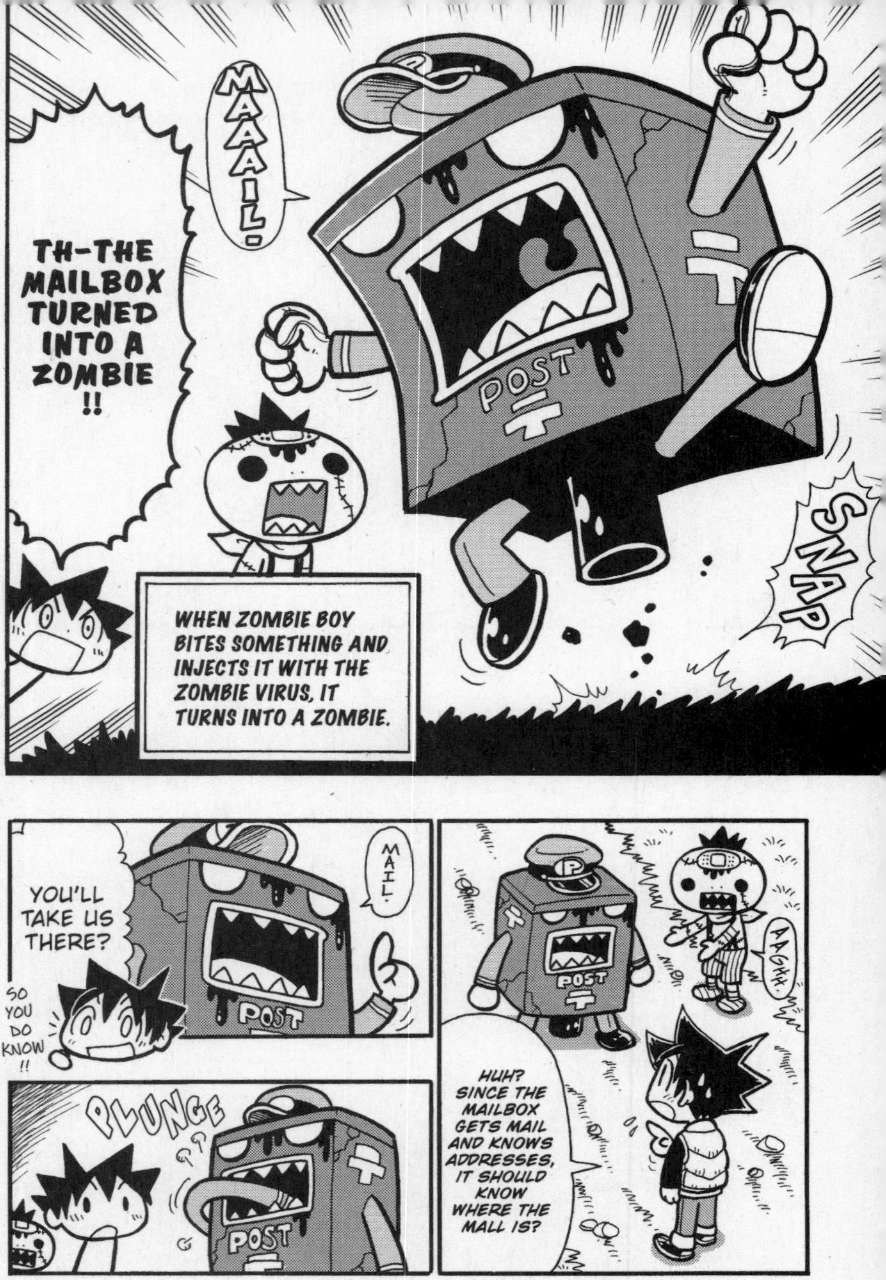
MAAAIL!
SNAP
TH-THE MAILBOX TURNED INTO A ZOMBIE!!
WHEN ZOMBIE BOY BITES SOMETHING AND INJECTS IT WITH THE ZOMBIE VIRUS, IT TURNS INTO A ZOMBIE.
AAGHH.
HUH? SINCE THE MAILBOX GETS MAIL AND KNOWS ADDRESSES, IT SHOULD KNOW WHERE THE MALL IS?
MAIL.
YOU'LL TAKE US THERE?
SO YOU DO KNOW!!
PLUNGE

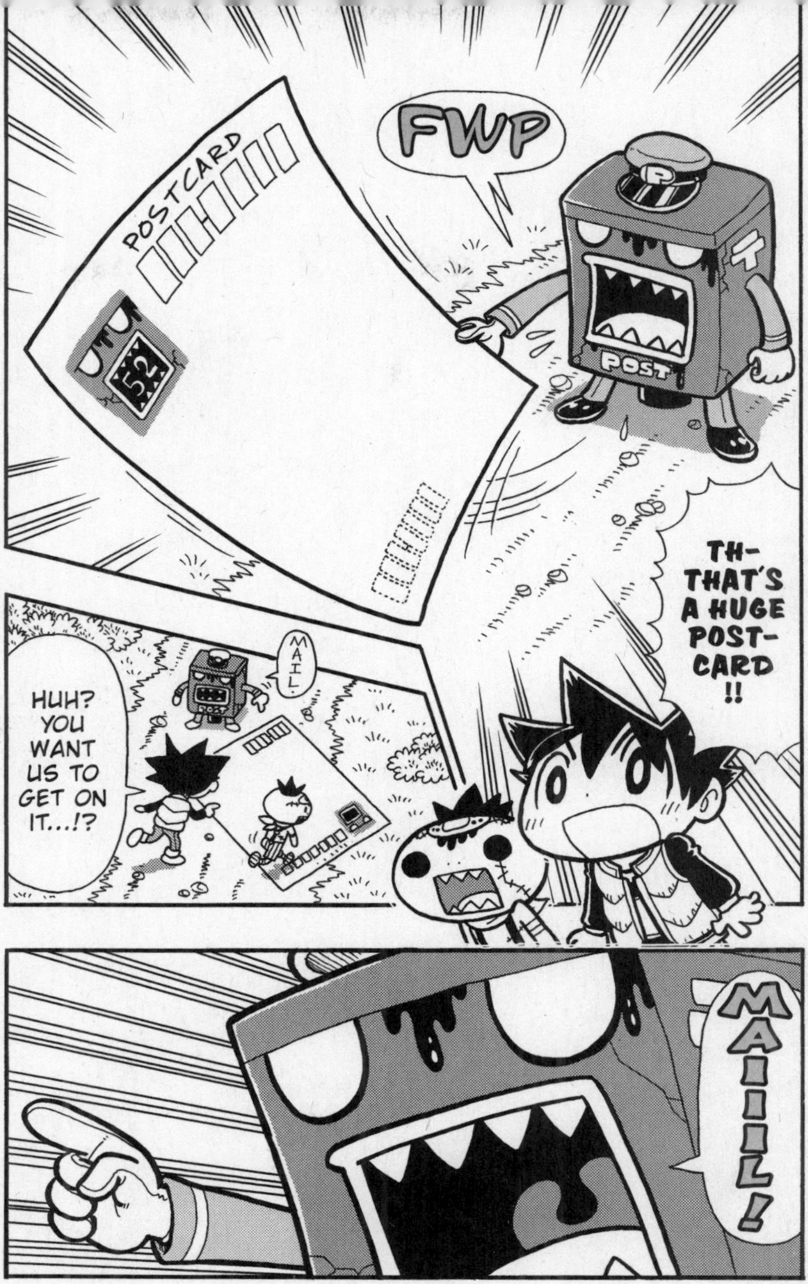
FWP
POSTCARD
POST
TH- THAT'S A HUGE POST-CARD!!
MAIL.
HUH? YOU WANT US TO GET ON IT...!?
MAIIIL!

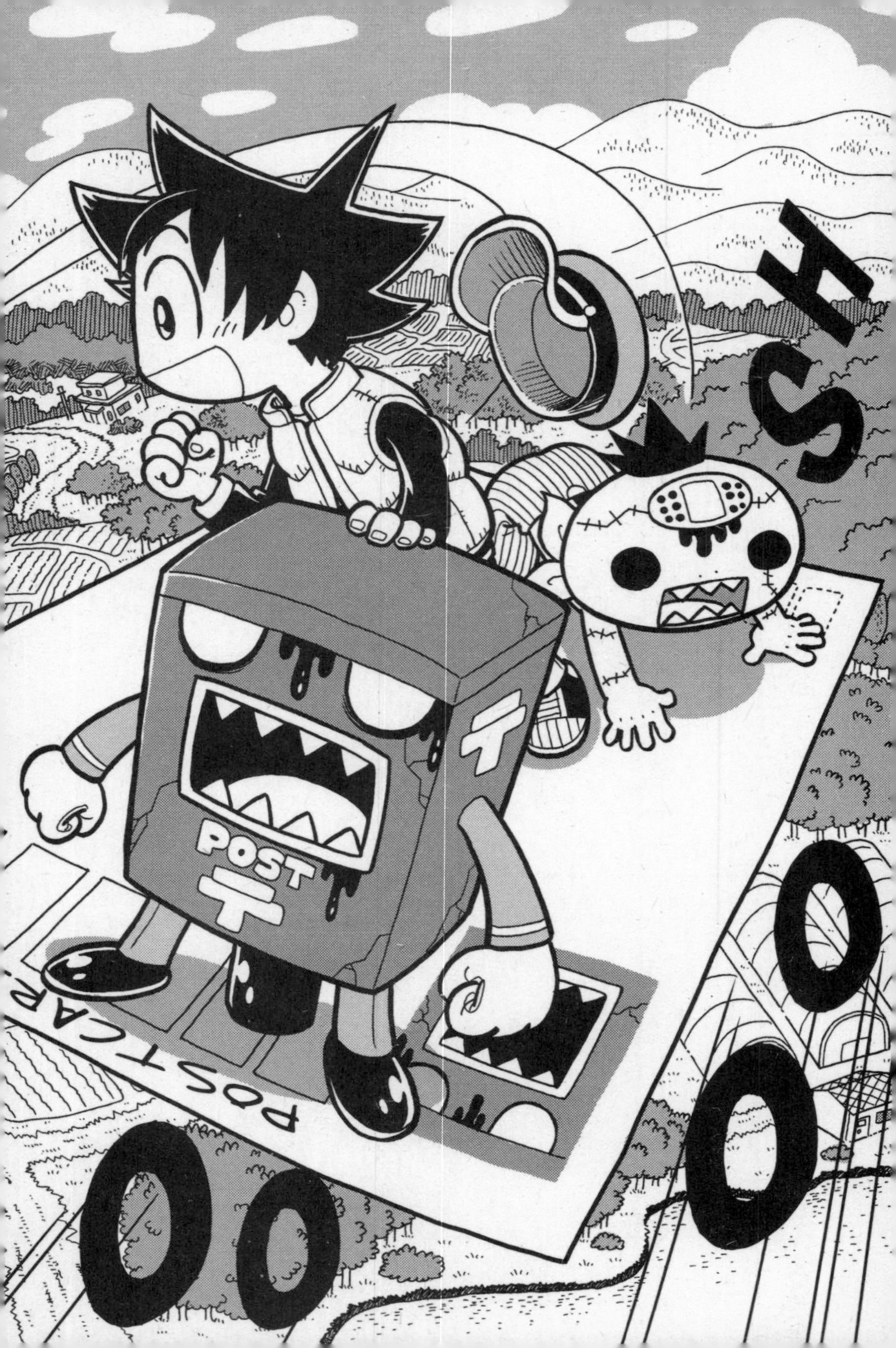
POST
POSTCAR
OOOOSH

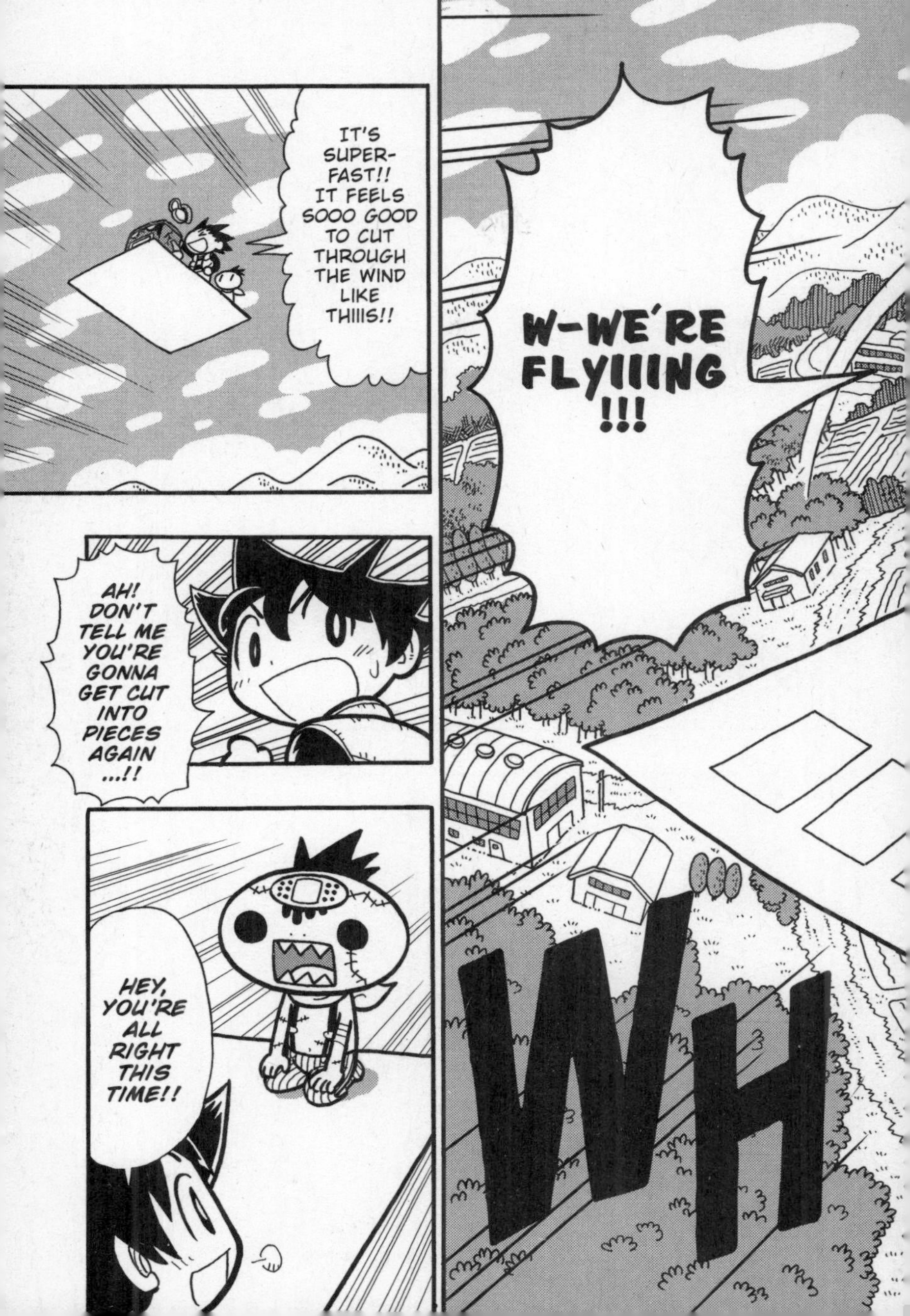
W-WE'RE FLYIIIING !!!
WH
IT'S SUPER-FAST!! IT FEELS SOOO GOOD TO CUT THROUGH THE WIND LIKE THIIIS!!
AH! DON'T TELL ME YOU'RE GONNA GET CUT INTO PIECES AGAIN ...!!
HEY, YOU'RE ALL RIGHT THIS TIME!!

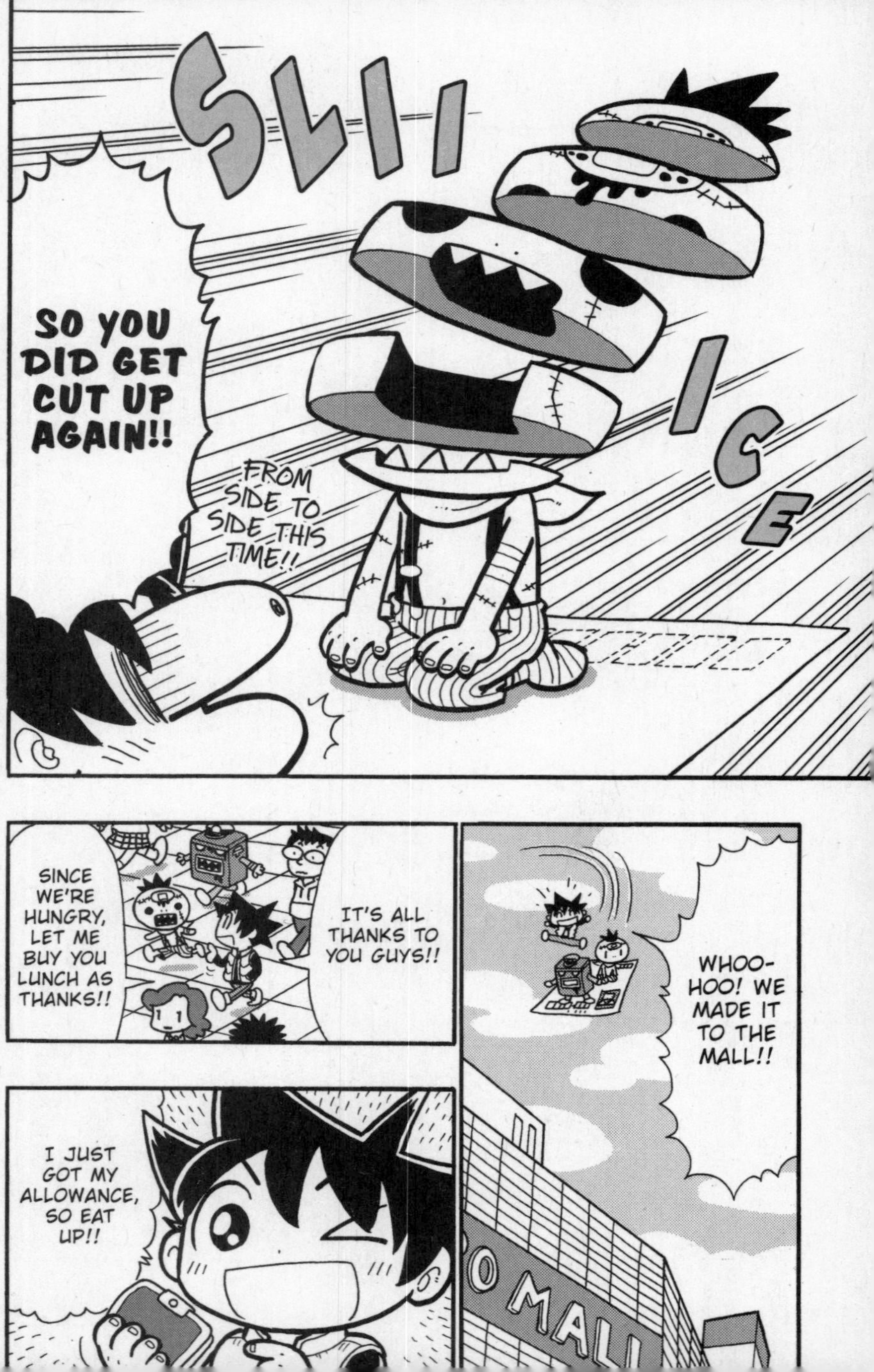
SLIIICE
SO YOU DID GET CUT UP AGAIN!!
FROM SIDE TO SIDE THIS TIME!!
WHOO-HOO! WE MADE IT TO THE MALL!!
MALL
IT'S ALL THANKS TO YOU GUYS!!
SINCE WE'RE HUNGRY, LET ME BUY YOU LUNCH AS THANKS!!
I JUST GOT MY ALLOWANCE, SO EAT UP!!

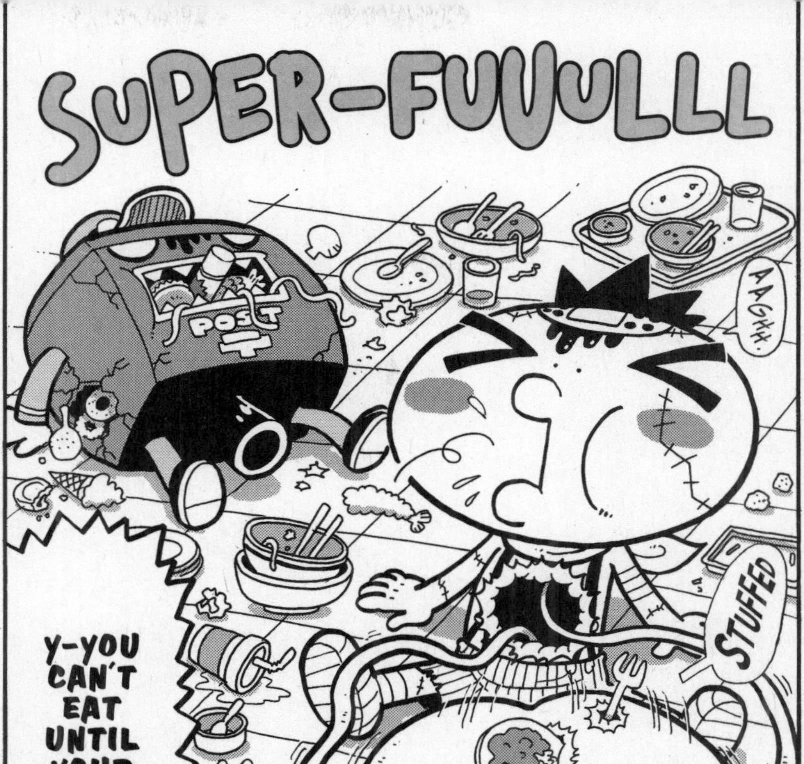
SUPER-FUUULLL
AAGHH.
STUFFED
FULL
EMPTY
STOMACH
Y-YOU CAN'T EAT UNTIL YOUR STOMACH POPS OUT!!!
THAT'S GOING OVER-BOARD!!

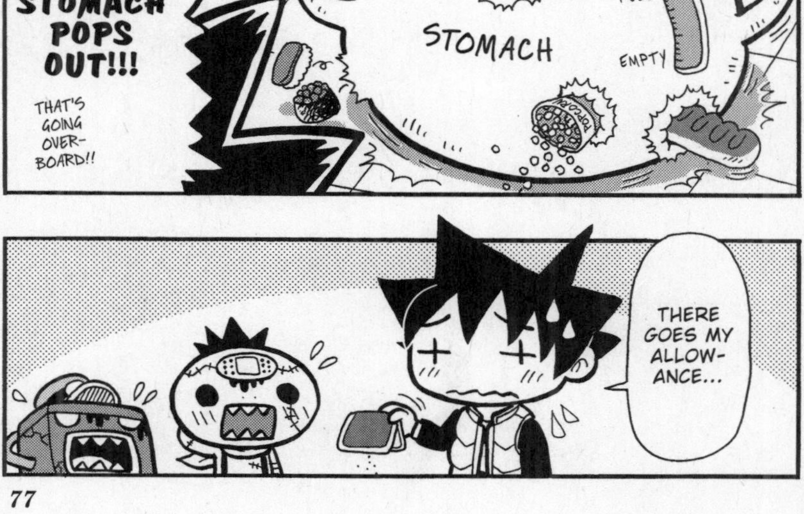
THERE GOES MY ALLOW-ANCE...

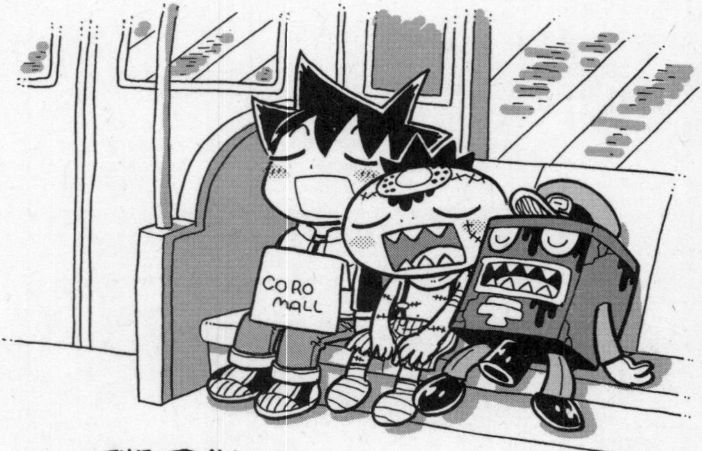
CORO MALL
THE TRAIN RIDE HOME

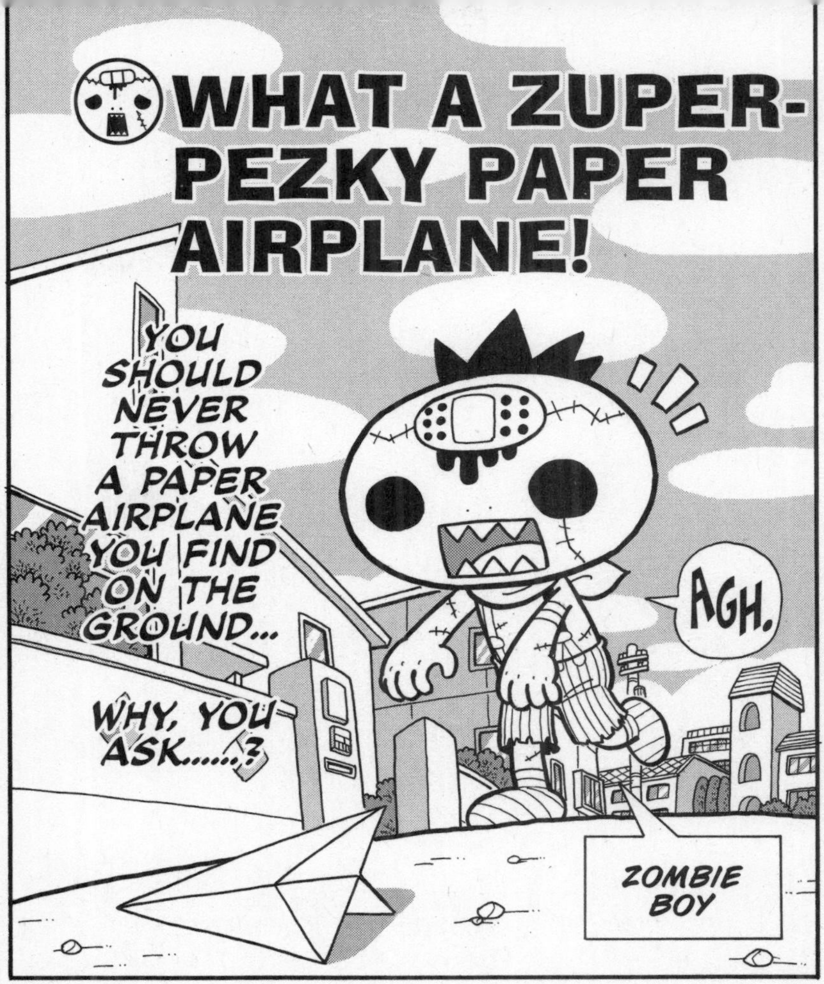
WHAT A ZUPER-PEZKY PAPER AIRPLANE!
AGH.
YOU SHOULD NEVER THROW A PAPER AIRPLANE YOU FIND ON THE GROUND...
WHY, YOU ASK......?
ZOMBIE BOY

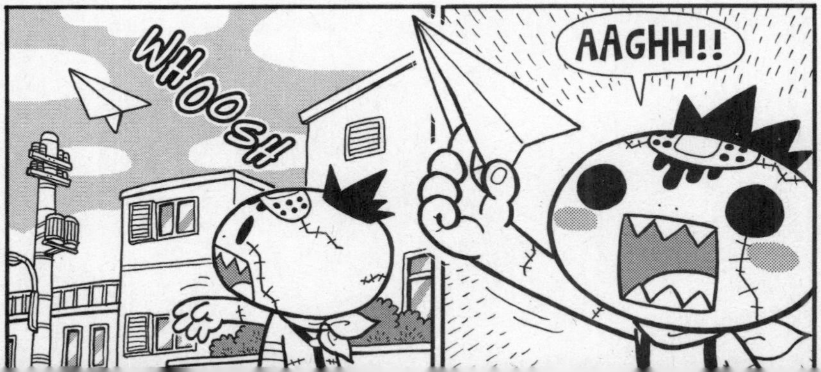
AAGHH!!
WHOOSH

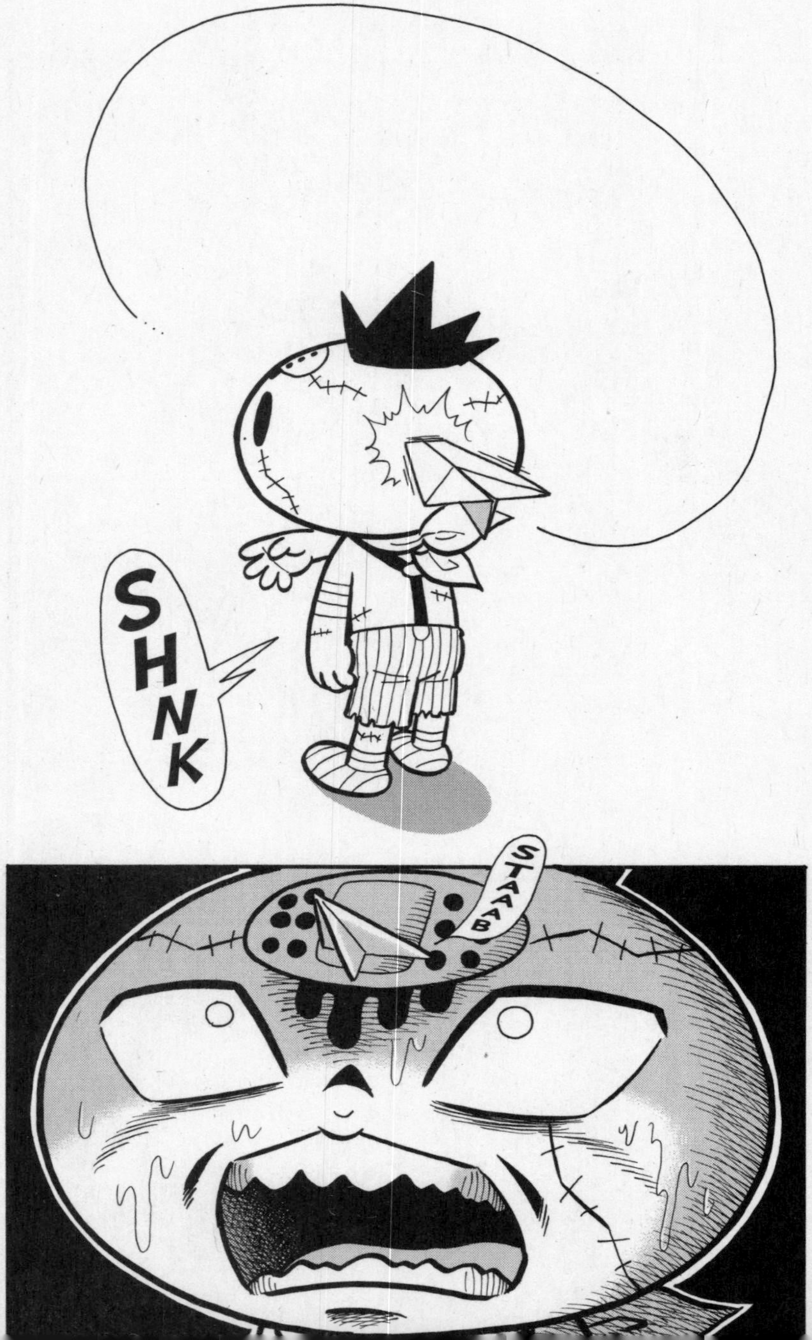
SHNK
STAAAB

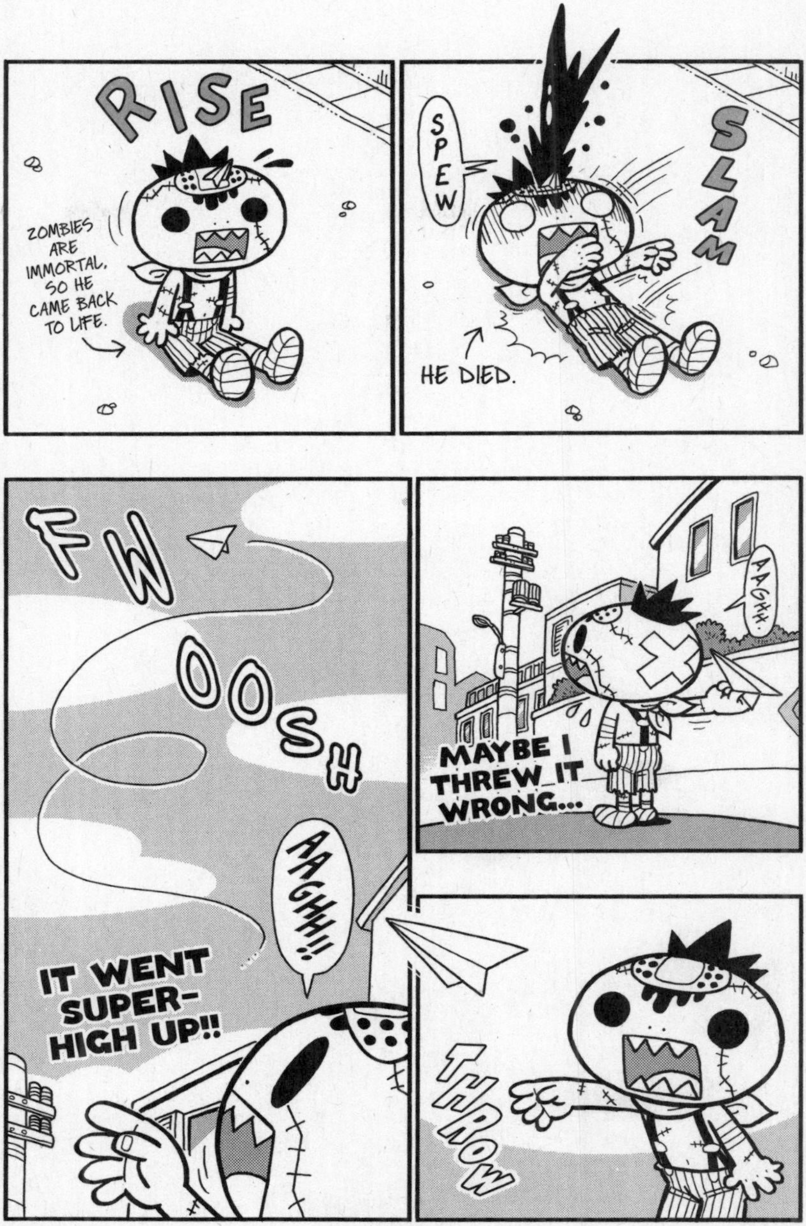
SLAM
SPEW
HE DIED.
RISE
ZOMBIES ARE IMMORTAL, SO HE CAME BACK TO LIFE.
AAGHH.
MAYBE I THREW IT WRONG...
THROW
FWOOSH
AAGHH!!
IT WENT SUPER-HIGH UP!!

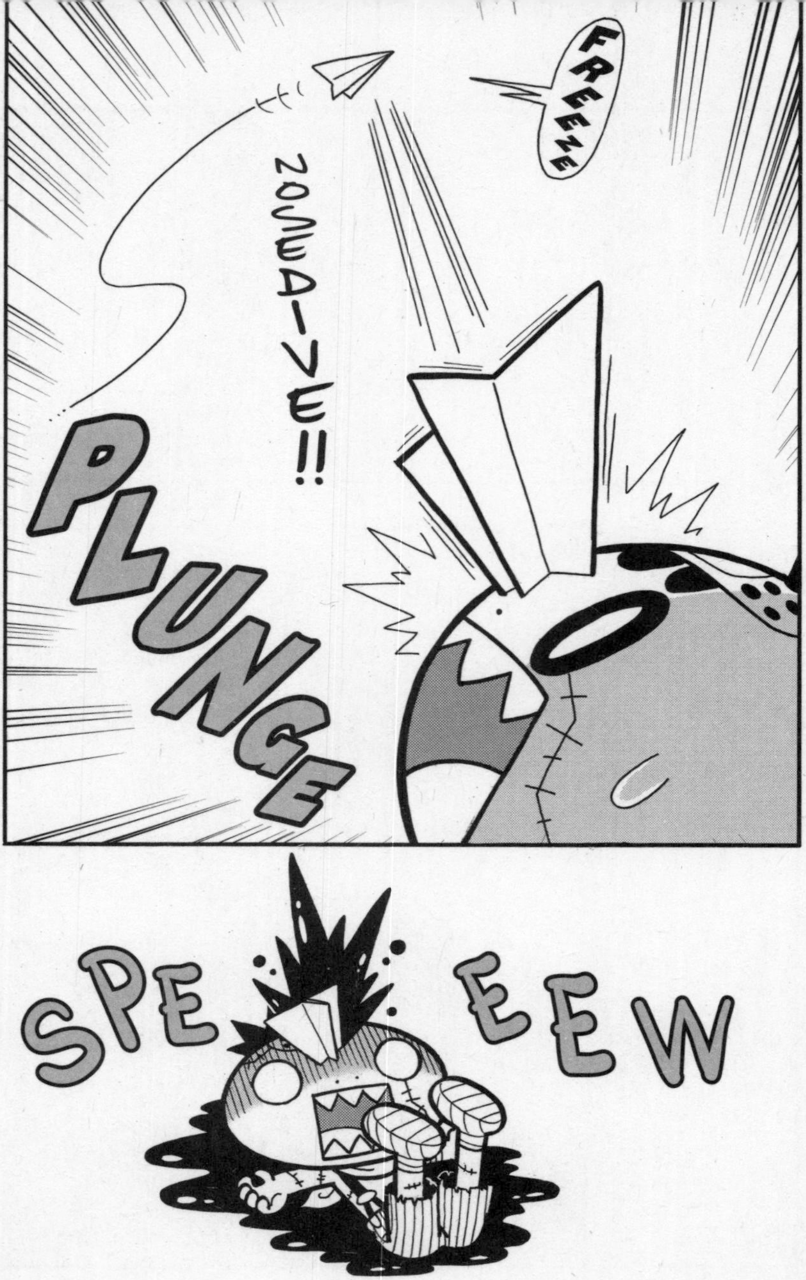
FREEZE
NOSEDIVE!!
PLUNGE
SPEEEW

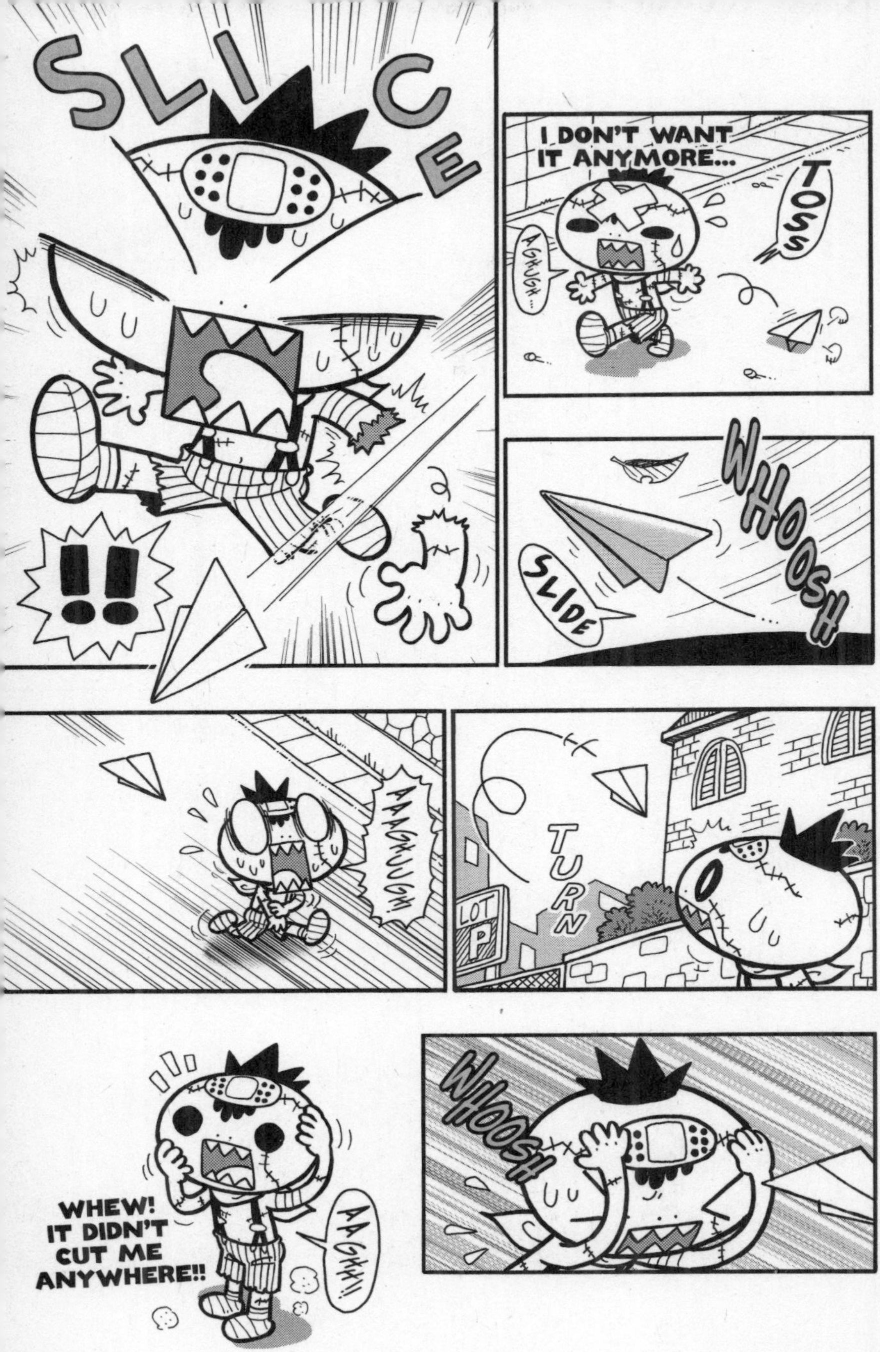
I DON'T WANT IT ANYMORE...
AGHUGH...
TOSS
WHOOSH
SLIDE
SLICE
!!
TURN
LOT
P
AAAGHUUGH!!
WHOOSH
AAGHH!!
WHEW! IT DIDN'T CUT ME ANYWHERE!!

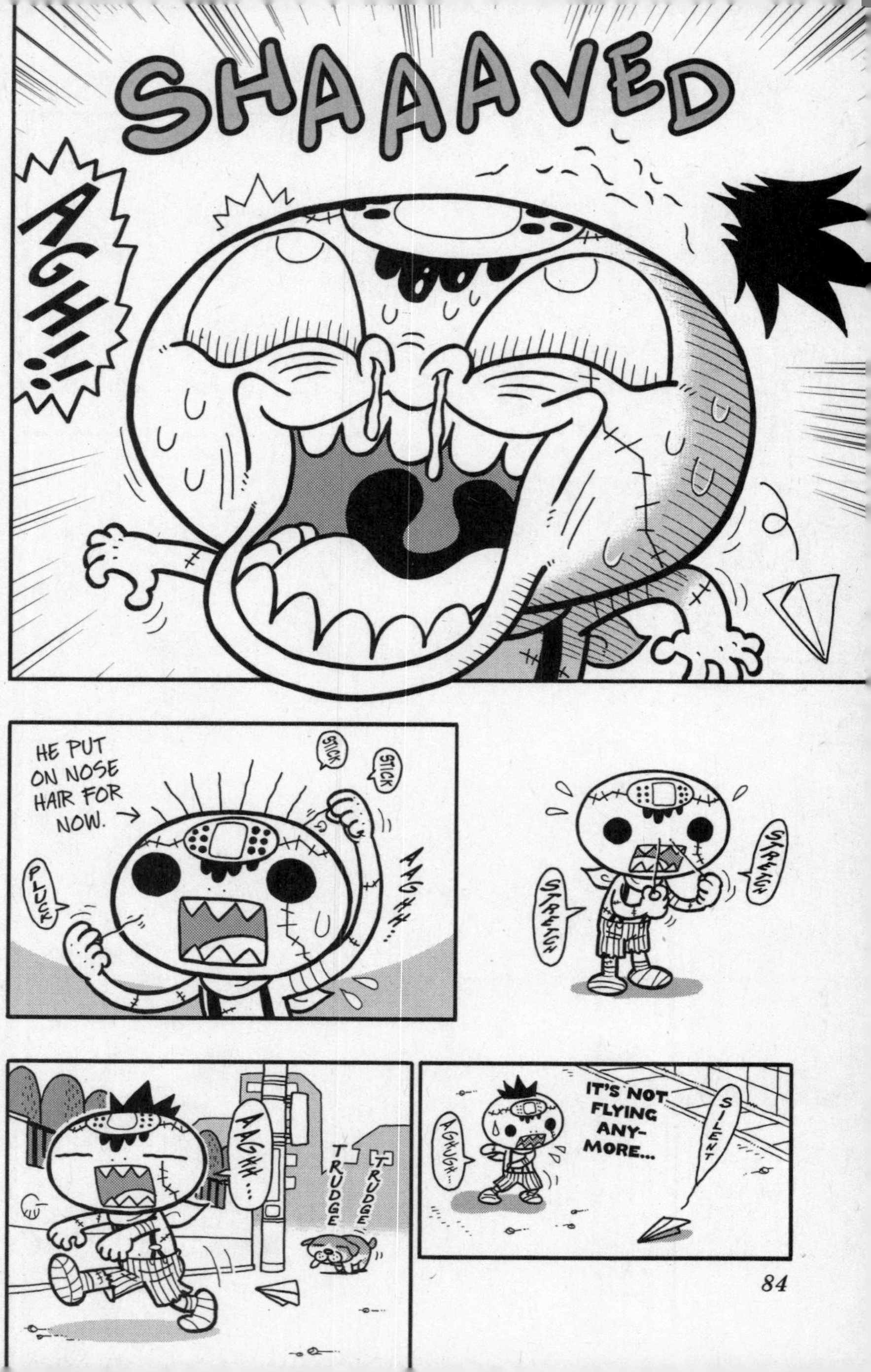
SHAAAVED
AGH!!!
STRETCH
STRETCH
STICK
STICK
HE PUT ON NOSE HAIR FOR NOW.
AAGHH...
PLUCK
SILENT
IT'S NOT FLYING ANYMORE...
AGHUGH...
TRUDGE
TRUDGE
AAGHH...

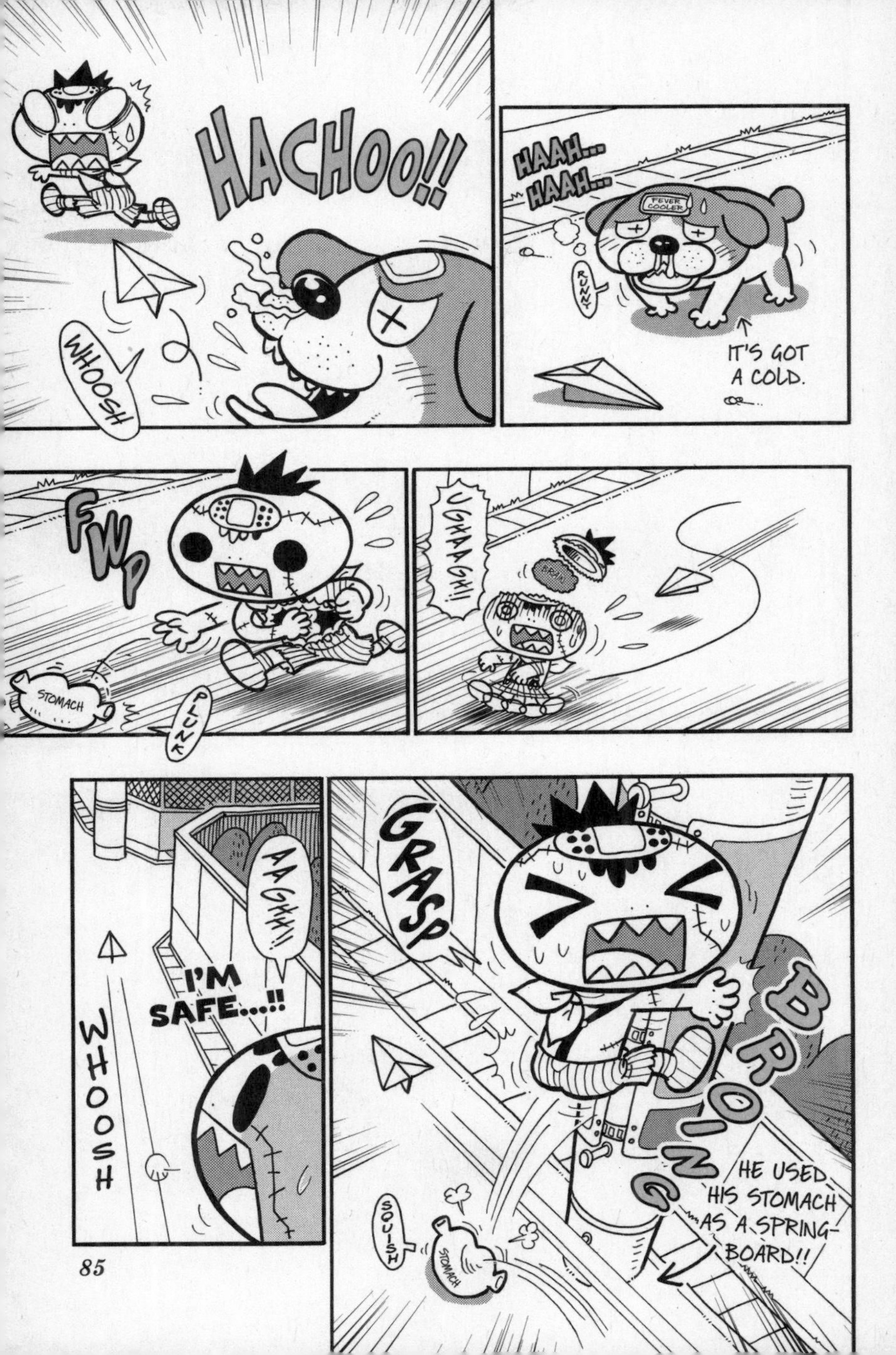
HAAH... HAAH...
FEVER COOLER
RUNNY
IT'S GOT A COLD.
HACHOO!!
WHOOSH
UGHAAGH!!
FWP
STOMACH
PLUNK
GRASP
BROING
HE USED HIS STOMACH AS A SPRING-BOARD!!
SQUISH
STOMACH
AAGHH!!
I'M SAFE...!!
WHOOSH

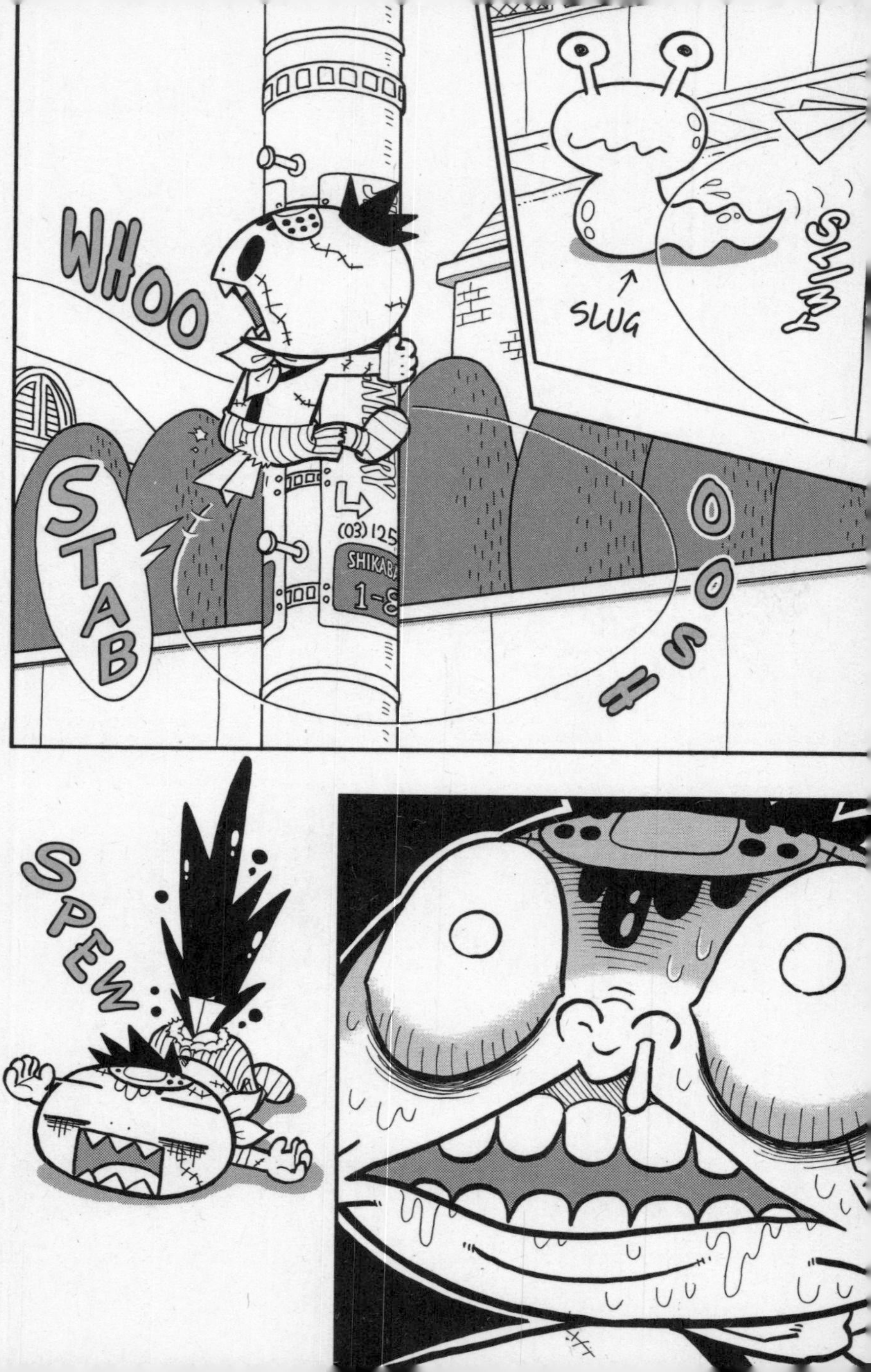
SLIMY
SLUG
OOSH
WHOO
STAB
(03) 125
SHIKABA
1-8
SPEW

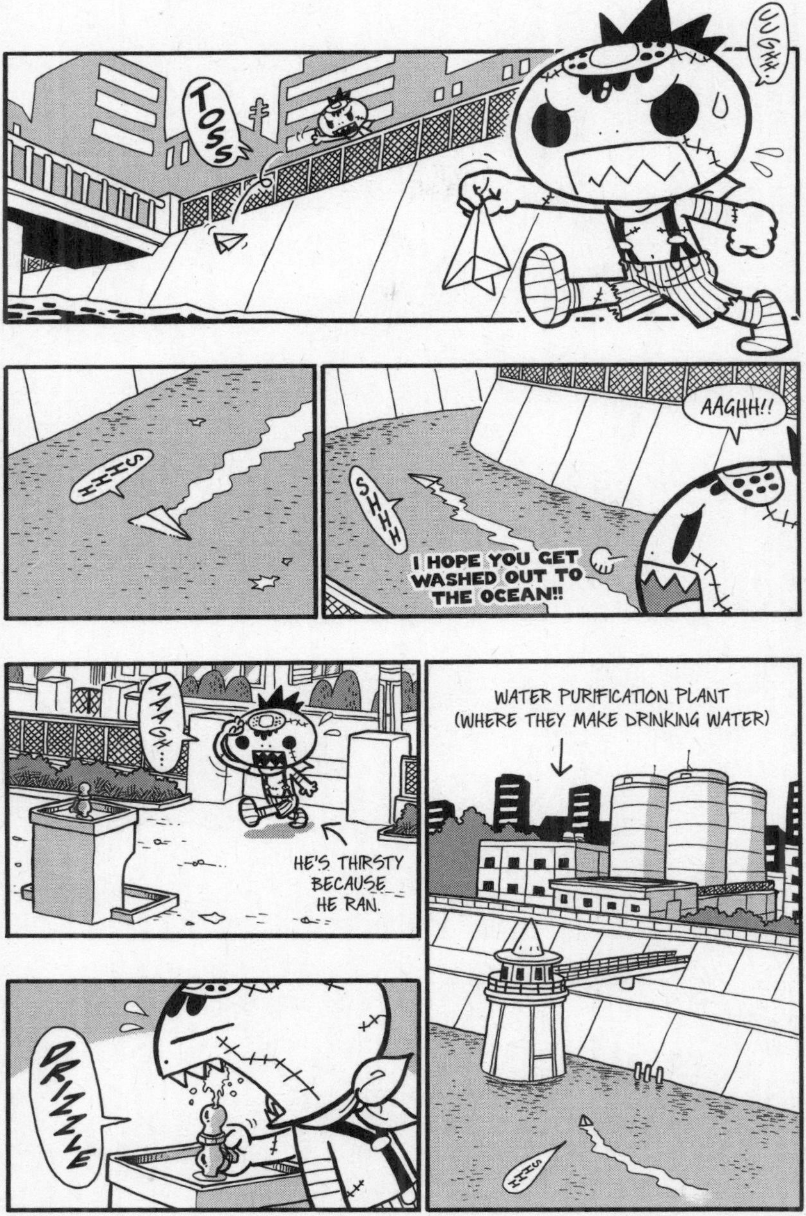
UUGHH...
TOSS
AAGHH!!
SHHH
I HOPE YOU GET WASHED OUT TO THE OCEAN!!
SHHH
WATER PURIFICATION PLANT (WHERE THEY MAKE DRINKING WATER)
SHHH
AAAGH...
HE'S THIRSTY BECAUSE HE RAN.
DRIZZLE

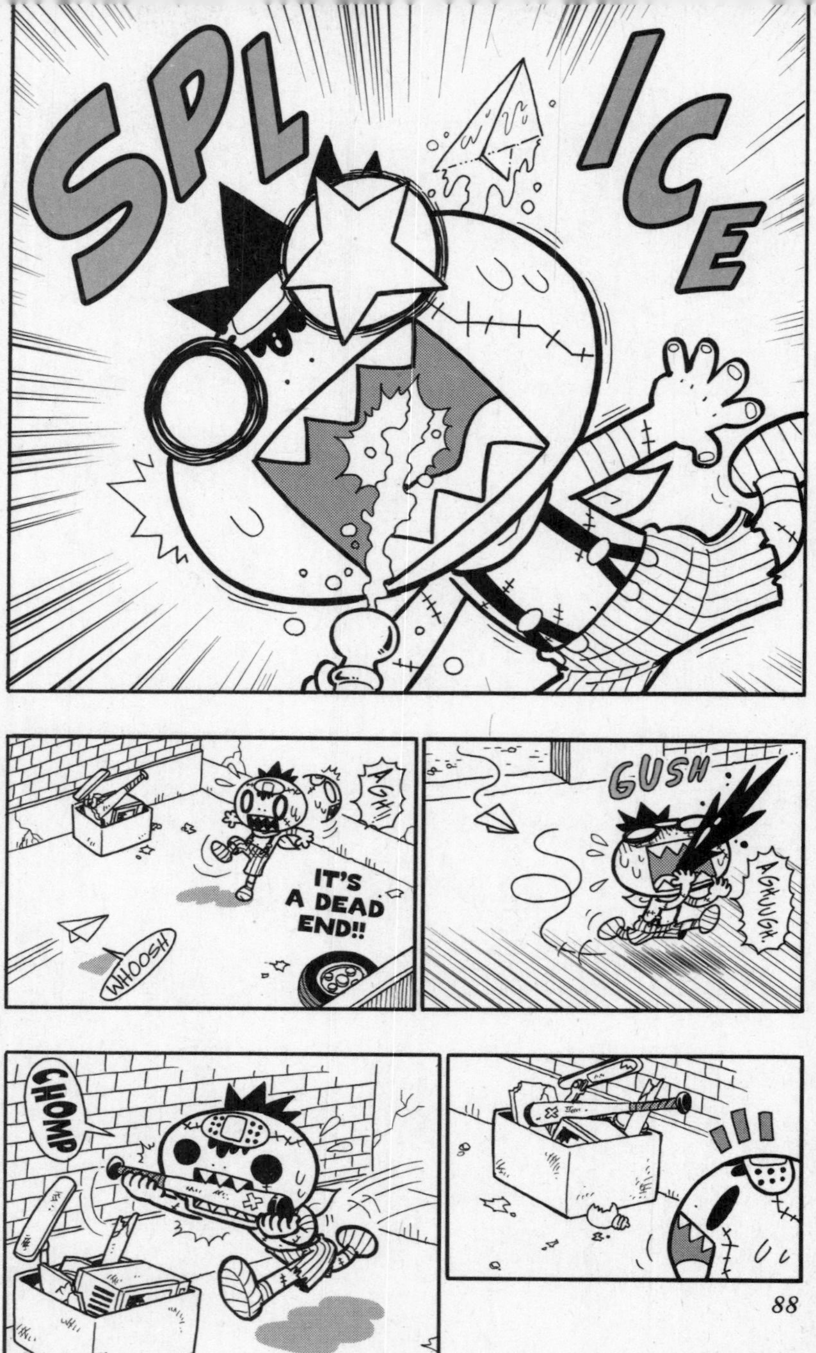
SPLICE
GUSH
AGHUUGH.
AGH!!
IT'S A DEAD END!!
WHOOSH
CHOMP

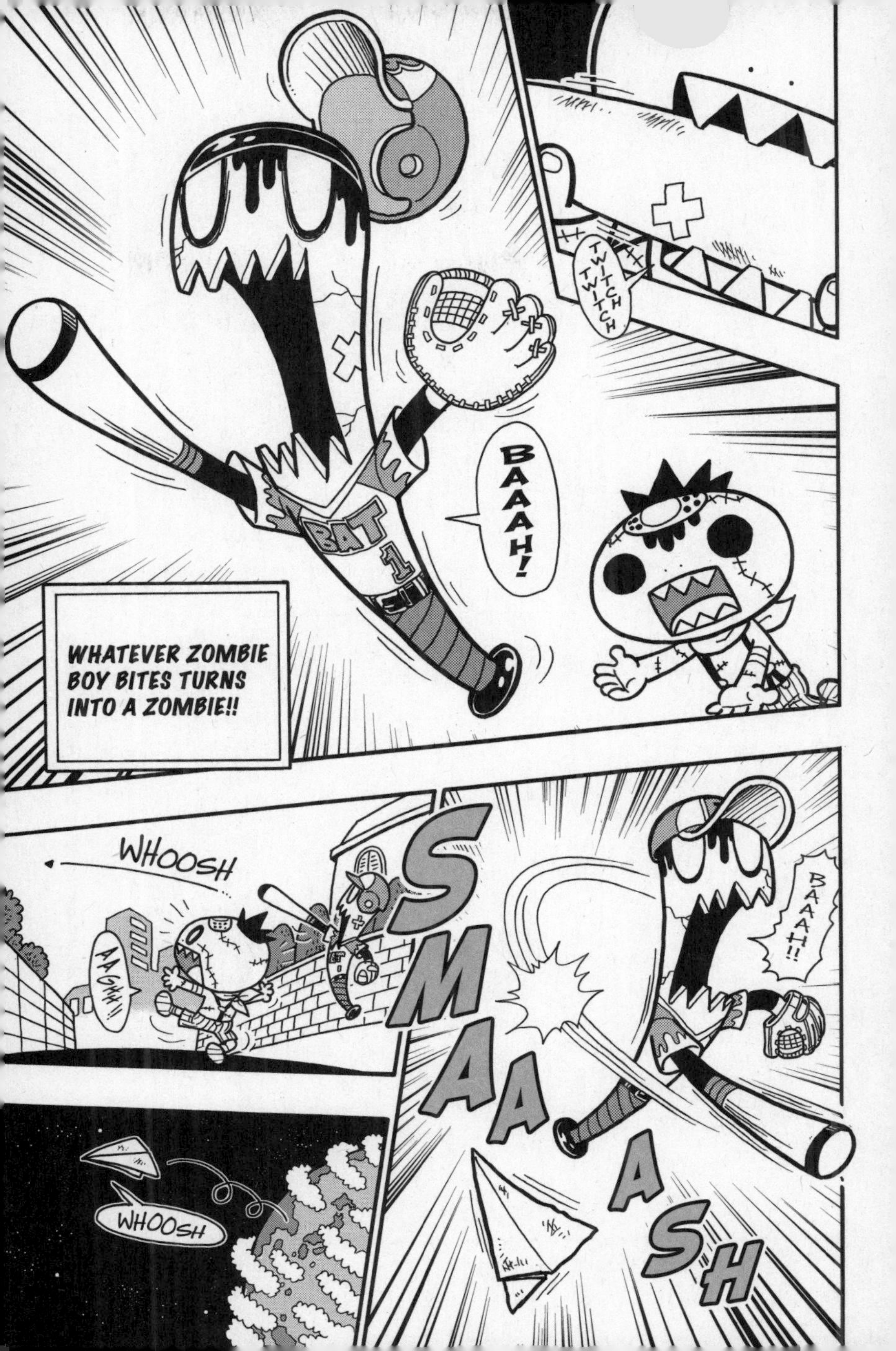
TWITCH TWITCH
BAAAH!
WHATEVER ZOMBIE BOY BITES TURNS INTO A ZOMBIE!!
SMAAAASH
BAAAAH!!
WHOOSH
AAGHH!!
WHOOSH

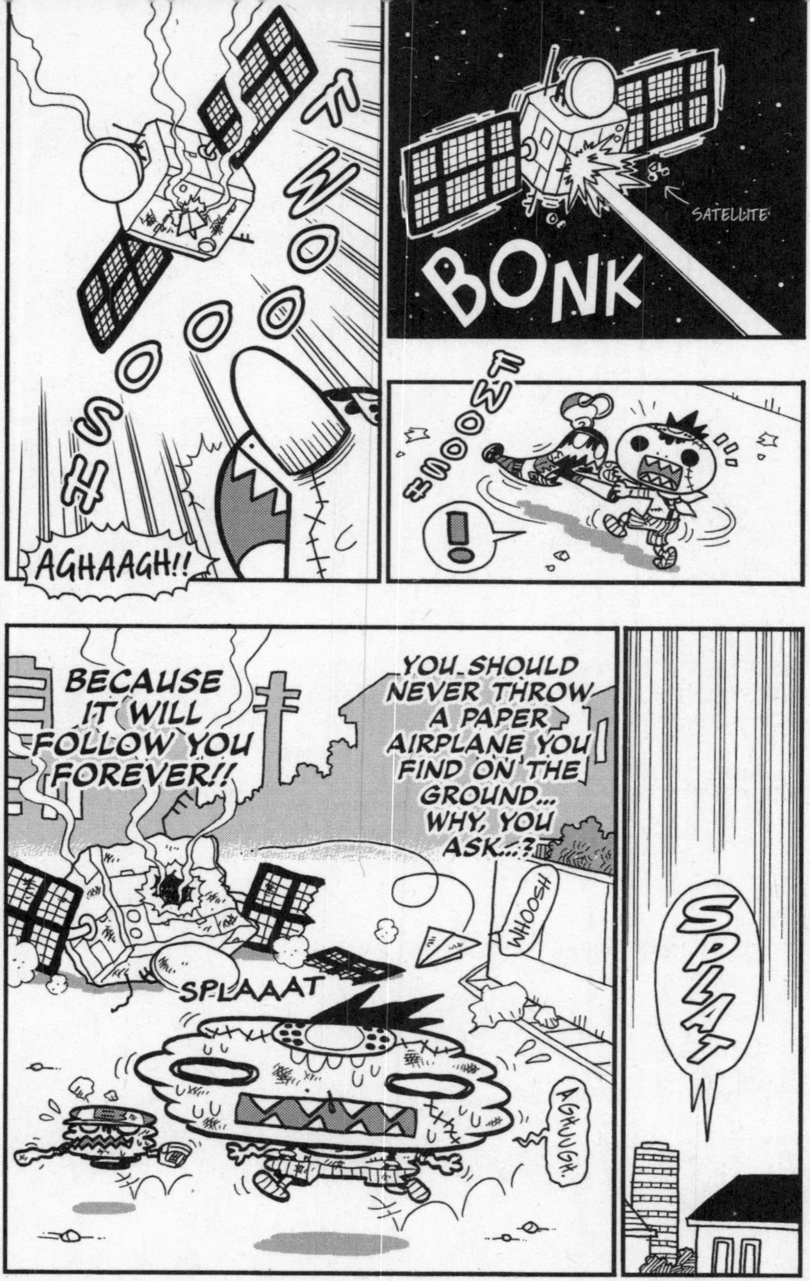
SATELLITE
BONK
FWOOSH
!
WHOOOOSH
AGHAAGH!!
SPLAT
YOU SHOULD NEVER THROW A PAPER AIRPLANE YOU FIND ON THE GROUND... WHY, YOU ASK...?
BECAUSE IT WILL FOLLOW YOU FOREVER!!
WHOOSH
SPLAAAT
AGHUUGH.

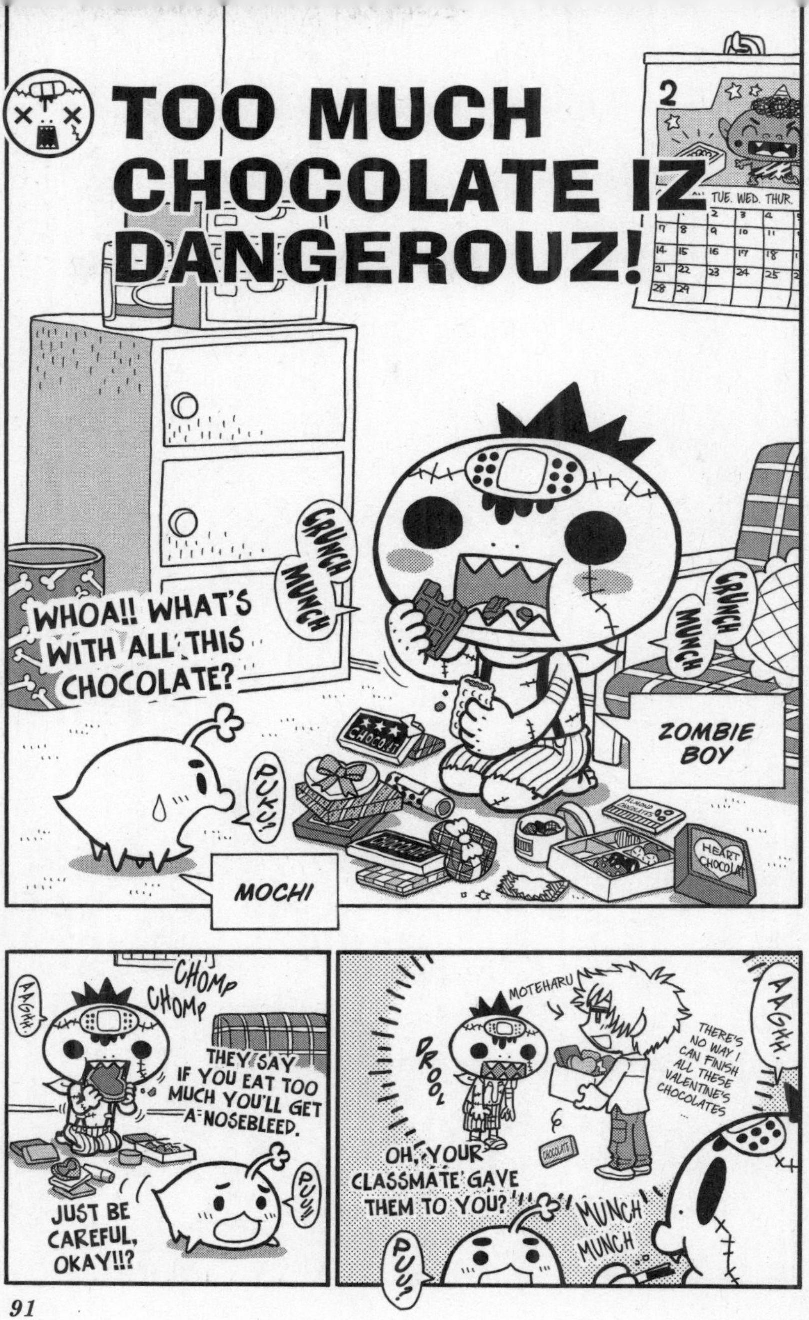
TOO MUCH CHOCOLATE IZ DANGEROUZ!
CRUNCH MUNCH
ZOMBIE BOY
CRUNCH MUNCH
WHOA!! WHAT'S WITH ALL THIS CHOCOLATE?
PUKU?
MOCHI
CHOCOLATE
ALMOND CHOCOLATES
HEART CHOCOLAT
AAGHH.
THERE'S NO WAY I CAN FINISH ALL THESE VALENTINE'S CHOCOLATES...
MOTEHARU
DROOL
OH, YOUR CLASSMATE GAVE THEM TO YOU?
MUNCH MUNCH
PUU?
CHOMP CHOMP
AAGHH.
THEY SAY IF YOU EAT TOO MUCH YOU'LL GET A NOSEBLEED.
PUU!
JUST BE CAREFUL, OKAY!!?

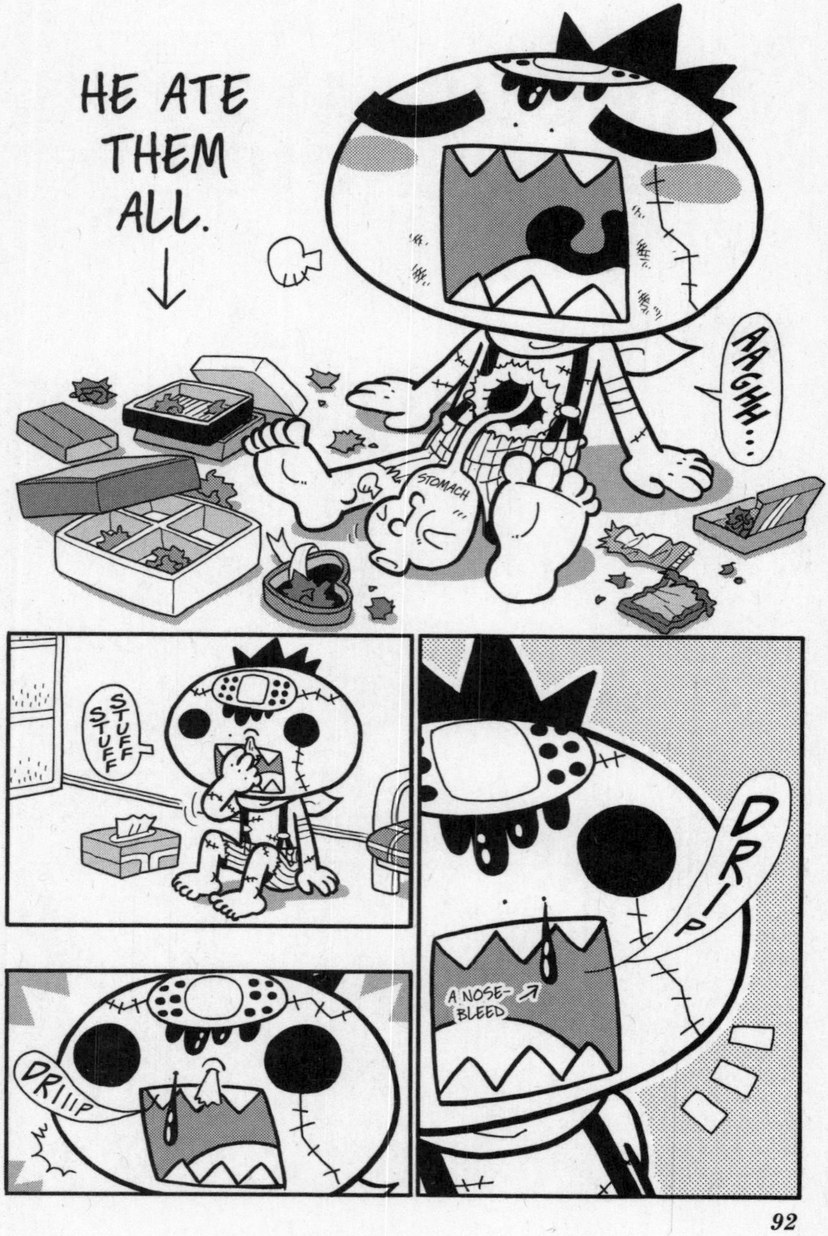
HE ATE THEM ALL.
AAGHH...
STOMACH
DRIP
A NOSE-BLEED
STUFF STUFF
DRIIIP

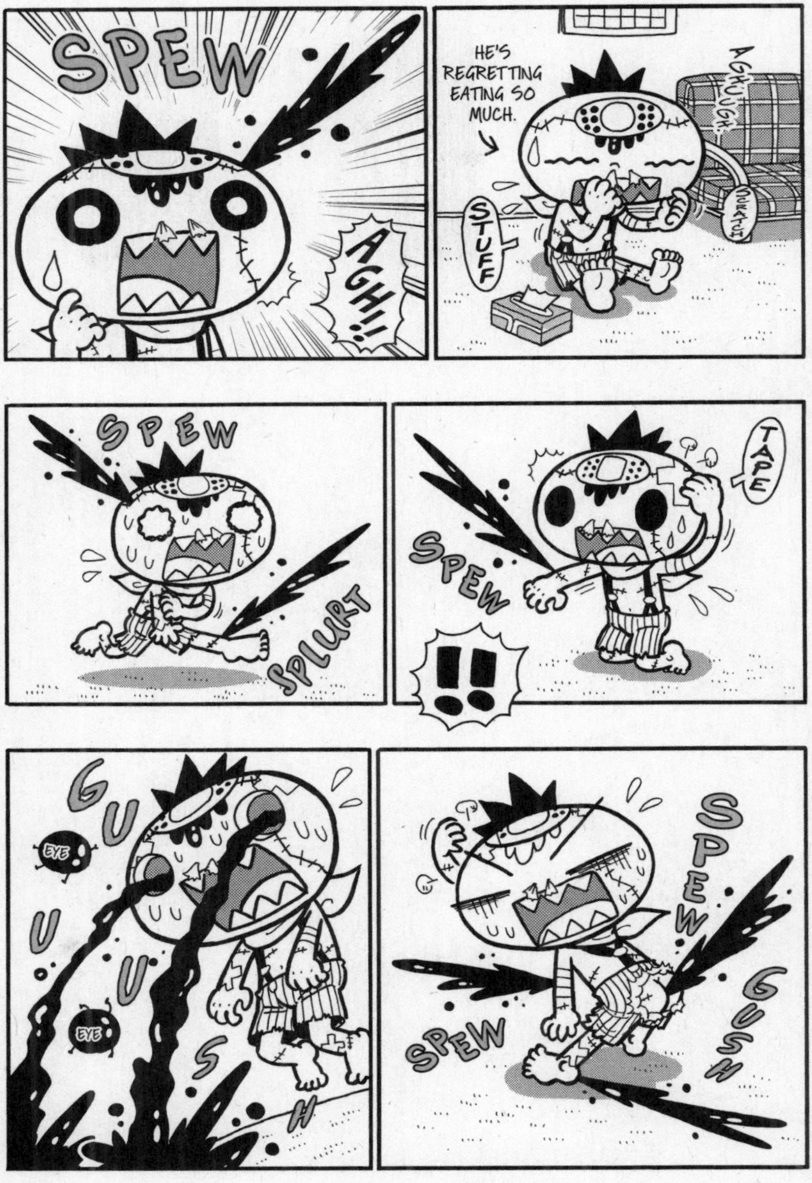

AGHUGH.
HE'S REGRETTING EATING SO MUCH.
SCRATCH
STUFF
SPEW
AGH!!
TAPE
SPEW
!!
SPEW
SPLURT
SPEW
SPEW
GUSH
GUUUSH
EYE
EYE

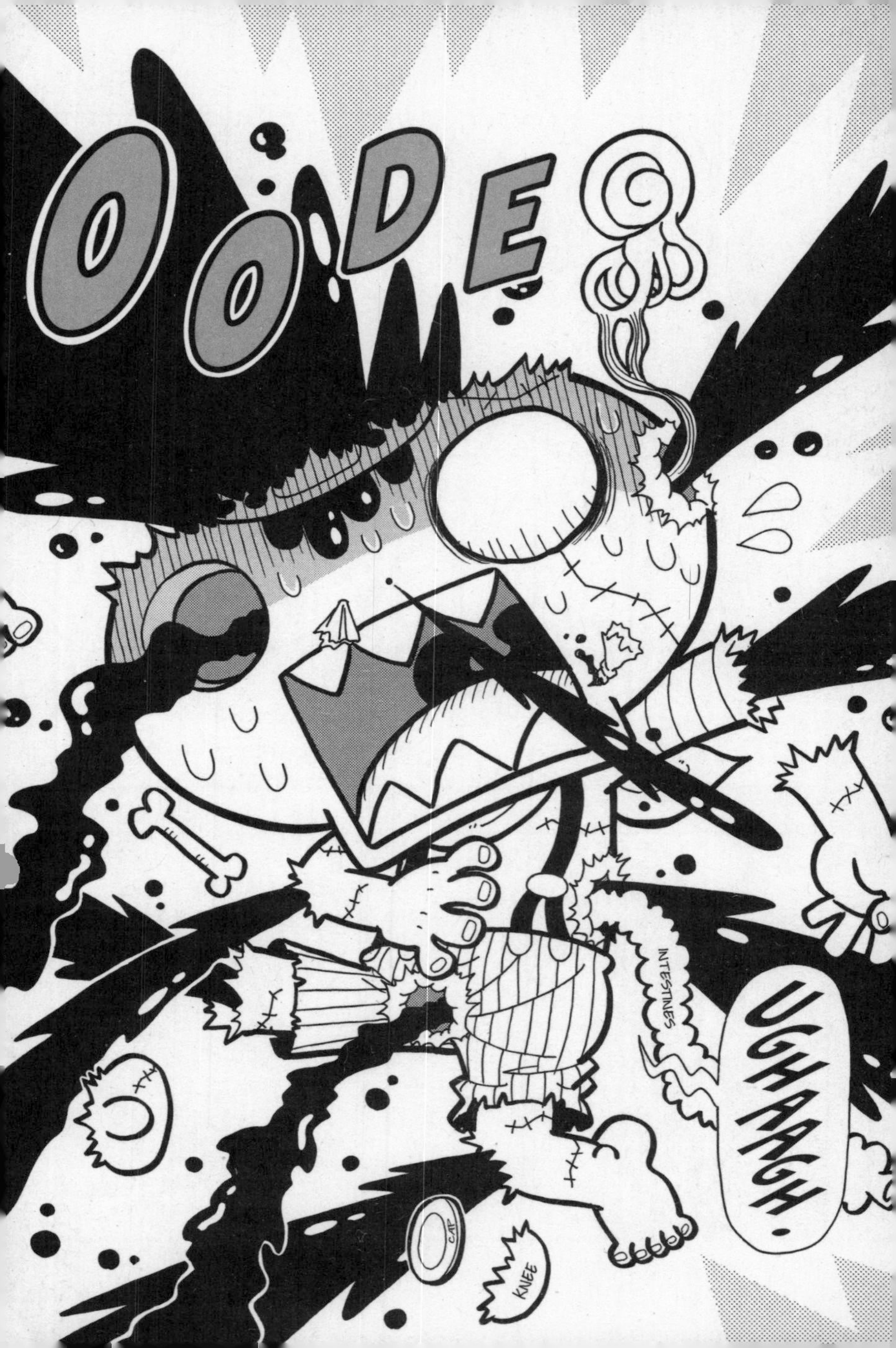
OODE
UGHAAGH.
INTESTINES
CAP
KNEE

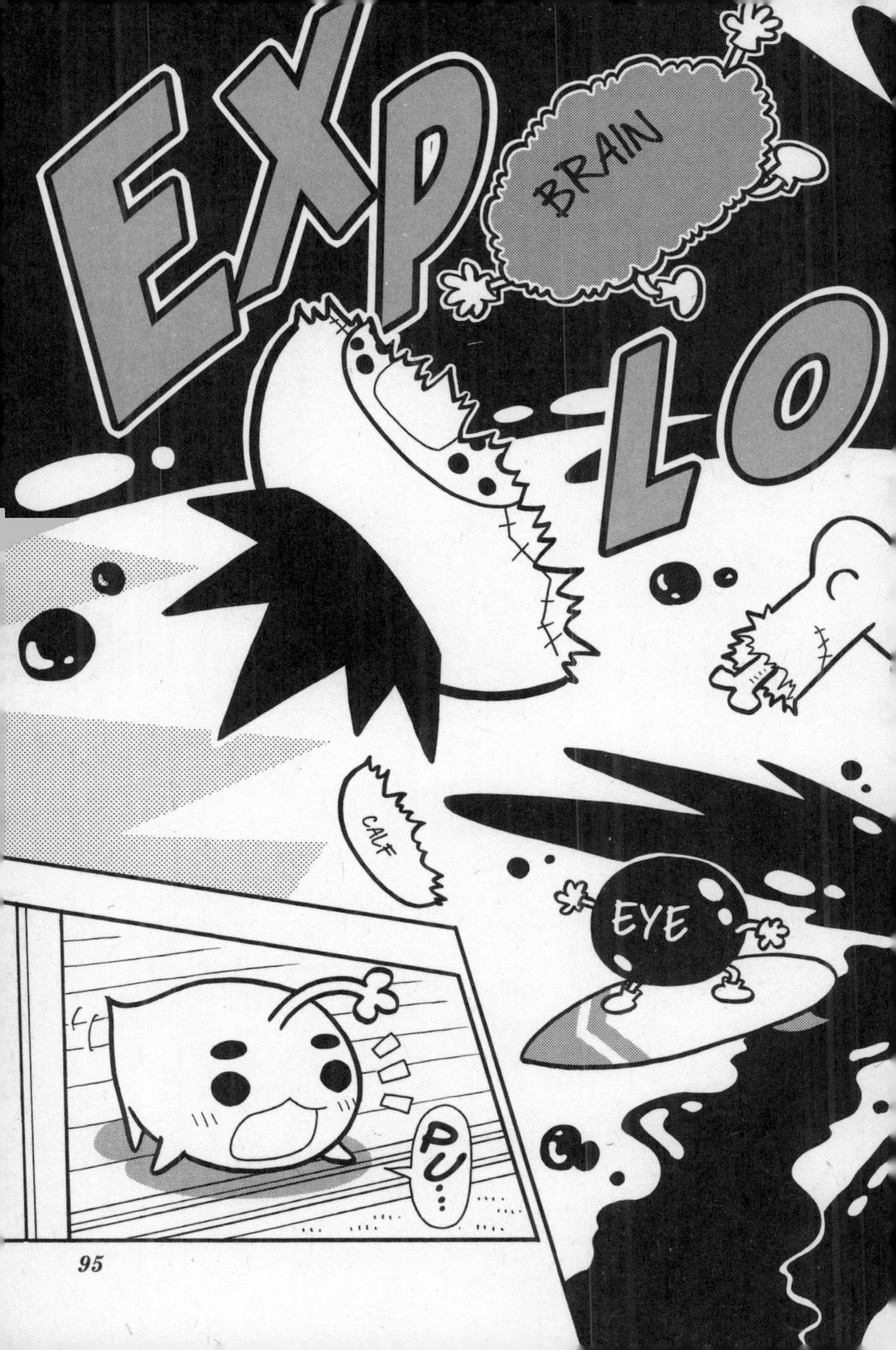
EXPLO
BRAIN
EYE
CALF
PU...

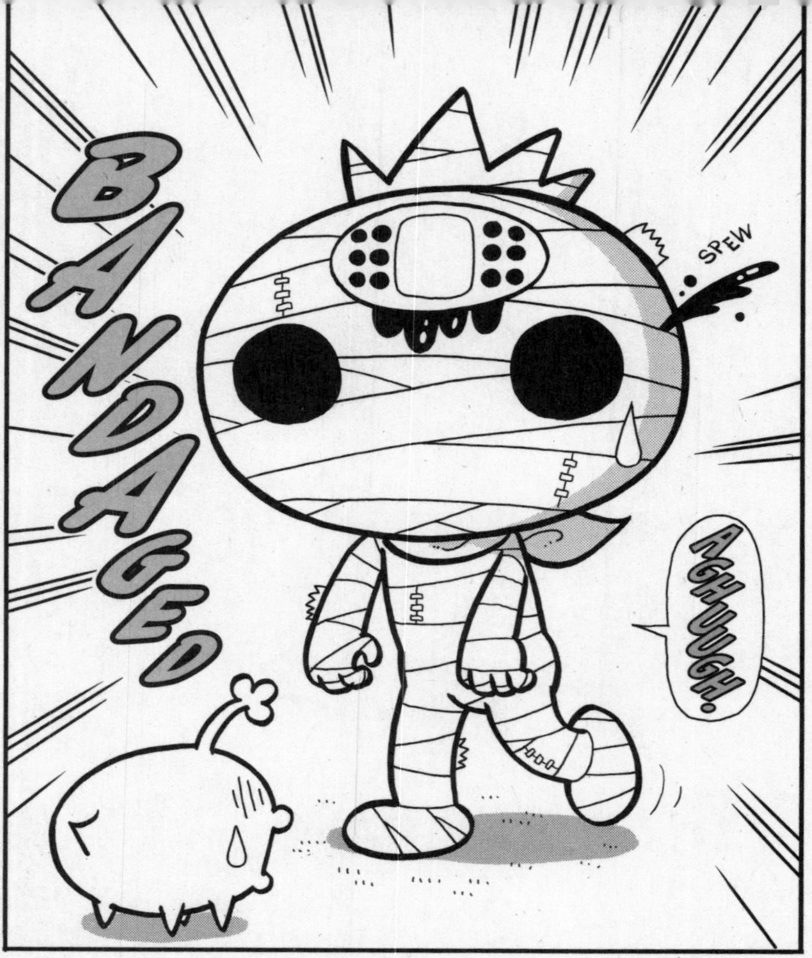
SPEW
BANDAGED
AGHUUGH!

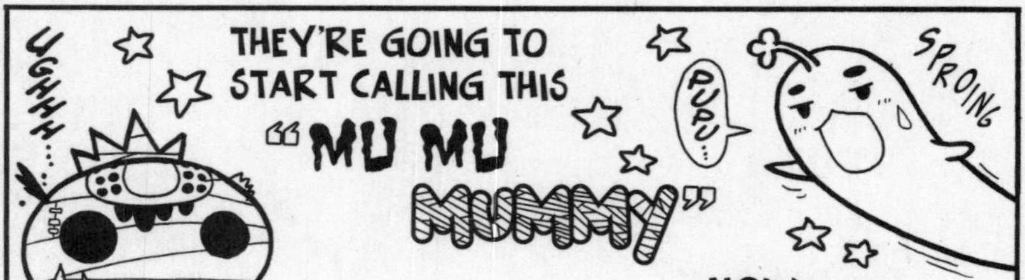
SPROING
PUPU...
THEY'RE GOING TO START CALLING THIS "MU MU MUMMY" NOW...
UGHHH...

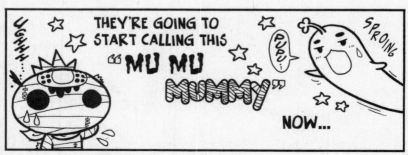

THANKS FOR EATING ALL THAT CHOCOLATE!!

← MOTEHARU

ISAMU'S CLASSMATES WHO RARELY EVER APPEAR.

WE'RE ON THE COVER OF THE NEXT CHAPTER, BUT WE DON'T ACTUALLY SHOW UP IN THE STORY...

WHAT'S UP WTIH THAT!?

I'D PLANNED TO PUT YOU BOTH IN IT BUT HAD TO CHANGE IT HALFWAY THROUGH. SORRY...

AUTHOR

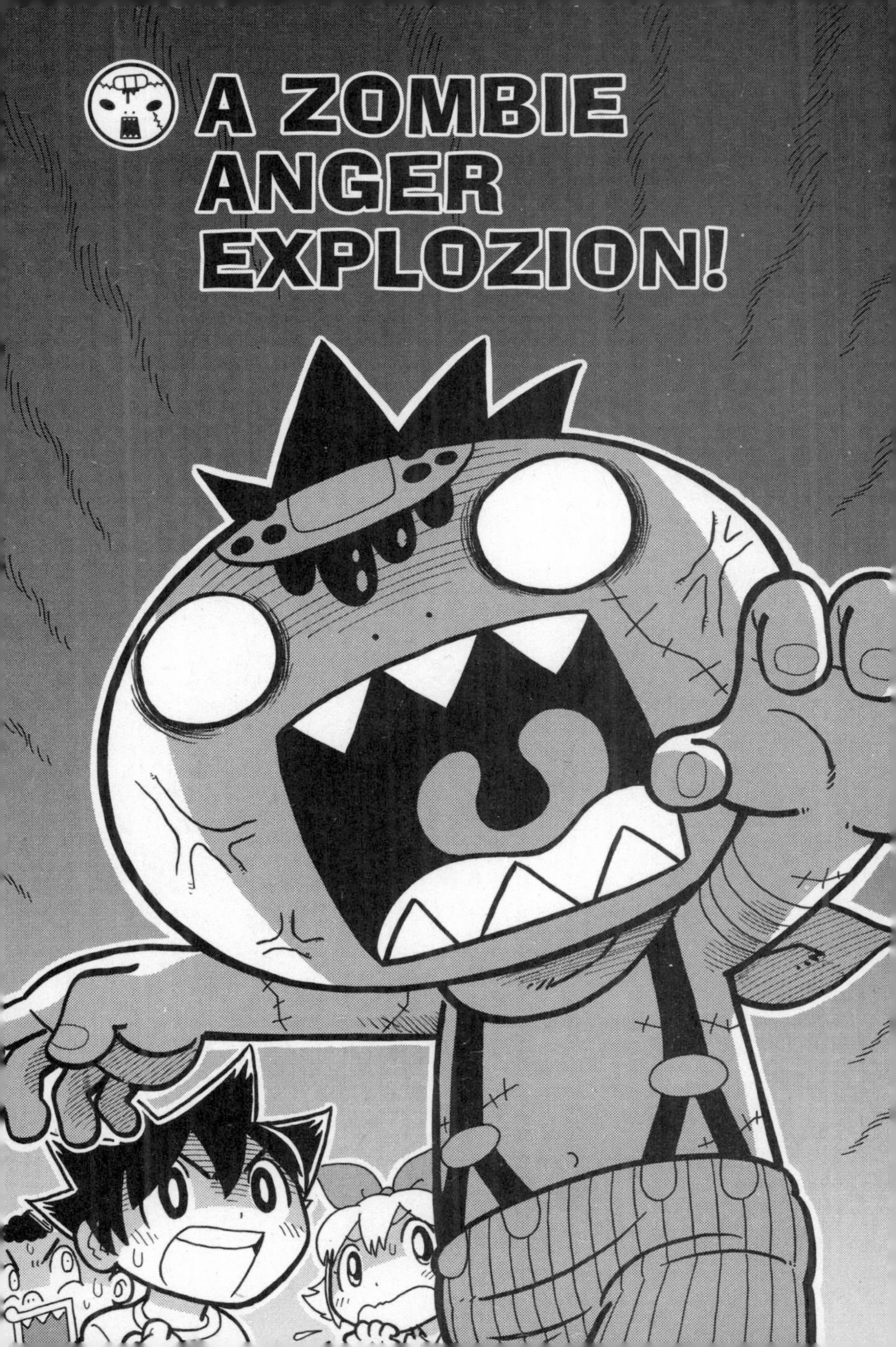
A ZOMBIE ANGER EXPLOZION!

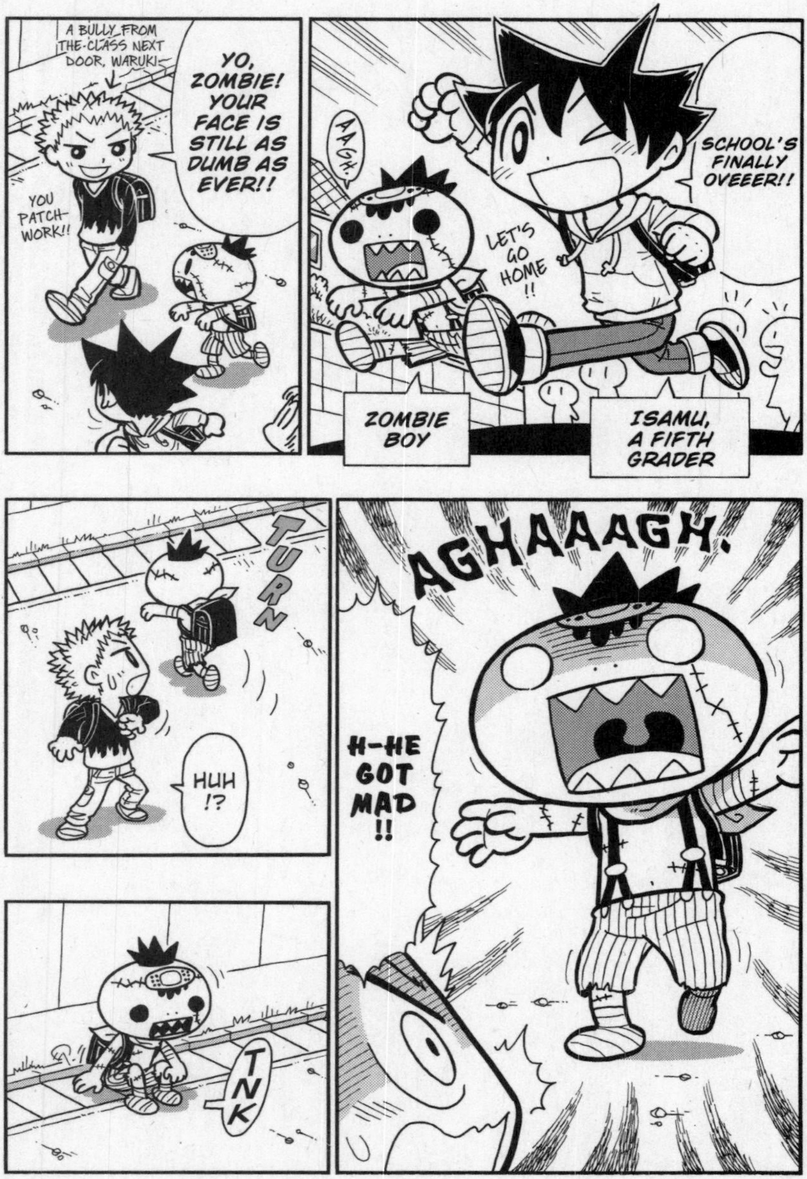
SCHOOL'S FINALLY OVEEER!!
AAGH.
LET'S GO HOME!!
ISAMU, A FIFTH GRADER
ZOMBIE BOY
A BULLY FROM THE CLASS NEXT DOOR, WARUKI
YO, ZOMBIE! YOUR FACE IS STILL AS DUMB AS EVER!!
YOU PATCHWORK!!
AGHAAAGH.
H-HE GOT MAD!!
TURN
HUH!?
TNK

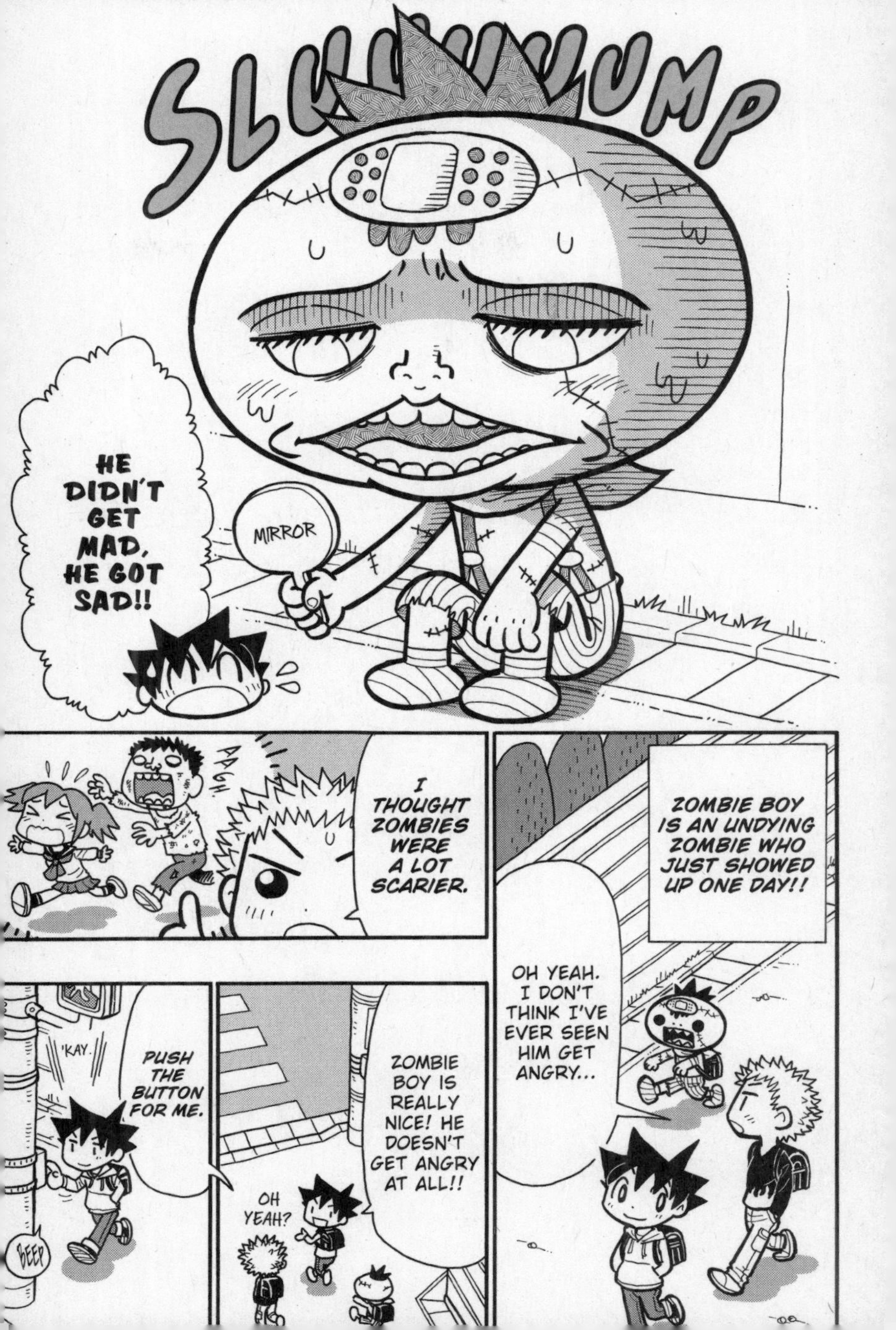
SLUUUUUMP
MIRROR
HE DIDN'T GET MAD, HE GOT SAD!!
ZOMBIE BOY IS AN UNDYING ZOMBIE WHO JUST SHOWED UP ONE DAY!!
OH YEAH. I DON'T THINK I'VE EVER SEEN HIM GET ANGRY...
AAGH
I THOUGHT ZOMBIES WERE A LOT SCARIER.
ZOMBIE BOY IS REALLY NICE! HE DOESN'T GET ANGRY AT ALL!!
OH YEAH?
PUSH THE BUTTON FOR ME.
'KAY.
BEEP

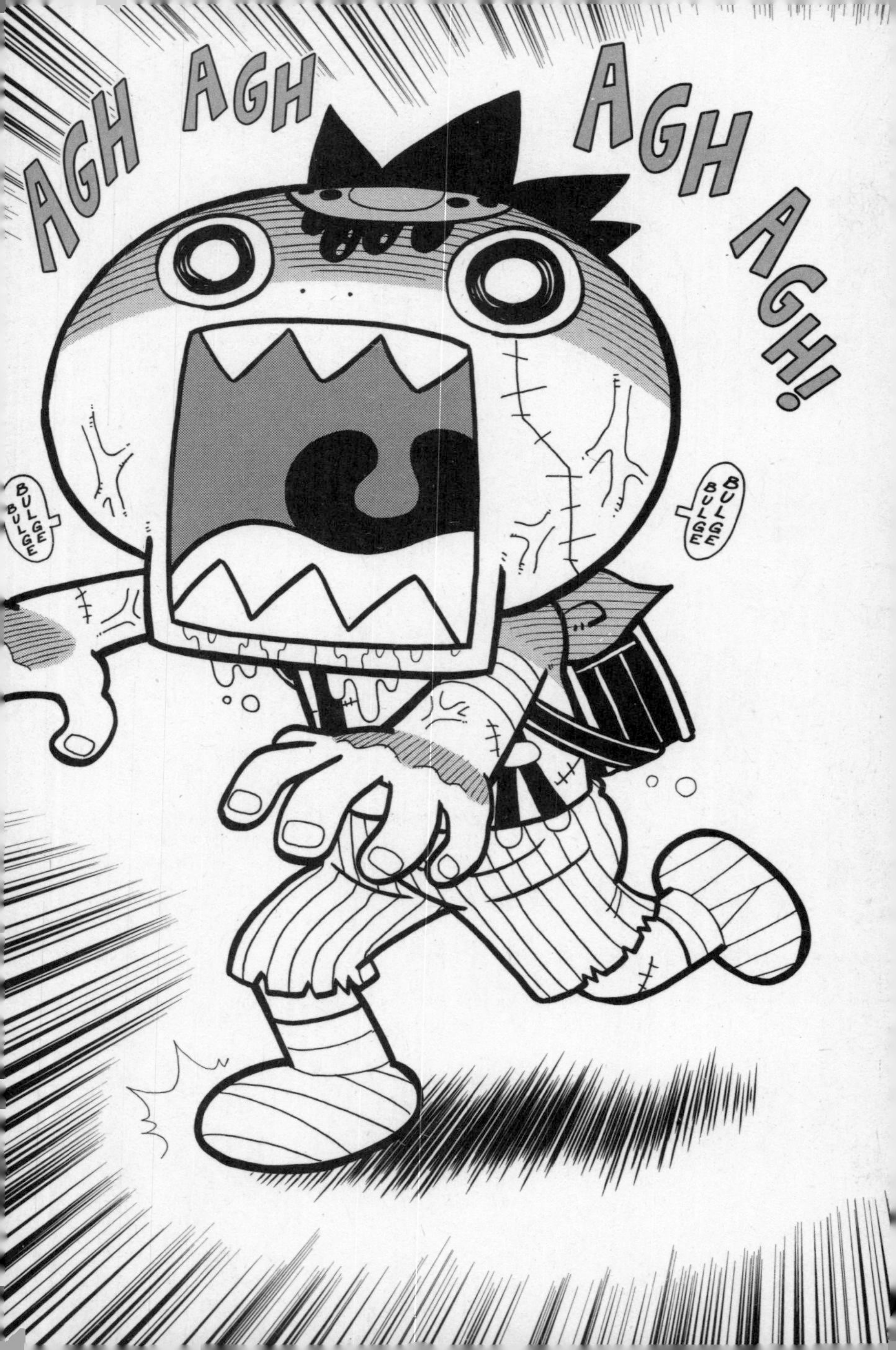
AGH AGH
AGH AGH AGH!
BULGE BULGE
BULGE BULGE

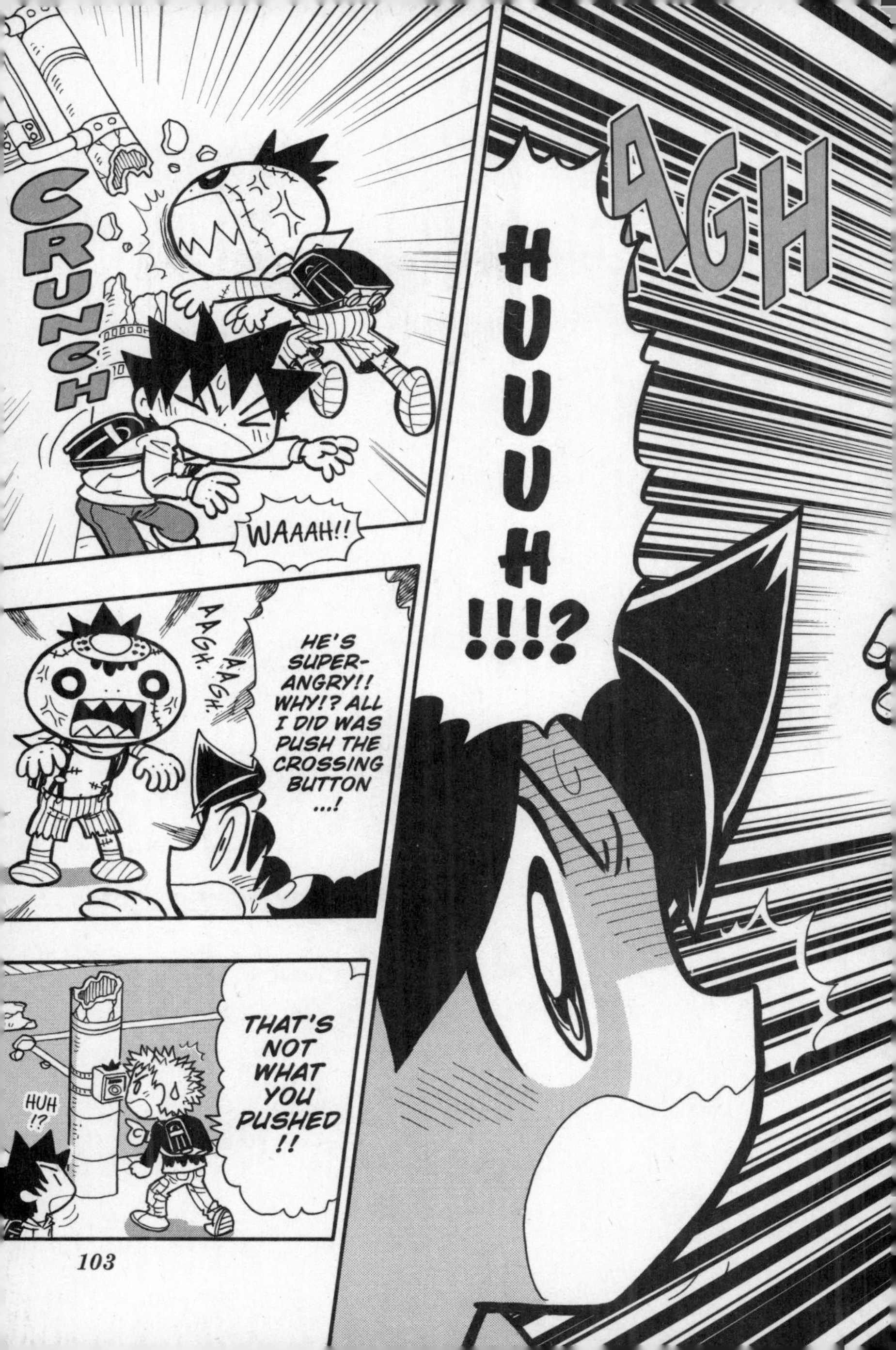
AGH
HUUUUH!!!?
CRUNCH
WAAAH!!
HE'S SUPER-ANGRY!! WHY!? ALL I DID WAS PUSH THE CROSSING BUTTON ...!
AAGH. AAGH.
THAT'S NOT WHAT YOU PUSHED!!
HUH!?

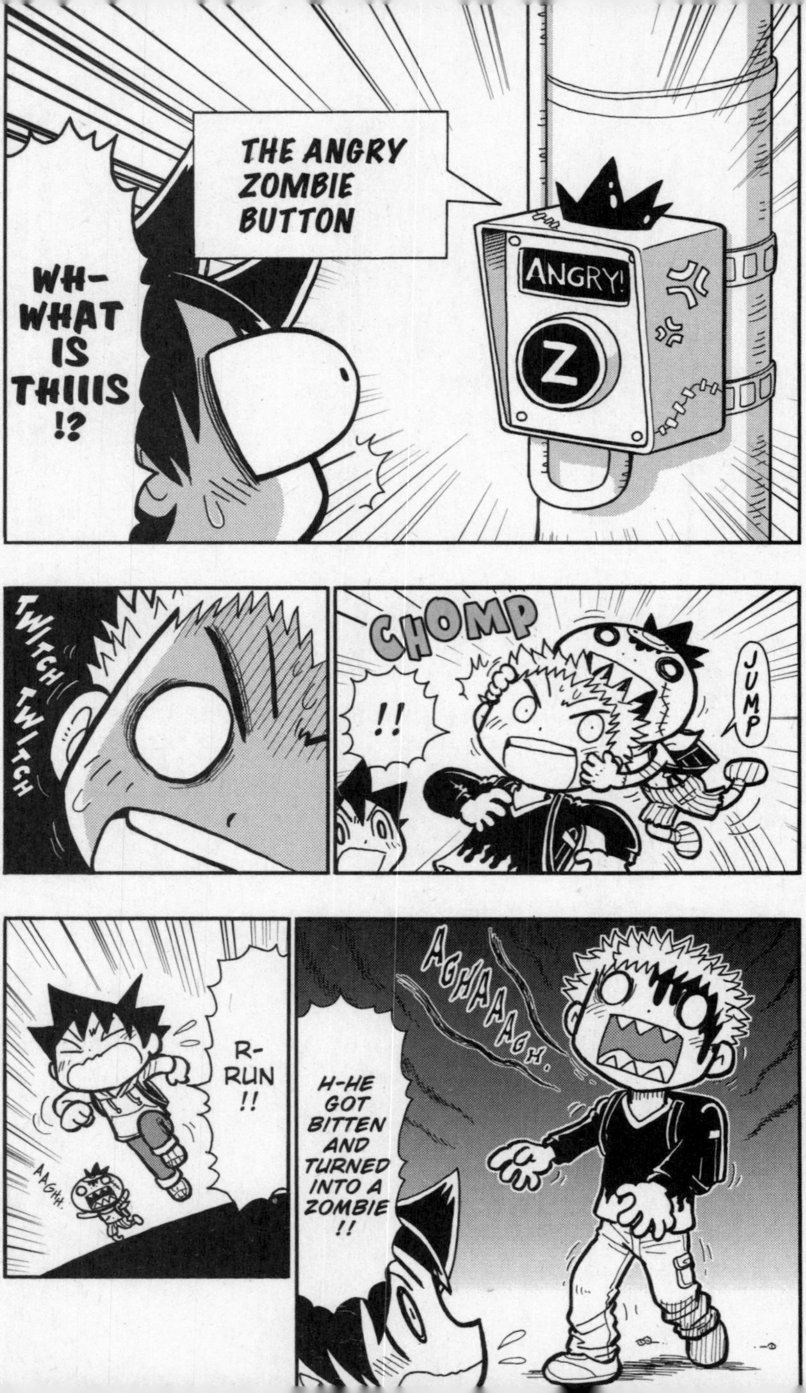
THE ANGRY ZOMBIE BUTTON
ANGRY!
Z
WH-WHAT IS THIIIS !?
JUMP
CHOMP
!!
TWITCH TWITCH
AGHAAAAGH.
H-HE GOT BITTEN AND TURNED INTO A ZOMBIE !!
R-RUN !!
AAGHH.

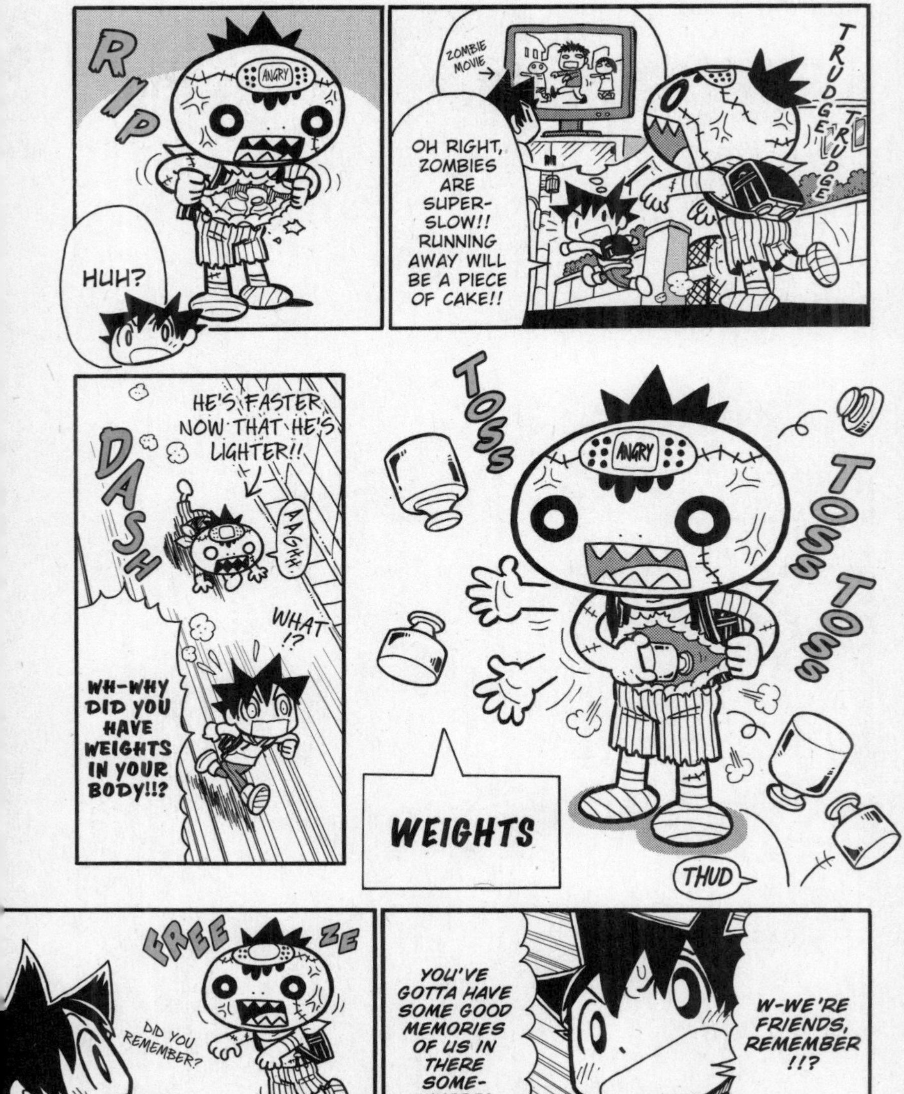
TRUDGE
TRUDGE
ZOMBIE MOVIE →
OH RIGHT, ZOMBIES ARE SUPER-SLOW!! RUNNING AWAY WILL BE A PIECE OF CAKE!!
RIP
ANGRY
HUH?
TOSS
TOSS
TOSS
ANGRY
WEIGHTS
THUD
HE'S FASTER NOW THAT HE'S LIGHTER!!
DASH
AAGHH
WHAT !?
WH-WHY DID YOU HAVE WEIGHTS IN YOUR BODY!!?
W-WE'RE FRIENDS, REMEMBER !!?
YOU'VE GOTTA HAVE SOME GOOD MEMORIES OF US IN THERE SOME-WHERE!
FREEZE
DID YOU REMEMBER?

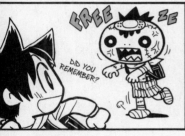

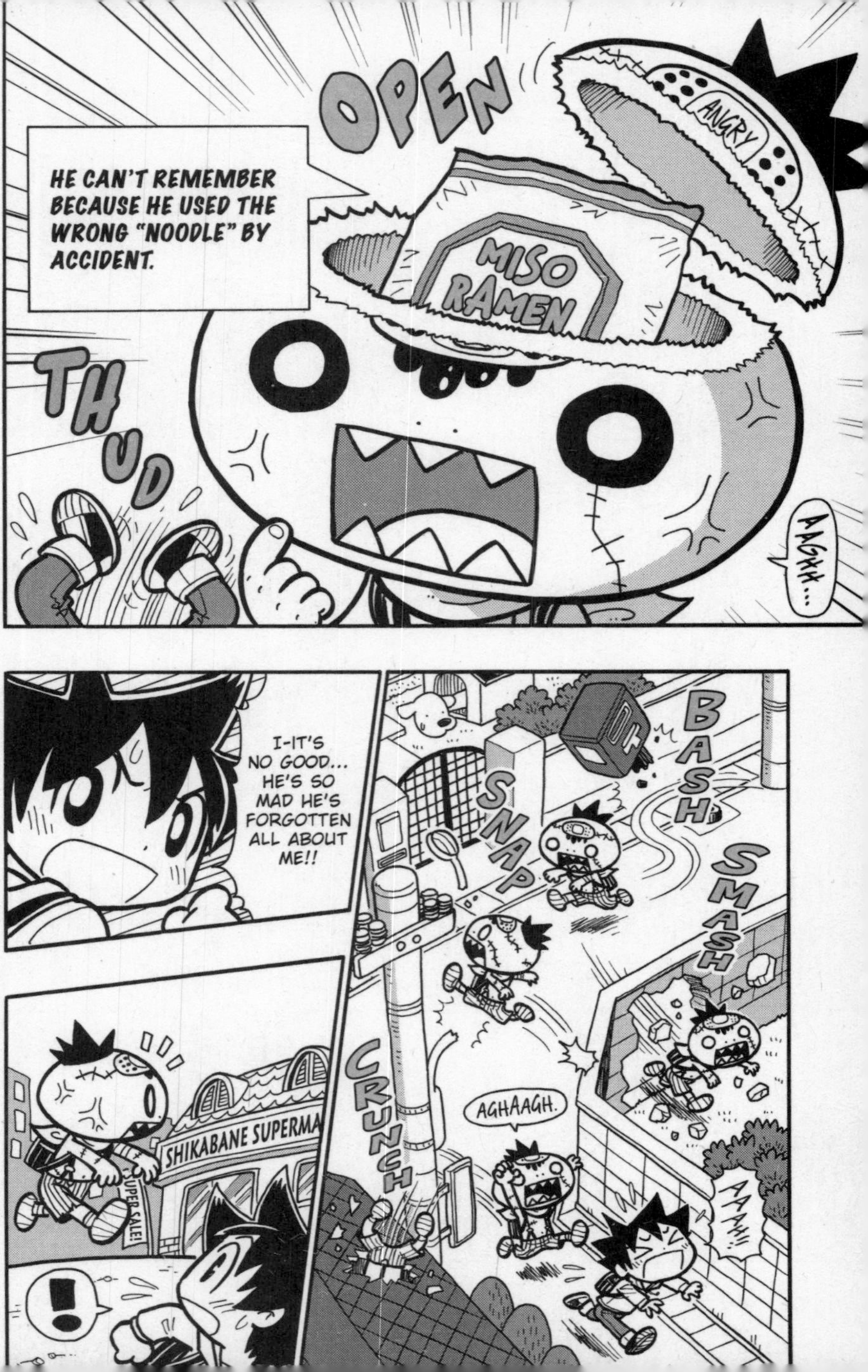
ANGRY
OPEN
HE CAN'T REMEMBER BECAUSE HE USED THE WRONG "NOODLE" BY ACCIDENT.
MISO RAMEN
AAGHH...
THUD
BASH
SMASH
SNAP
AAAH!!
AGHAAGH.
CRUNCH
I-IT'S NO GOOD... HE'S SO MAD HE'S FORGOTTEN ALL ABOUT ME!!
SHIKABANE SUPERMA
SUPER SALE!
!

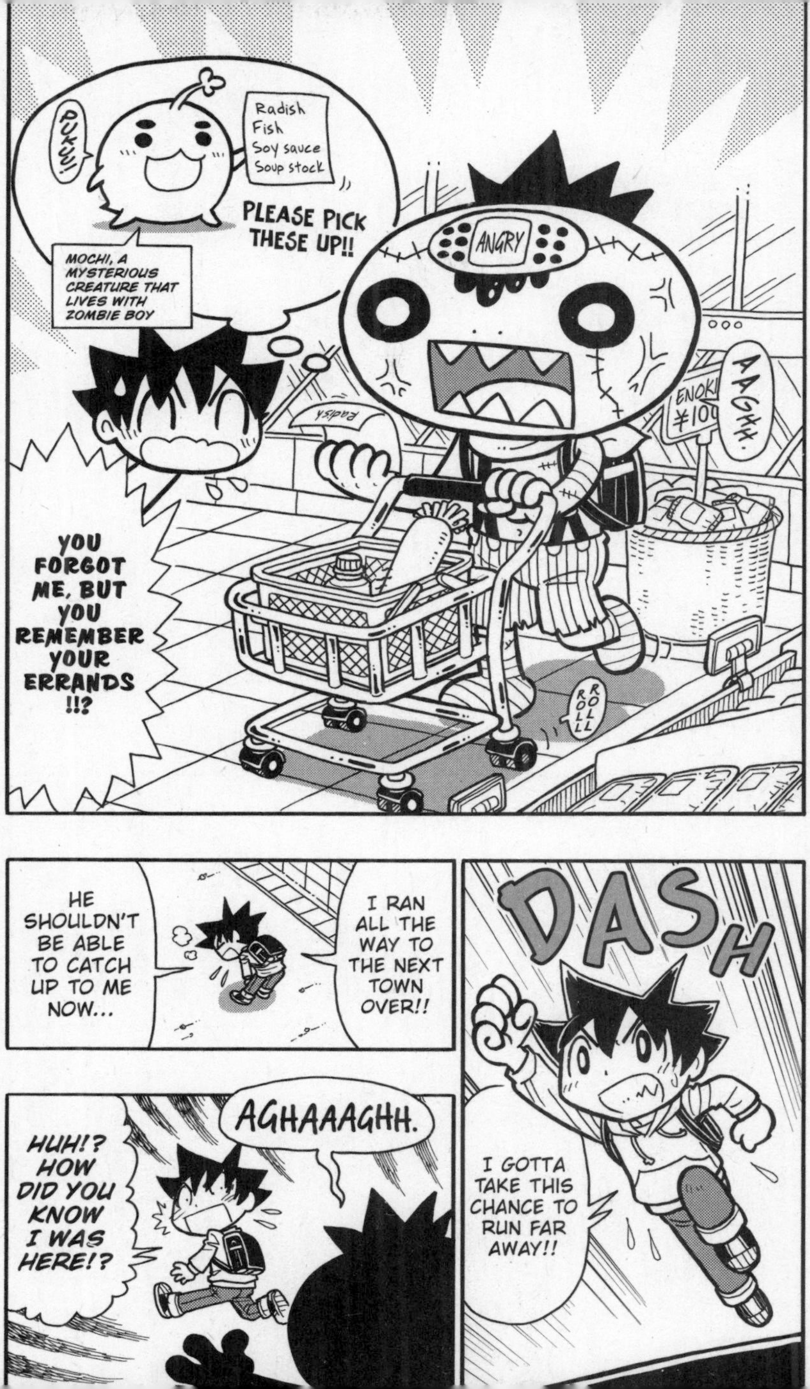

AAGHH.
ENOKI ¥10
ANGRY
PUKUU!
Radish Fish Soy sauce Soup stock
PLEASE PICK THESE UP!!
MOCHI, A MYSTERIOUS CREATURE THAT LIVES WITH ZOMBIE BOY
Radish
ROLL ROLL
YOU FORGOT ME, BUT YOU REMEMBER YOUR ERRANDS!!?
DASH
I GOTTA TAKE THIS CHANCE TO RUN FAR AWAY!!
I RAN ALL THE WAY TO THE NEXT TOWN OVER!!
HE SHOULDN'T BE ABLE TO CATCH UP TO ME NOW...
AGHAAAGHH.
HUH!? HOW DID YOU KNOW I WAS HERE!?

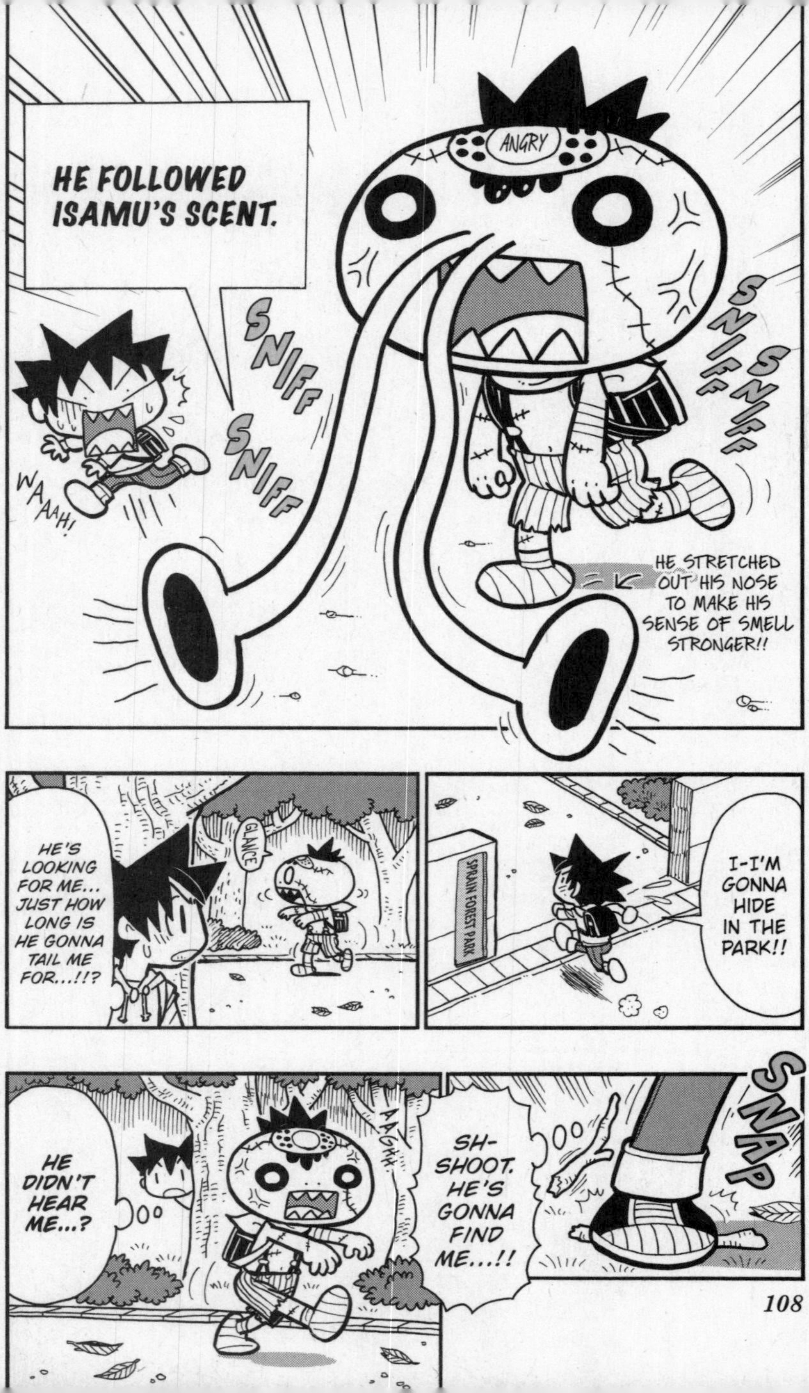
ANGRY
SNIFF SNIFF
HE FOLLOWED ISAMU'S SCENT.
SNIFF SNIFF
WAAAH!
HE STRETCHED OUT HIS NOSE TO MAKE HIS SENSE OF SMELL STRONGER!!
I-I'M GONNA HIDE IN THE PARK!!
SPRAIN FOREST PARK
GLANCE
HE'S LOOKING FOR ME... JUST HOW LONG IS HE GONNA TAIL ME FOR...!!?
SNAP
SH-SHOOT. HE'S GONNA FIND ME...!!
AAGH...
HE DIDN'T HEAR ME...?

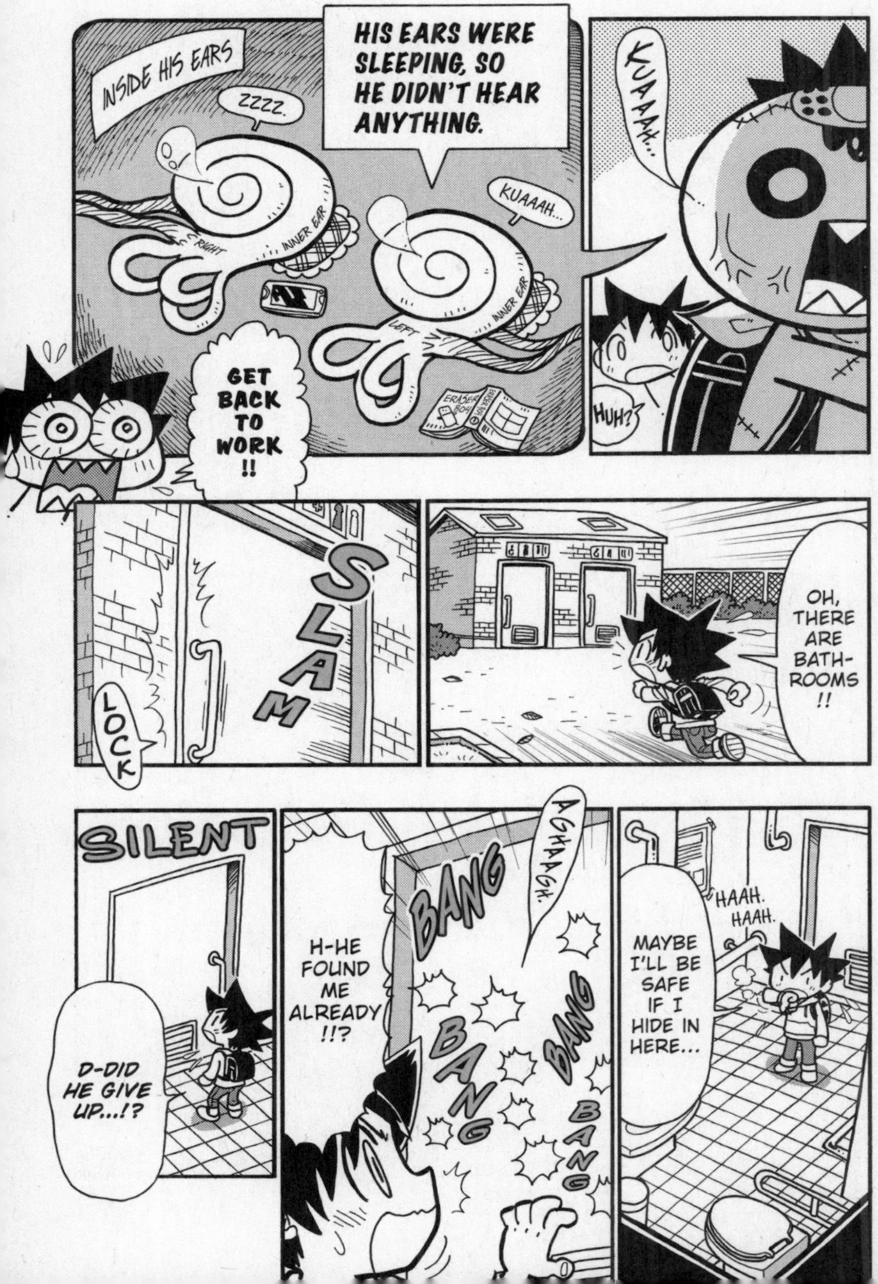
KUAAAAH...
HUH?
HIS EARS WERE SLEEPING, SO HE DIDN'T HEAR ANYTHING.
KUAAAH...
INSIDE HIS EARS
ZZZZ.
RIGHT
INNER EAR
LEFT
INNER EAR
ERASER BOX
GET BACK TO WORK!!
OH, THERE ARE BATH-ROOMS!!
SLAM
LOCK
HAAH. HAAH.
MAYBE I'LL BE SAFE IF I HIDE IN HERE...
AGHAAAGH.
BANG
BANG
BANG
BANG
BANG
H-HE FOUND ME ALREADY!!?
SILENT
D-DID HE GIVE UP...!?

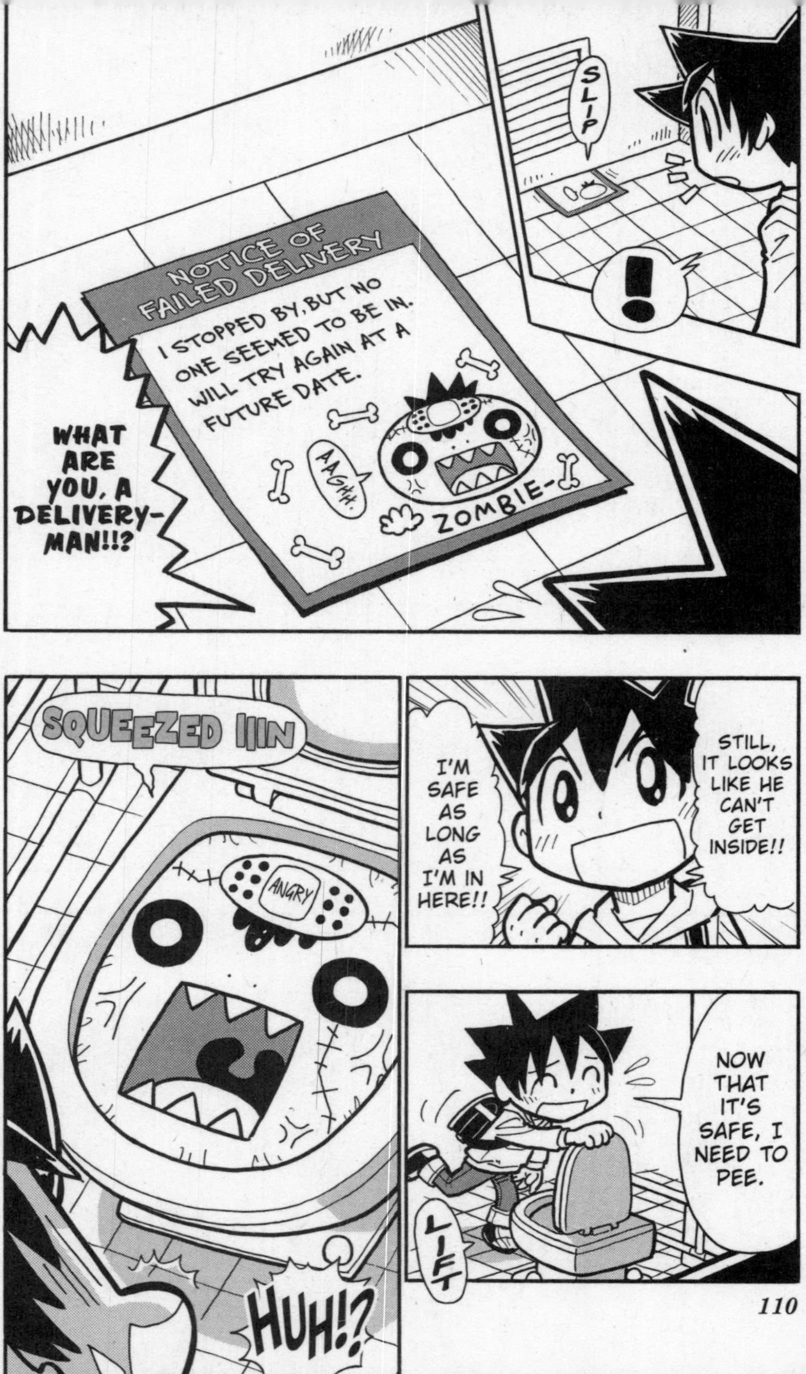
SLIP
!
NOTICE OF FAILED DELIVERY
I STOPPED BY, BUT NO ONE SEEMED TO BE IN. WILL TRY AGAIN AT A FUTURE DATE.
AAGHH.
ZOMBIE-
WHAT ARE YOU, A DELIVERYMAN!!?
STILL, IT LOOKS LIKE HE CAN'T GET INSIDE!!
I'M SAFE AS LONG AS I'M IN HERE!!
NOW THAT IT'S SAFE, I NEED TO PEE.
LIFT
SQUEEZED IIIN
ANGRY
HUH!?

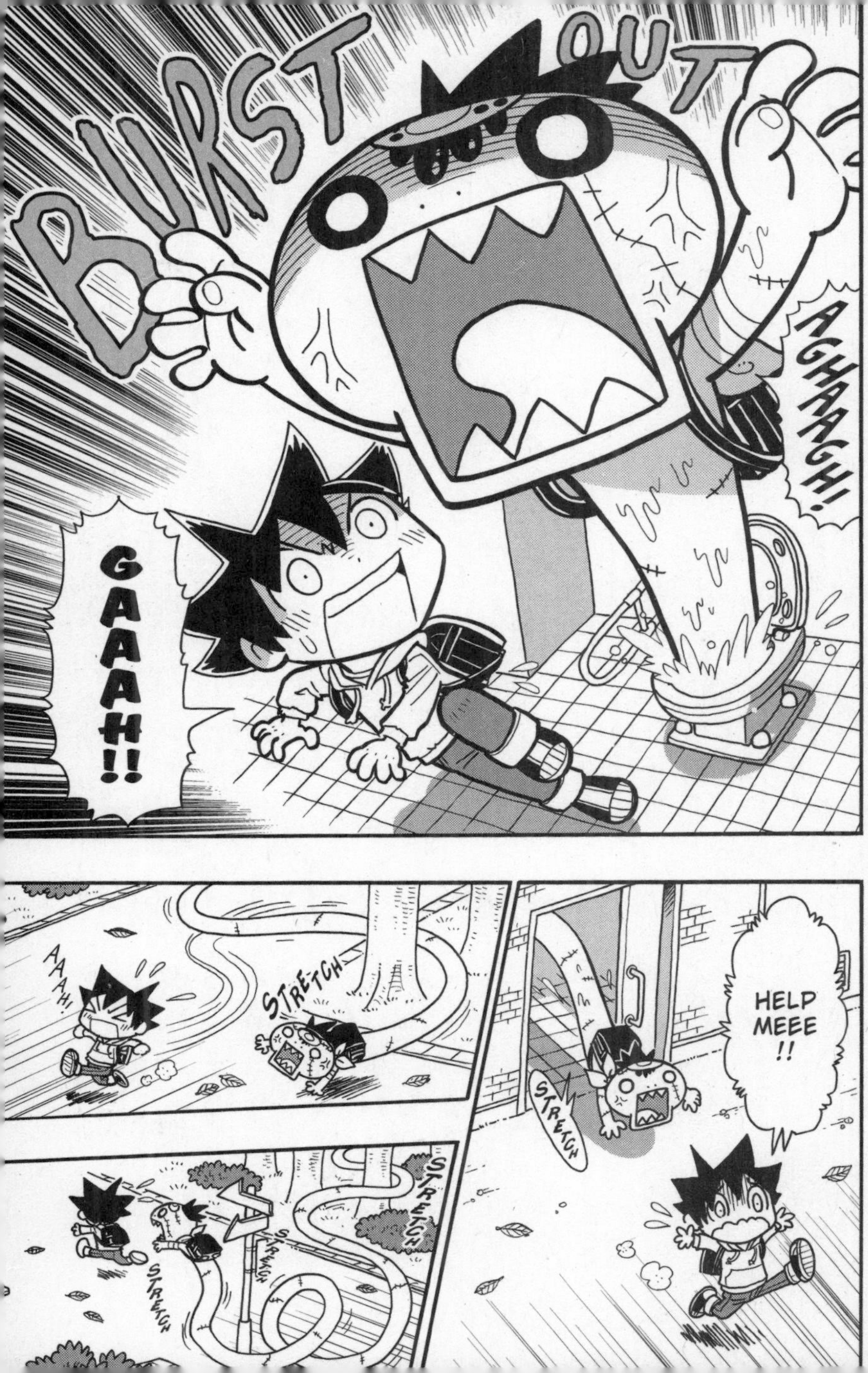
BURST OUT
AGHRAAGH!
GAAAAH!!
HELP MEEE!!
STRETCH
AAAH!
STRETCH
STRETCH
STRETCH
STRETCH

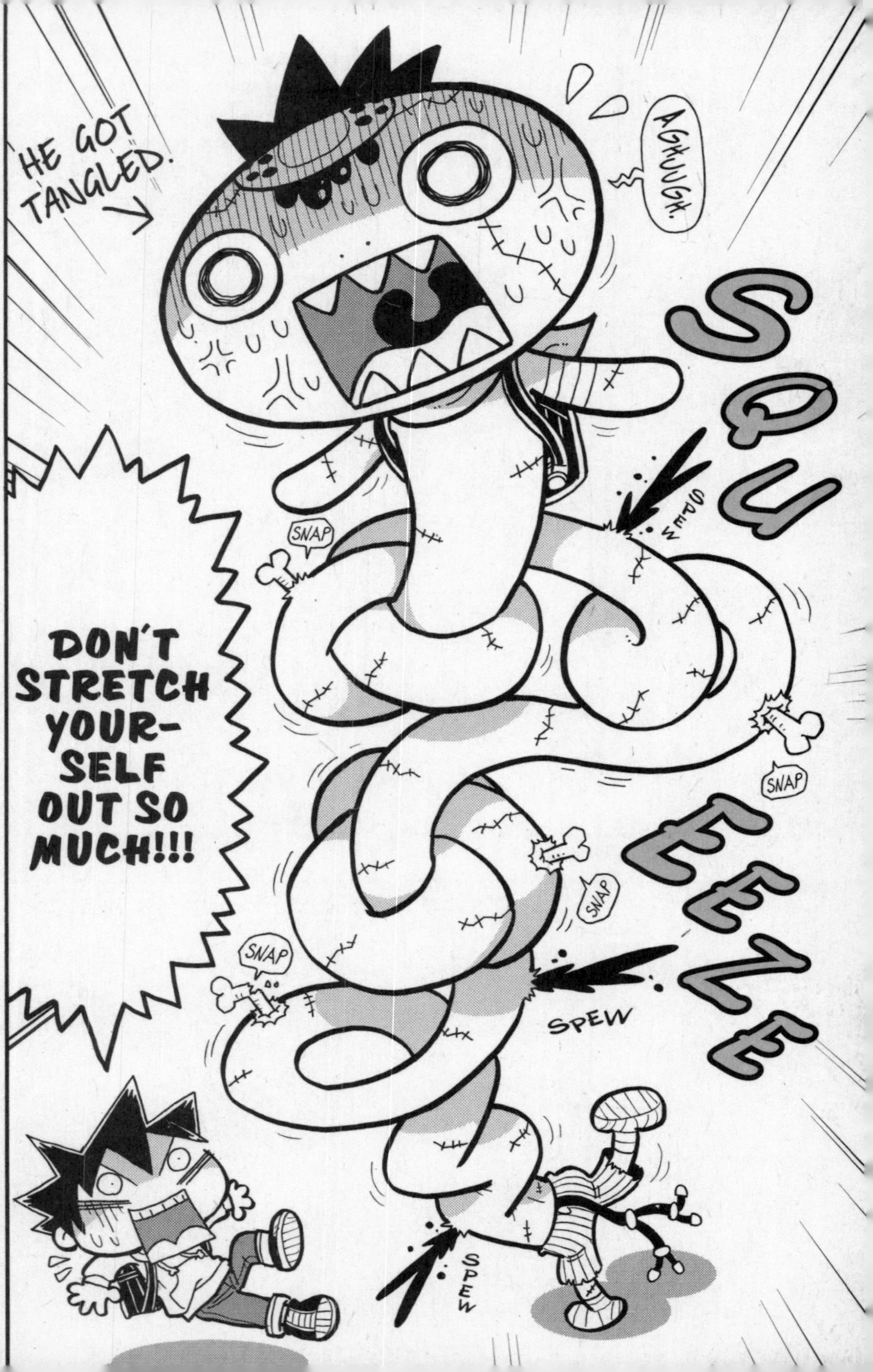
AGHUUGH.
HE GOT TANGLED.
SQUEEZE
SPEW
SNAP
SNAP
SNAP
SNAP
SPEW
SPEW
DON'T STRETCH YOURSELF OUT SO MUCH!!!

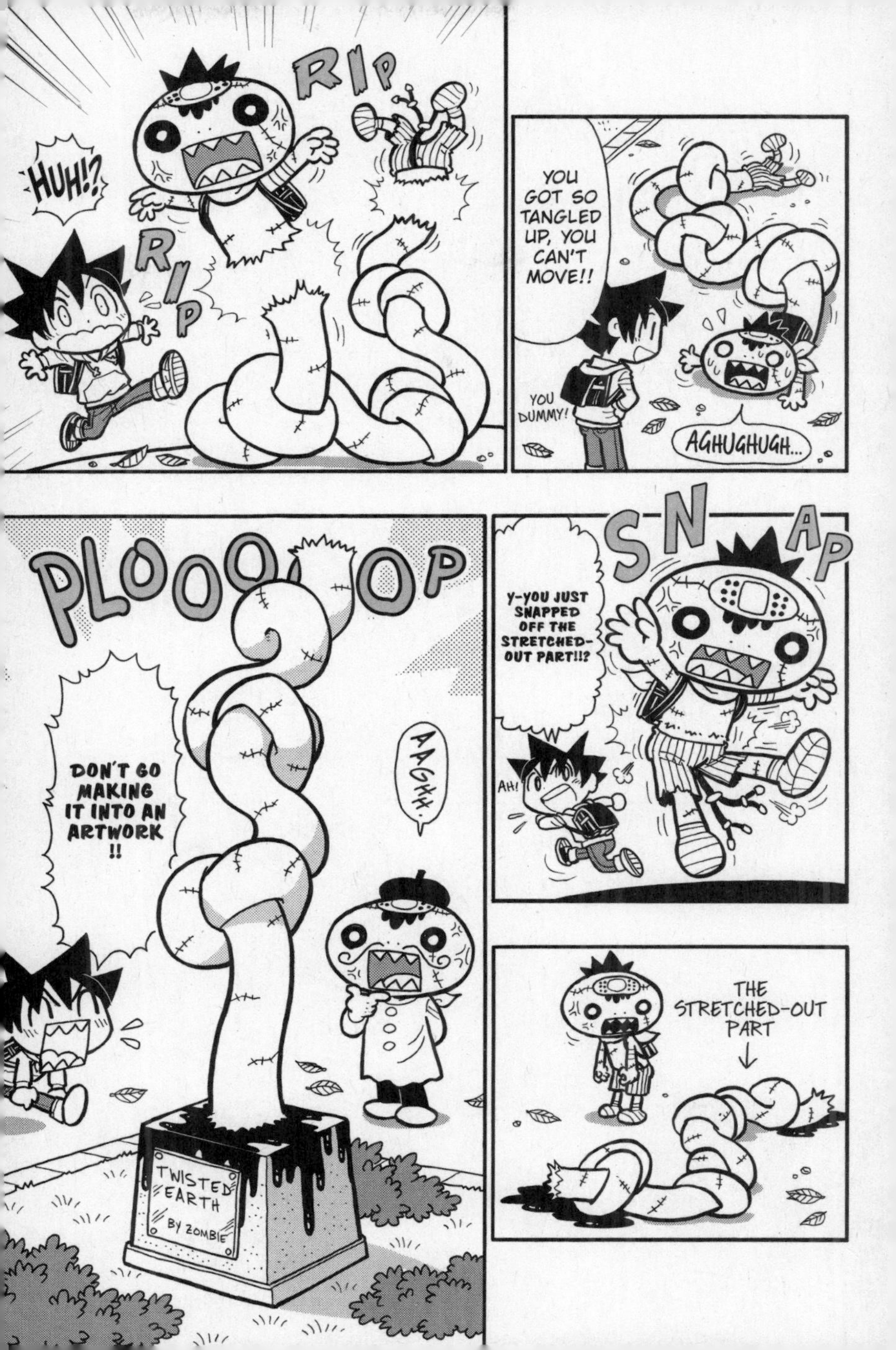
YOU GOT SO TANGLED UP, YOU CAN'T MOVE!!
YOU DUMMY!
AGHUGHUGH...
RIP
HUH!?
RIP
SNAP
Y-YOU JUST SNAPPED OFF THE STRETCHED-OUT PART!!?
AH!
THE STRETCHED-OUT PART
PLOOOOP
AAGHH.
DON'T GO MAKING IT INTO AN ARTWORK !!
TWISTED EARTH
BY ZOMBIE

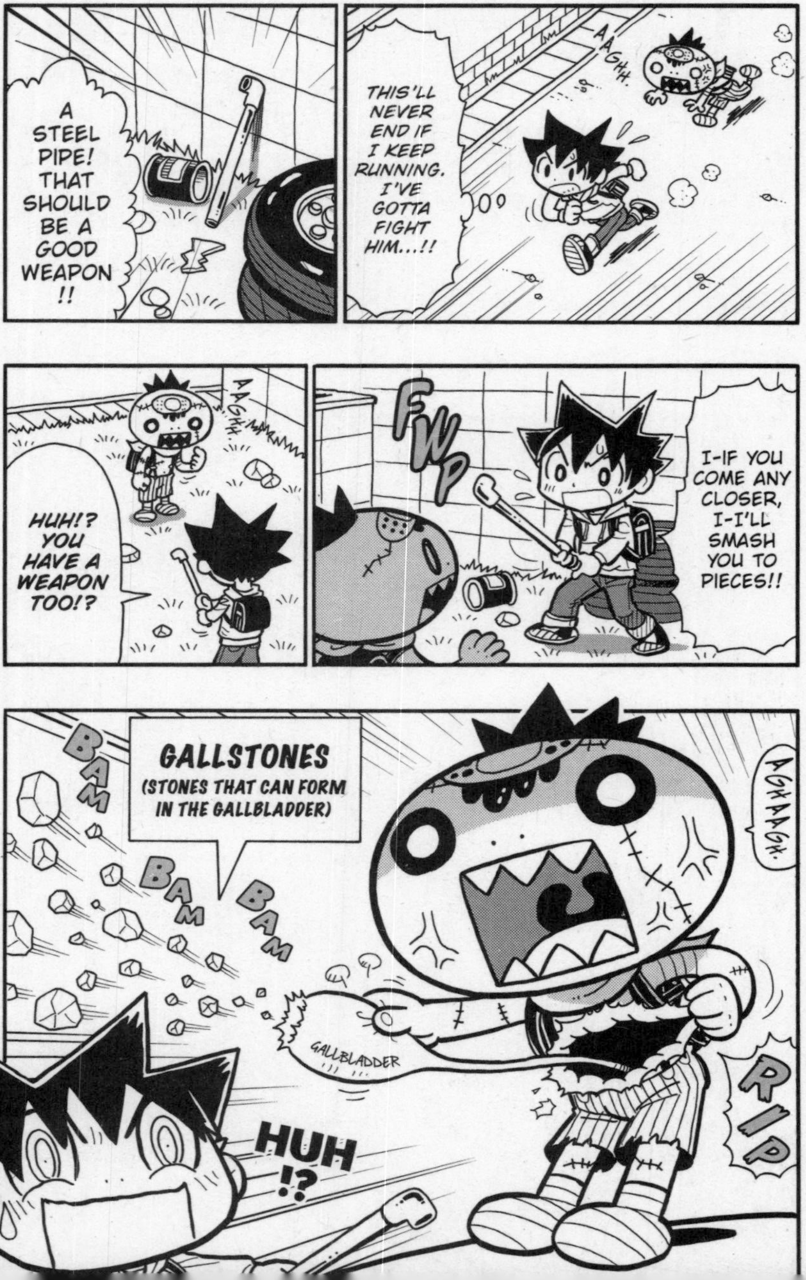
AAGHH.
THIS'LL NEVER END IF I KEEP RUNNING. I'VE GOTTA FIGHT HIM...!!
A STEEL PIPE! THAT SHOULD BE A GOOD WEAPON!!
FWP
I-IF YOU COME ANY CLOSER, I-I'LL SMASH YOU TO PIECES!!
AAGHH.
HUH!? YOU HAVE A WEAPON TOO!?
AGHAAGH.
RIP
GALLSTONES
(STONES THAT CAN FORM IN THE GALLBLADDER)
BAM
BAM
BAM
GALLBLADDER
HUH!?

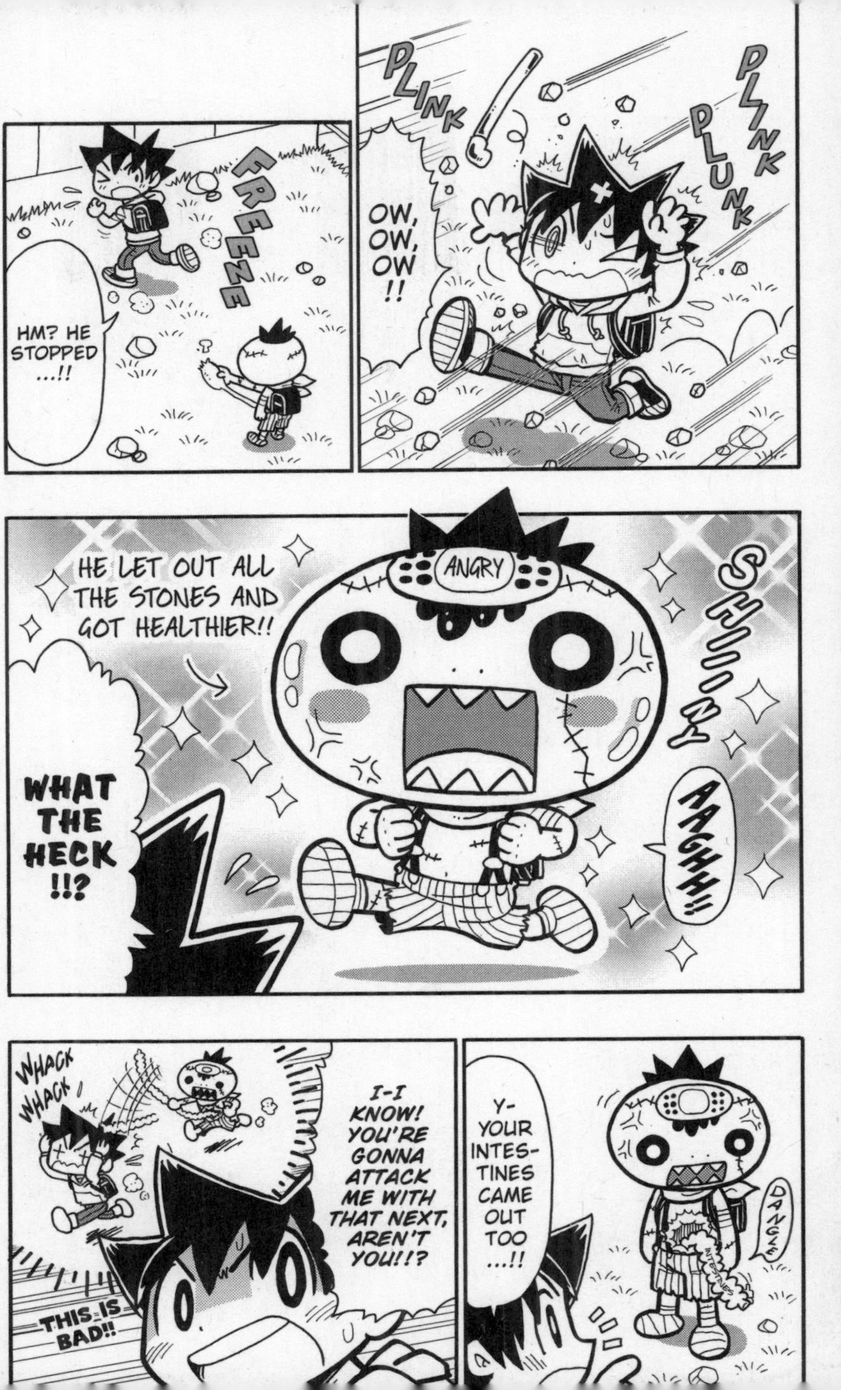
PLINK PLINK
PLUNK
PLINK
OW, OW, OW!!
FREEZE
HM? HE STOPPED ...!!
SHIIIINY
AAGHH!!
ANGRY
HE LET OUT ALL THE STONES AND GOT HEALTHIER!!
WHAT THE HECK!!?
DANGLE
Y-YOUR INTES-TINES CAME OUT TOO ...!!
INTESTINES
I-I KNOW! YOU'RE GONNA ATTACK ME WITH THAT NEXT, AREN'T YOU!!?
WHACK WHACK
THIS IS BAD!!

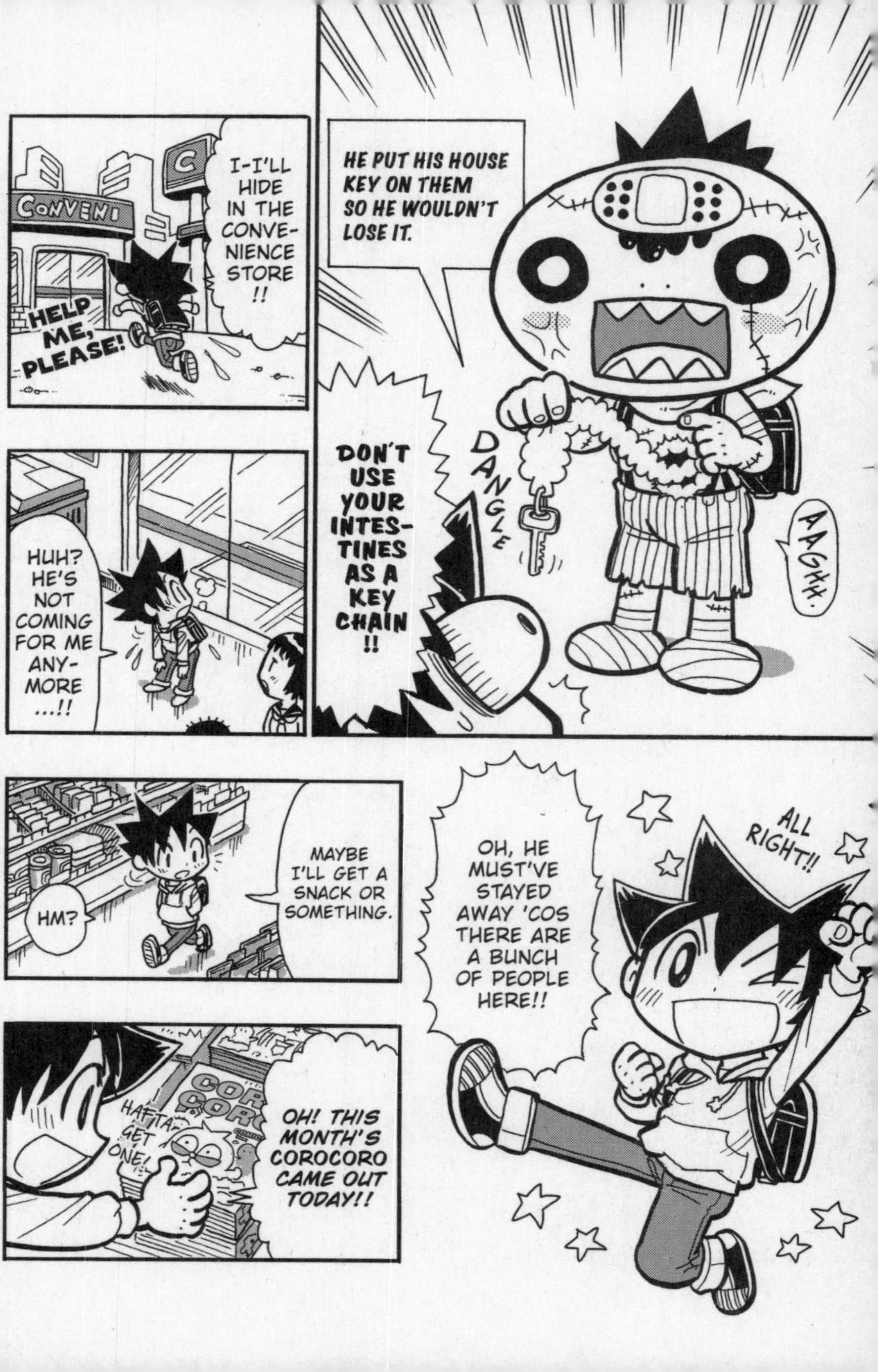
HE PUT HIS HOUSE KEY ON THEM SO HE WOULDN'T LOSE IT.
DON'T USE YOUR INTES-TINES AS A KEY CHAIN!!
DANGLE
AAGKK.
CONVENI
I-I'LL HIDE IN THE CONVE-NIENCE STORE!!
HELP ME, PLEASE!
HUH? HE'S NOT COMING FOR ME ANY-MORE...!!
ALL RIGHT!!
OH, HE MUST'VE STAYED AWAY 'COS THERE ARE A BUNCH OF PEOPLE HERE!!
MAYBE I'LL GET A SNACK OR SOMETHING.
HM?
OH! THIS MONTH'S COROCORO CAME OUT TODAY!!
I HAFTA GET ONE!

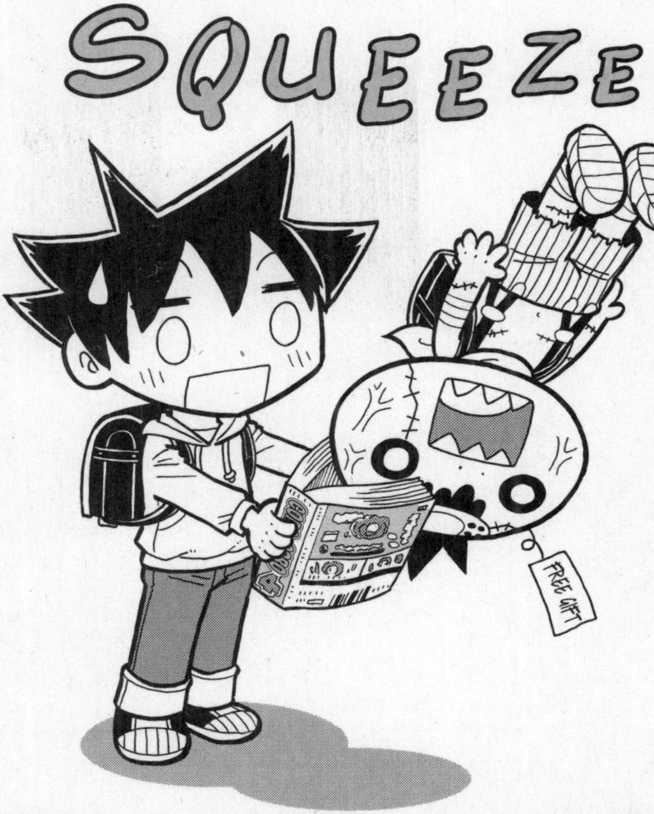
SQUEEZE
FREE GIFT
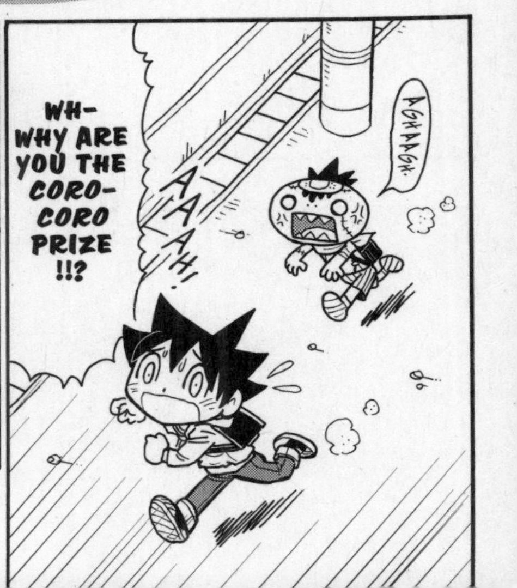
AGHAAGH.
AAAH!
WH-
WHY ARE
YOU THE
CORO-
CORO
PRIZE
!!?
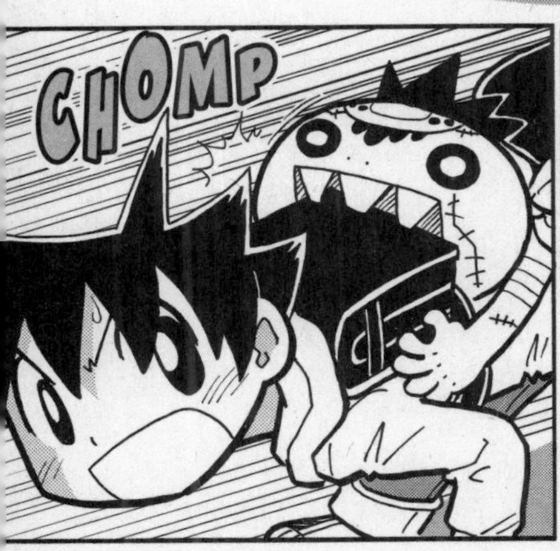
CHOMP

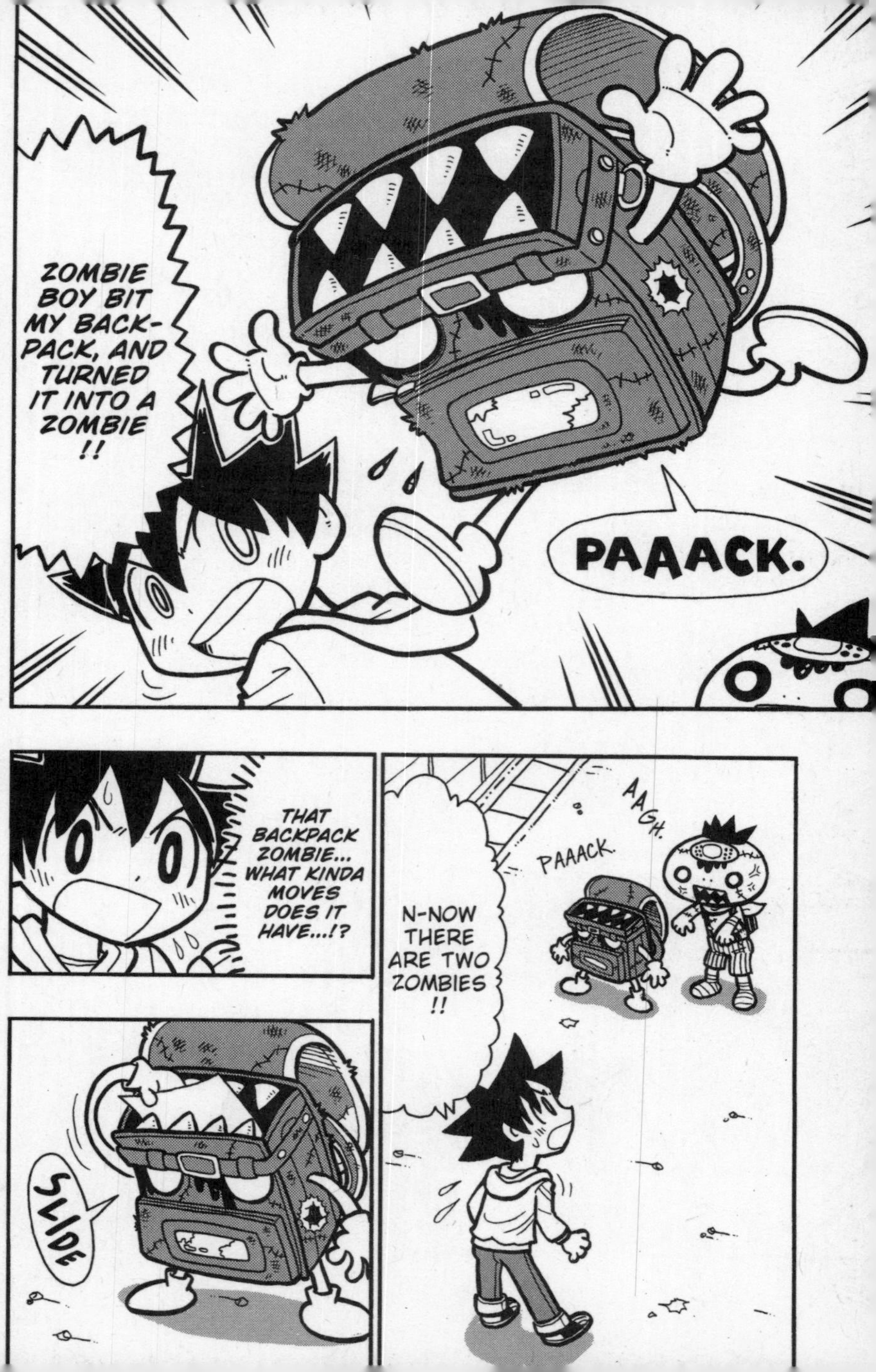
PAAACK.
ZOMBIE BOY BIT MY BACK-PACK, AND TURNED IT INTO A ZOMBIE !!
AAAGH.
PAAACK.
N-NOW THERE ARE TWO ZOMBIES !!
THAT BACKPACK ZOMBIE... WHAT KINDA MOVES DOES IT HAVE...!?
SLIDE

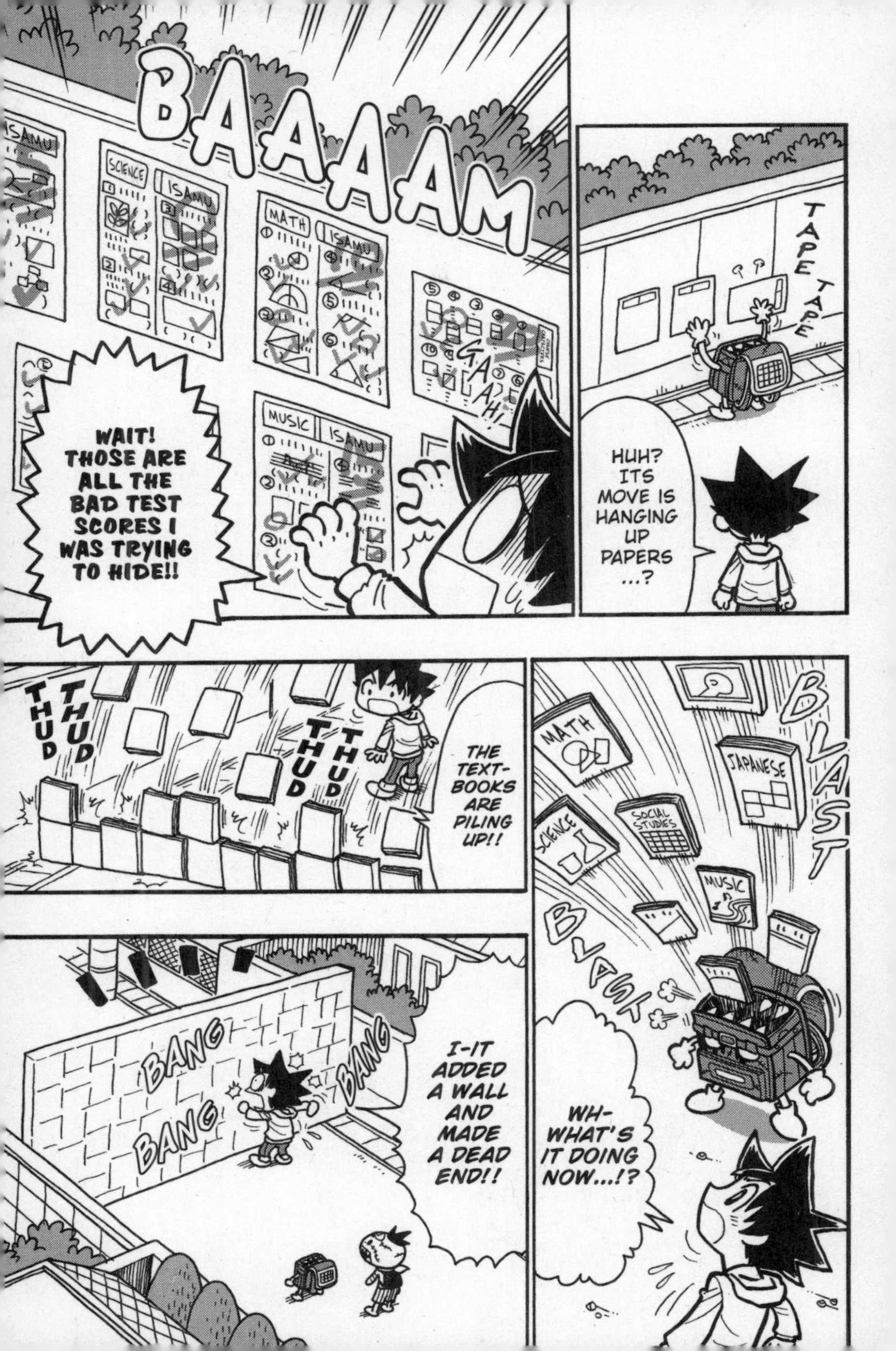
TAPE TAPE
HUH? ITS MOVE IS HANGING UP PAPERS ...?
BAAAAAM
SCIENCE
ISAMU
MATH
ISAMU
MUSIC
ISAMU
GAAAH!
WAIT! THOSE ARE ALL THE BAD TEST SCORES I WAS TRYING TO HIDE!!
BLAST
MATH
JAPANESE
SOCIAL STUDIES
SCIENCE
MUSIC
BLAST
WH-WHAT'S IT DOING NOW...!?
THUD THUD
THUD THUD
THE TEXT-BOOKS ARE PILING UP!!
BANG BANG BANG
I-IT ADDED A WALL AND MADE A DEAD END!!

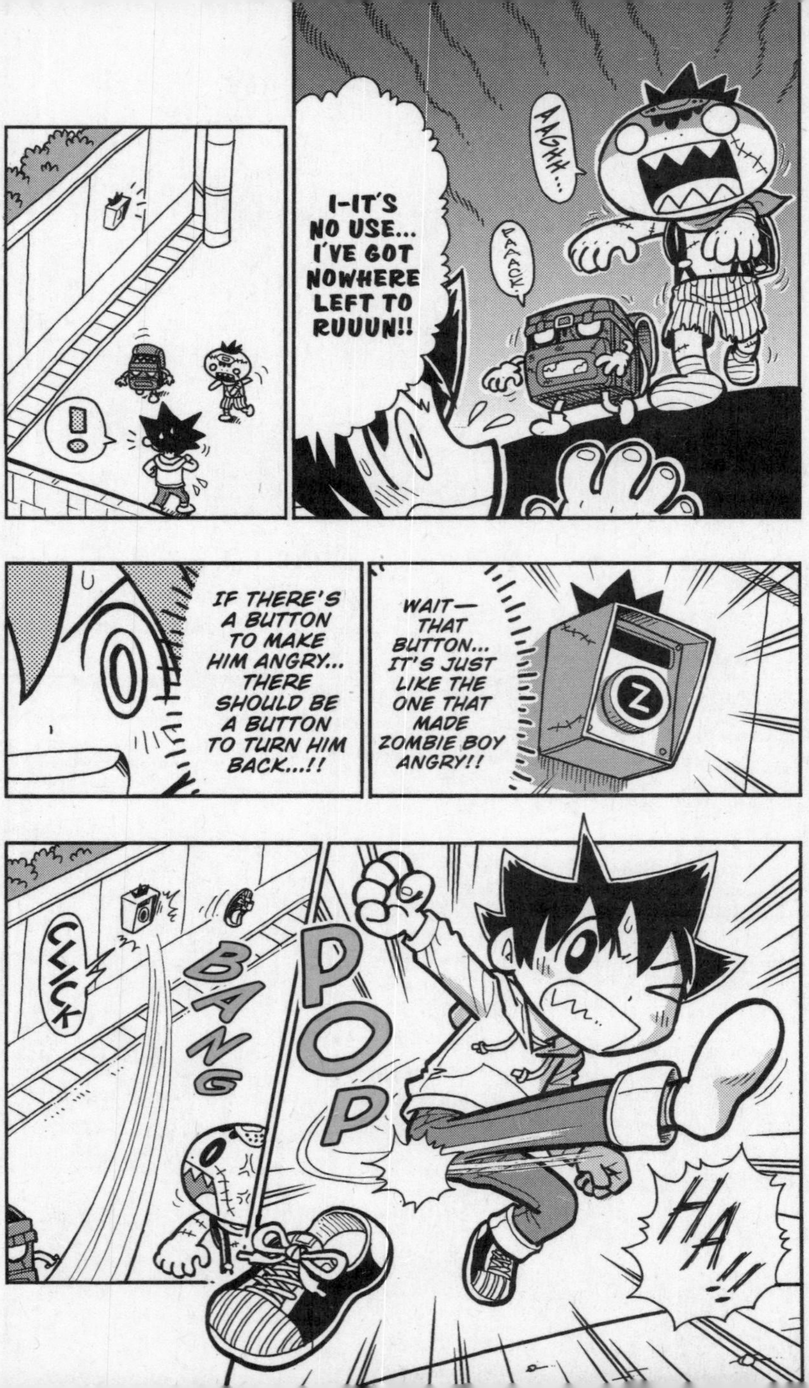
AAGHH...
PAAACK
I-IT'S NO USE... I'VE GOT NOWHERE LEFT TO RUUUN!!
!
WAIT— THAT BUTTON... IT'S JUST LIKE THE ONE THAT MADE ZOMBIE BOY ANGRY!!
IF THERE'S A BUTTON TO MAKE HIM ANGRY... THERE SHOULD BE A BUTTON TO TURN HIM BACK...!!
HA!!
POP
BANG
CLICK

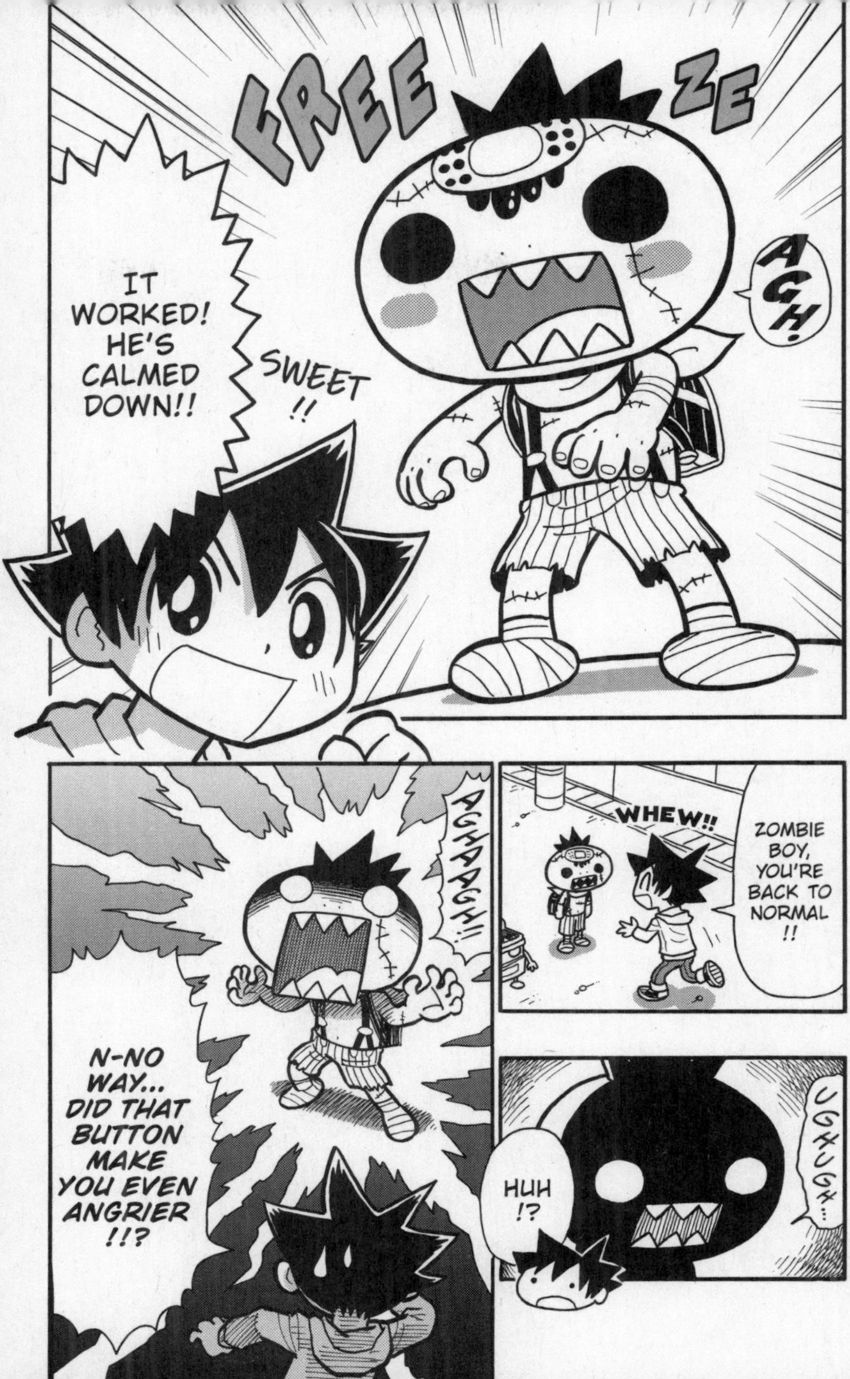
FREEZE
ACH!
SWEET!!
IT WORKED! HE'S CALMED DOWN!!
ZOMBIE BOY, YOU'RE BACK TO NORMAL!!
WHEW!!
UGXUGX...
HUH!?
AGHAAAGH!!
N-NO WAY... DID THAT BUTTON MAKE YOU EVEN ANGRIER!!?

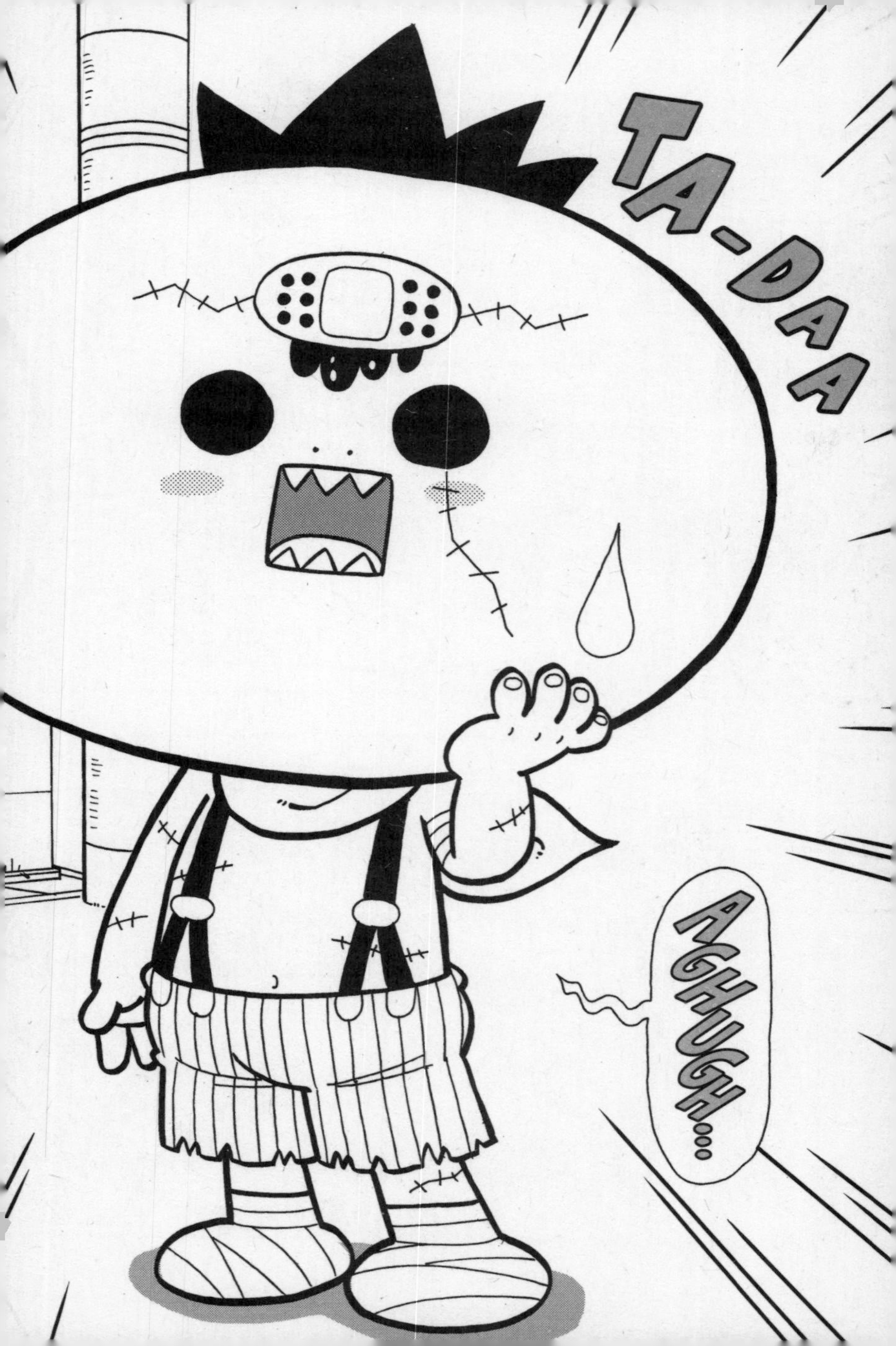
TA-DAA
AGHUGH...

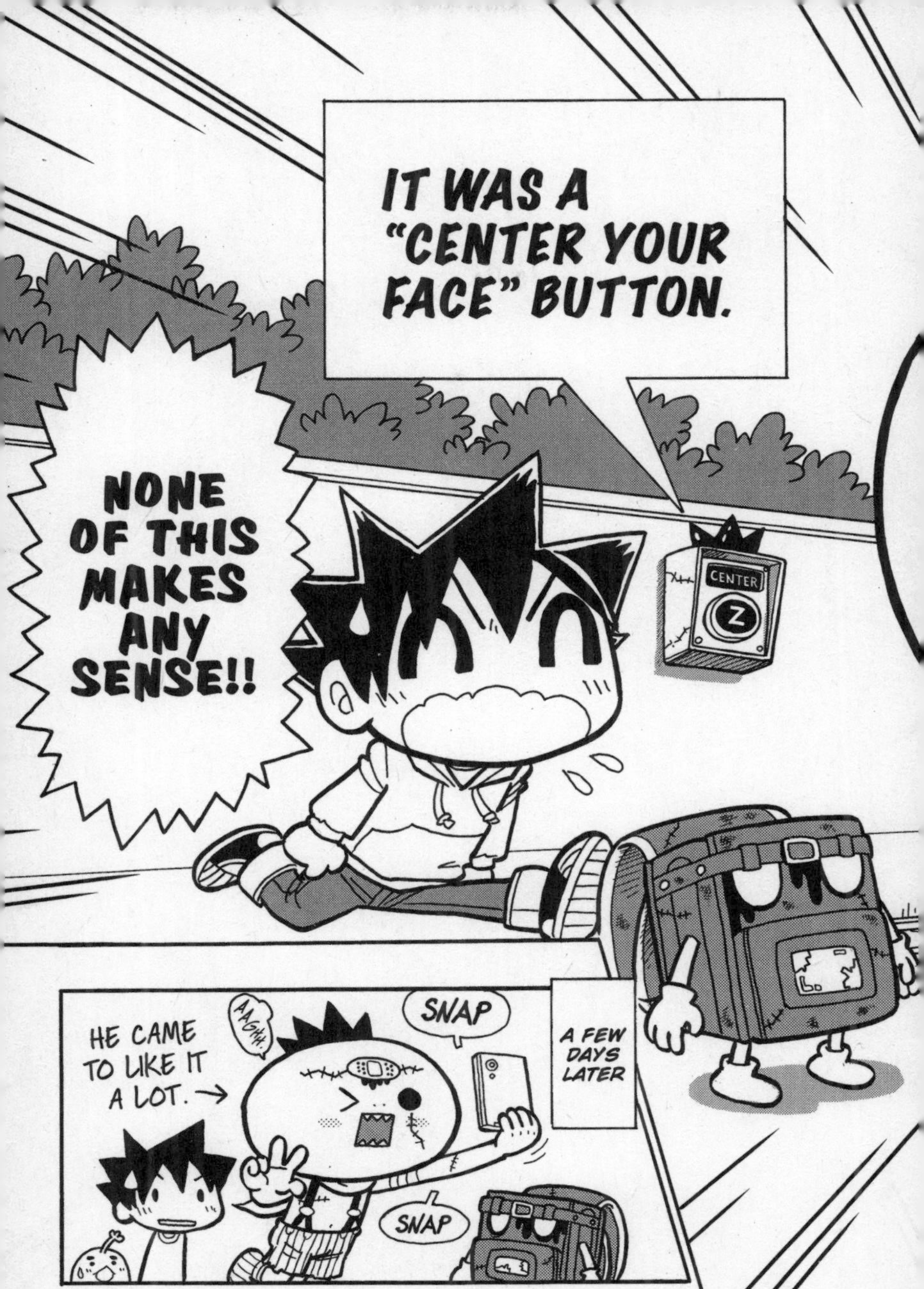

IT WAS A "CENTER YOUR FACE" BUTTON.
NONE OF THIS MAKES ANY SENSE!!
CENTER
Z
A FEW DAYS LATER
SNAP
AAGHH.
HE CAME TO LIKE IT A LOT. →
SNAP

DON'T BE LATE FOR ZCHOOL—OR ELZE!

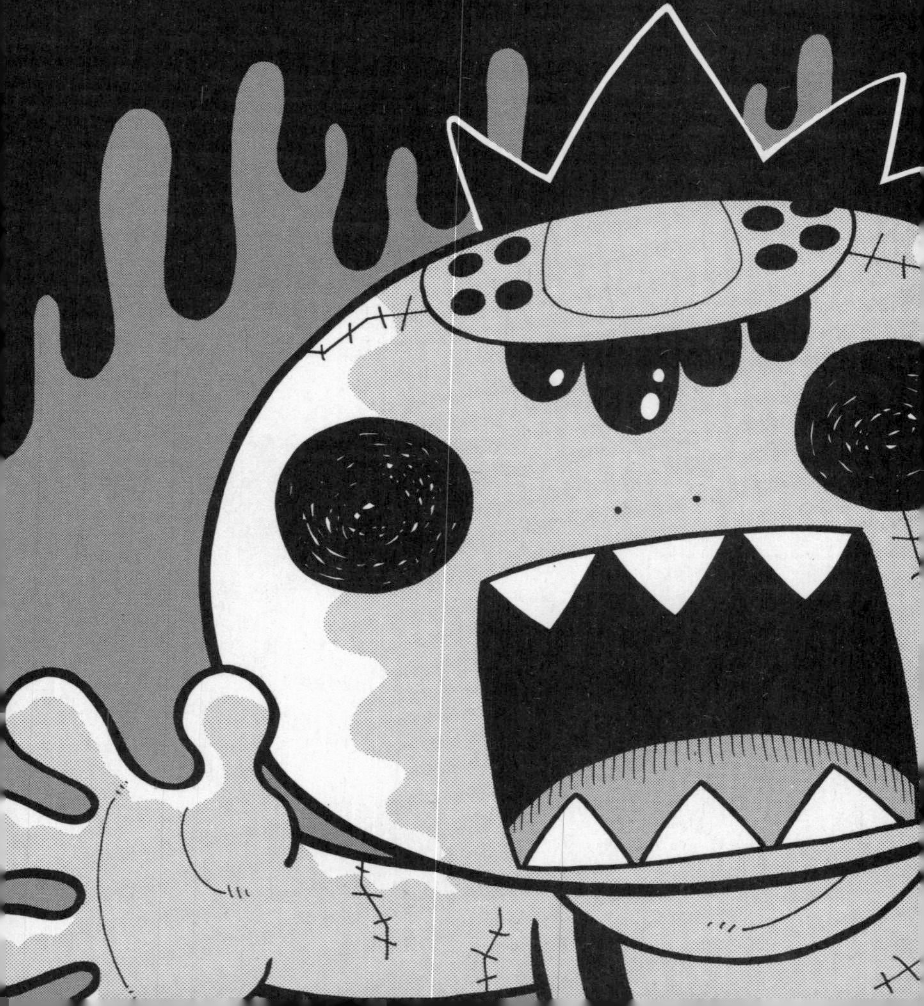

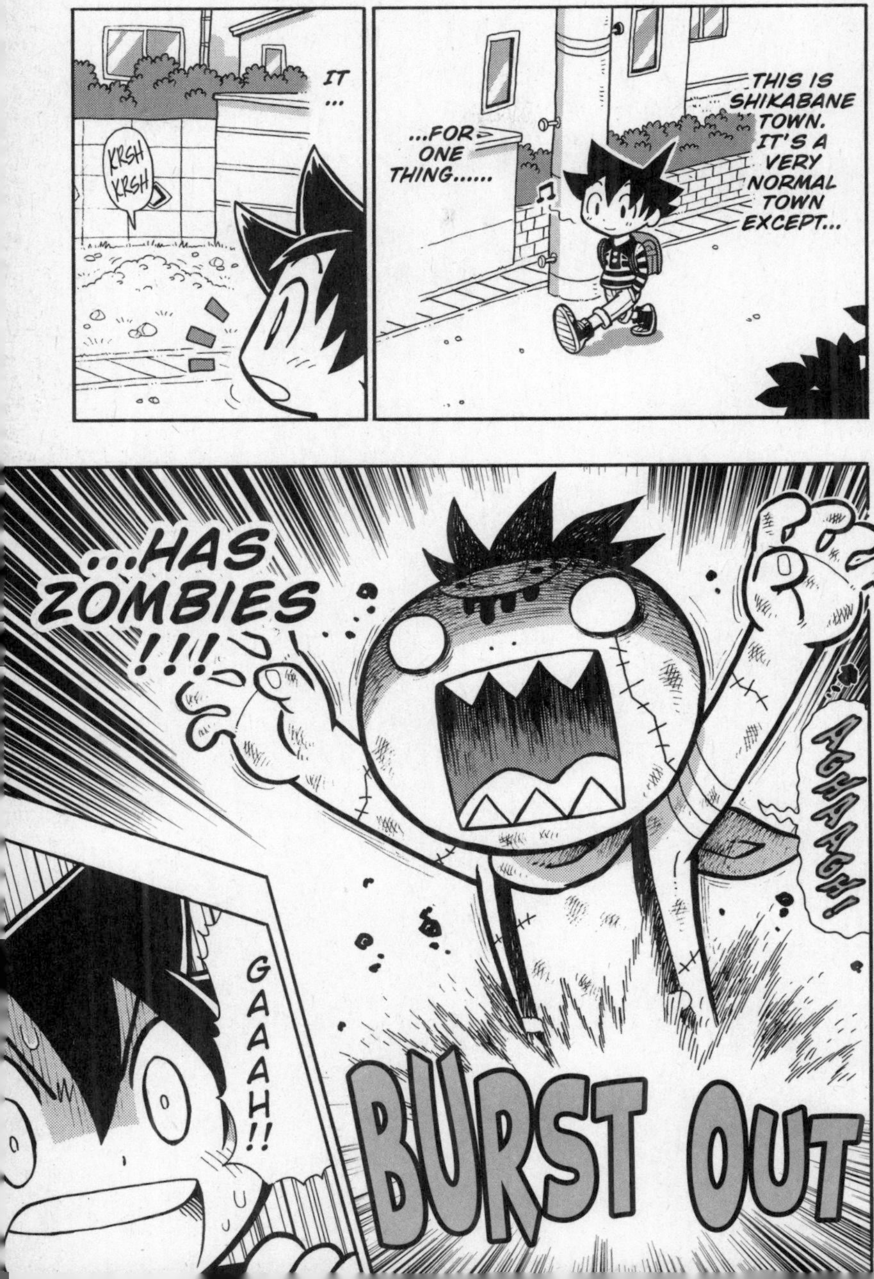
THIS IS SHIKABANE TOWN. IT'S A VERY NORMAL TOWN EXCEPT...
...FOR ONE THING......
IT ...
KRSH KRSH
AGHAAAGH!
...HAS ZOMBIES!!!
BURST OUT
GAAAAH!!

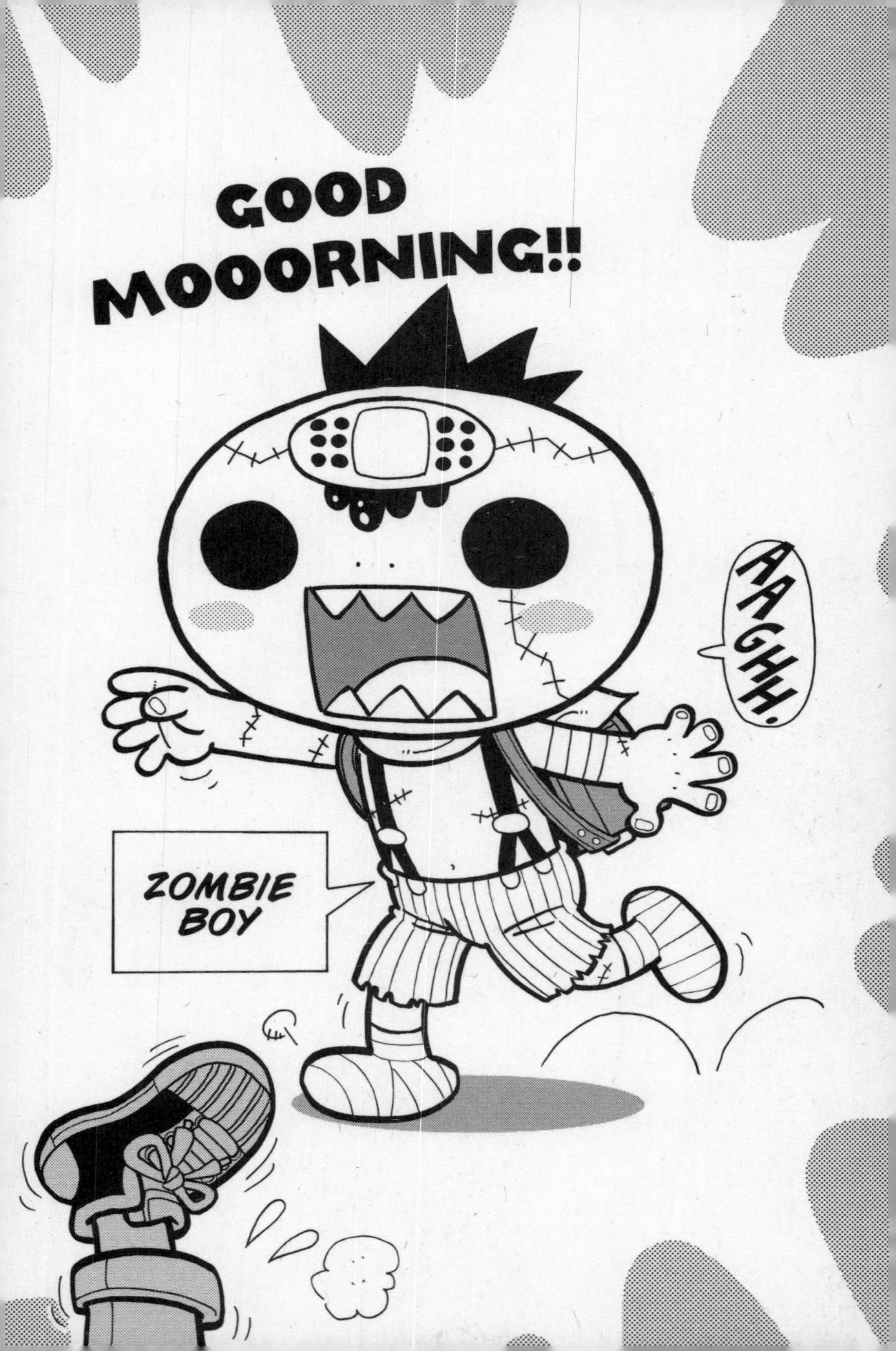
GOOD MOOORNING!!
AAGHH.
ZOMBIE BOY

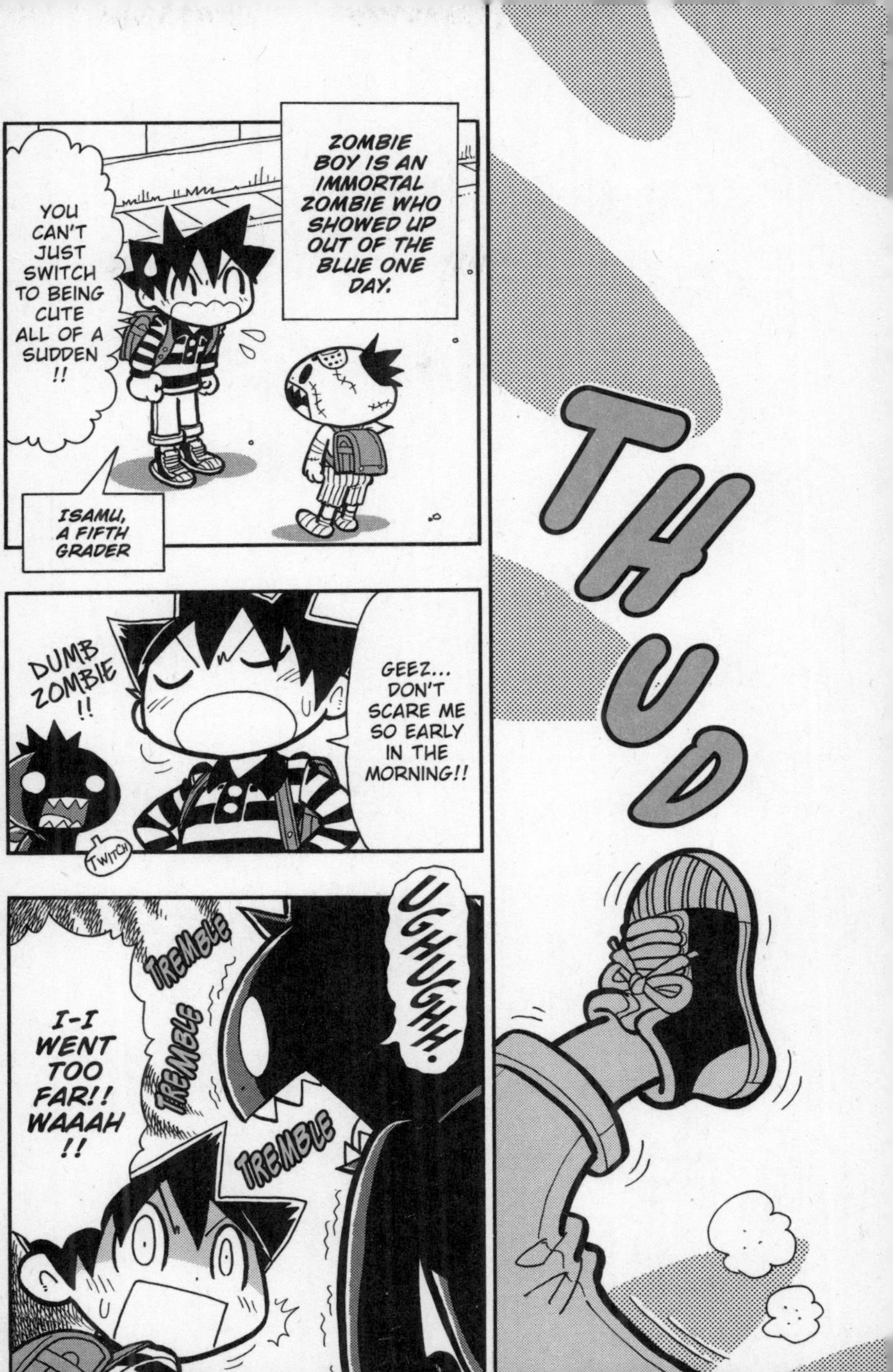
THUD
ZOMBIE BOY IS AN IMMORTAL ZOMBIE WHO SHOWED UP OUT OF THE BLUE ONE DAY.
YOU CAN'T JUST SWITCH TO BEING CUTE ALL OF A SUDDEN!!
ISAMU, A FIFTH GRADER
GEEZ... DON'T SCARE ME SO EARLY IN THE MORNING!!
DUMB ZOMBIE!!
TWITCH
UGHUGHH.
TREMBLE
TREMBLE
TREMBLE
I-I WENT TOO FAR!! WAAAH!!

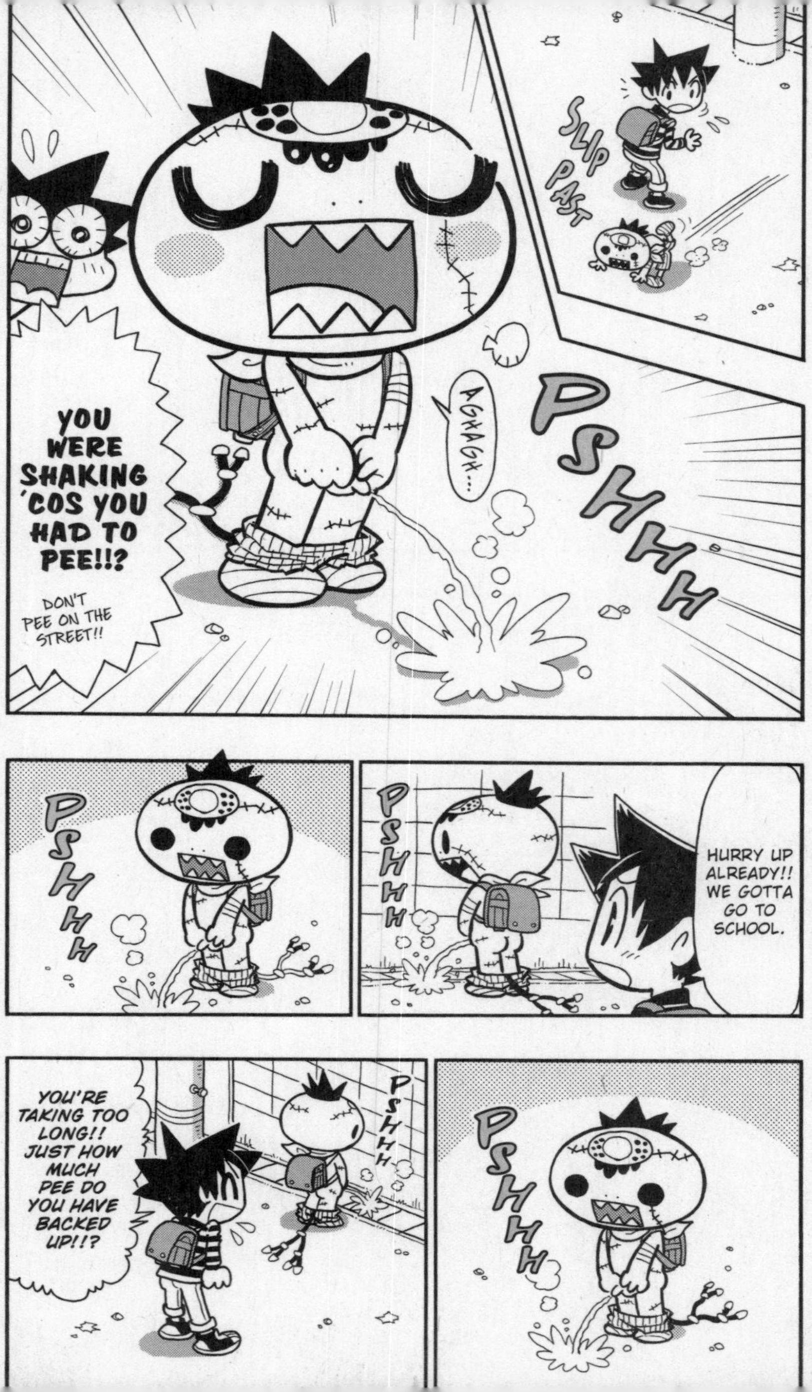
SLIP PAST
AGHAGH...
PSHHH
YOU WERE SHAKING 'COS YOU HAD TO PEE!!?
DON'T PEE ON THE STREET!!
HURRY UP ALREADY!! WE GOTTA GO TO SCHOOL.
PSHHH
PSHHH
PSHHH
PSHHH
YOU'RE TAKING TOO LONG!! JUST HOW MUCH PEE DO YOU HAVE BACKED UP!!?

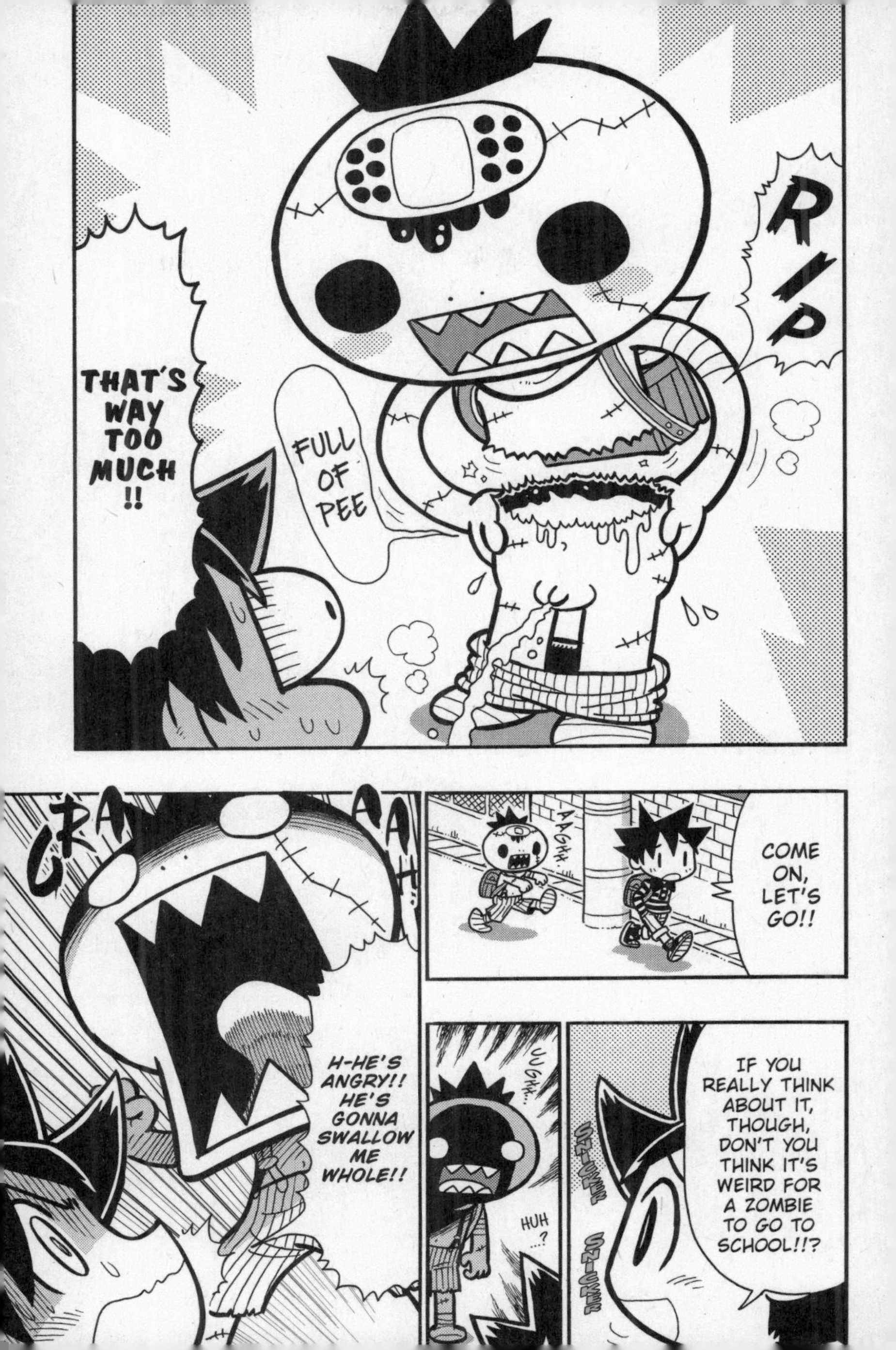
RIP
FULL OF PEE
THAT'S WAY TOO MUCH!!
COME ON, LET'S GO!!
IF YOU REALLY THINK ABOUT IT, THOUGH, DON'T YOU THINK IT'S WEIRD FOR A ZOMBIE TO GO TO SCHOOL!!?
SNICKER
SNICKER
HUH...?
GRAAAH
H-HE'S ANGRY!! HE'S GONNA SWALLOW ME WHOLE!!

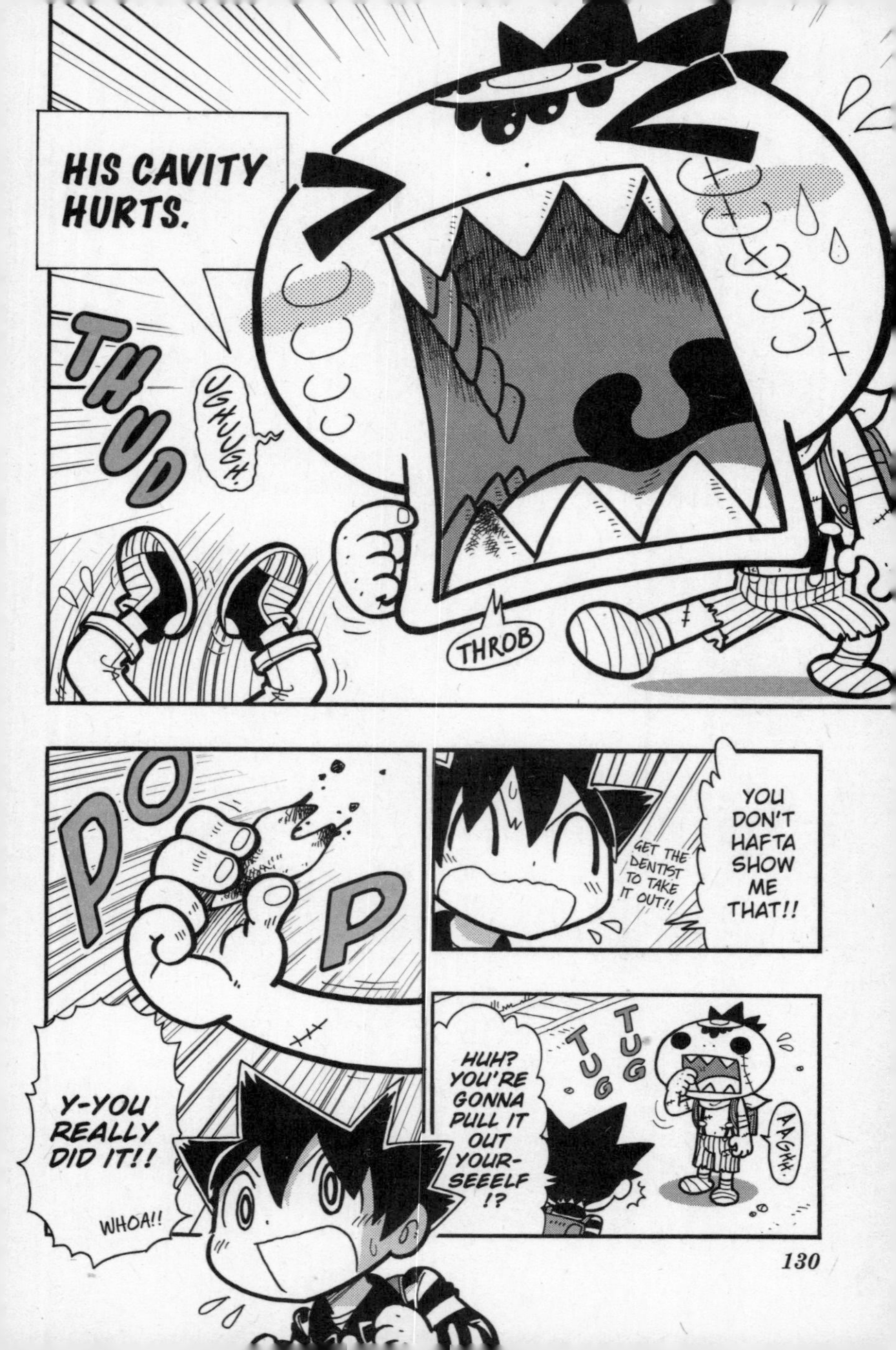
HIS CAVITY HURTS.
UGHUGH
THUD
THROB
YOU DON'T HAFTA SHOW ME THAT!!
GET THE DENTIST TO TAKE IT OUT!!
TUG TUG
HUH? YOU'RE GONNA PULL IT OUT YOURSEEELF!?
AAGHH
POP
Y-YOU REALLY DID IT!!
WHOA!!

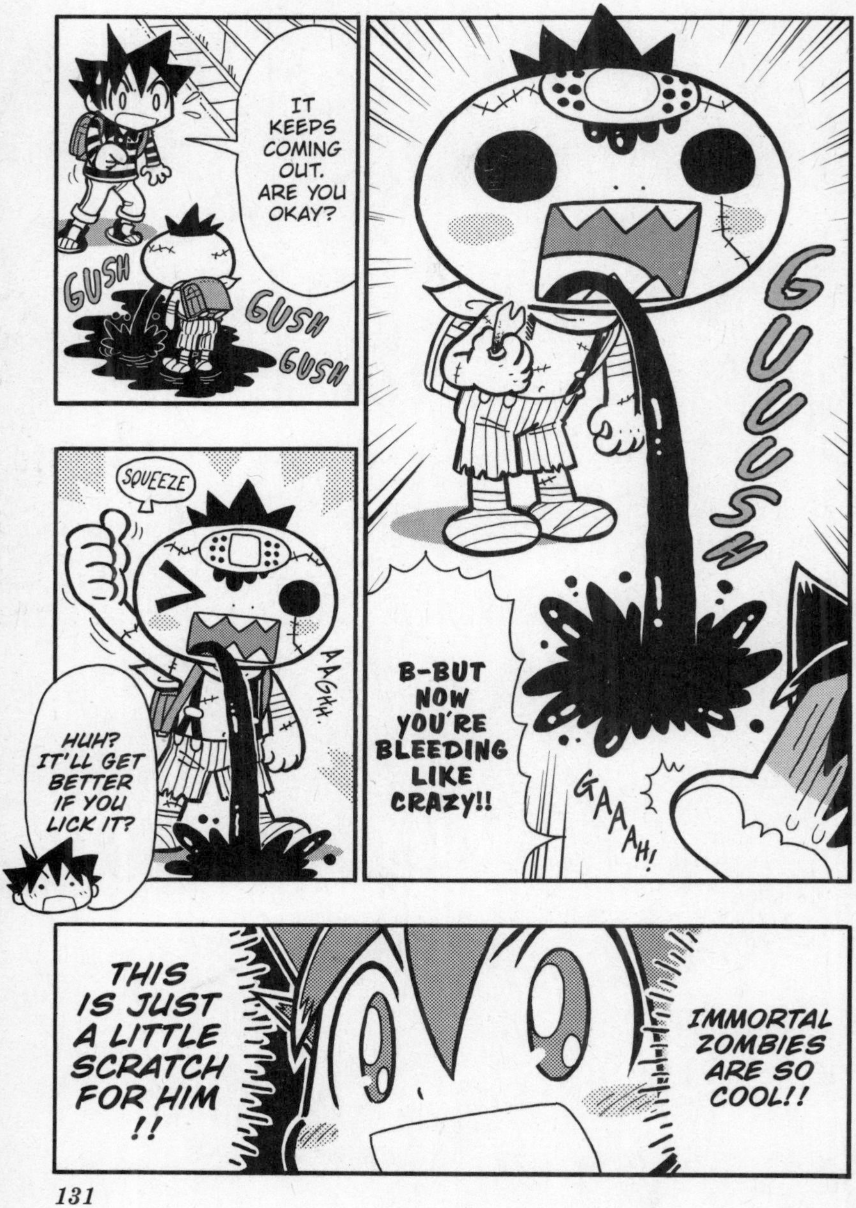
GUUUUSH
B-BUT NOW YOU'RE BLEEDING LIKE CRAZY!!
GAAAAH!
IT KEEPS COMING OUT. ARE YOU OKAY?
GUSH
GUSH
GUSH
SQUEEZE
AAGHH.
HUH? IT'LL GET BETTER IF YOU LICK IT?
IMMORTAL ZOMBIES ARE SO COOL!!
THIS IS JUST A LITTLE SCRATCH FOR HIM!!

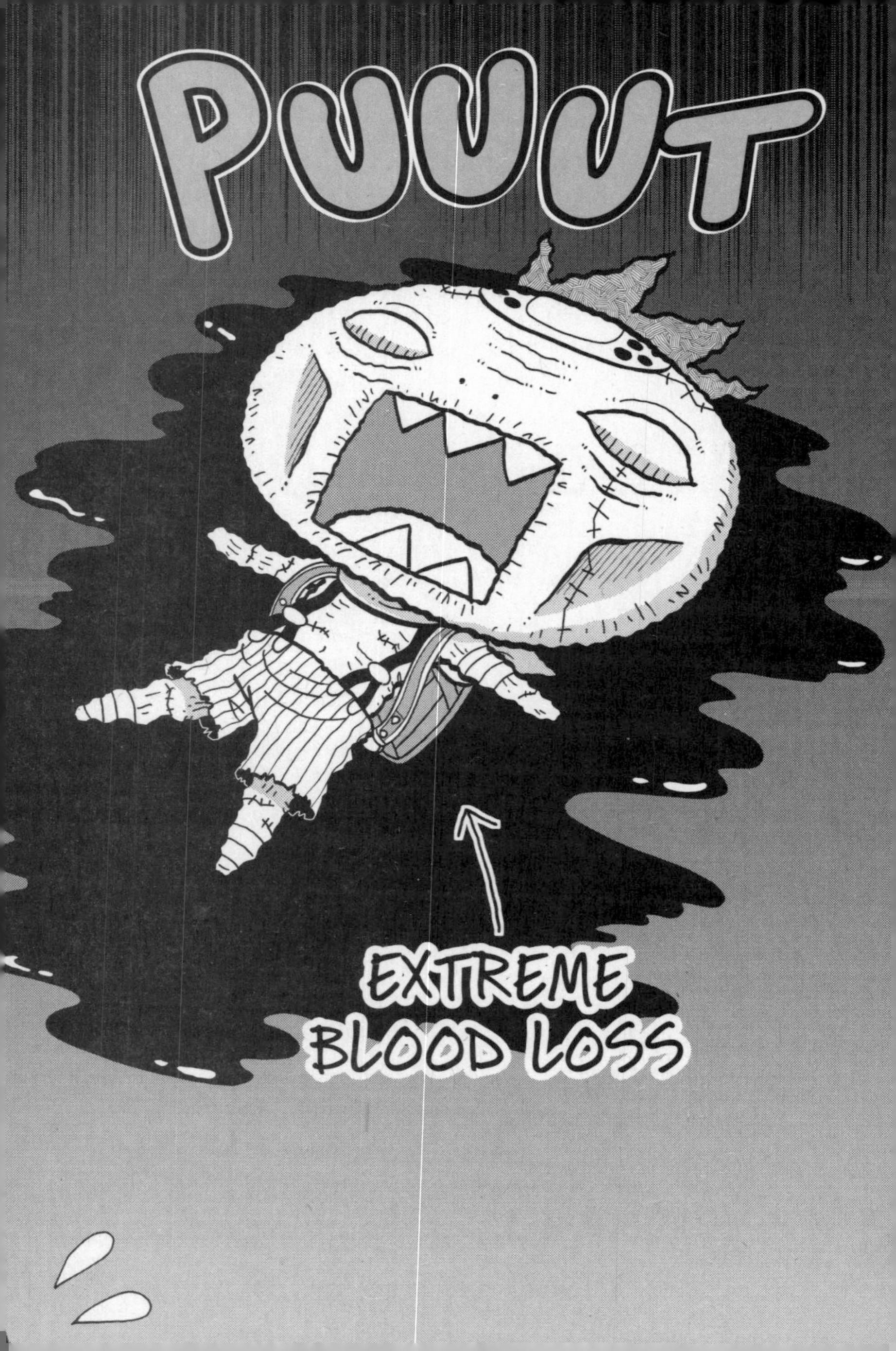
PUUUT
EXTREME BLOOD LOSS

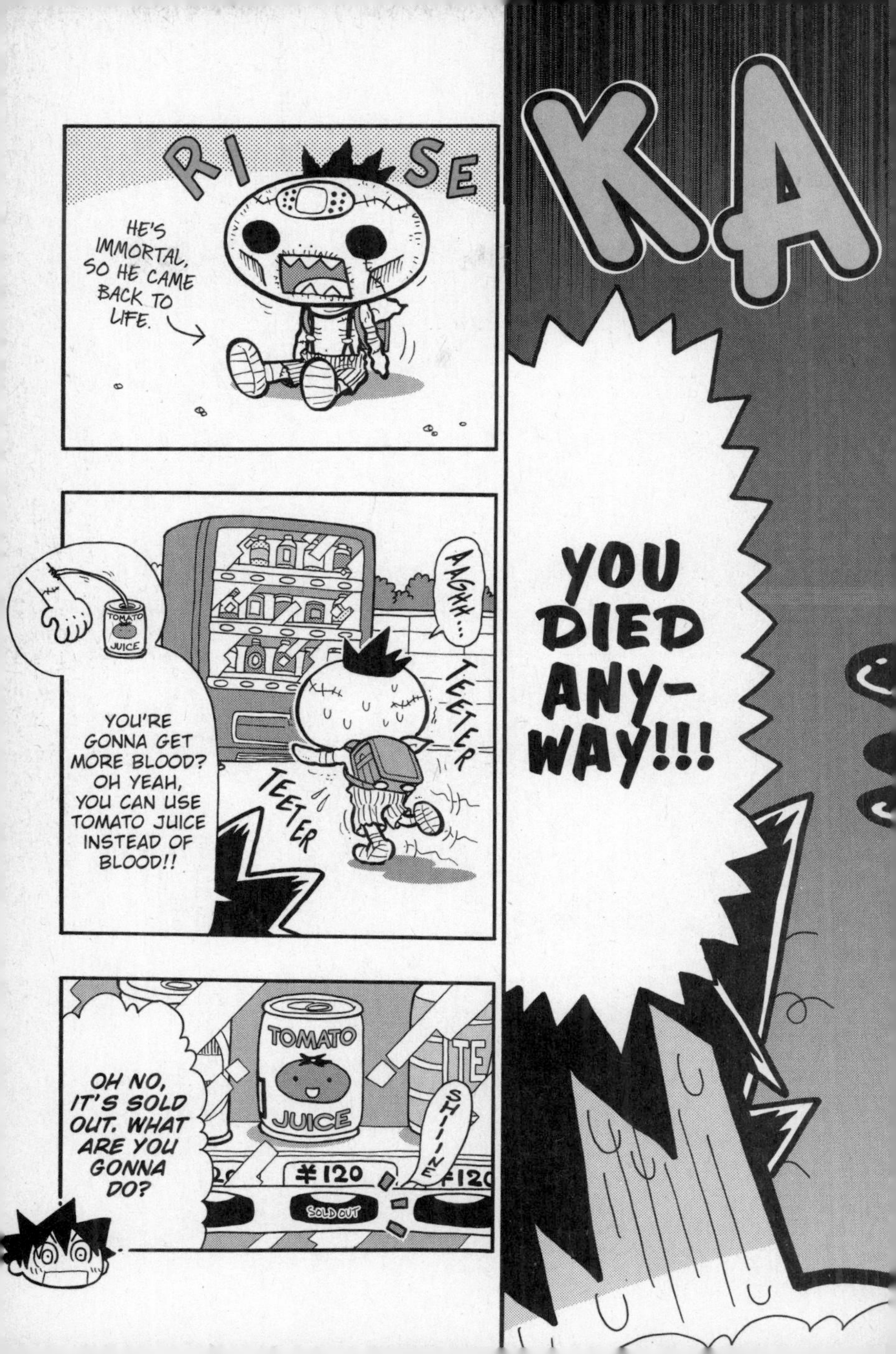
KA
YOU DIED ANY-WAY!!!
RISE
HE'S IMMORTAL, SO HE CAME BACK TO LIFE.
AAGHH...
TEETER
TEETER
TOMATO JUICE
YOU'RE GONNA GET MORE BLOOD? OH YEAH, YOU CAN USE TOMATO JUICE INSTEAD OF BLOOD!!
TOMATO JUICE
SHIIINE
¥120
SOLD OUT
OH NO, IT'S SOLD OUT. WHAT ARE YOU GONNA DO?

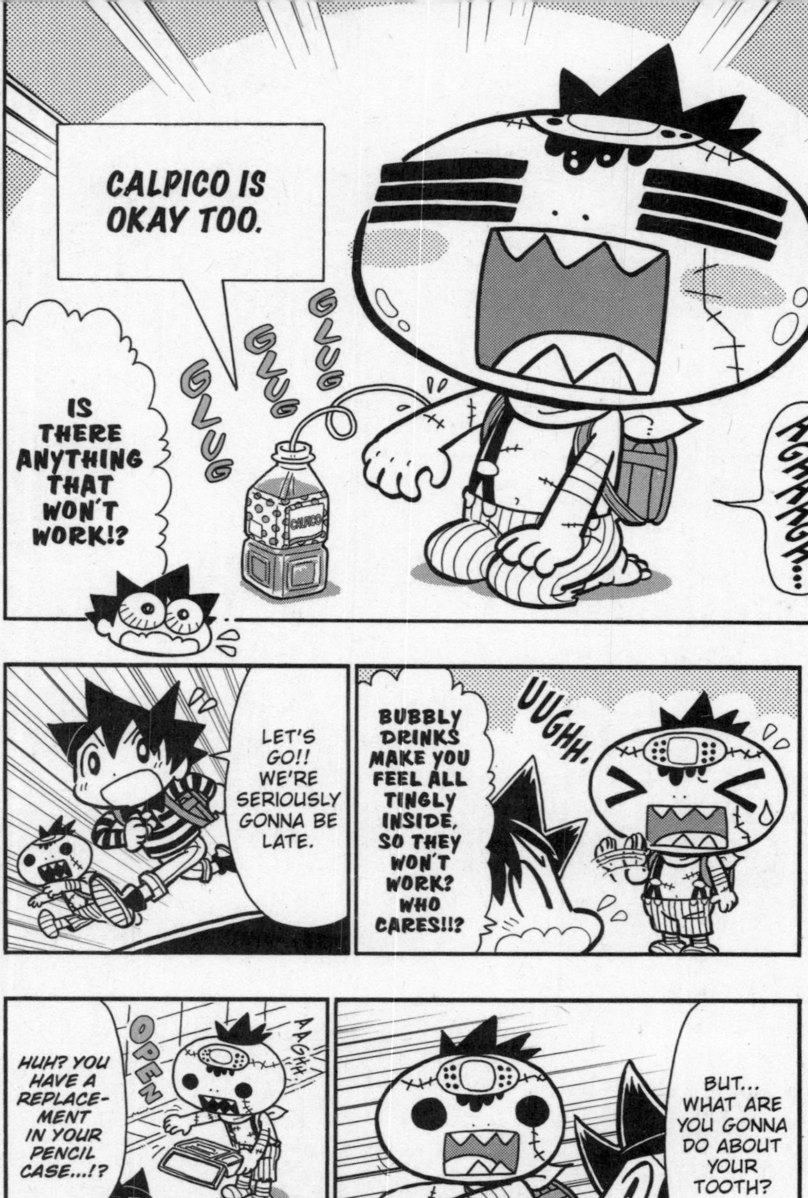
CALPICO IS OKAY TOO.
GLUG GLUG GLUG
CALPICO
AGHAAAGH...
IS THERE ANYTHING THAT WON'T WORK!?
UUGHH.
BUBBLY DRINKS MAKE YOU FEEL ALL TINGLY INSIDE, SO THEY WON'T WORK? WHO CARES!!?
LET'S GO!! WE'RE SERIOUSLY GONNA BE LATE.
BUT... WHAT ARE YOU GONNA DO ABOUT YOUR TOOTH?
AAGHH
OPEN
HUH? YOU HAVE A REPLACE-MENT IN YOUR PENCIL CASE...!?

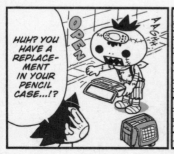

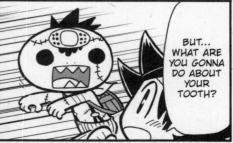

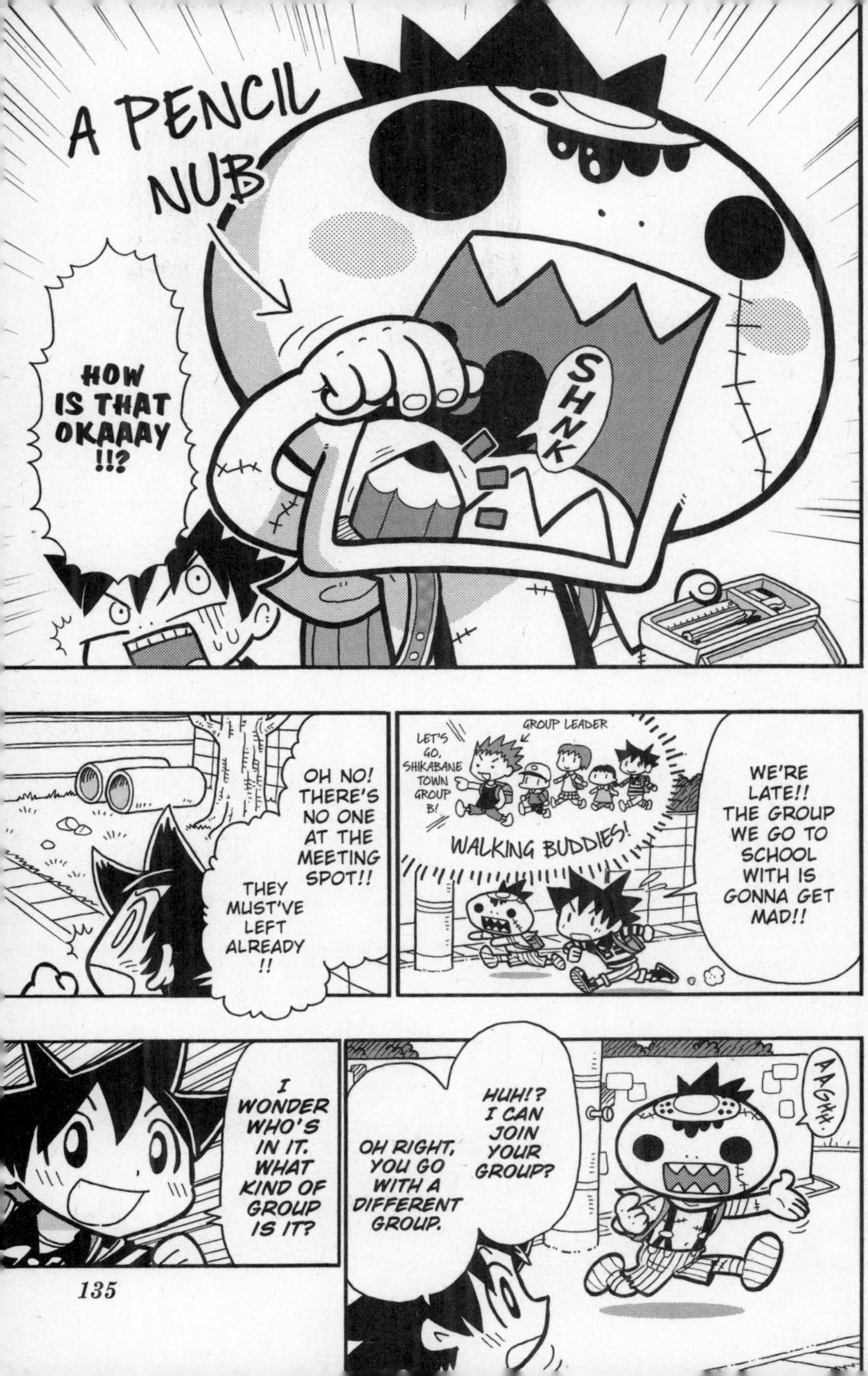
A PENCIL NUB
SHNK
HOW IS THAT OKAAAY!!?
WE'RE LATE!! THE GROUP WE GO TO SCHOOL WITH IS GONNA GET MAD!!
GROUP LEADER
LET'S GO, SHIKABANE TOWN GROUP B!
WALKING BUDDIES!
OH NO! THERE'S NO ONE AT THE MEETING SPOT!!
THEY MUST'VE LEFT ALREADY!!
AAGH.
HUH!? I CAN JOIN YOUR GROUP?
OH RIGHT, YOU GO WITH A DIFFERENT GROUP.
I WONDER WHO'S IN IT. WHAT KIND OF GROUP IS IT?

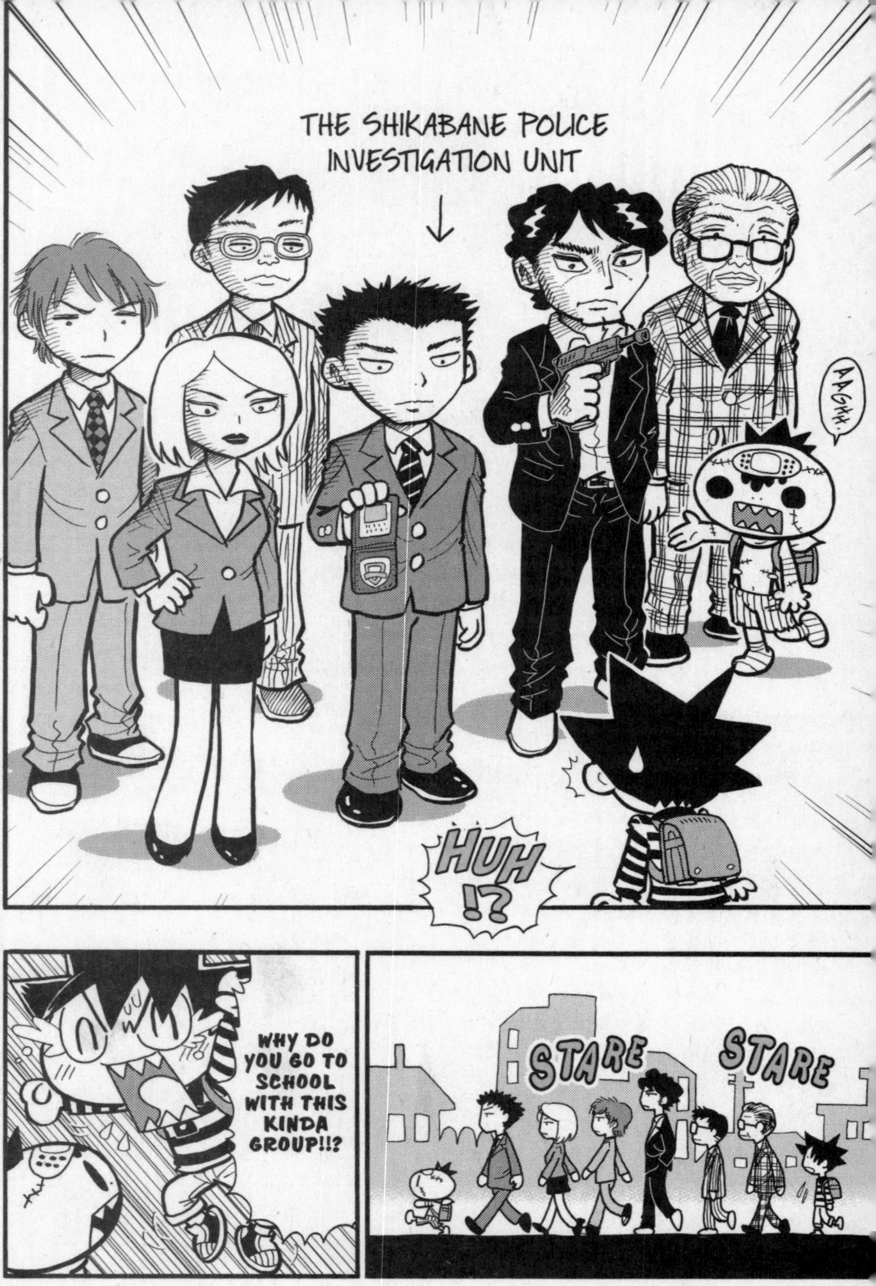
THE SHIKABANE POLICE INVESTIGATION UNIT
AAGHH.
HUH!?
STARE STARE
WHY DO YOU GO TO SCHOOL WITH THIS KINDA GROUP!!?

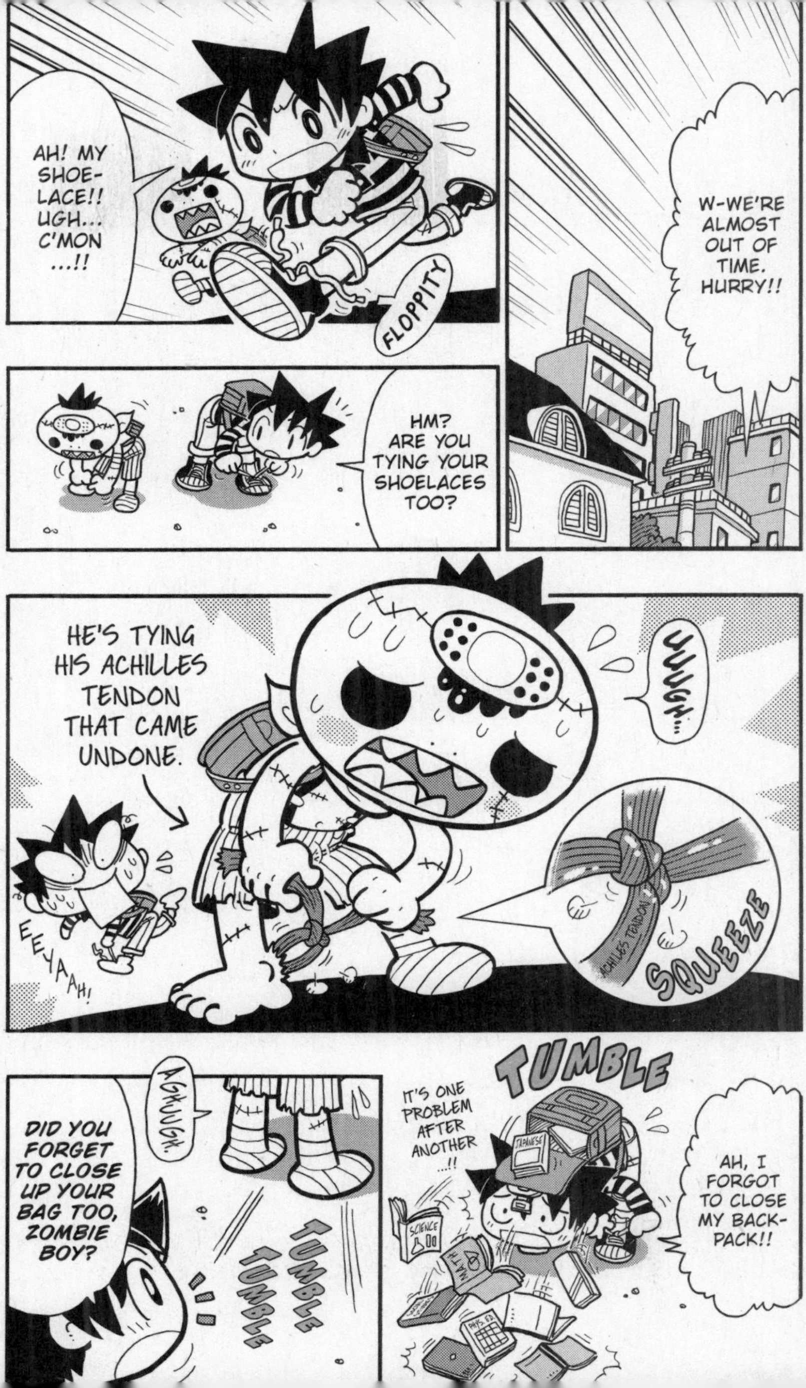
W-WE'RE ALMOST OUT OF TIME. HURRY!!
AH! MY SHOE-LACE!! UGH... C'MON ...!!
FLOPPITY
HM? ARE YOU TYING YOUR SHOELACES TOO?
UUUGH...
HE'S TYING HIS ACHILLES TENDON THAT CAME UNDONE.
ACHILLES TENDON
SQUEEEZE
EEYAAAH!
AH, I FORGOT TO CLOSE MY BACK-PACK!!
TUMBLE
IT'S ONE PROBLEM AFTER ANOTHER ...!!
JAPANESE
SCIENCE
MATH
PHYS ED
AGHUUGH.
DID YOU FORGET TO CLOSE UP YOUR BAG TOO, ZOMBIE BOY?
TUMBLE TUMBLE TUMBLE

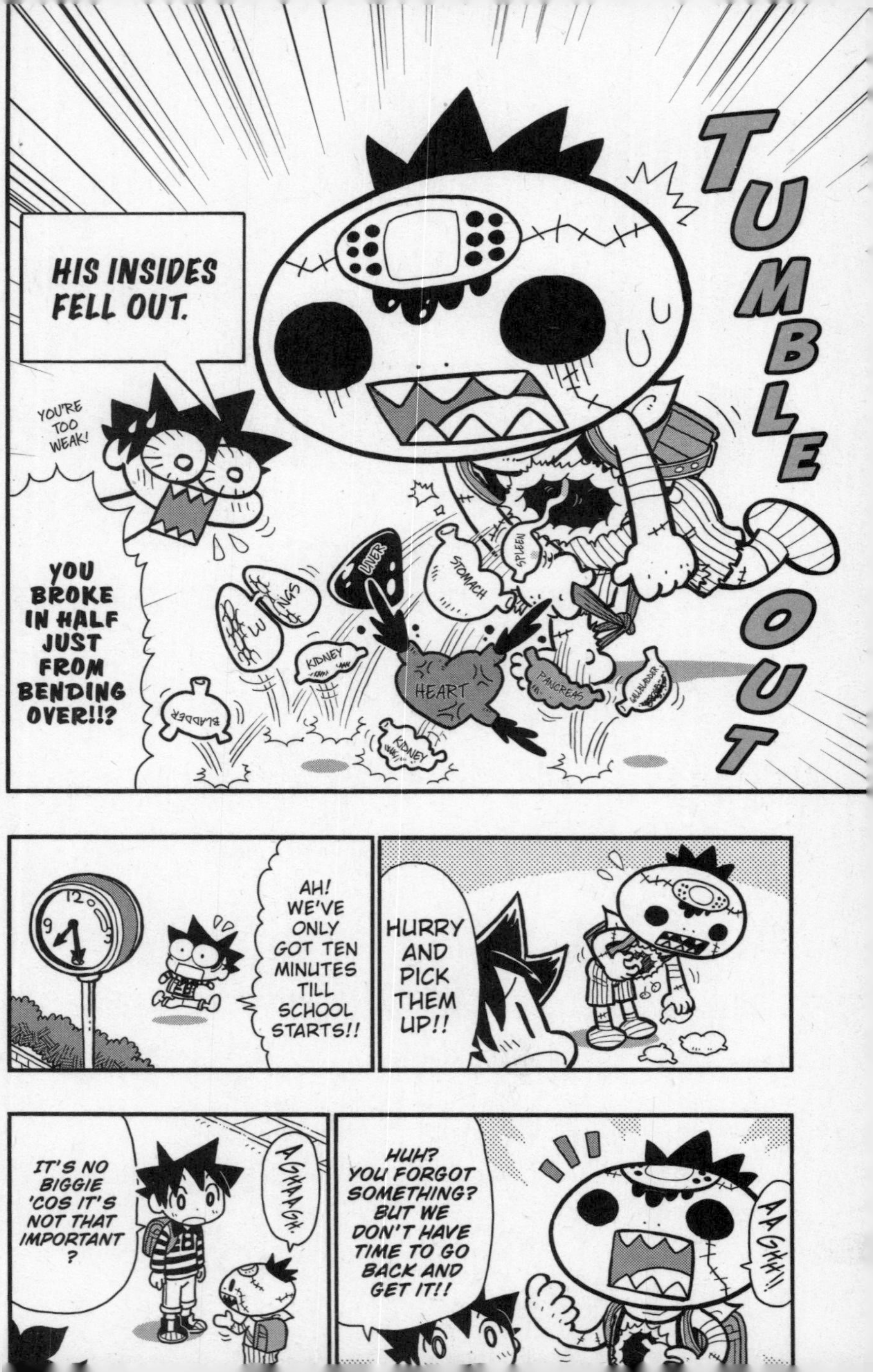
TUMBLE OUT
SPLEEN
STOMACH
LIVER
LUNGS
KIDNEY
HEART
PANCREAS
GALLBLADDER
KIDNEY
BLADDER
HIS INSIDES FELL OUT.
YOU'RE TOO WEAK!
YOU BROKE IN HALF JUST FROM BENDING OVER!!?
HURRY AND PICK THEM UP!!
AH! WE'VE ONLY GOT TEN MINUTES TILL SCHOOL STARTS!!
AAGHK!!
HUH? YOU FORGOT SOMETHING? BUT WE DON'T HAVE TIME TO GO BACK AND GET IT!!
AGHAAGH.
IT'S NO BIGGIE 'COS IT'S NOT THAT IMPORTANT?

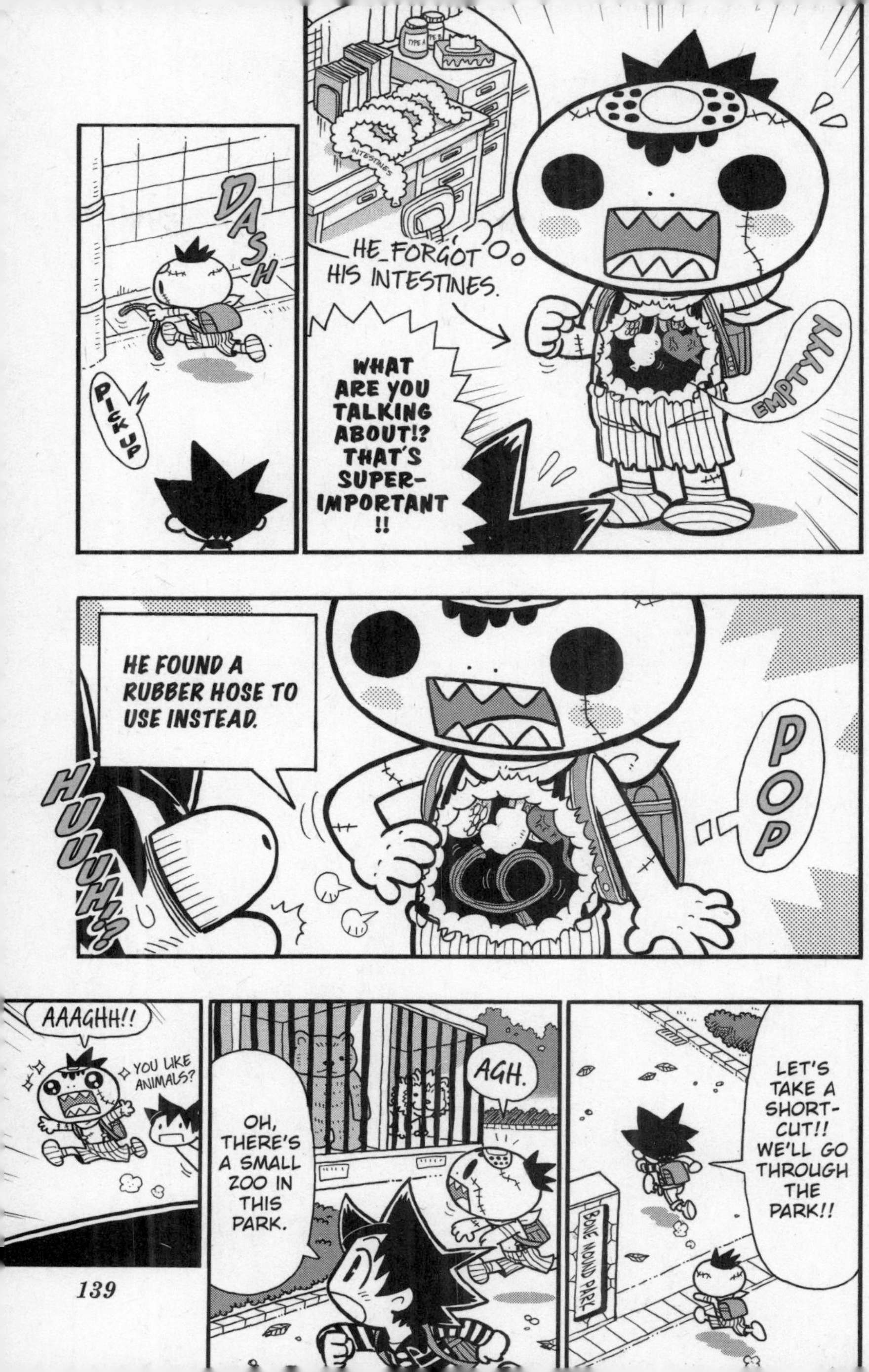

TYPE A
TYPE B
INTESTINES
HE FORGOT HIS INTESTINES.
EMPTYYY
WHAT ARE YOU TALKING ABOUT!? THAT'S SUPER-IMPORTANT!!
DASH
PICK UP
POP
HE FOUND A RUBBER HOSE TO USE INSTEAD.
HUUUH!?
LET'S TAKE A SHORT-CUT!! WE'LL GO THROUGH THE PARK!!
BONE MOUND PARK
AGH.
OH, THERE'S A SMALL ZOO IN THIS PARK.
AAAGHH!!
YOU LIKE ANIMALS?

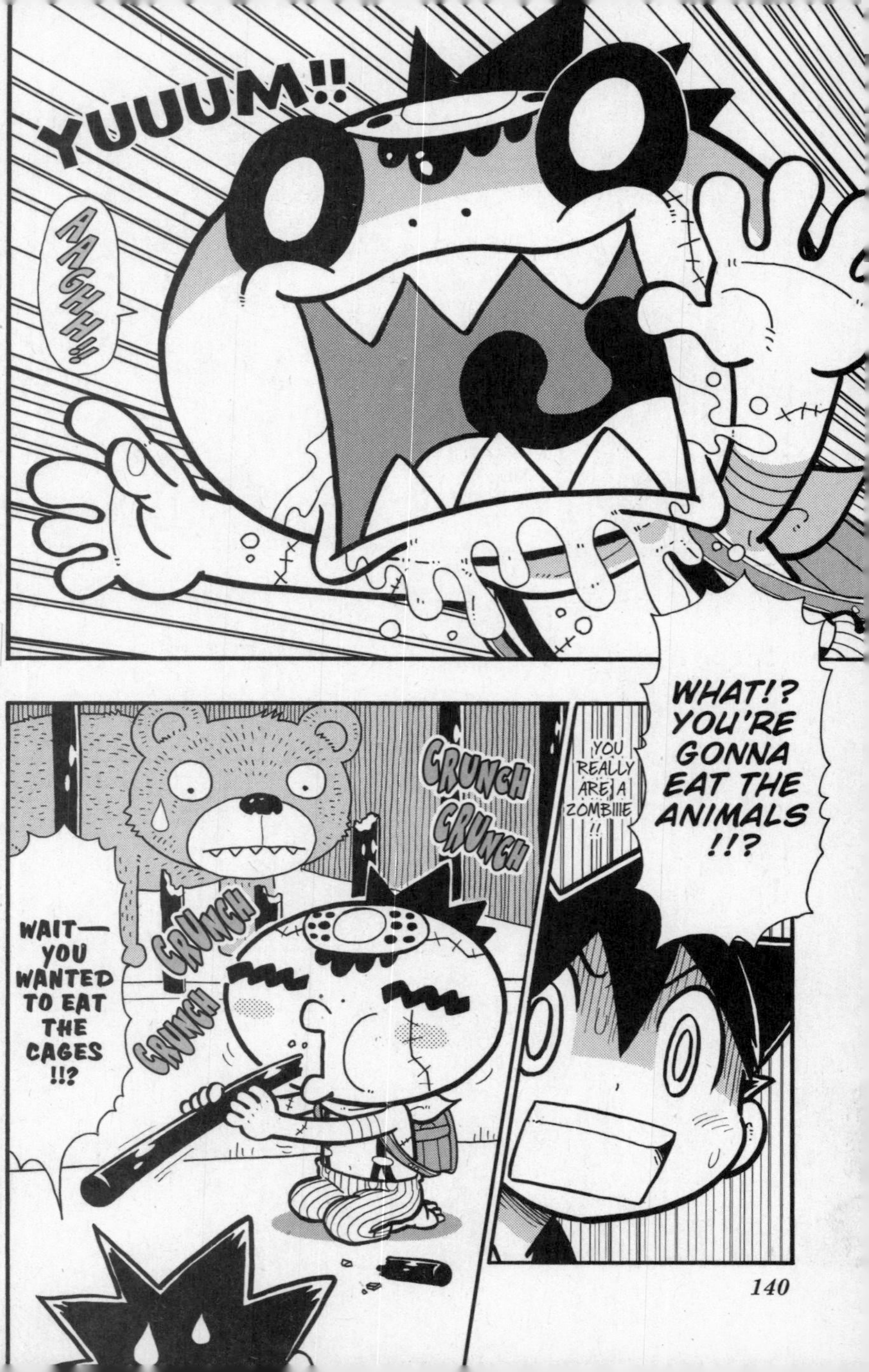
YUUUM!!
AAGHHH!!
WHAT!? YOU'RE GONNA EAT THE ANIMALS!!?
YOU REALLY ARE A ZOMBIIIE!!
CRUNCH
CRUNCH
CRUNCH
CRUNCH
WAIT— YOU WANTED TO EAT THE CAGES!!?

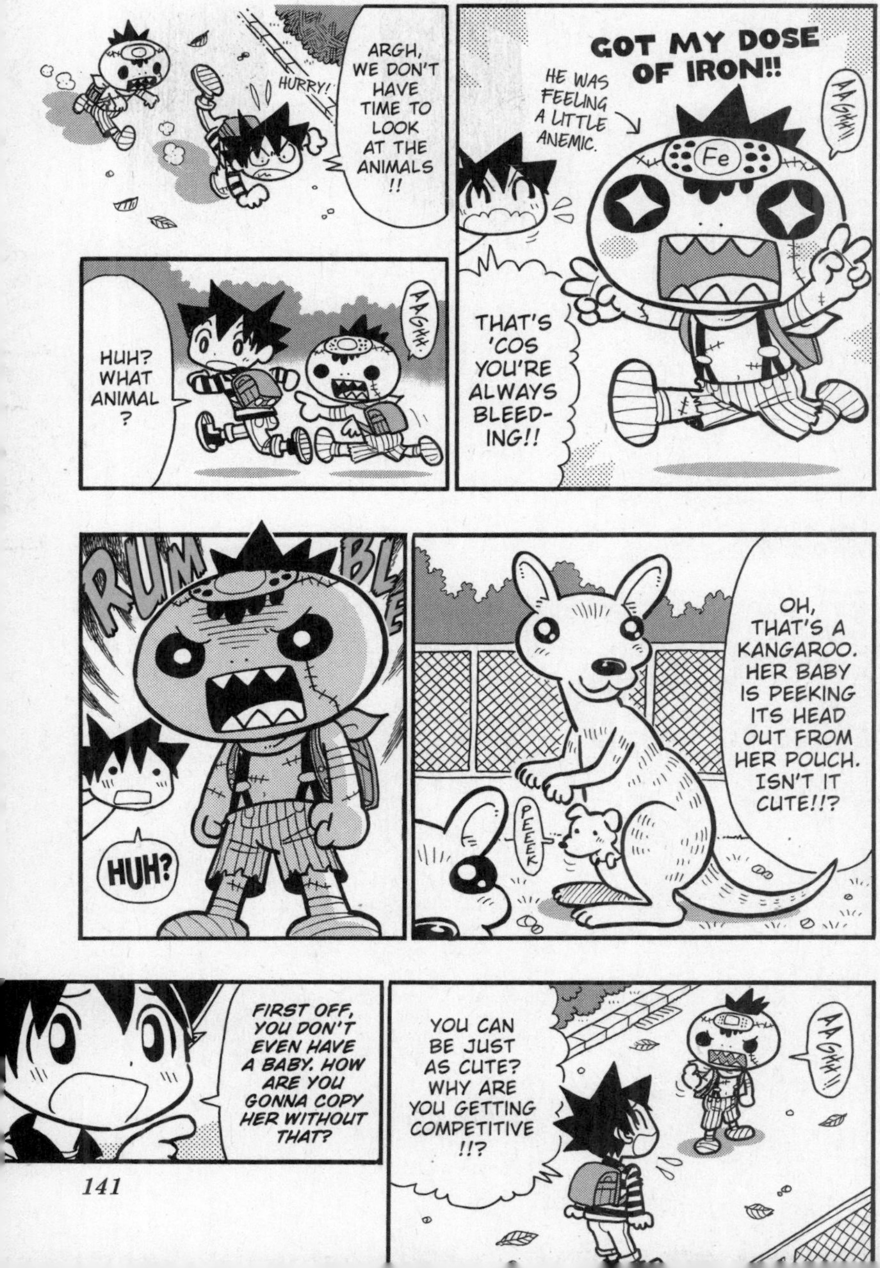
GOT MY DOSE OF IRON!!
AAGHH!!
HE WAS FEELING A LITTLE ANEMIC.
THAT'S 'COS YOU'RE ALWAYS BLEEDING!!
ARGH, WE DON'T HAVE TIME TO LOOK AT THE ANIMALS!!
HURRY!
AAGHH.
HUH? WHAT ANIMAL?
OH, THAT'S A KANGAROO. HER BABY IS PEEKING ITS HEAD OUT FROM HER POUCH. ISN'T IT CUTE!!?
PEEEK
RUMBLE
HUH?
AAGHH!!
YOU CAN BE JUST AS CUTE? WHY ARE YOU GETTING COMPETITIVE!!?
FIRST OFF, YOU DON'T EVEN HAVE A BABY. HOW ARE YOU GONNA COPY HER WITHOUT THAT?

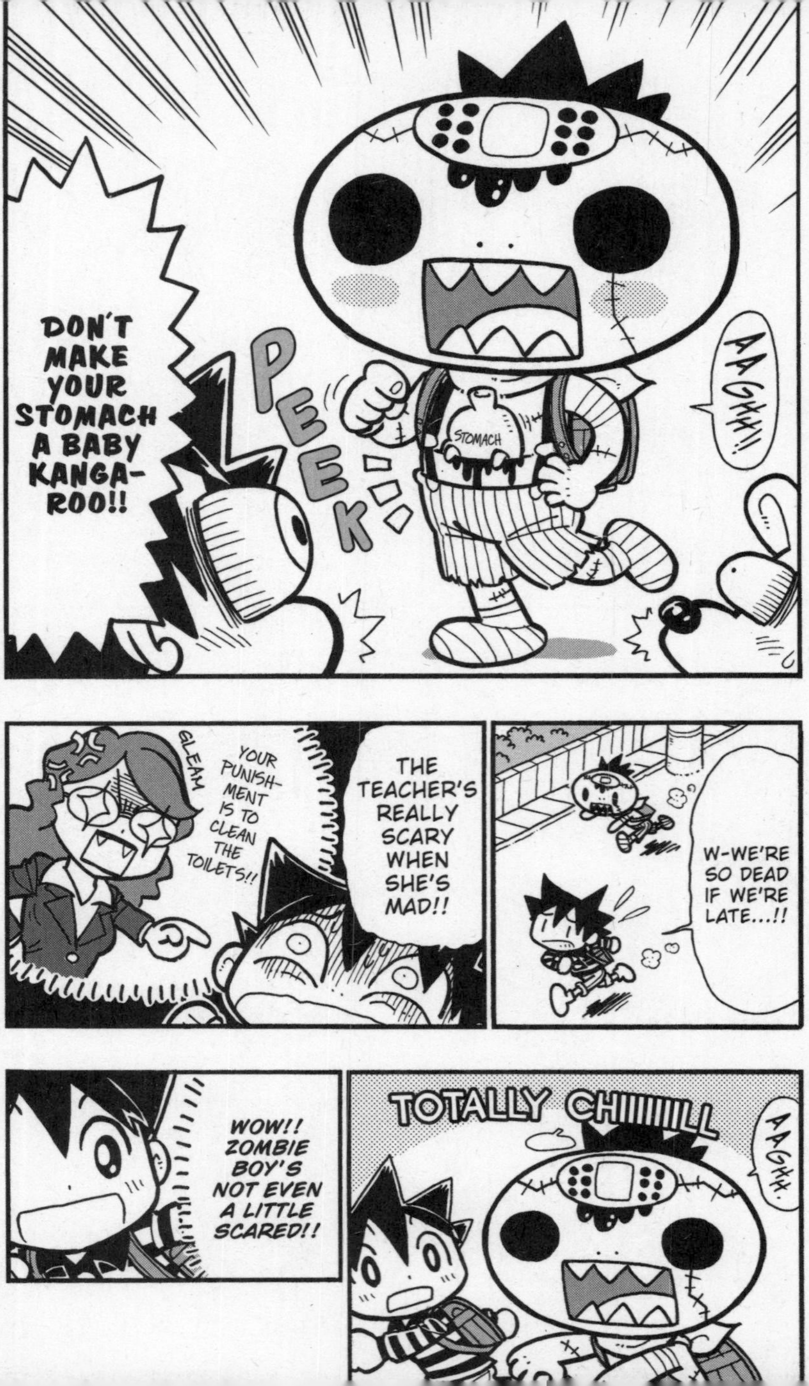
AAGHH!!
PEEK
STOMACH
DON'T MAKE YOUR STOMACH A BABY KANGA-ROO!!
W-WE'RE SO DEAD IF WE'RE LATE...!!
THE TEACHER'S REALLY SCARY WHEN SHE'S MAD!!
YOUR PUNISH-MENT IS TO CLEAN THE TOILETS!!
GLEAM
TOTALLY CHIIIIIIILL
AAGHH.
WOW!! ZOMBIE BOY'S NOT EVEN A LITTLE SCARED!!

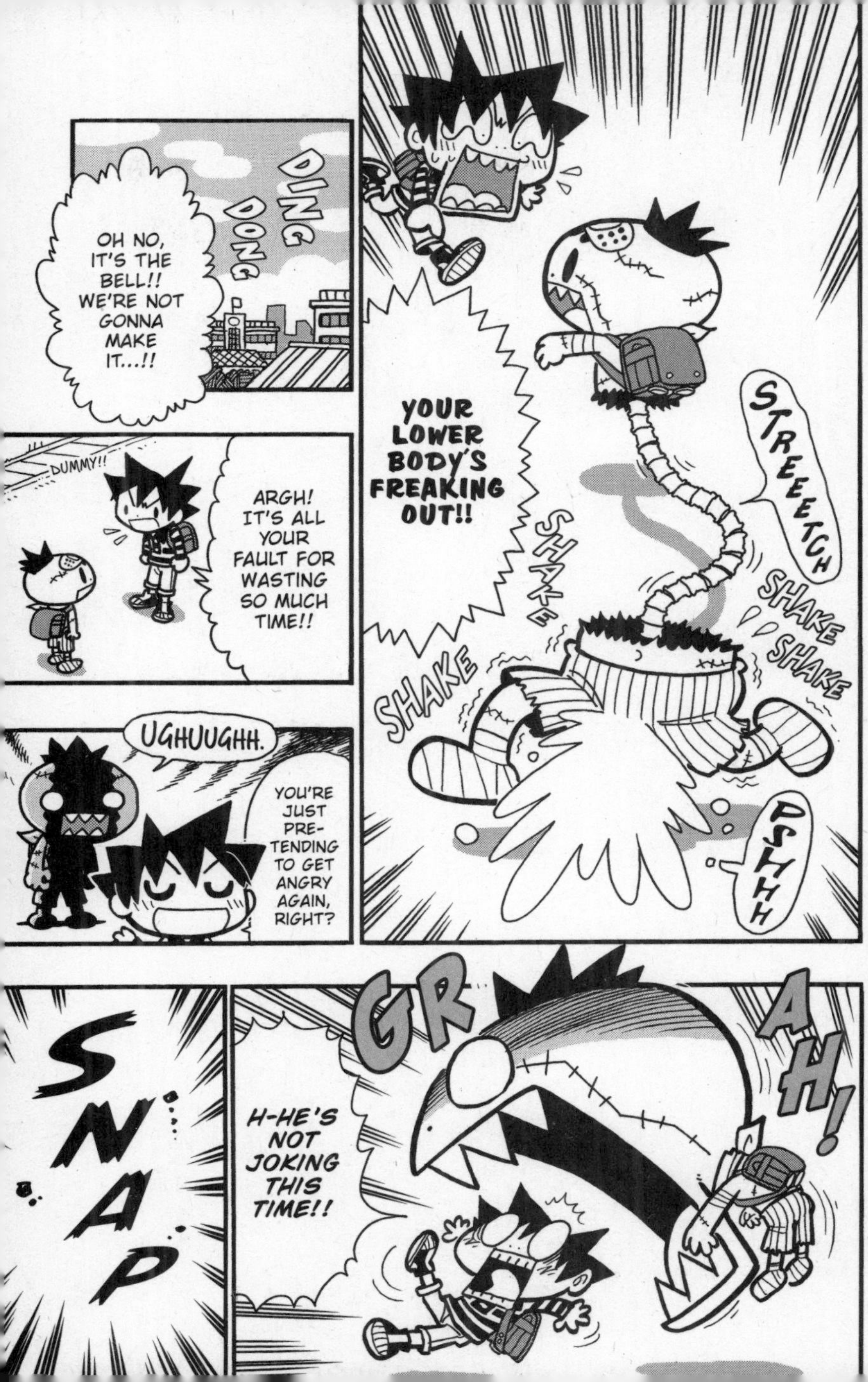
STREEETCH
SHAKE SHAKE
SHAKE
YOUR LOWER BODY'S FREAKING OUT!!
SHAKE
SHAKE
PSHHH
DING DONG
OH NO, IT'S THE BELL!! WE'RE NOT GONNA MAKE IT...!!
ARGH! IT'S ALL YOUR FAULT FOR WASTING SO MUCH TIME!!
DUMMY!!
UGHUUGHH.
YOU'RE JUST PRE-TENDING TO GET ANGRY AGAIN, RIGHT?
GRAH!
H-HE'S NOT JOKING THIS TIME!!
SNAP

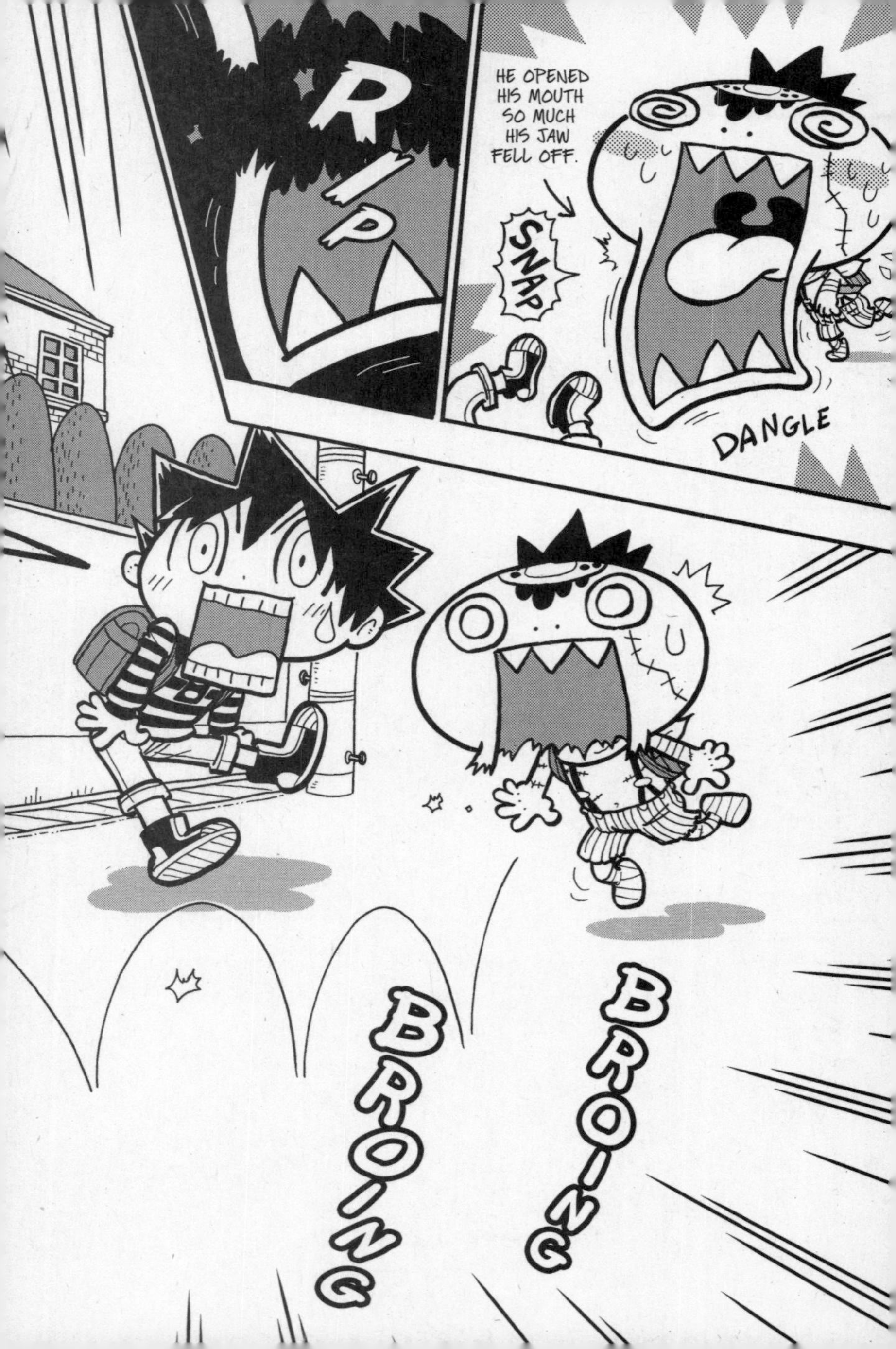
HE OPENED HIS MOUTH SO MUCH HIS JAW FELL OFF.
SNAP
DANGLE
RIP
BROING
BROING

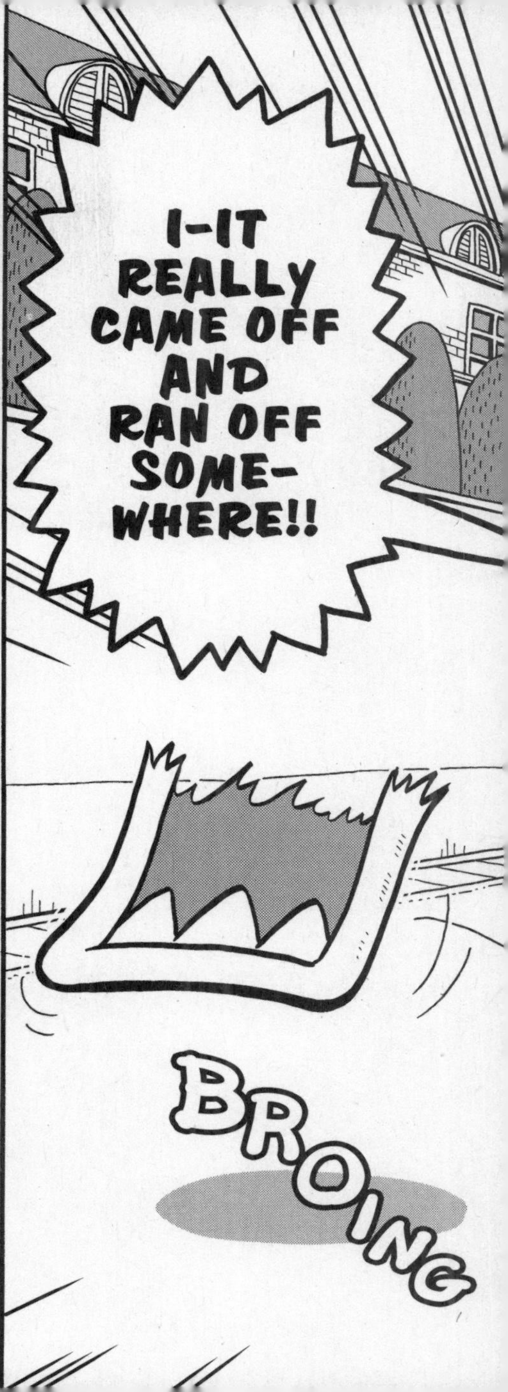
I-IT REALLY CAME OFF AND RAN OFF SOME-WHERE!!
BROING

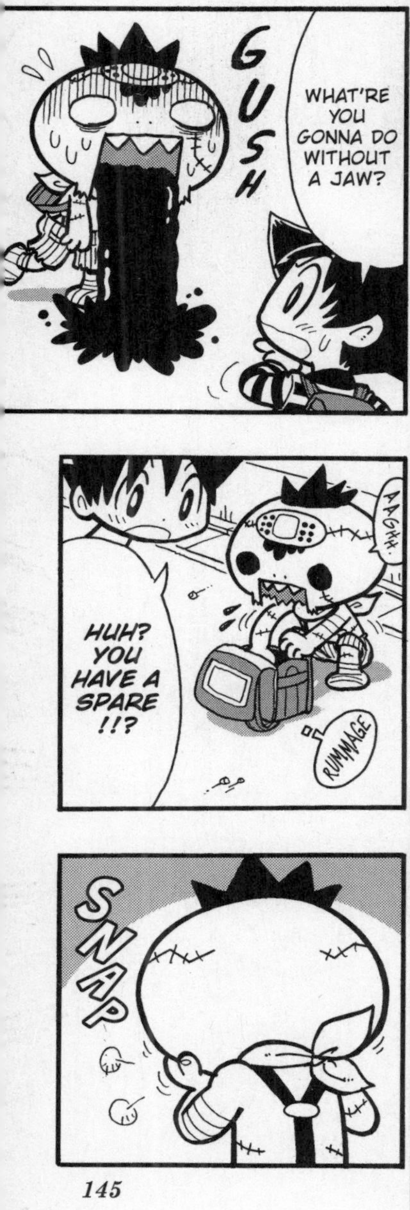
WHAT'RE YOU GONNA DO WITHOUT A JAW?
GUSH
AAGHH.
HUH? YOU HAVE A SPARE !!?
RUMMAGE
SNAP

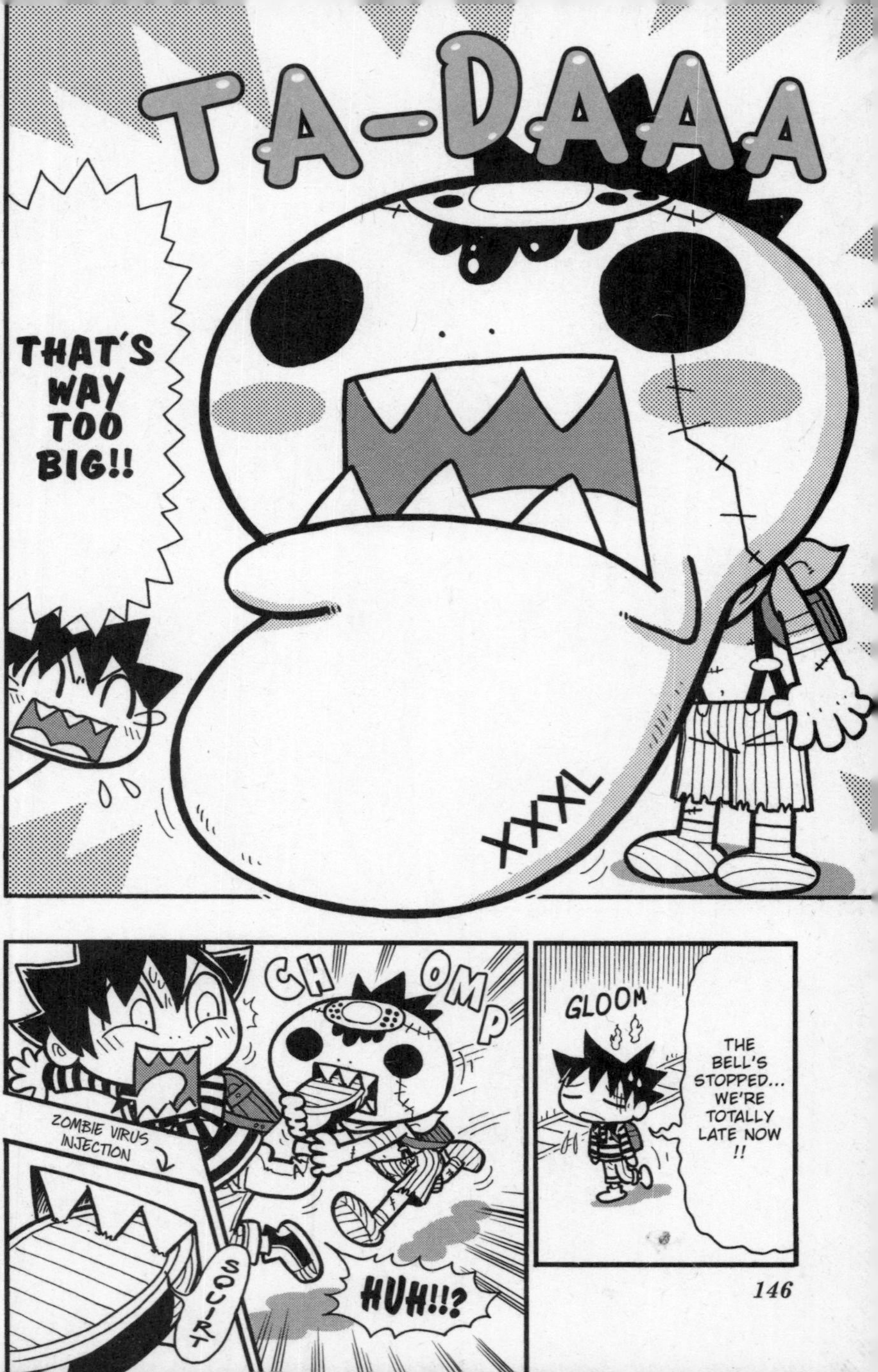
TA-DAAA
THAT'S WAY TOO BIG!!
XXXL
GLOOM
THE BELL'S STOPPED... WE'RE TOTALLY LATE NOW !!
CH OMP
ZOMBIE VIRUS INJECTION
HUH!!?
SQUIRT

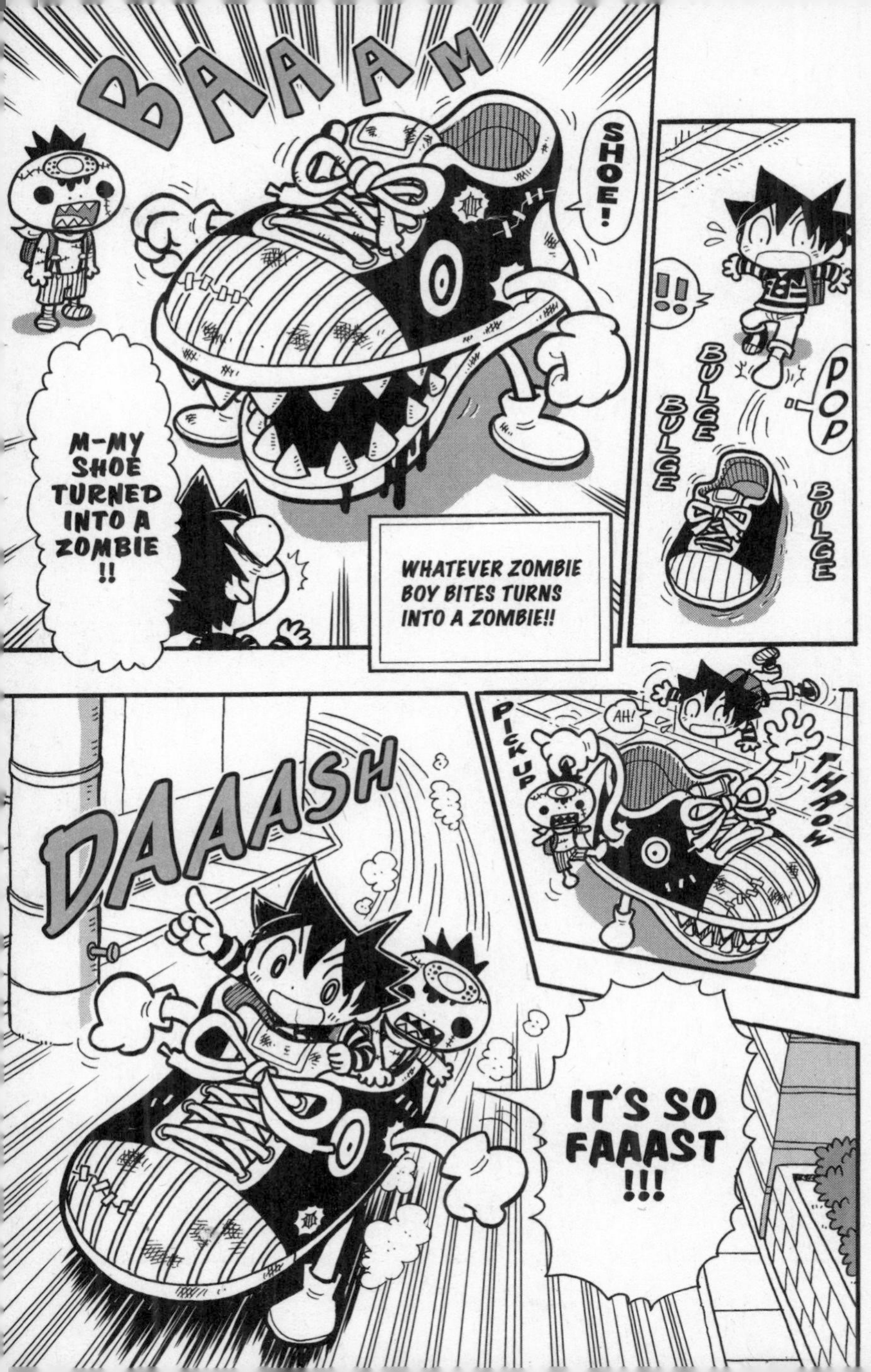
!!
POP
BULGE
BULGE
BULGE
BAAAM
SHOE!
M-MY SHOE TURNED INTO A ZOMBIE !!
WHATEVER ZOMBIE BOY BITES TURNS INTO A ZOMBIE!!
AH!
PICK UP
THROW
DAAASH
IT'S SO FAAAST !!!

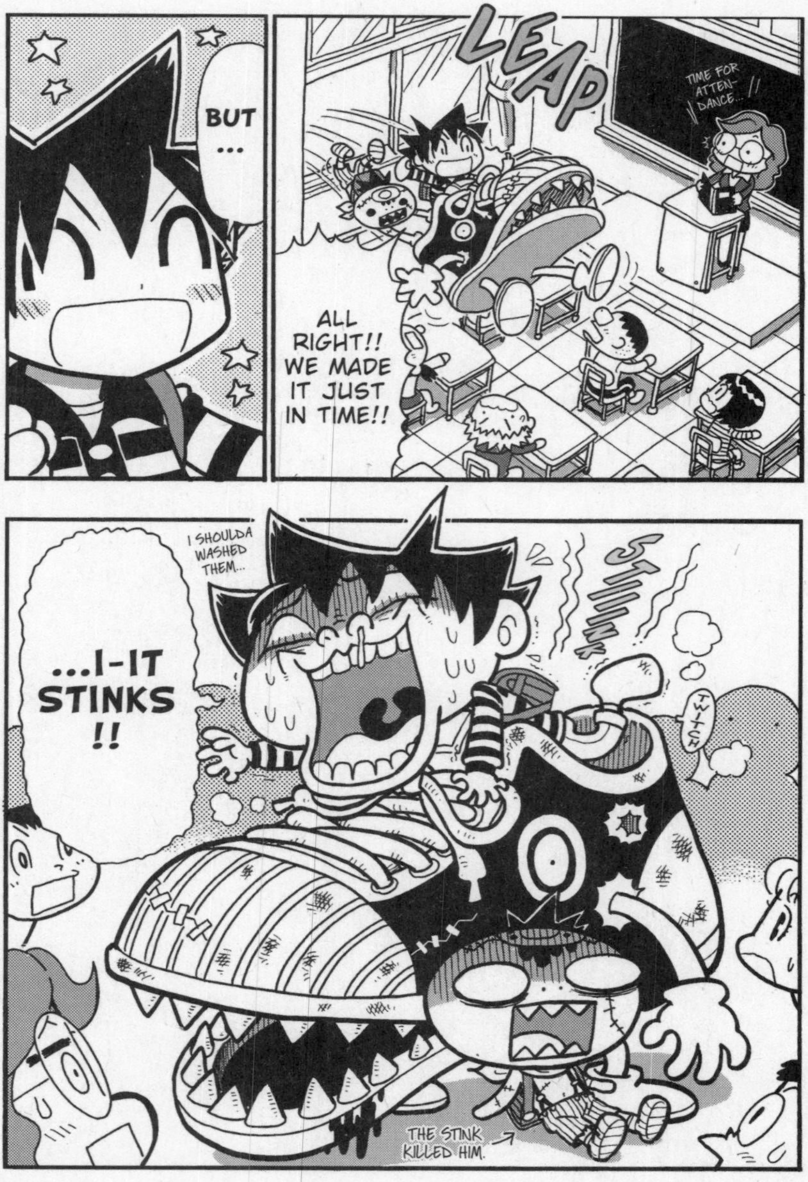
LEAP
TIME FOR ATTEN-DANCE...
ALL RIGHT!! WE MADE IT JUST IN TIME!!
BUT ...
STIIINK
TWITCH
I SHOULDA WASHED THEM...
...I-IT STINKS!!
THE STINK KILLED HIM.

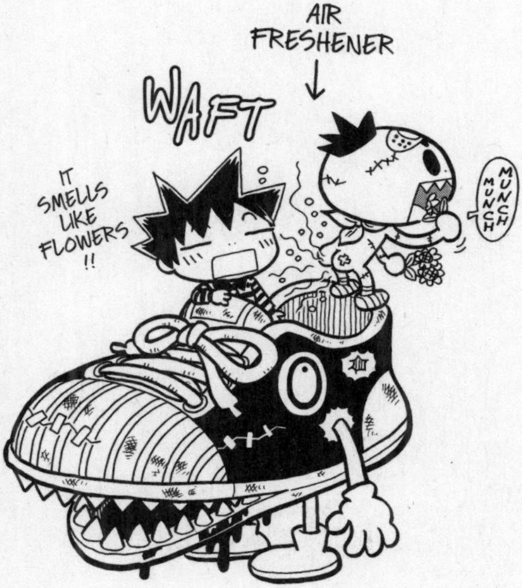
AIR FRESHENER
WAFT
IT SMELLS LIKE FLOWERS!!
MUNCH MUNCH

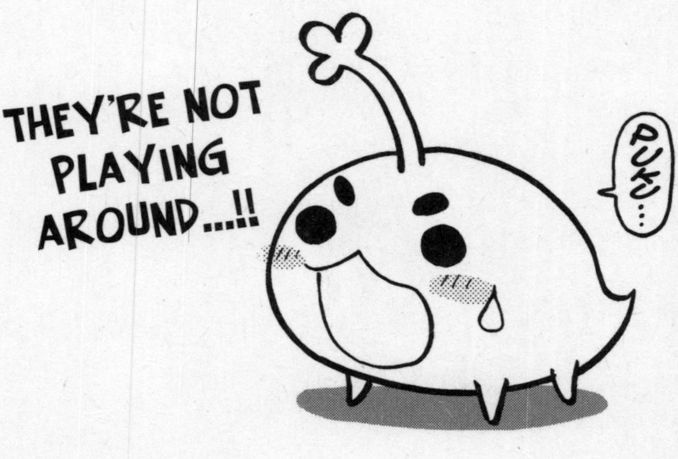
THEY'RE NOT PLAYING AROUND...!!
PUKU...

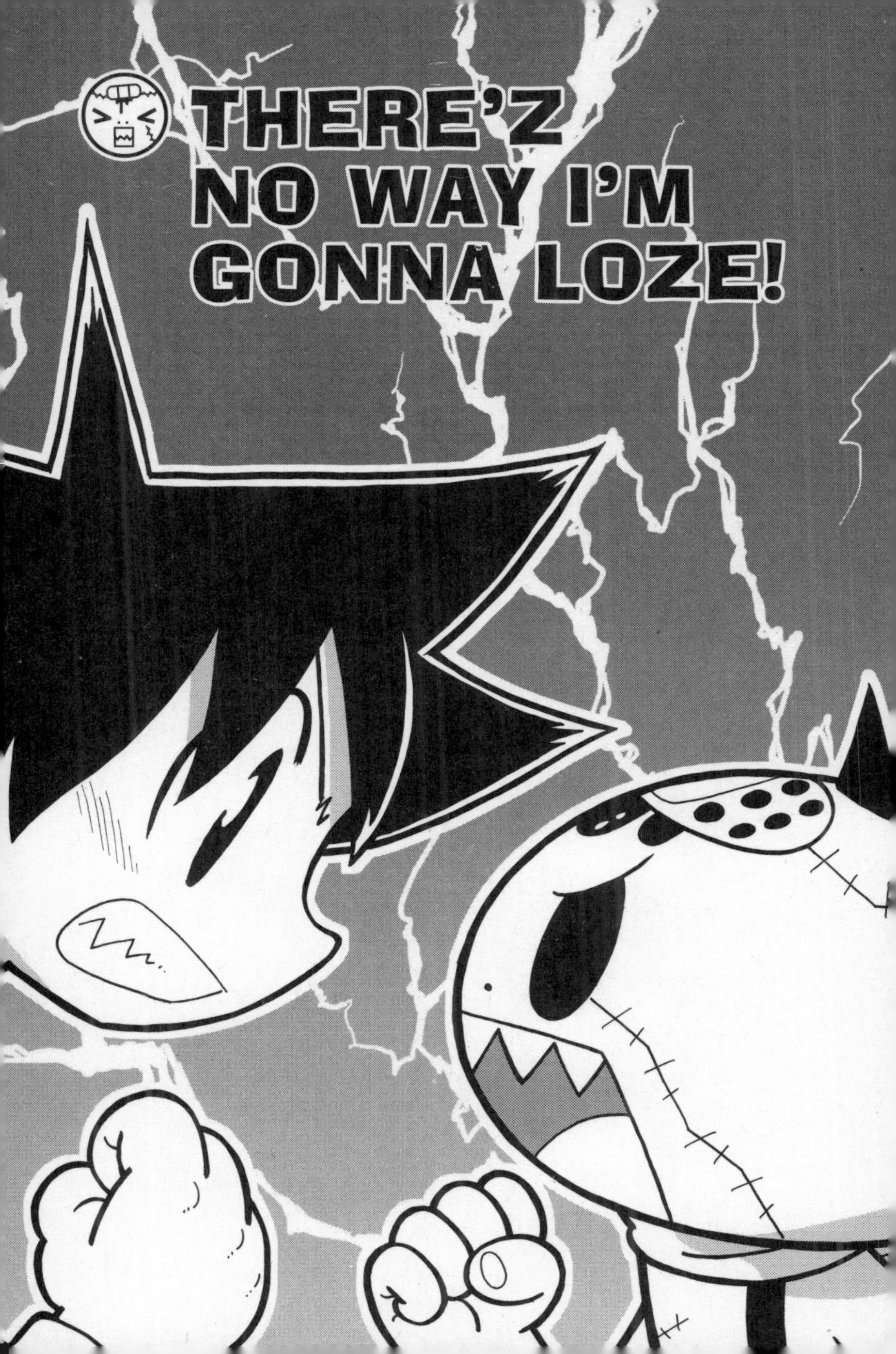
THERE'Z NO WAY I'M GONNA LOZE!

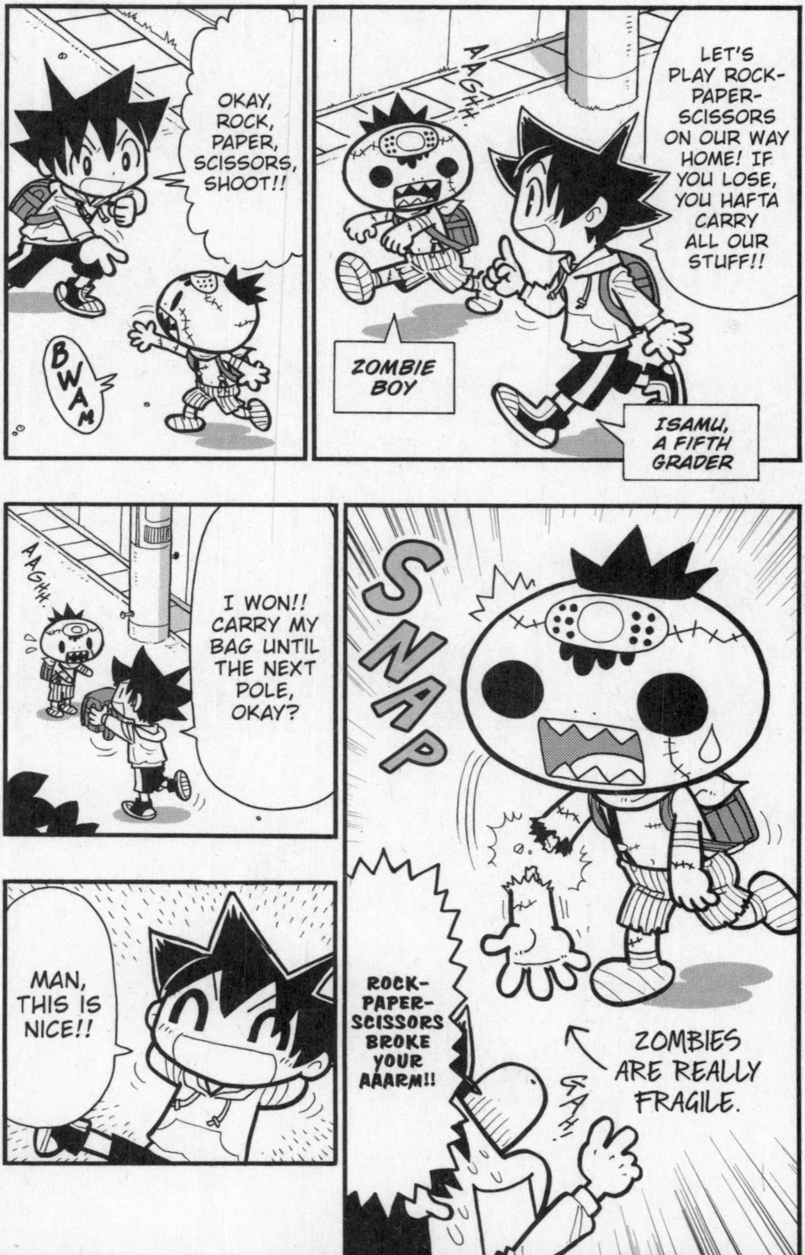
AAGHH.
LET'S PLAY ROCK-PAPER-SCISSORS ON OUR WAY HOME! IF YOU LOSE, YOU HAFTA CARRY ALL OUR STUFF!!
ZOMBIE BOY
ISAMU, A FIFTH GRADER
OKAY, ROCK, PAPER, SCISSORS, SHOOT!!
BWAM
SNAP
ZOMBIES ARE REALLY FRAGILE.
GAH!
ROCK-PAPER-SCISSORS BROKE YOUR AAARM!!
AAGHH.
I WON!! CARRY MY BAG UNTIL THE NEXT POLE, OKAY?
MAN, THIS IS NICE!!

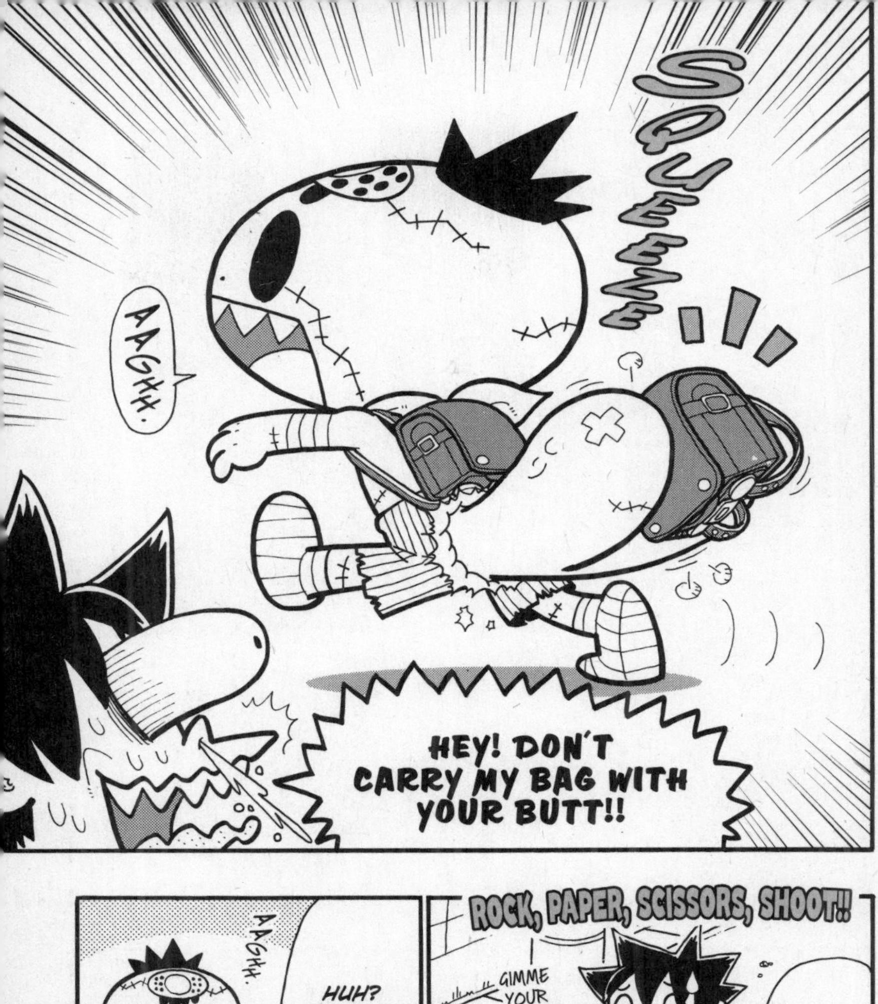
SQUEEZE
AAGHH.
HEY! DON'T CARRY MY BAG WITH YOUR BUTT!!
ROCK, PAPER, SCISSORS, SHOOT!!
OH, I LOST THIS TIME.
GIMME YOUR BACKPACK.
HUH? YOU HAVE OTHER STUFF TOO...!?
AAGHH.

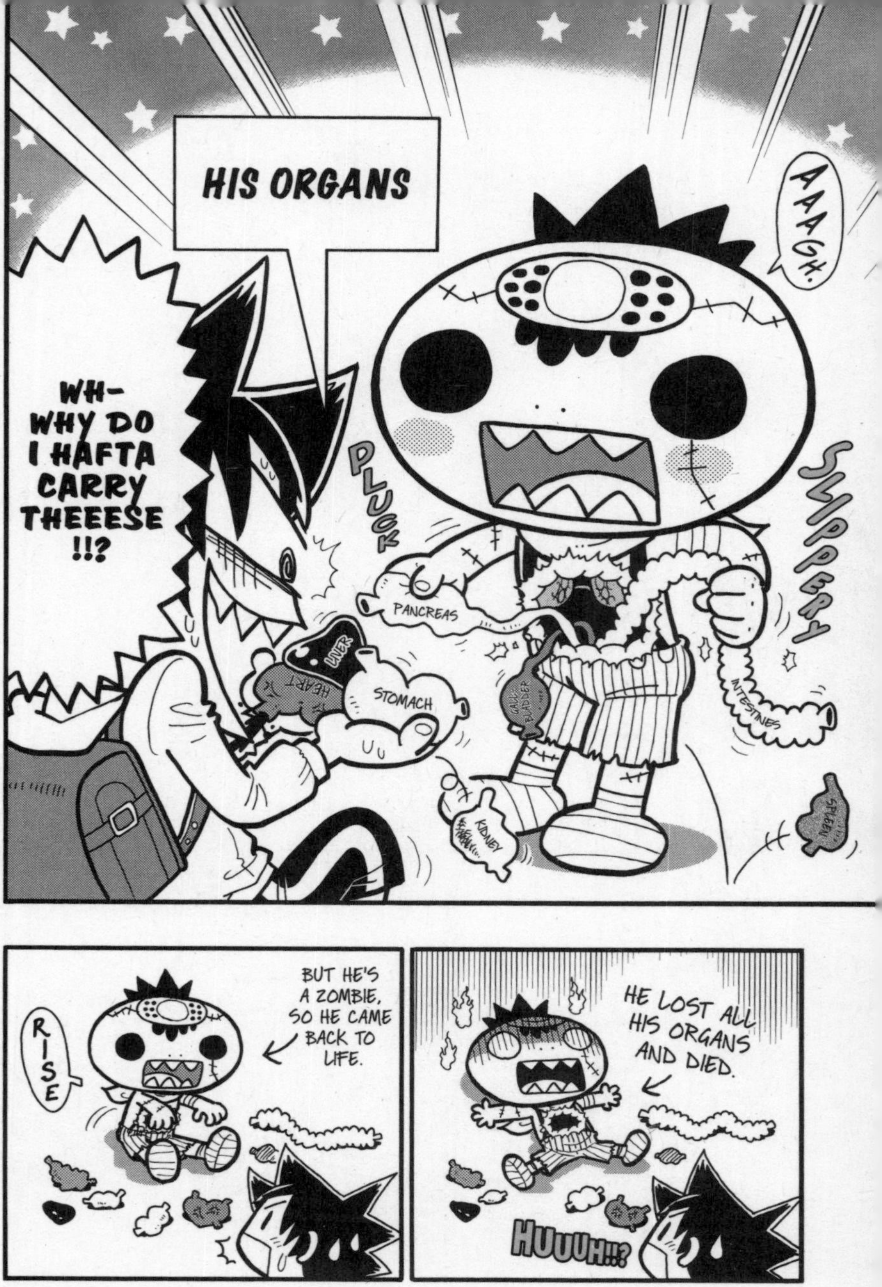

AAAGH.
HIS ORGANS
SLIPPERY
PLUCK
WH- WHY DO I HAFTA CARRY THEEESE !!?
PANCREAS
INTESTINES
GALL-BLADDER
LIVER
HEART
STOMACH
SPLEEN
KIDNEY
HE LOST ALL HIS ORGANS AND DIED.
HUUUH!!?
BUT HE'S A ZOMBIE, SO HE CAME BACK TO LIFE.
RISE

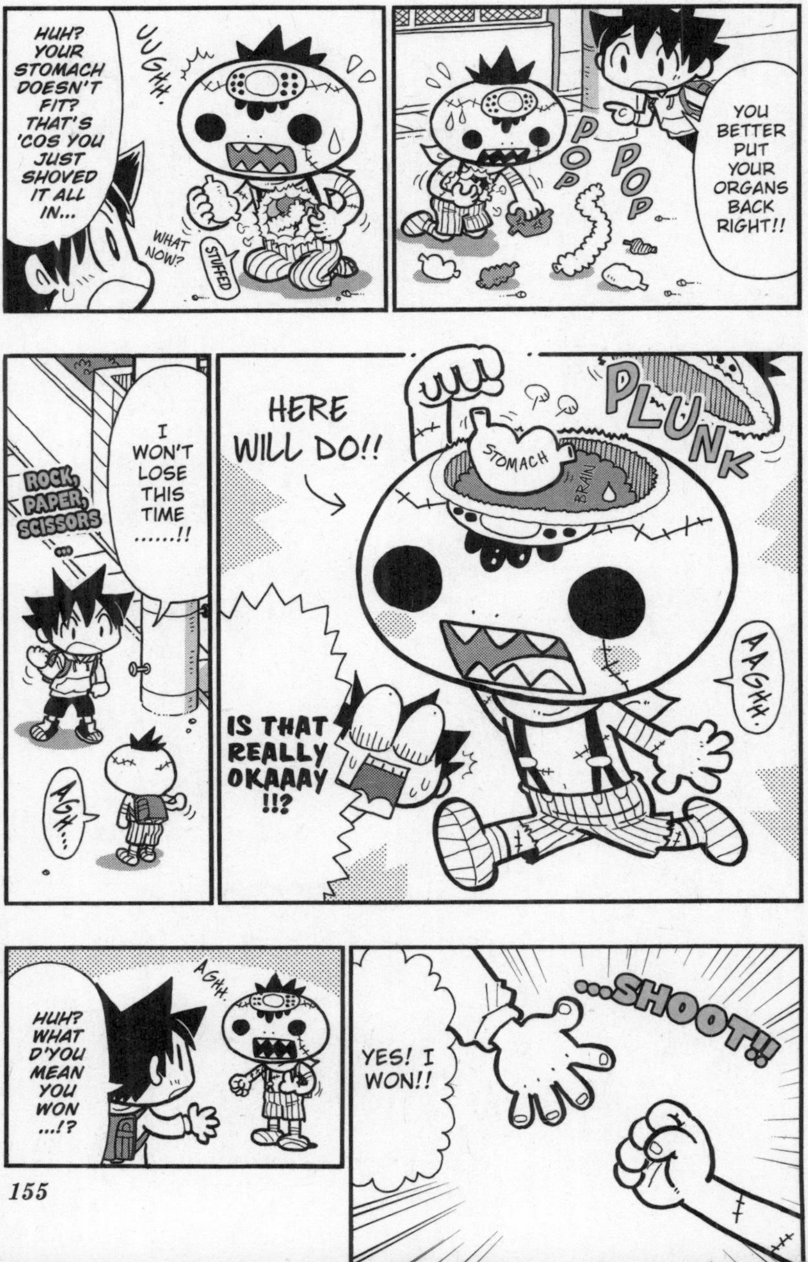

POP
POP
POP
YOU BETTER PUT YOUR ORGANS BACK RIGHT!!
HUH? YOUR STOMACH DOESN'T FIT? THAT'S 'COS YOU JUST SHOVED IT ALL IN...
UUGHH.
WHAT NOW?
STUFFED
PLUNK
HERE WILL DO!!
STOMACH
BRAIN
AAGHH.
IS THAT REALLY OKAAAY!!?
I WON'T LOSE THIS TIME......!!
ROCK, PAPER, SCISSORS...
AGH...
...SHOOT!!
YES! I WON!!
AGHH.
HUH? WHAT D'YOU MEAN YOU WON...!?

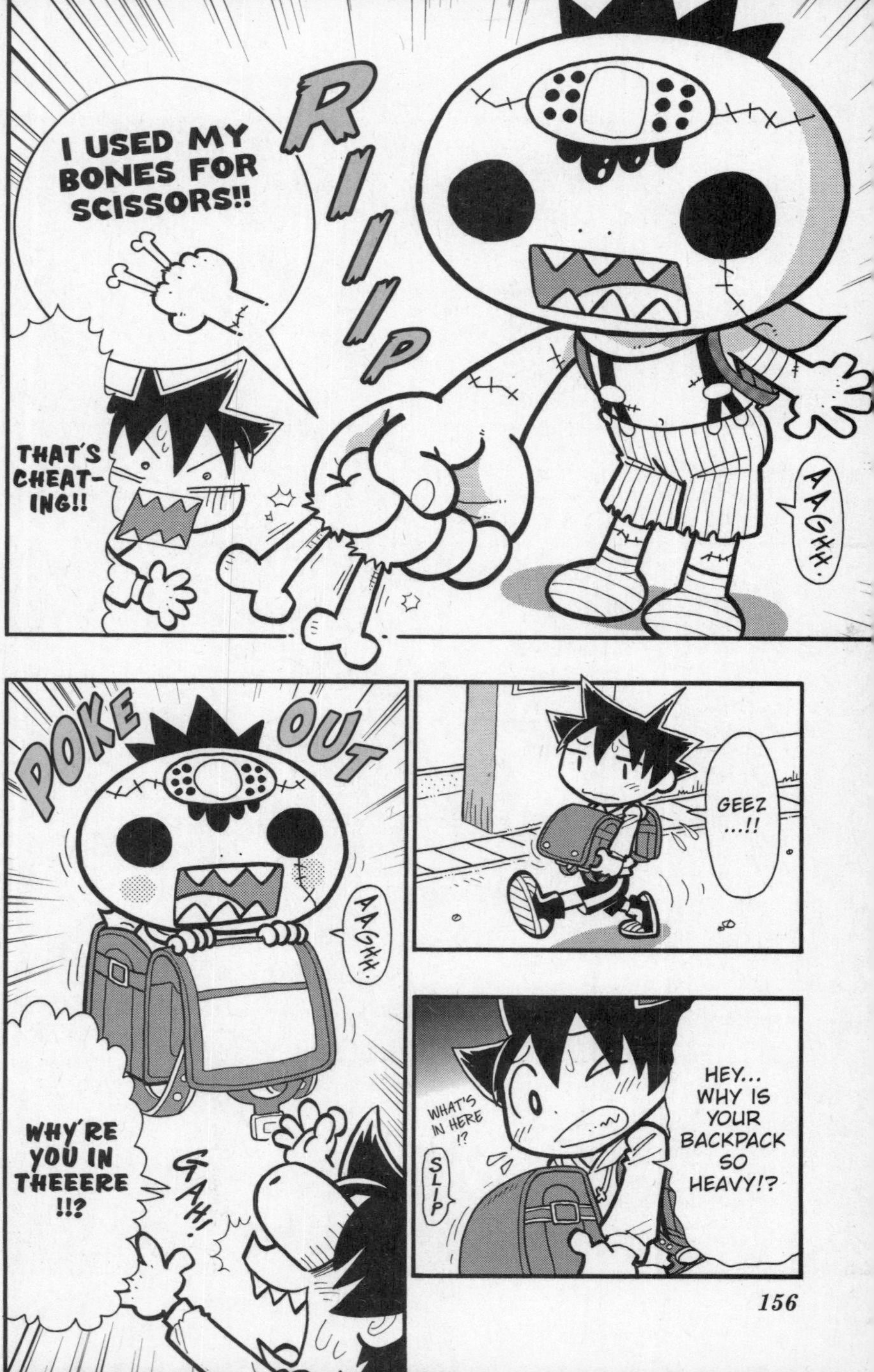
RIIP
I USED MY BONES FOR SCISSORS!!
AAGHH.
THAT'S CHEATING!!
GEEZ ...!!
HEY... WHY IS YOUR BACKPACK SO HEAVY!?
WHAT'S IN HERE !?
SLIP
POKE OUT
AAGHH.
WHY'RE YOU IN THEEERE !!?
GAH!

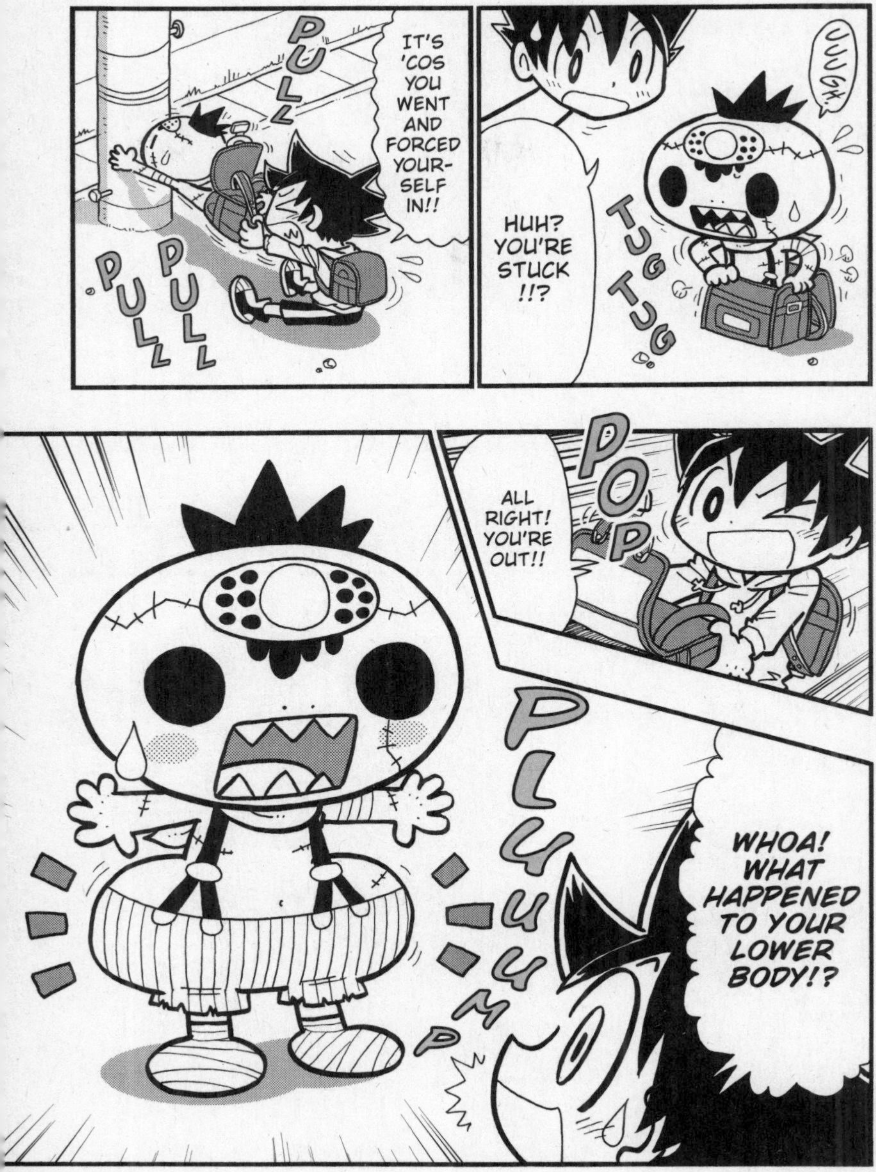
UUUGH.
TUG TUG
HUH? YOU'RE STUCK!!?
IT'S 'COS YOU WENT AND FORCED YOURSELF IN!!
PULL
PULL PULL
POP
ALL RIGHT! YOU'RE OUT!!
WHOA! WHAT HAPPENED TO YOUR LOWER BODY!?
PLUUUUMP

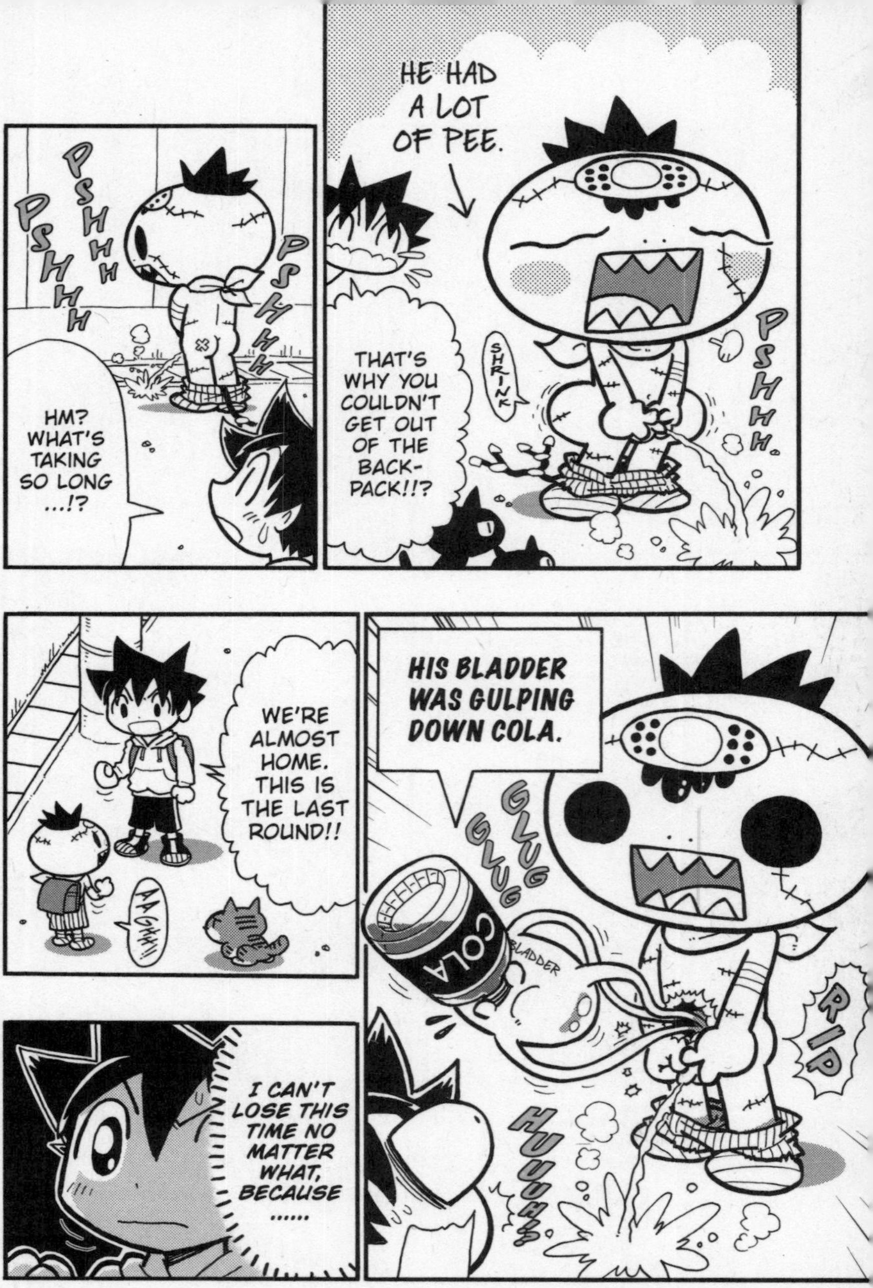
HE HAD A LOT OF PEE.
THAT'S WHY YOU COULDN'T GET OUT OF THE BACK-PACK!!?
SHRINK
PSHHH
PSHHH
PSHHH
PSHHH
HM? WHAT'S TAKING SO LONG ...!?
HIS BLADDER WAS GULPING DOWN COLA.
GLUG GLUG
COLA
BLADDER
RIP
HUUUUH!?
WE'RE ALMOST HOME. THIS IS THE LAST ROUND!!
AAGH!!
I CAN'T LOSE THIS TIME NO MATTER WHAT, BECAUSE ......

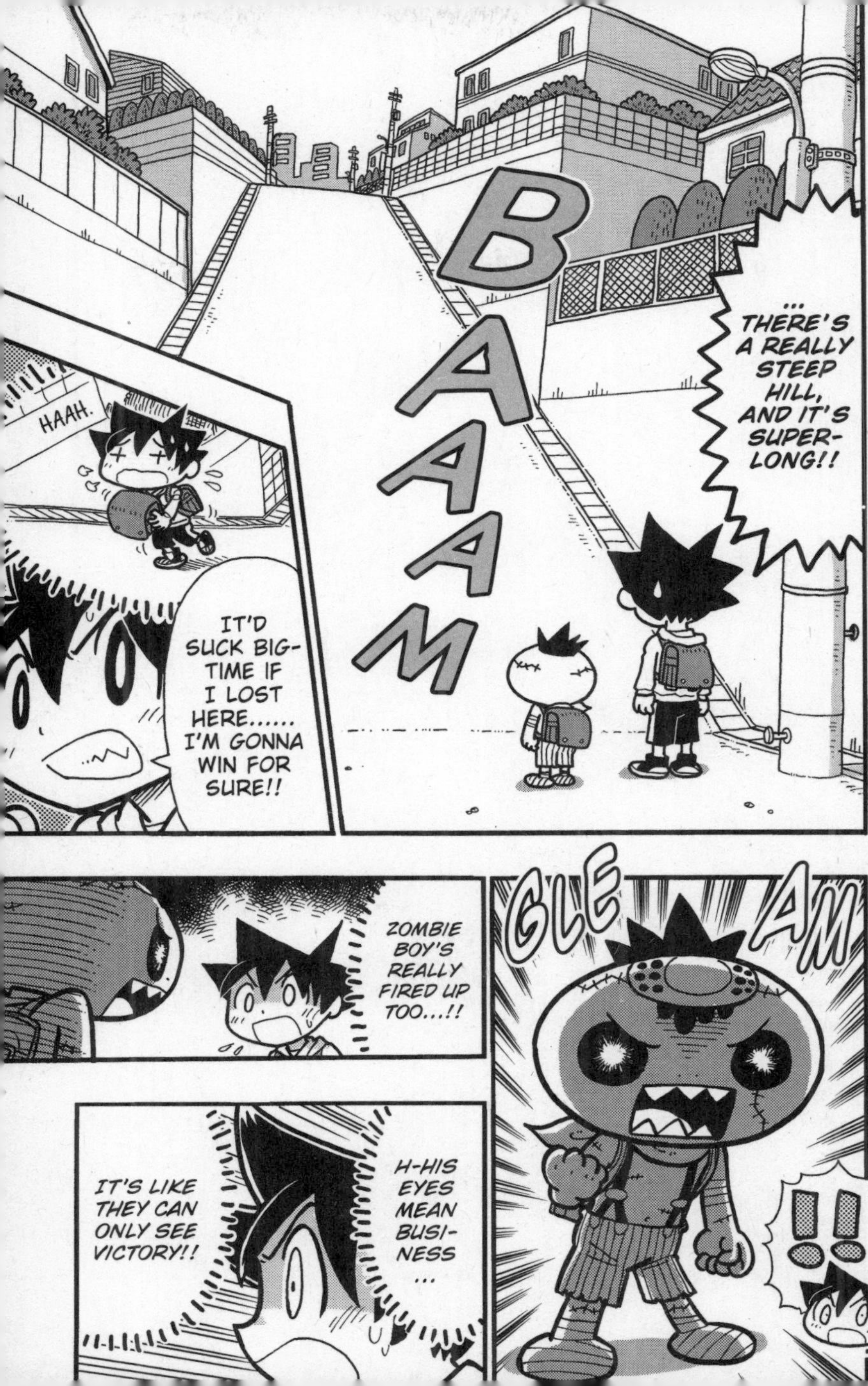

... THERE'S A REALLY STEEP HILL, AND IT'S SUPER-LONG!!
BAAAAM
HAAH.
IT'D SUCK BIG-TIME IF I LOST HERE...... I'M GONNA WIN FOR SURE!!
GLEAM
!!
ZOMBIE BOY'S REALLY FIRED UP TOO...!!
H-HIS EYES MEAN BUSINESS...
IT'S LIKE THEY CAN ONLY SEE VICTORY!!

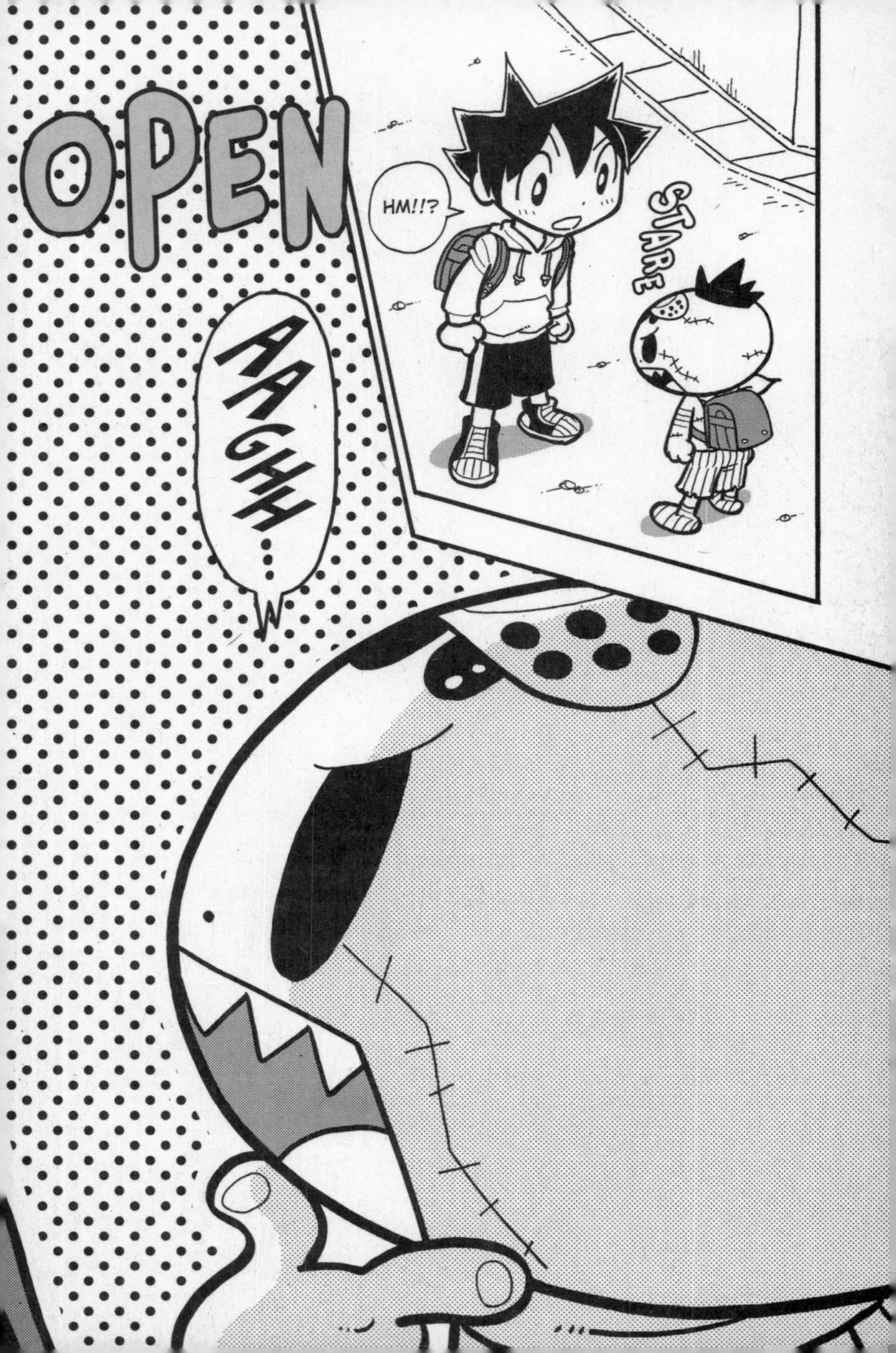
STARE
HM!!?
OPEN
AAGHH

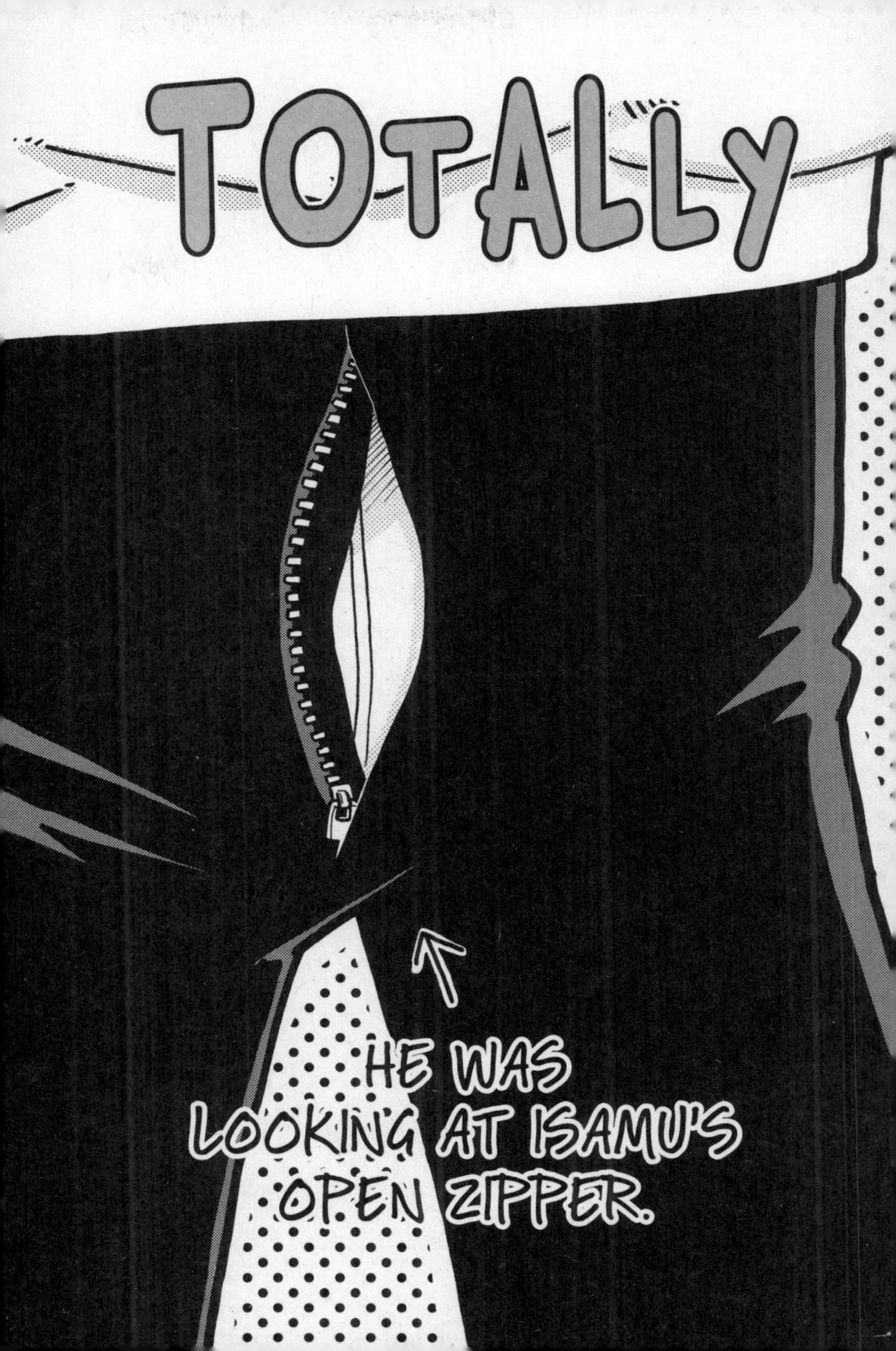
TOTALLY
HE WAS LOOKING AT ISAMU'S OPEN ZIPPER.

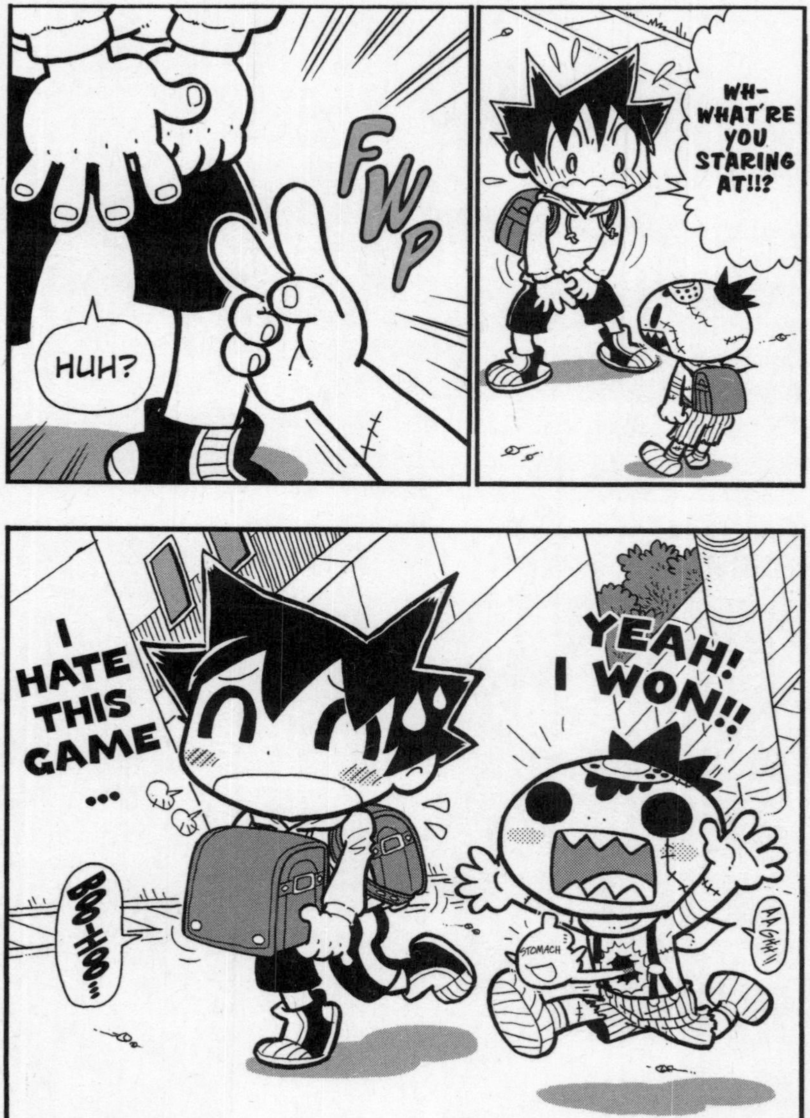
WH- WHAT'RE YOU STARING AT!!?
FWP
HUH?
YEAH! I WON!!
I HATE THIS GAME...
AAGHH!!
STOMACH
BOO-HOO...

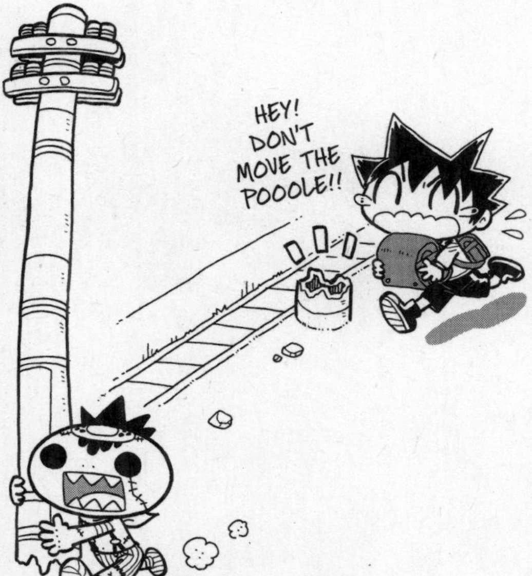
HEY! DON'T MOVE THE POOOLE!!

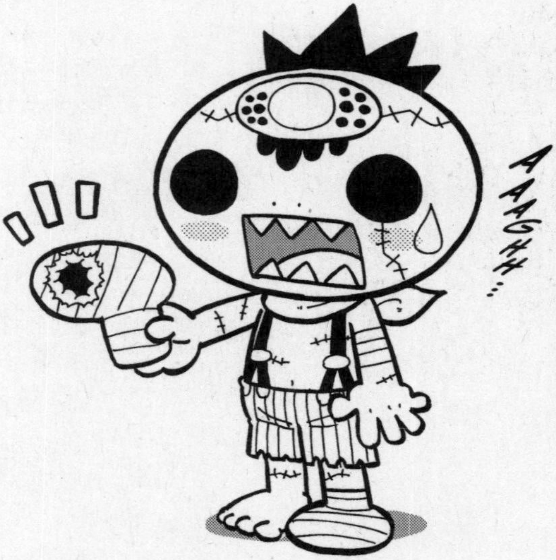
AAAGHH...

A ZTEP INTO ZOMETHING ZHOCKING!

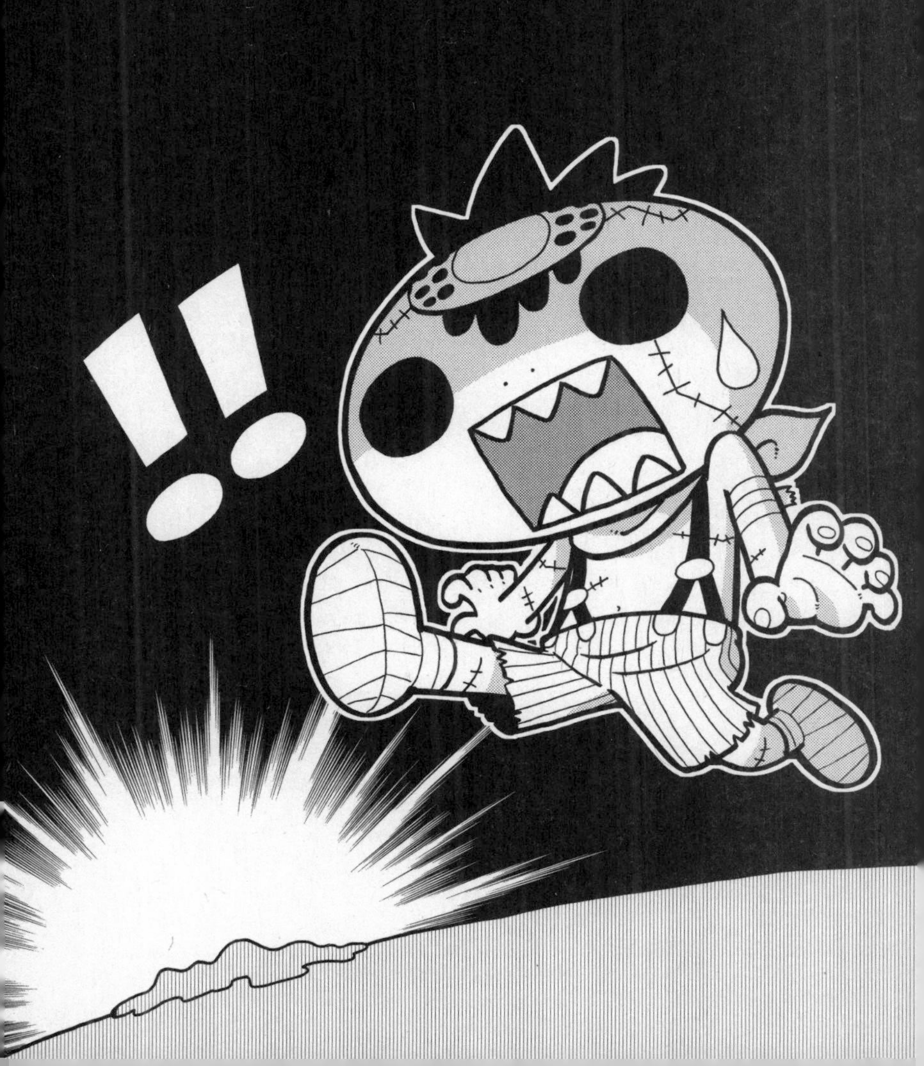
!!

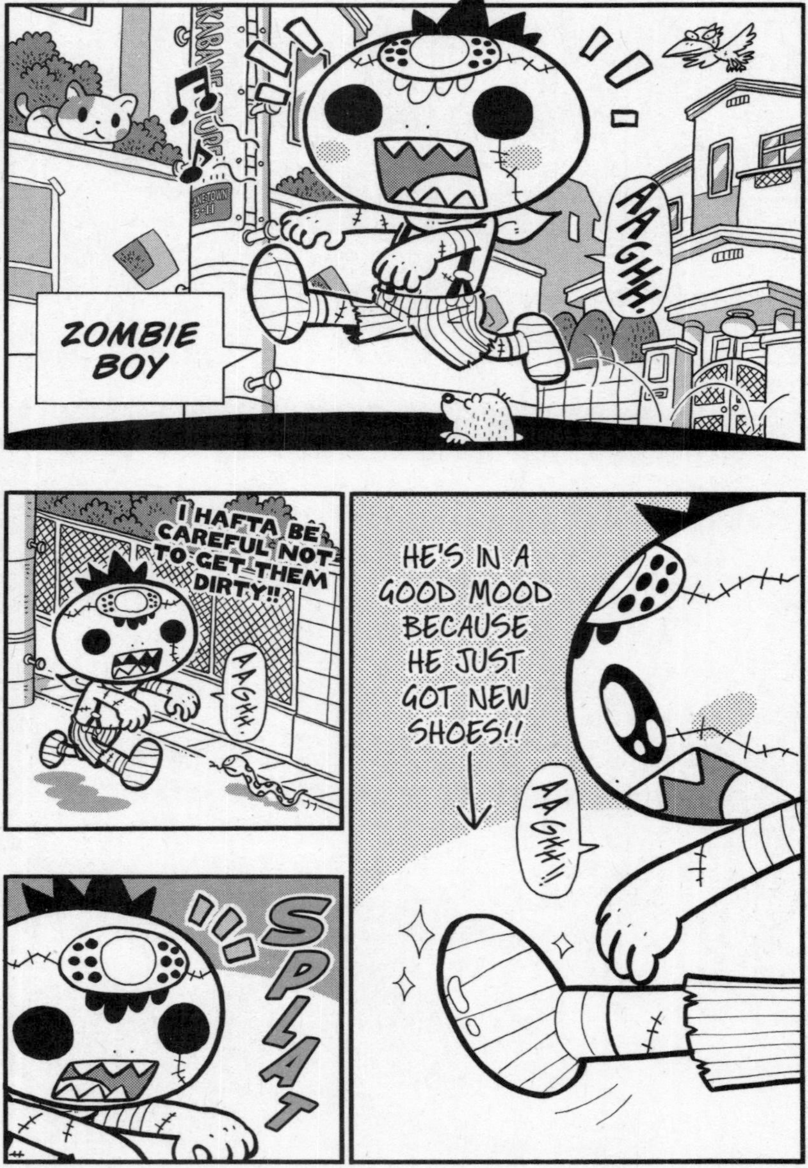

ZOMBIE BOY
AAGHH.
HE'S IN A GOOD MOOD BECAUSE HE JUST GOT NEW SHOES!!
AAGHH!!
I HAFTA BE CAREFUL NOT TO GET THEM DIRTY!!
AAGHH.
SPLAT

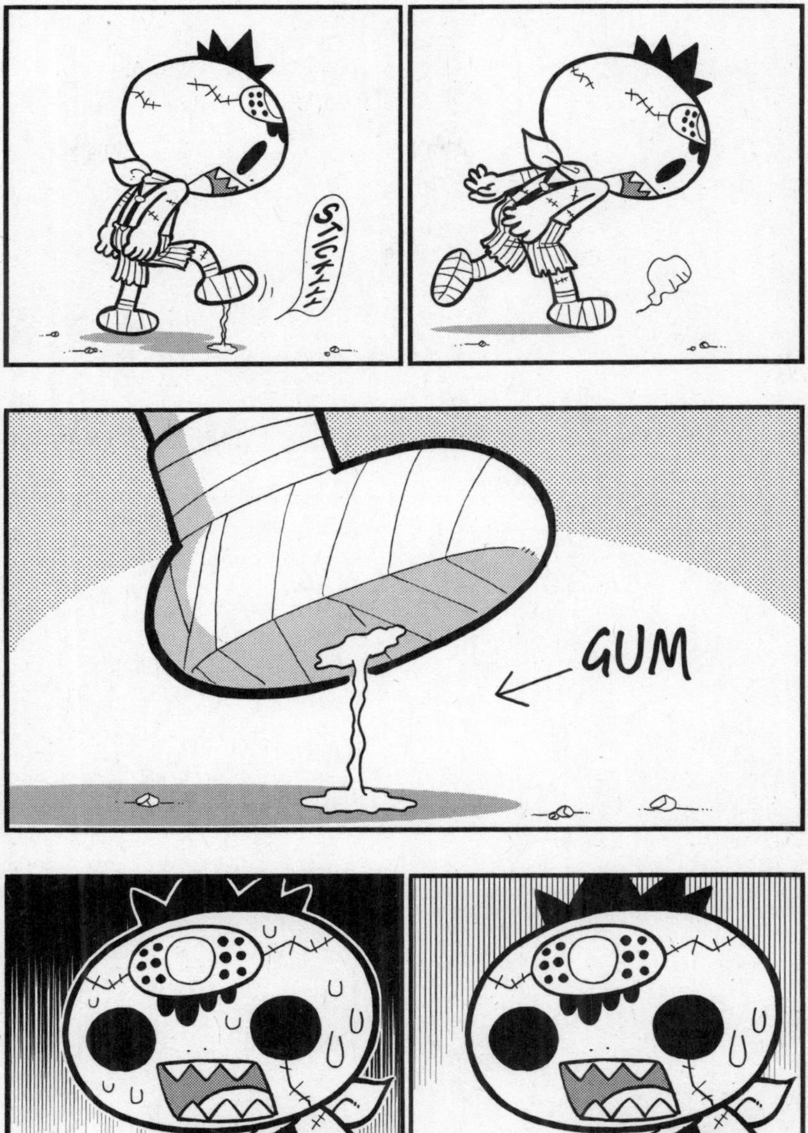
STICKYYY
GUM

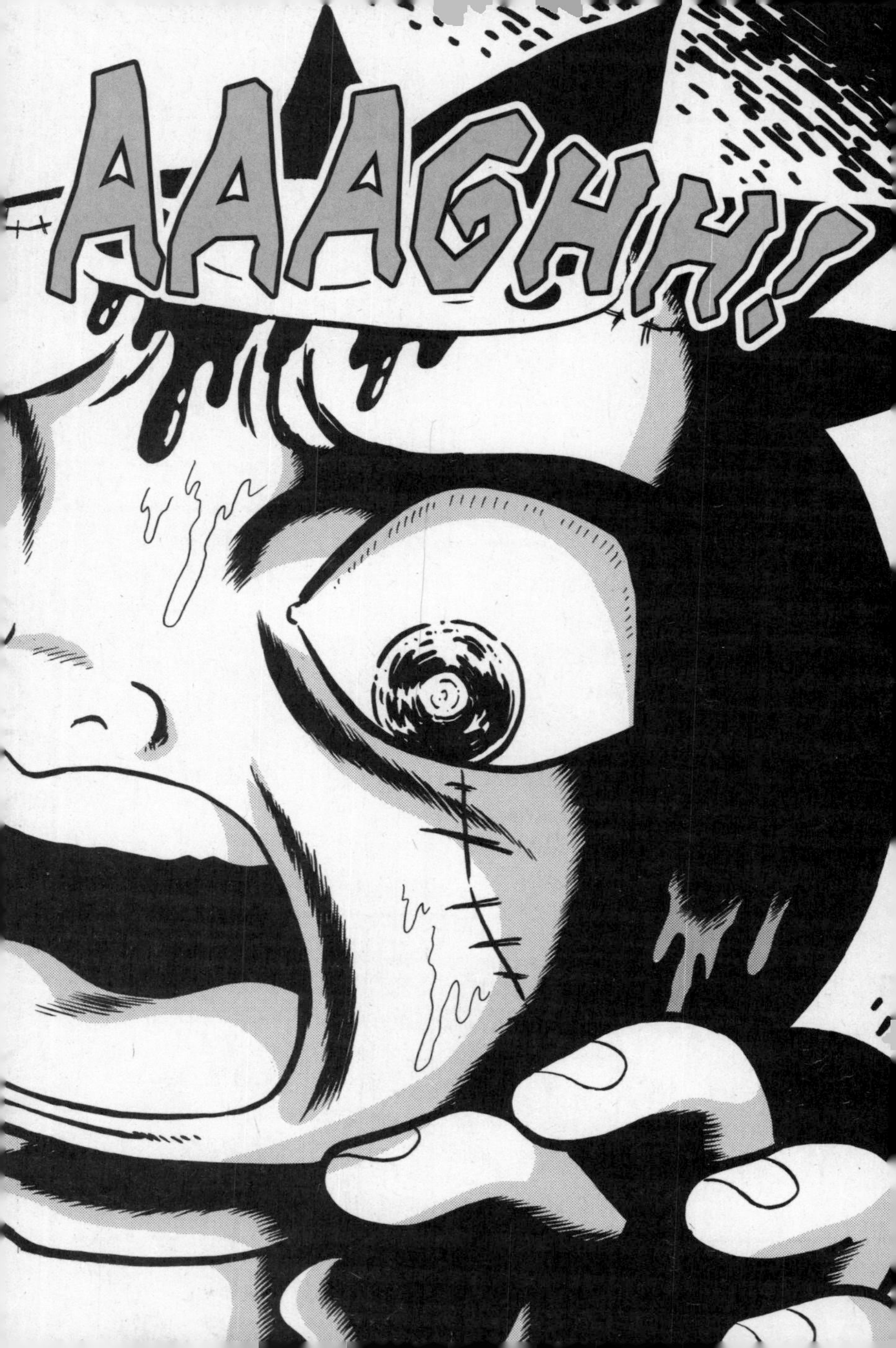
AAAGHH!!

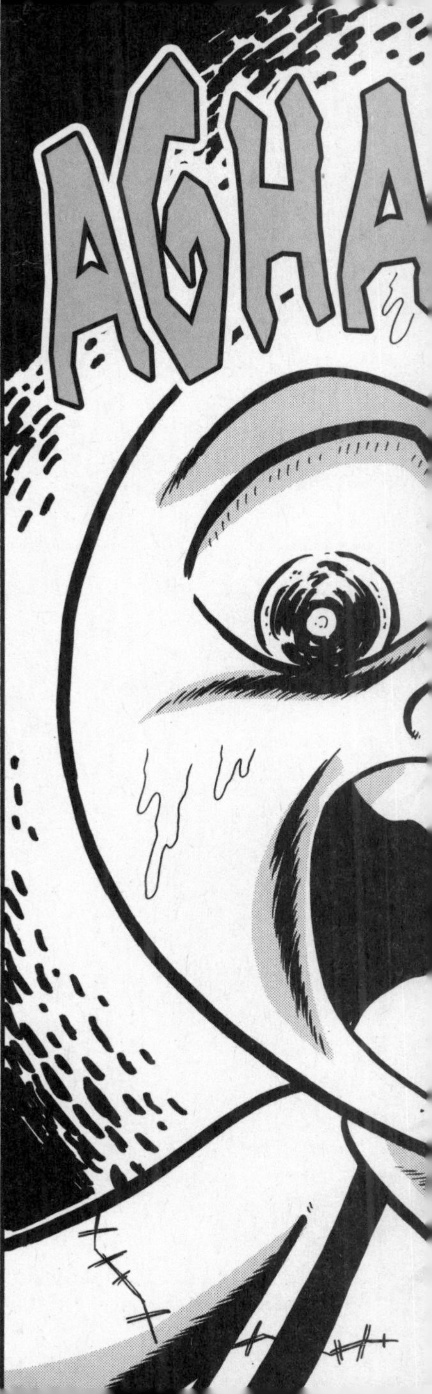
AGHA

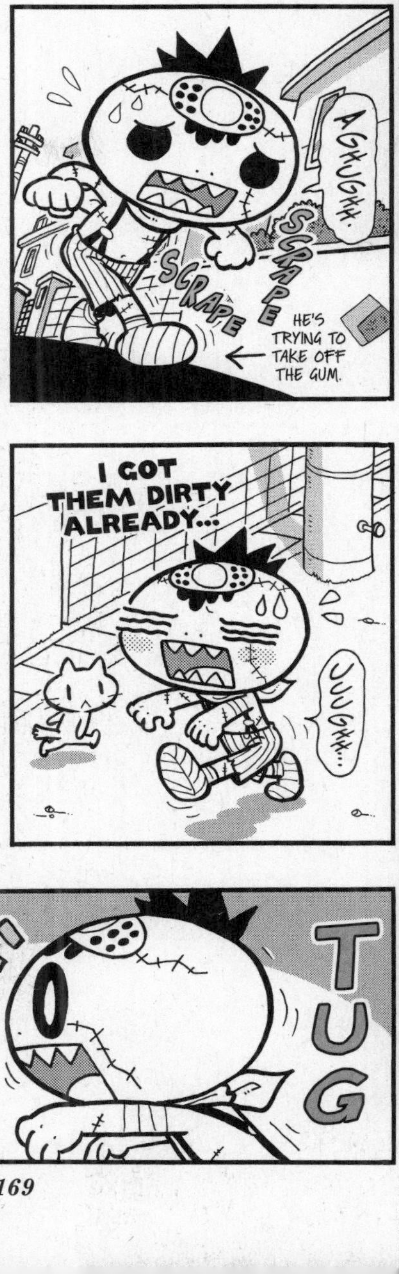
AGHUGHH.
SCRAPE
SCRAPE
HE'S TRYING TO TAKE OFF THE GUM.
I GOT THEM DIRTY ALREADY...
UUUGHHH...
TUG

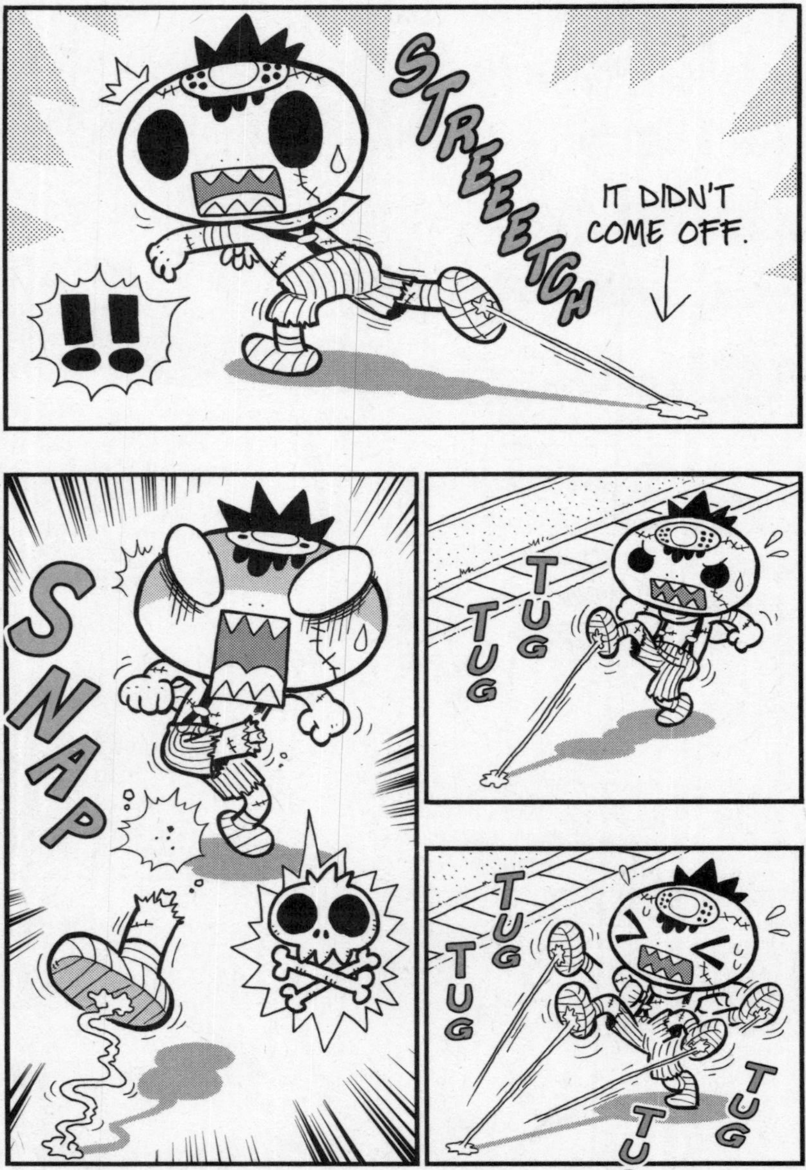
STREEETCH
IT DIDN'T
COME OFF.
!!
TUG
TUG
TUG
TUG
TUG
TUG
SNAP

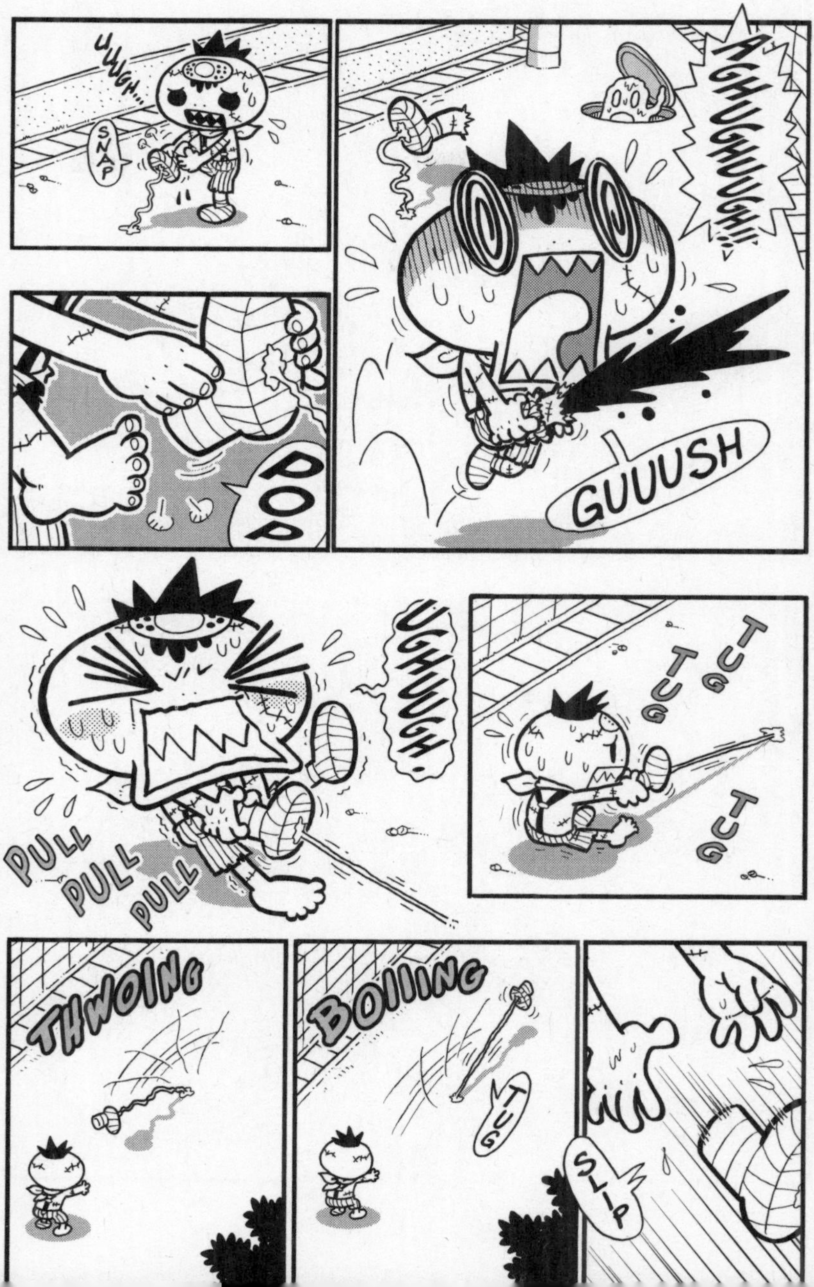
AGHUGHUUGH!!!
GUUUSH
UUUGH...
SNAP
POP
TUG TUG
TUG TUG
UGHUUGH.
PULL PULL PULL
SLIP
BOIIING
TUG
THWOING

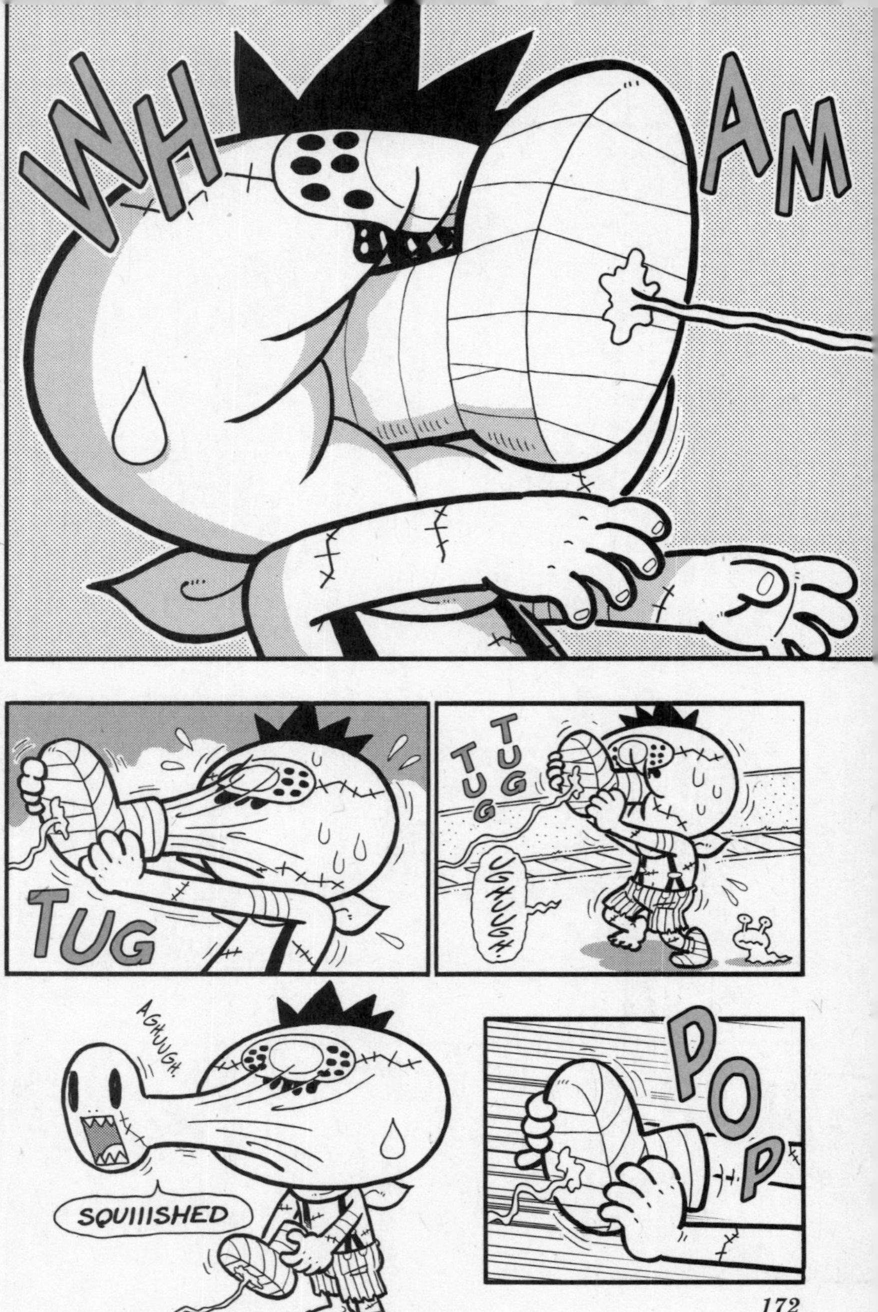
WH
AM
TUG
TUG
UGHUUGH.
TUG
POP
AGHUUGH.
SQUIIISHED

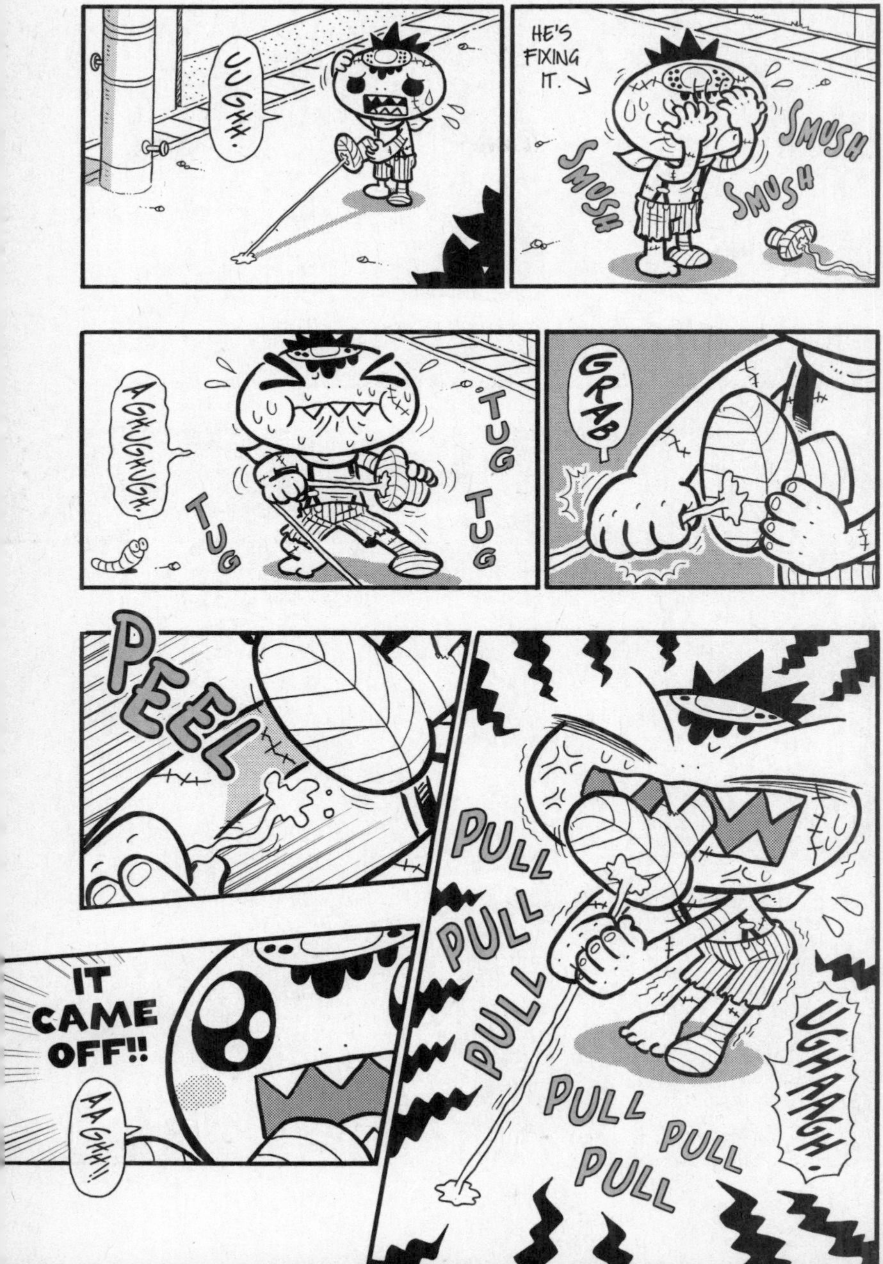
HE'S FIXING IT.
SMUSH
SMUSH
SMUSH
UUGHH.
GRAB
TUG
TUG
TUG
AGHUGHUGH.
PULL
PULL
PULL
PULL
PULL
PULL
UGHAAAGH.
PEEL
IT CAME OFF!!
AAGHH!!

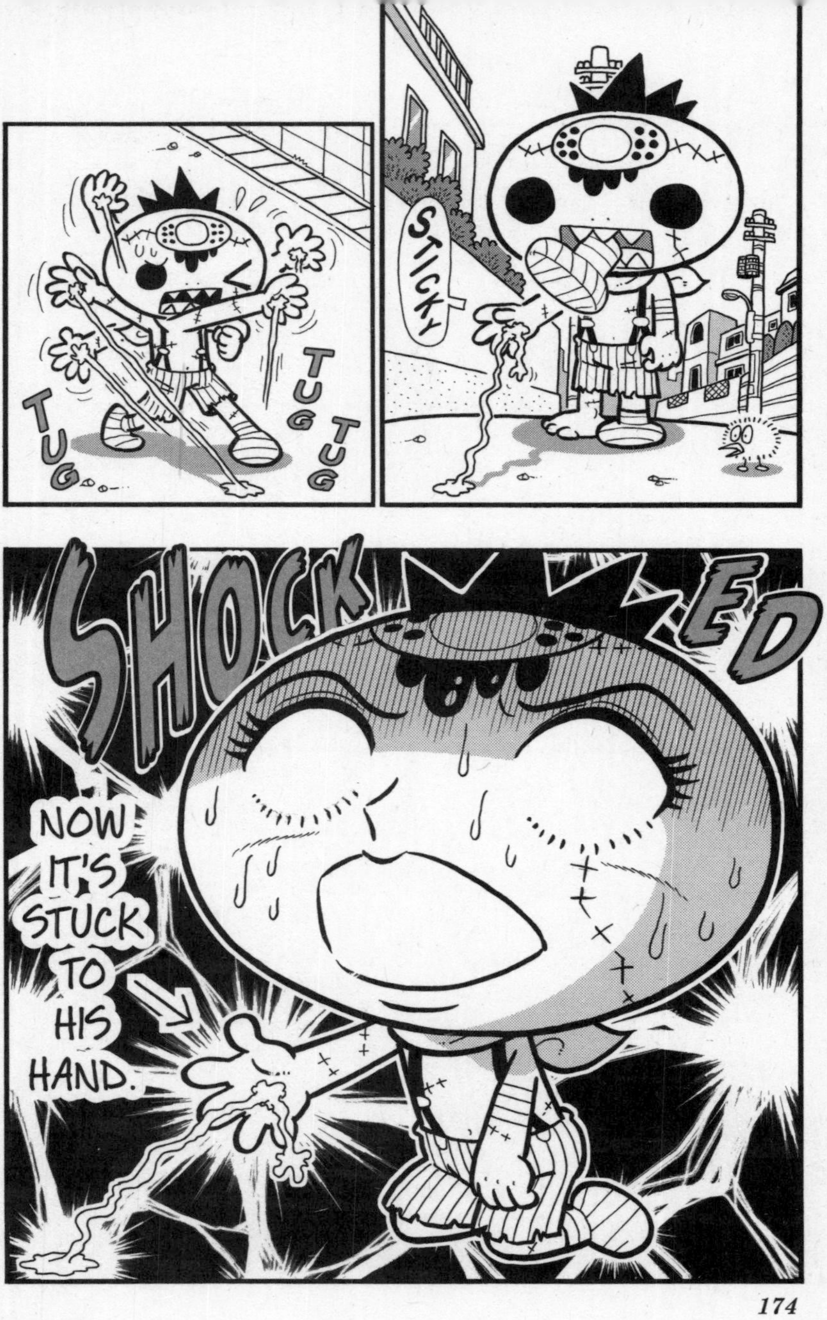
STICKY
TUG
TUG
TUG
SHOCKED
NOW IT'S STUCK TO HIS HAND.

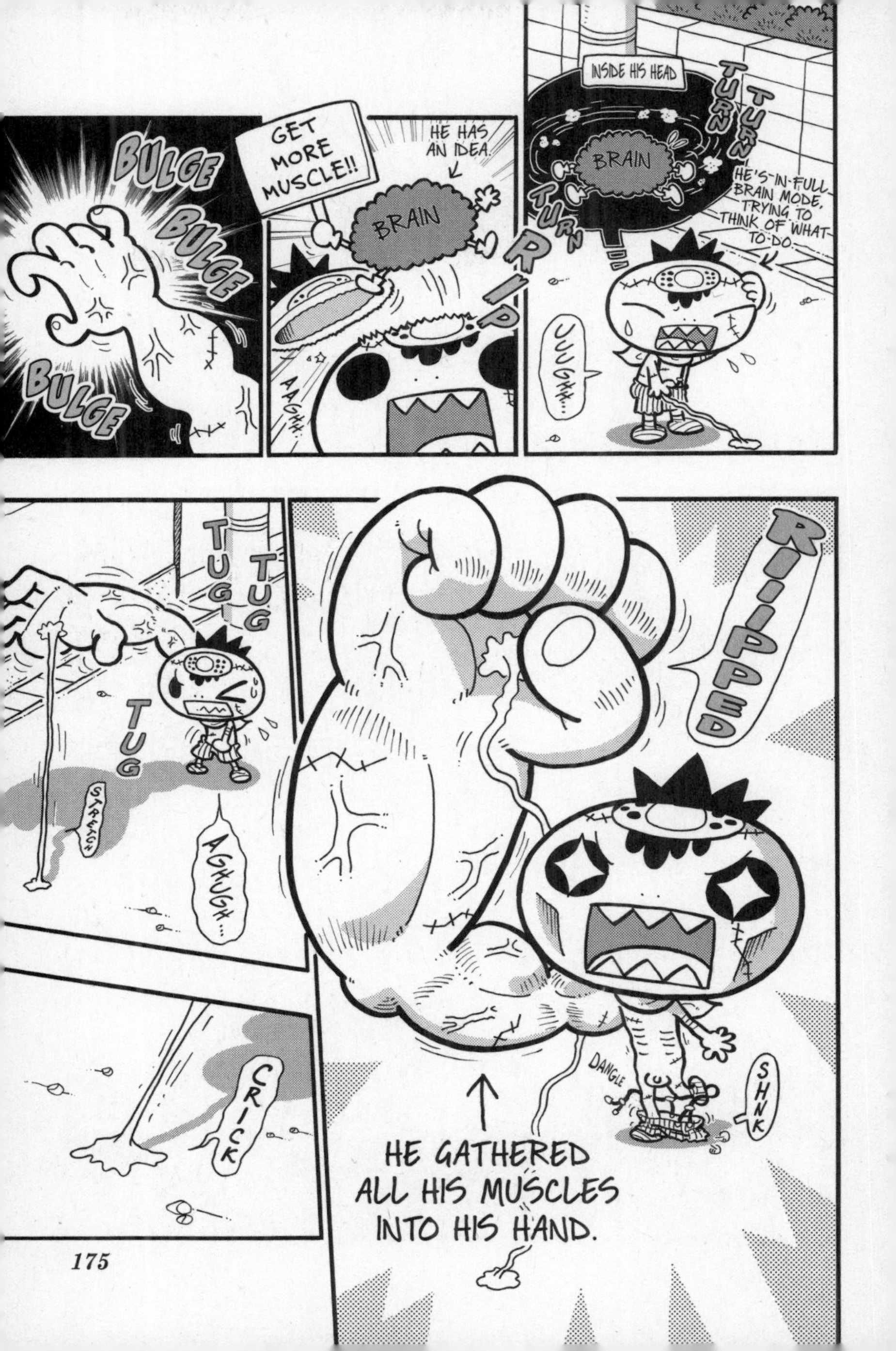
INSIDE HIS HEAD
TURN TURN
BRAIN
TURN TURN
HE'S IN FULL BRAIN MODE, TRYING TO THINK OF WHAT TO DO.
UUUGHH...
HE HAS AN IDEA.
GET MORE MUSCLE!!
BRAIN
RIP
AAGHH.
BULGE
BULGE
BULGE
BULGE
RIIIPPED
DANGLE
SHNK
HE GATHERED ALL HIS MUSCLES INTO HIS HAND.
TUG TUG
TUG TUG
STREECH
AGHUGH...
CRICK

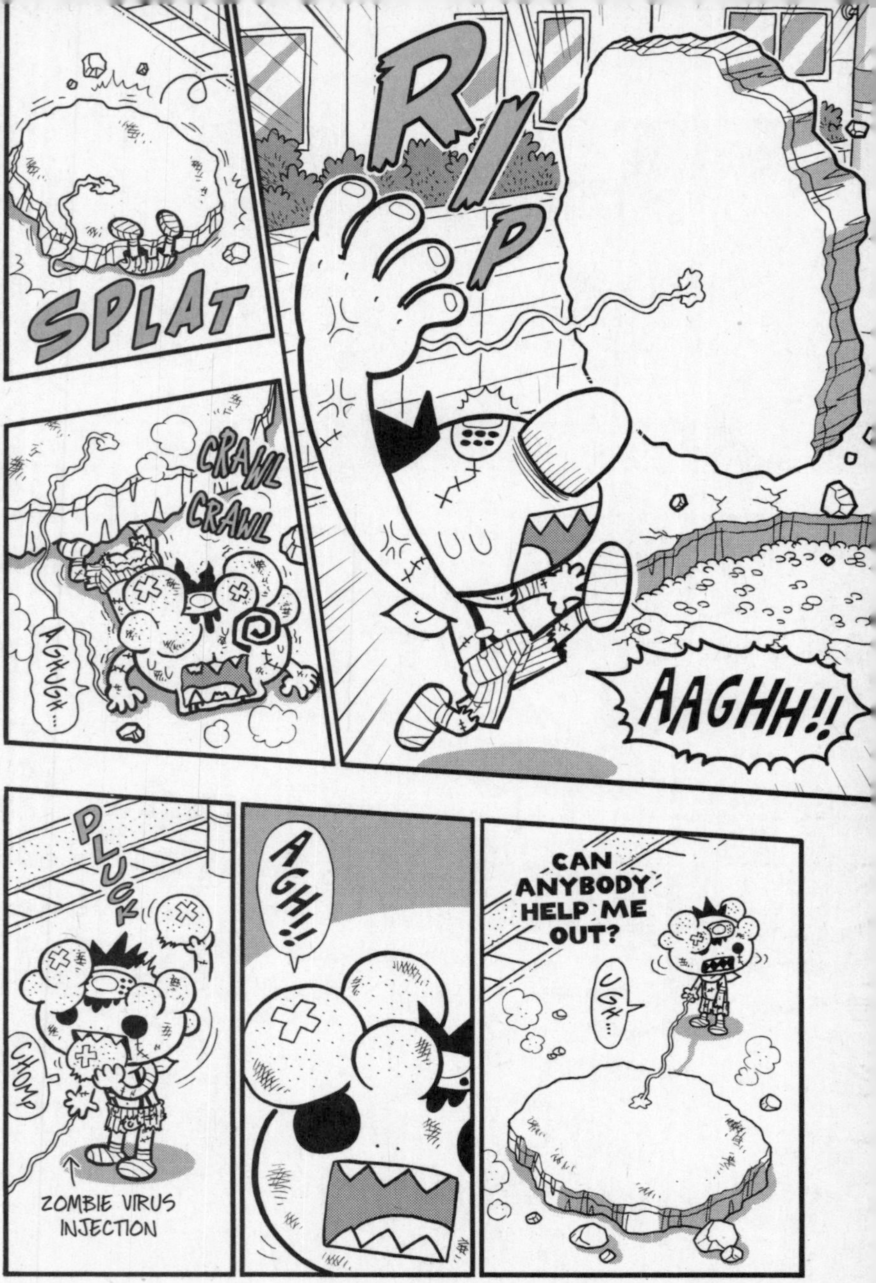
RIP
AAGHH!!
SPLAT
CRAWL CRAWL
AGHUGH...
CAN ANYBODY HELP ME OUT?
UGH...
AGH!!
PLUCK
CHOMP
ZOMBIE VIRUS INJECTION

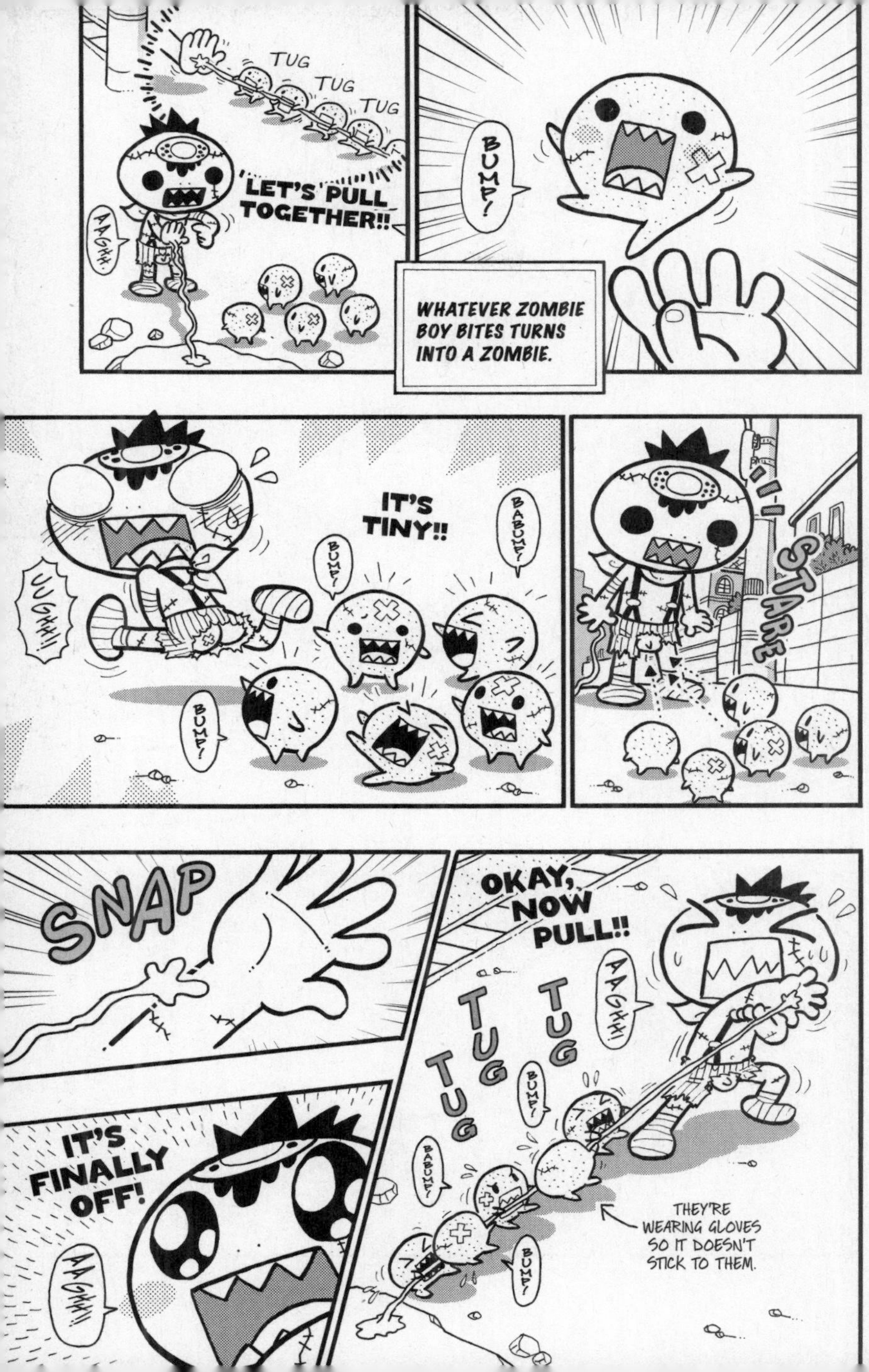
BUMP!
WHATEVER ZOMBIE BOY BITES TURNS INTO A ZOMBIE.
TUG
TUG
TUG
LET'S PULL TOGETHER!!
AAGHH.
STARE
IT'S TINY!!
BABUMP!
BUMP!
UUGHH!!
BUMP!
OKAY, NOW PULL!!
AAGHH!
TUG
TUG
TUG
TUG
BUMP!
BABUMP!
BUMP!
THEY'RE WEARING GLOVES SO IT DOESN'T STICK TO THEM.
SNAP
IT'S FINALLY OFF!
AAGHH!!

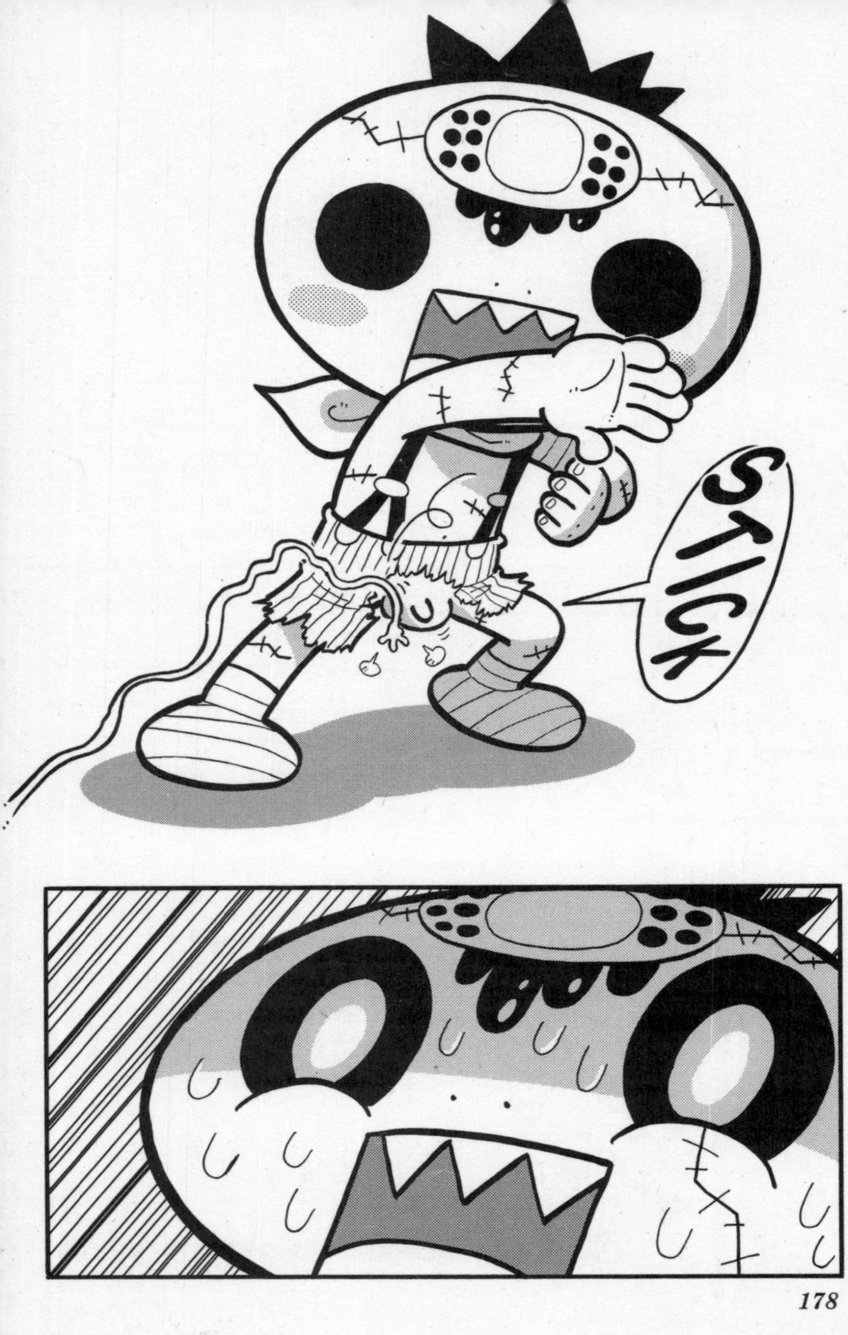
STICK

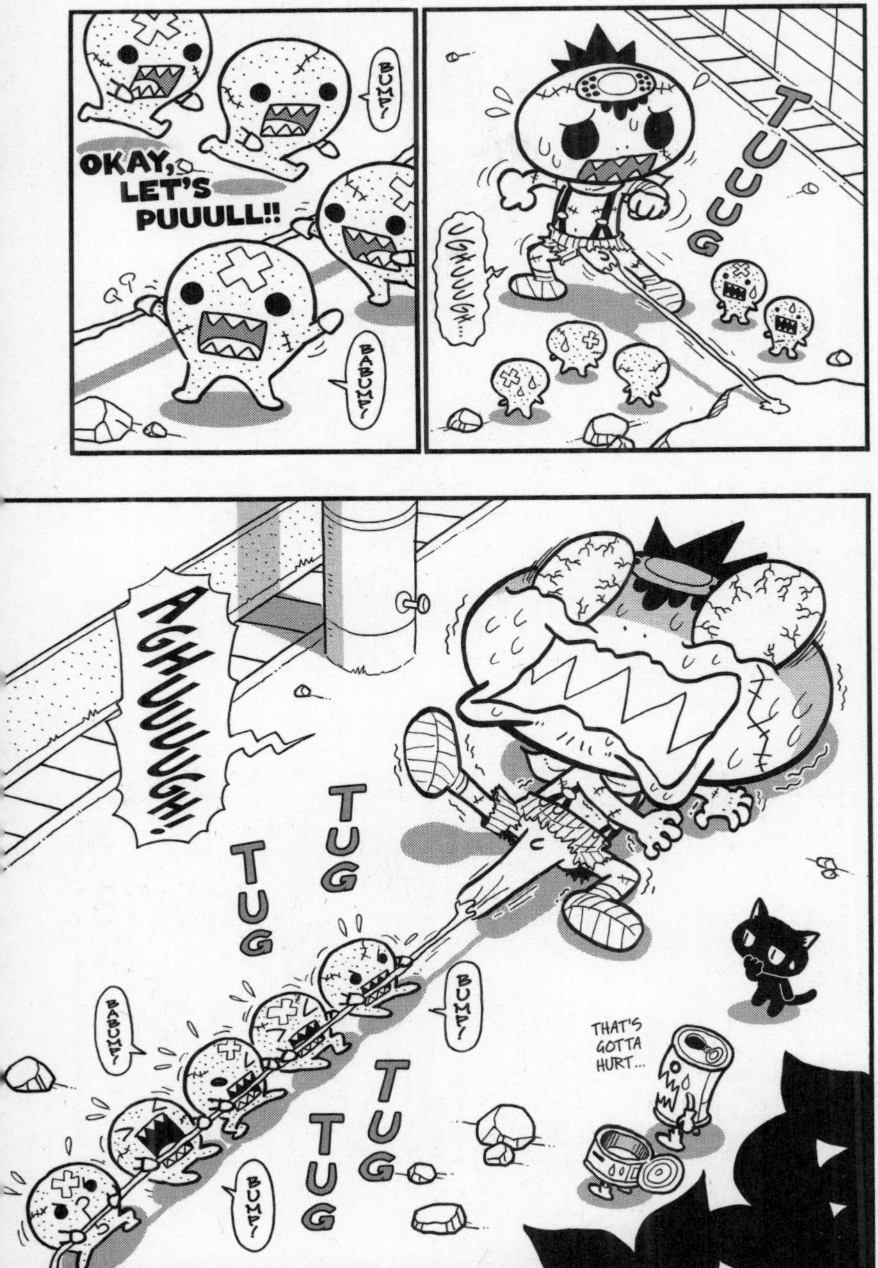
TUUUG
UGHUUUGH...
BUMP!
OKAY, LET'S PUUULL!!
BABUMP!
AGHUUUUUGH!
TUG
TUG
BUMP!
BABUMP!
THAT'S GOTTA HURT...
TUG
TUG
BUMP!

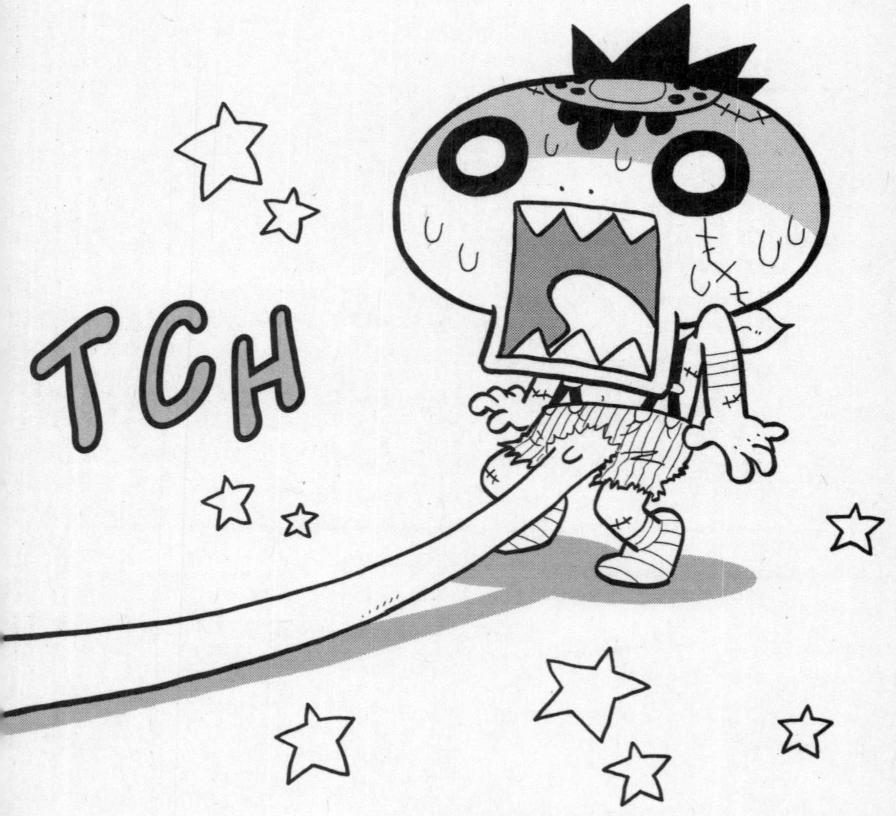
TCH

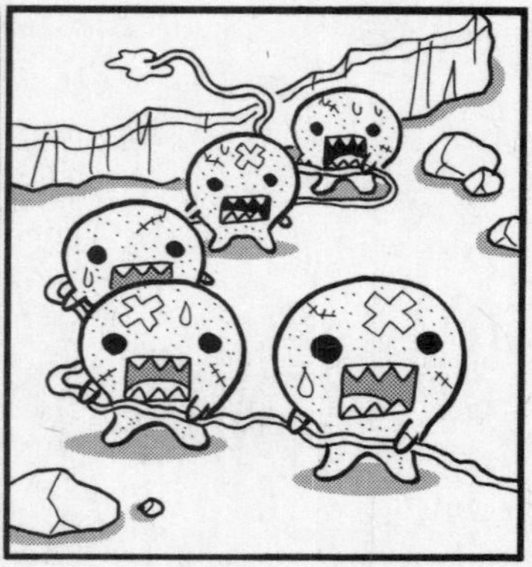

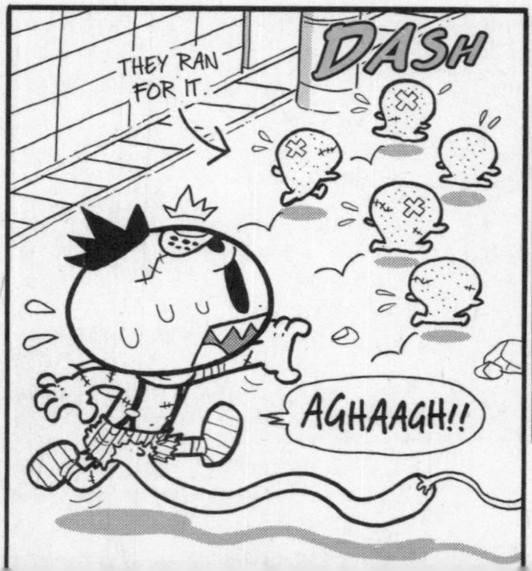
DASH
THEY RAN FOR IT.
AGHAAGH!!

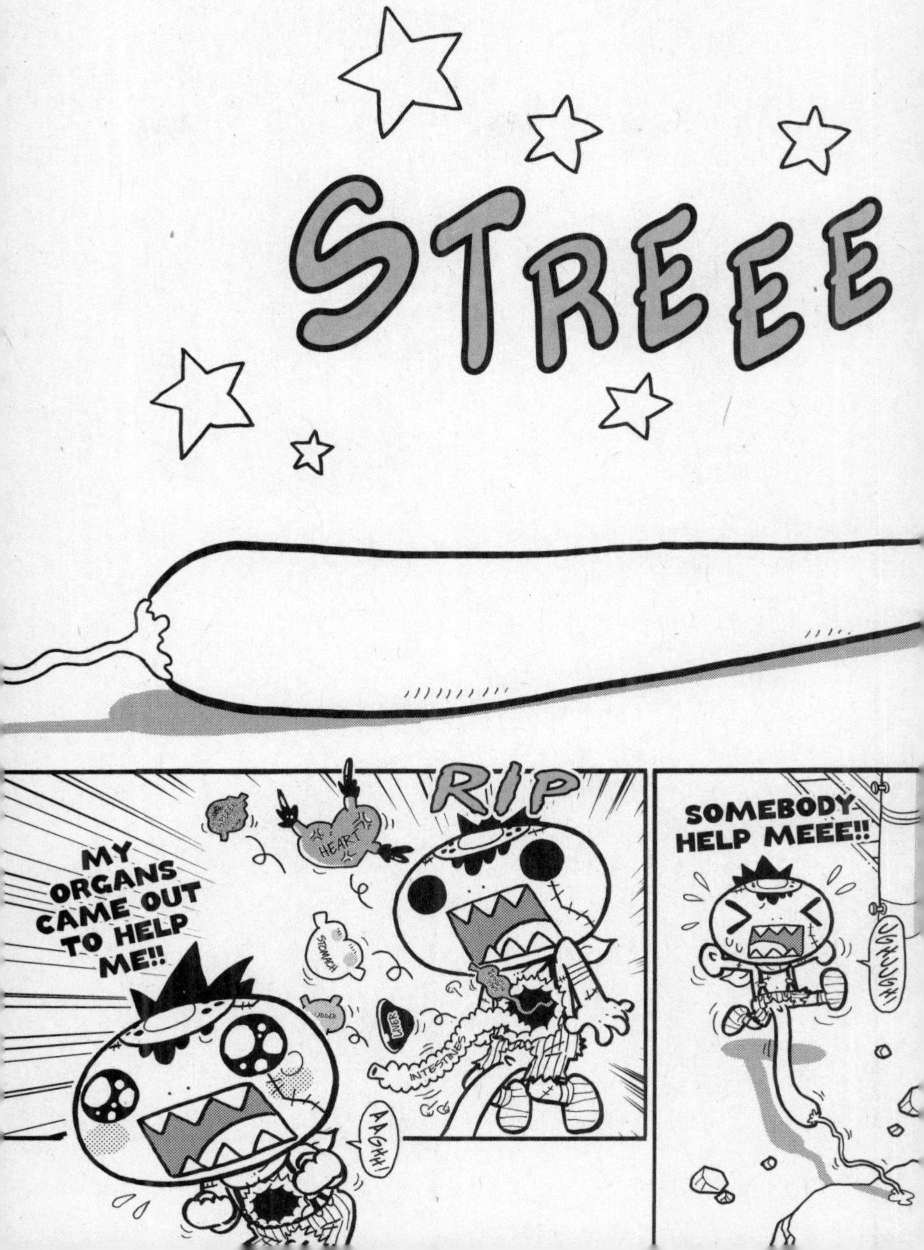
STREEE
SOMEBODY HELP MEEE!!
UGHUGH!
RIP
SPLEEN
HEART
STOMACH
LIVER
INTESTINES
MY ORGANS CAME OUT TO HELP ME!!
AAGH!

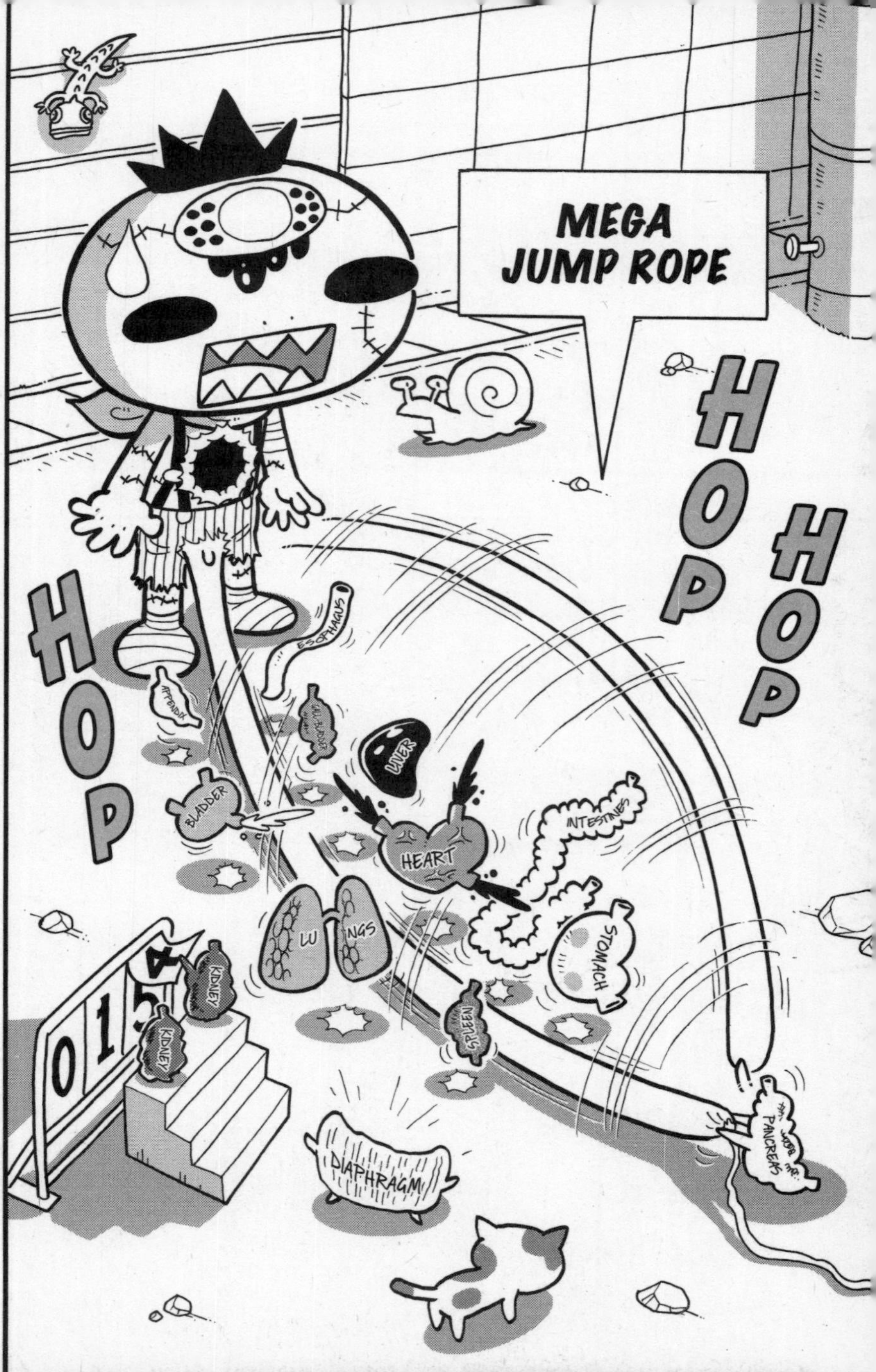
MEGA JUMP ROPE
HOP
HOP
HOP
ESOPHAGUS
APPENDIX
LIVER
BLADDER
HEART
INTESTINES
LU NGS
STOMACH
KIDNEY
KIDNEY
SPLEEN
DIAPHRAGM
PANCREAS
015
4

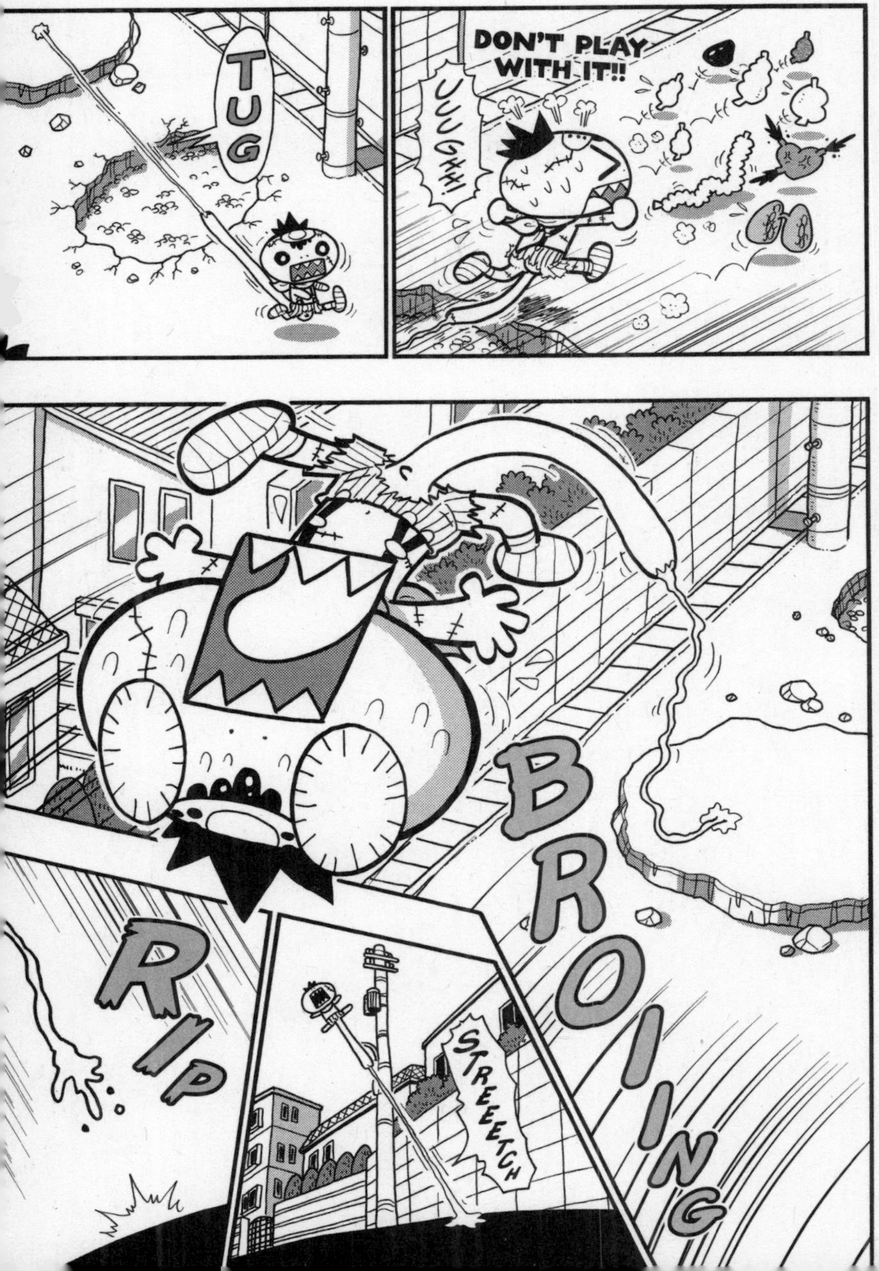
DON'T PLAY WITH IT!!
UUUGHH!
TUG
BROING
RIP
STREEETCH

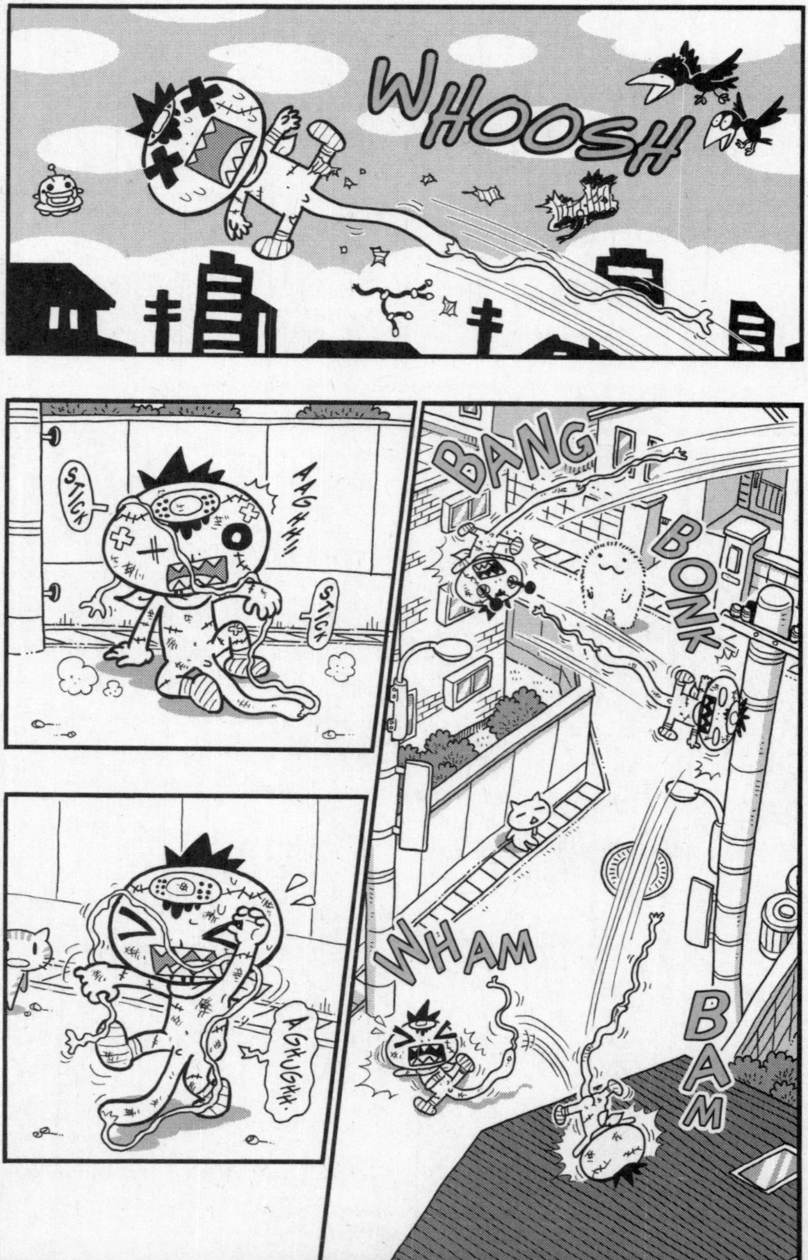
WHOOSH
BANG
BONK
WHAM
BAM
STICK
AAGHHH!!
STICK
AGHUGHH.

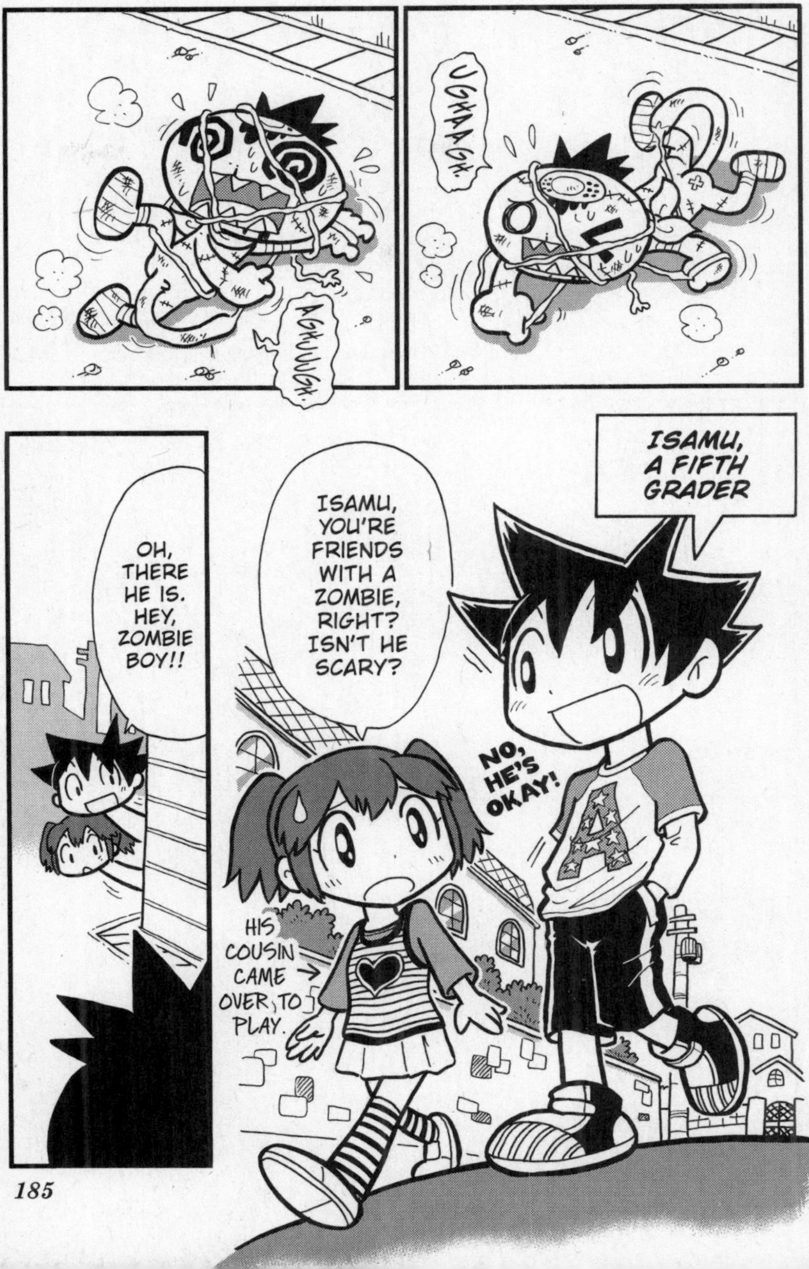
UGHAAAGH.
AGHUUUGH.
ISAMU, A FIFTH GRADER
ISAMU, YOU'RE FRIENDS WITH A ZOMBIE, RIGHT? ISN'T HE SCARY?
NO, HE'S OKAY!
HIS COUSIN CAME OVER TO PLAY.
OH, THERE HE IS. HEY, ZOMBIE BOY!!

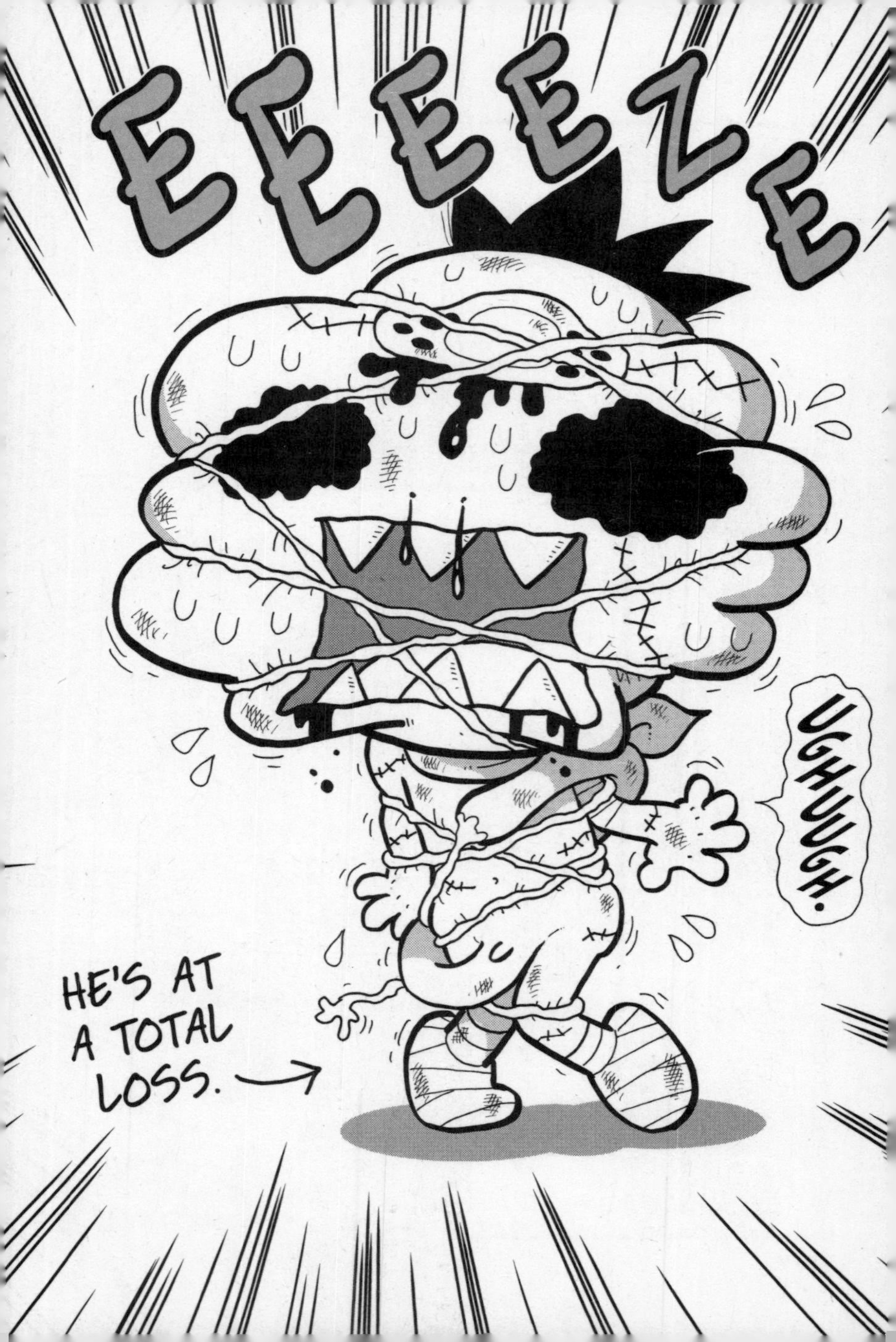
EEEEZE
UGHUUGH.
HE'S AT A TOTAL LOSS.

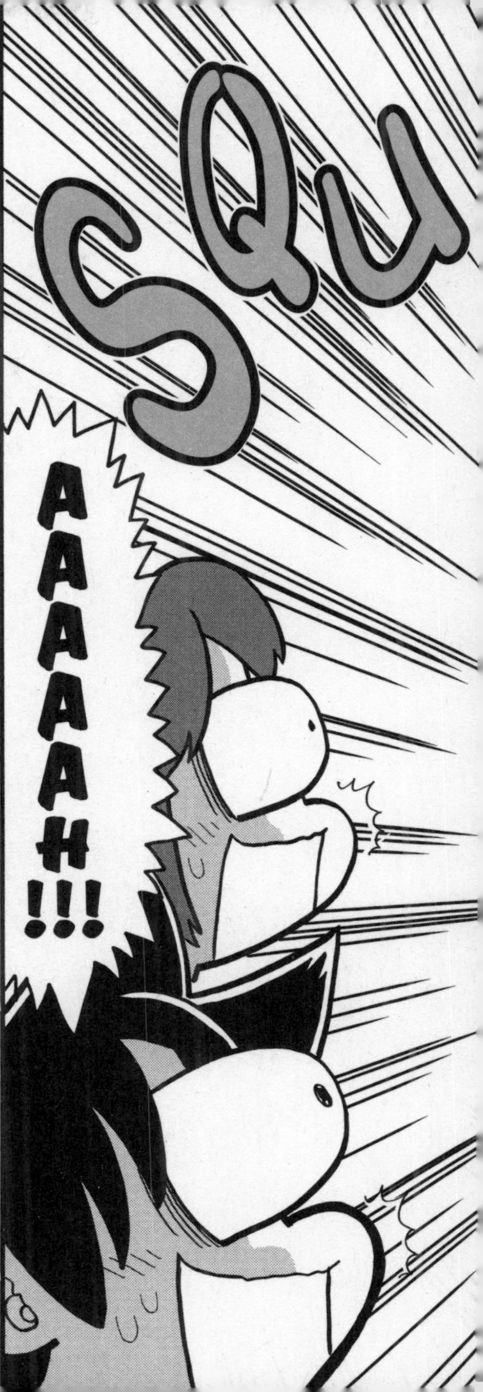
SQU
AAAAAAH!!!
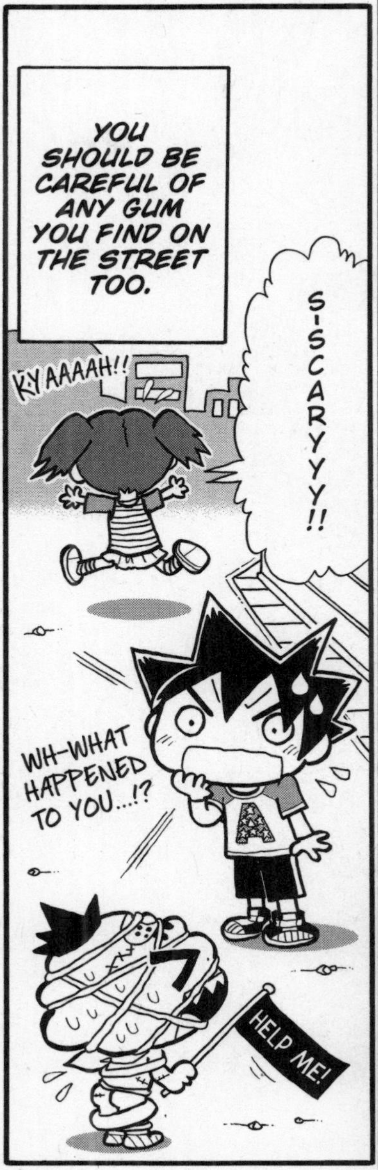
YOU SHOULD BE CAREFUL OF ANY GUM YOU FIND ON THE STREET TOO.
S-SCARYYYY!!
KYAAAAH!!
WH-WHAT HAPPENED TO YOU...!?
HELP ME!

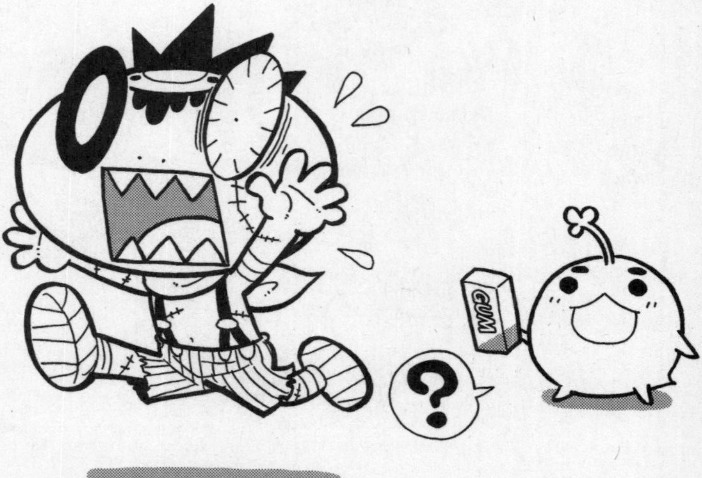
GUM
?

SEE YOU AGAIN IN VOLUME 9!!

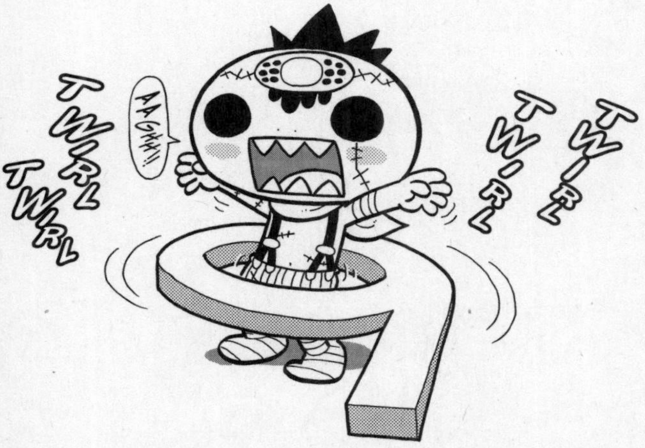
TWIRL TWIRL
AAGHH!!
TWIRL TWIRL

★ SEND YOUR LETTERS FOR YASUNARI NAGATOSHI TO ▼

JY
150 West 30th Street, 19th Floor, New York, NY 10001

ZO ZO ZOMBIE 8 THE END

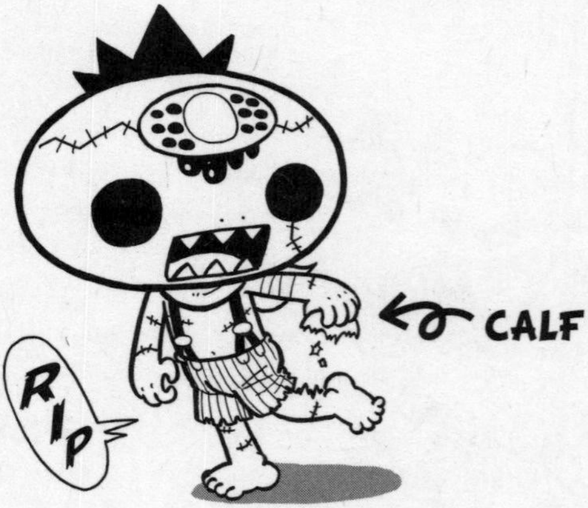
RIP
CALF

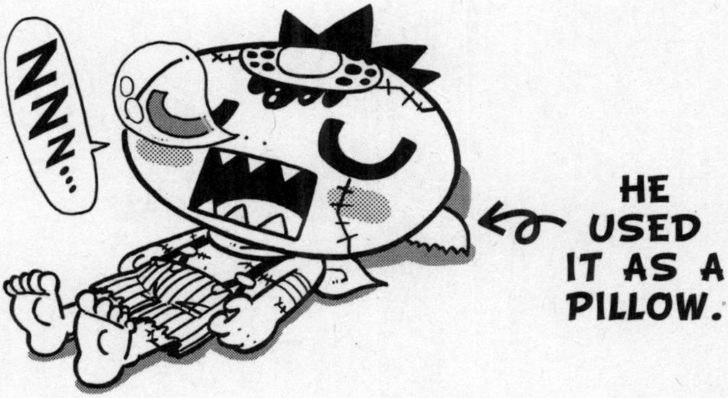
ZZZ...
HE USED IT AS A PILLOW.

Keep up with all their adventures in this award-winning series!

AWKWARD
ISBN: 9780316381307
(Paperback)

ISBN: 9780316381321
(Hardcover)

ISBN: 9780316381314
(Ebook)

BRAVE
ISBN: 9780316363181
(Paperback)

ISBN: 9780316363174
(Hardcover)

ISBN: 9780316363167
(Ebook)

CRUSH
ISBN: 9780316363242
(Paperback)

ISBN: 9780316363235
(Hardcover)

ISBN: 9780316363198
(Ebook)

Have you met the kids from Berrybrook Middle School yet?

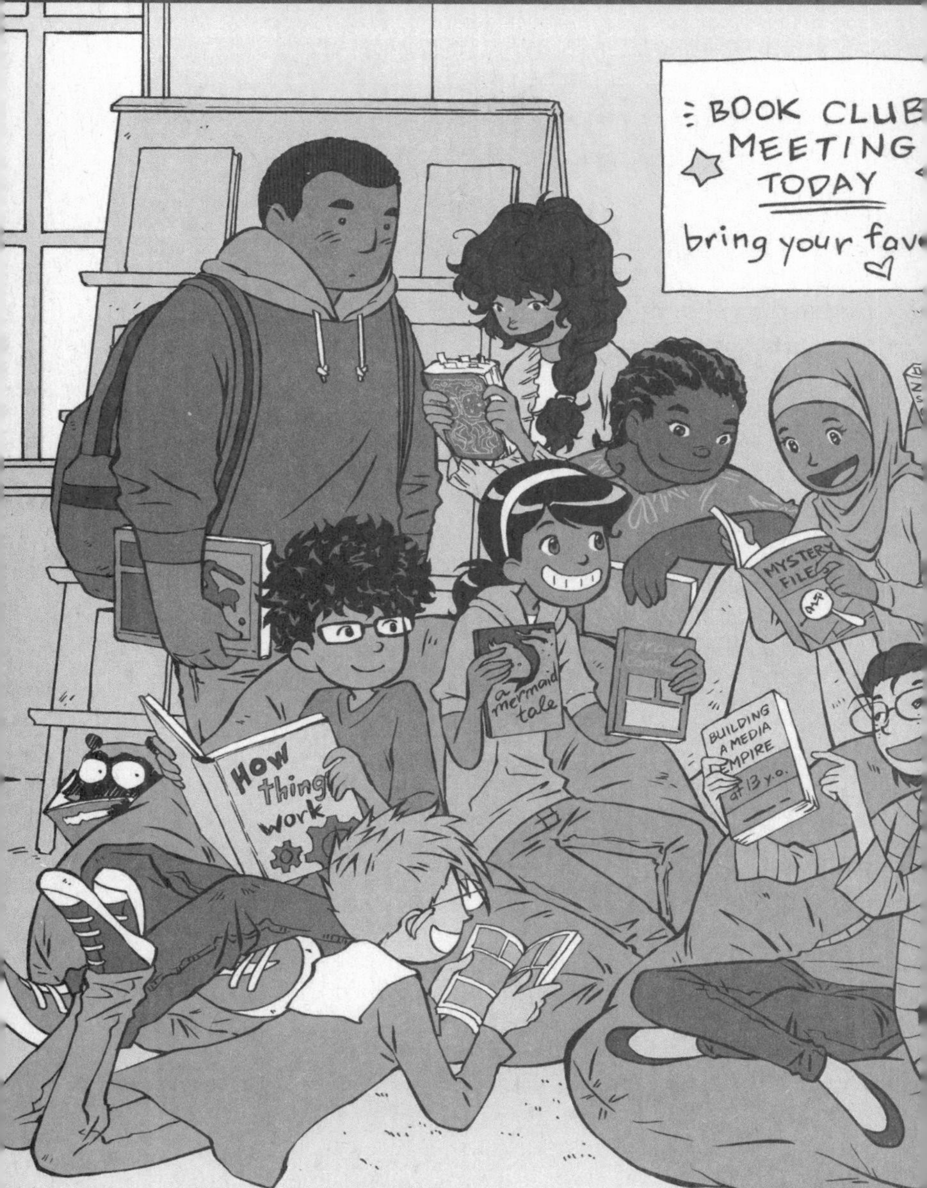
BOOK CLUB MEETING TODAY
bring your fav
MYSTERY FILES
a mermaid tale
HOW thing work
BUILDING A MEDIA EMPIRE at 13 y.o.

ZOMBIE 8

YASUNARI NAGATOSHI

Translation: ALEXANDRA MCCULLOUGH-GARCIA ♣ Lettering: BIANCA PISTILLO

ZOZOZO ZOMBIE-KUN Vol. 8
by Yasunari NAGATOSHI
© 2013 Yasunari NAGATOSHI
All rights reserved.
Original Japanese edition published by SHOGAKUKAN.
English translation rights in the United States of America, Canada, the United Kingdom, Ireland, Australia and New Zealand arranged with SHOGAKUKAN through Tuttle-Mori Agency, Inc.

English translation © 2020 by Yen Press, LLC

JY
150 West 30th Street, 19th Floor
New York, NY 10001

Visit us at jyforkids.com ♣ facebook.com/jyforkids
twitter.com/jyforkids ♣ jyforkids.tumblr.com ♣ instagram.com/jyforkids

First JY Edition: August 2020

JY is an imprint of Yen Press, LLC.
The JY name and logo are trademarks of Yen Press, LLC.

The publisher is not responsible for websites (or their content) that are not owned by the publisher.

Library of Congress Control Number: 2018948323

ISBNs: 978-1-9753-5348-3 (paperback)
978-1-9753-8636-8 (ebook)

10 9 8 7 6 5 4 3 2 1

WOR

Printed in the United States of America